SUSPICION

SUSPICION

JAKE BUSSOLINI

EDITED BY: C. H. WEBER

ARPress
45 Dan Road Suite 36
Canton MA 02021

Hotline: 1(800) 220-7660
Fax: 1(855) 752-6001

Ordering Information:
Quantity sales. Special discounts are available on quantity purchases by corporations, associations, and others. For details, contact the publisher at the address above.

Printed in the United States of America.

ISBN-13:   Paperback   979-8-89389-608-4
           eBook   979-8-89389-609-1

Library of Congress Control Number: 2024921471

CHAPTER 1

HIS EYES OPENED very slowly because he wasn't exactly sure whether he was opening them himself or being assisted by some unknown force within him. He wasn't even sure if he was alive, a human or some form of animal life, because he had absolutely no feeling, no senses, no memories, and no awareness of why his eyes had been closed. Perhaps they were not closed at all; maybe his brain just started working or perhaps he was just being born. As he began to gain focus of the view in front of him, he was sure that he had just died and passed on to a much better place because he was looking at a beautiful sight as far as he could see.

His eyes were focused on a small lake-like water body, lying there as still as a huge mirror—not a ripple, not a movement, just beauty. The trees that surrounded the shoreline were in full bloom and the majestic mountains in the distance provided a picture that surely was painted by one of the world's greatest artists. He felt no breeze, no heat, no cold, just amazingly soothing calm surrounding him.

It seemed that his brain had no function because he couldn't move. Everything just seemed a huge blank, no memory, feelings, not even the urge to understand where he was or how he got here. If this was Hell, he thought, it wouldn't be this nice; it would be very unpleasant. Heaven, he thought, should have more people around; it wouldn't be this quiet. But why were Heaven and Hell his first thoughts, the only things in this newly hatched brain? There was nothing else there. He could feel his feet, his arms, his body, but the feeling was like everything was just beginning to come alive.

He wasn't confused because he didn't know what confusion really was. He was clothed in what seemed to be normal attire, but then what would he know about that? He had no knowledge! Hell, he didn't even know he had a name—or, for that matter, whether names actually existed in this new world that he was in.

He remained in this somewhat catatonic state for quite a while because he really didn't want to disturb it. Disturb it? Hell, he didn't even know he was in any unusual state of being. He was suddenly feeling this enormous fatigue, like everything in his being needed to rest. He allowed his eyes to close and he fell into this beautiful deep sleep.

There were no dreams or nightmares, no tossing or wanting to move as far as he could tell. The only thing he suddenly felt was a soft hand moving over his head. In a soft and somewhat hesitant female voice, he heard the words, "Mitch, are you okay? Can you open your eyes for me?"

As his eyes opened, he noticed this charming lady sitting by his side, half facing him and also looking directly at the sights in front of them. She seemed to know him, and she called him by the name Mitch. Who the hell was Mitch, he thought, and who was this strange woman sitting by his side acting as tender to him as the tenderness of the surroundings that they were both viewing?

He didn't even know if he could respond to her question or even if words were possible for him. He looked at her with a blank stare, as blank as his mind seemed to be. "Mitch? Mitch?" He mumbled as he shook his head, as though giving the signal that he didn't know what she was talking about.

She leaned over and gently kissed his lips, and while gently rubbing his face, she said, "Wake up Mitch. You must have fallen into a very deep sleep. Please wake up for me."

Her voice was very seductive and the touch of her lips to his must have been some kind of trigger because now he was suddenly able to feel his body, move his arms and legs, and collect enough intellect to ask, "Who are you, and who is Mitch?" Was he actually speaking or imagining these words, he thought. For a moment she didn't respond, so he thought he was just imagining that he had spoken.

She turned to face him directly and quietly replied in a tender and understanding voice, "I'm Jessica, and you are Mitch Waters. Don't you have any recollection of the time that we have spent together here on this mountain?"

Time, he thought. Hell I was just born. "I don't know," he mumbled. "I can't seem to remember anything before that kiss that you just gave me. Am I really alive and here in some strange place with a woman that I don't even know?"

"You are alive. Your name is Mitch Waters. Our helicopter crashed into this mountain several days ago. Hank Farber and I were with you in that plane. Hank was killed in the crash, and you were unconscious for some time." She suddenly stopped short and a look of fear and disappointment came over her face. "I'm going too fast," she said. "You can't remember anything before I woke you up a few minutes ago, can you?" "No, not a thing," he replied.

"Then we must take this very slow. So much has happened to us both in the last few days, alone here on this mountain. You cannot remember any of that, nor can you remember any of your life before that accident, can you?"

"Nope," he responded, "as far as I know my life just started when you kissed me a few minutes ago. By the way, I'm not even sure what a good kiss is supposed to feel like, but I think that was a really good one."

They walked slowly up a narrow path, arm in arm. It didn't seem like the arms entangled meant anything, it was like Jessica was kind of holding him up, knowing that he had just had some sort of seizure. At least, that was the only explanation that he could rationalize that would explain his weird behavior. "We'll walk up to the cabin and talk about this situation a little more," she said. She realized that he was apparently strong enough to hold himself up. She walked a little faster, kind of in a slight hurry. That was the first time he really had a chance to view her by herself in front of him. She was about his height and well-built. Her attire was a pair of properly fitted jeans and a red blouse, and from the rear she seemed fairly shapely. He tried to keep up with her, but even if he thought he was at full strength, he still seemed short on energy. She noticed that as she pulled away from him, and she stopped when she looked back at him and realized that he was falling behind.

As he caught up with her, he suddenly remembered that she had said that they were going to a cabin. What cabin, he thought. How the hell do we have a cabin in what seems to be a remote location high on some unknown mountain? "How on Earth do we have a cabin?" he asked. Then he realized that asking that question was only one of about a million questions that he had that needed answers. They came to the end of the path and entered a field of beautiful green grass.

"That's our cabin," she giggled as she sort of danced and hopped at the same time as though demonstrating her excitement that she was showing him the place for the first time. It struck him as a sort of very small hideaway, a place where one could survive off of the grid for a short time, or even a tiny remote summer place to be used as a getaway from a high-pressure job. The small size of this structure certainly did not show any capability for survival for any long period of time. "The cabin is one of many stories about which I need to refresh your memory," she laughed, "but that's a really complicated story, and I think that before I start bringing you up to date, we have to talk about what you actually remember about the past." "Not much to talk about," he replied. "There's nothing in my head that I can recall before you gave me that kiss back there." At that point, they were standing face to face and a strange look came across her face, as though his comment had thrown her back a little, almost like she didn't believe him. "We can do this any way you like," he said, "but I don't even remember my name. Everything in my head is blank; there's nothing there. Why would I kid you about something like that? You look confused, and I don't know why. You seem to know everything about me, and I don't know a thing about you." She walked slowly around the cabin, fussing here and there with little things as though she was trying to get her thoughts together, but also acting as though she was thinking up the next phase of her explanation.

Now he began to get a little suspicious about her actions. He suddenly realized that he didn't even know what suspicion was as a feeling, but he was feeling strange doubts about her. Was he getting some emotions back in his brain? He was thinking. "Am I coming out of some deep sleep now and starting to regain some brain power?" He was totally confused with everything that was happening. His whole life seemed to be the last hour or so. No matter how hard he tried, he just didn't have the key to open the door to the rest of his life.

They both sat at a small table near the front window of the cabin. Jessica had brewed a pot of coffee, and she got up, grabbed two cups from a crowded shelf and poured them each a cup. Somehow, her movements in this simple task of making and pouring coffee gave him the feeling that serving another person was not something that she was skilled at. He slowly sipped the first few drops, not knowing if he even liked to drink coffee, but Jessica seemed to know that he liked it black. The first taste was not to his liking, but he didn't say anything. Perhaps it was just too hot, so he let it cool a little. The second sip was slightly more than a sip, and he nearly could not swallow it. The taste was simply too strong.

"Would you like me to add some sugar?" Jessica asked. There was a small glass container filled with sugar already on the table. She added a spoonful into his cup and slowly stirred it while staring directly into his eyes. This time her stare was so terribly warm, almost seductive. Her seductive manner seemed to be drawing him toward her, but he didn't even know that it was happening. "Try this," she said softly, and she handed him his cup. This tasted better to him, and they both sat back in their chairs to begin to talk.

"I have to think seriously how to begin our discussion," Jessica said. "There is so much to tell, and if I don't get it all in the right order, I may only confuse you more."

She slid back in her chair and pulled the chair closer to the table and looked as if she was assuming a deep-thinking position, kind of rubbing her small hand over the side of her cheek. A slight wrinkle appeared above her eyes as though she was trying to really think this out before getting started.

Mitch suddenly leaned back quickly as though something had come to his mind. He thought, if they had lived alone in this cabin for several days, she would certainly have known that he liked sugar in his coffee—but she gave it to him without sugar, why?

Was she testing him with the coffee? *Here I go with that feeling of suspicion again. I don't even know what feelings are, and the first feelings that I develop are feelings of suspicion. Why should I suspect Jessica of anything? She apparently saved my life.*

"Look," she responded as she pulled her chair closer to the table as though wanting to share a secret. "The past few days have been very complicated and knowing what I know requires me to be very careful with you."

"What do you mean, careful?" He responded

"In the next few days, as I unveil your recent life to you, we each have to develop a mutual trust in the other. For several days we have lived here together alone, with no one else around us and no way to know what the hell was going on in the rest of the world. I tried to nurse you back to some normalcy. We lived in an atmosphere of great mutual trust. You had no option but to trust me; it was the only thing you had. I've been trying to re-build your life for you, and so far, I have had to rebuild it around this little cabin. I grew to like the way we survived here, and I believed that you also were totally comfortable with it. Like it or not, I want to continue to work with you to revive your past, but I don't want to say anything to you that might cause a setback for you.

"There were a whole series of events that led up to us being here, and I am afraid that if I trigger something in your mind the wrong way, you might stop moving forward with your memory."

At this point, his head was spinning. There had been nothing in his brain that had previously triggered any emotions except that kiss. Now, it seemed that there were a great many emotions, a lot of learning of the past that Jessica felt might destroy their relationship or even destroy him mentally. Apparently, they both had a complicated past that somehow came together. Jessica's kiss was the only thing that stimulated any of his emotions. Did he have feelings for her? The only thing he knew was that he needed to start learning about himself. He simply wanted to re-enter the real world. The only thing that would permit him to do that was to start learning about himself through Jessica's knowledge of him, and it was just as important to learn about Jessica and the world in which she lived. He was just going to have to trust what she tells him without hesitation or doubt for the time being He reached across the table. His first instinctive motion was to take her hands in his and look directly into her eyes. "You have my total trust, not because I have no other alternative, but because that kiss back there gave me the warmest feeling I have ever felt. I believe that kiss triggered something in my brain that is related to something that we had in the past. That emotion is the only emotion that I remember ever feeling in this latest phase of my life." Instinctively, they both rose from their chairs and came together in a warm embrace. Jessica kissed him, and he returned the kiss. "Now perhaps we can get on with the next segment of our lives," he told her.

CHAPTER 2

THE OUTWARD APPEARANCE of Ivan Schwarz could best be described as non-descript. If you passed him on the street, he would probably give you no reason to look twice, just an average American in his late 30s with a little prematurely gray hair. Ivan, his wife Erma, and their son Michael lived in a small ranch house in Medfield, Massachusetts, a few miles south of Boston.

Ivan worked for the Calbro Corporation a mid-sized data information company located in Medfield. The company was founded twenty years ago in San Francisco, California, by two brothers, Jim and Thomas Whitney, and hence the name Calbro. The company moved to the Boston area a few years ago because it was doing a great deal of business with several companies located on Rt. 128, where most of the East Coast MIT brains were located. Calbro had about three hundred employees, mostly postgraduate technical types. Some would call a company of this type a "brain trust," and nearly all of the company's business was highly classified government contract work.

Ivan himself was an MIT graduate who had specialized in artificial intelligence studies while in college. He earned his master's degree in that specialty and eventually his doctorate.

Ivan, like most Calbro employees, rarely talked about his work because it too was highly classified and very specialized. He usually worked alone in his small private laboratory and was often permitted to work at home as long as that work could be separated from the details of the work he did in his laboratory.

The laboratory that housed Ivan's work at Calbro was wall-to-wall computers and other electronic devices, all seemingly tied together with thousands of small wires. His associates, who rarely got a peek at this laboratory, would joke with him about this, since interconnecting electronics was normally done with the wires hidden in the rear of the equipment. His laboratory was named "the spaghetti factory" by his associates whenever they got a peek inside.

Ivan had become an expert in the field of neural networks which involved the study of the human nervous system, the brain, and how they work together. Scientists in this highly specialized field were normally trying to develop a computer that could actually think like a human, make judgments and decisions based on facts presented, and have reactions to this information much like a human did. No one had yet developed such a computer, although Ivan's work was very advanced, and within his small circle of scientific peers, he had a world-wide reputation.

Calbro had been awarded a contract by the government to develop a system that could be added to electronically guided bombs that would navigate the bombs and missiles to their target once the proper data was provided. If information changed once the missile was launched, the missile system could automatically make the necessary changes putting the weapon back on its target. This wasn't exactly what Ivan wanted to be doing because it detracted him from the neuroscience work that was his specialty. There was, in fact, a close relationship between the two assignments. Because of this, he was granted permission to do the work on the "brain system," as he called it, in his laboratory and work on the guidance system for the government from his home, provided that the proper security precautions were taken. These precautions included a completely locked facility with camera sensors linked to a monitoring system at the Calbro facility. No one but Ivan was to be permitted in this private room.

Ivan called his work room his private sanctuary, but his wife Erma called it "the destroyer" because she felt that it was destroying their marriage, taking up all of his time and emotional energy and leaving nothing for their relationship.

Ivan had written and presented several technical papers on the work that he was doing with neurosystems through the National Association of Neuroscientists. He was regularly invited to travel throughout the world presenting papers on this subject. He had become quite famous in his field, but like most true scientists, the fame was not a big concern to him

To the public and to his work associates, Ivan probably seemed quite normal, as normal as a neuroscientist can be. To his wife Erma and son Michael, however, it was quite another thing. Ivan was born in 1939 and lived in Germany with his mother and father for two years. He really did not have a clear recollection of the events of 1941, but it was then that he was sent to the United States to live with his aunt and uncle.

Both of Ivan's parents were tortured and killed in 1942 during the Holocaust. His father was a fairly wealthy businessman and his mother was a schoolteacher. Between 1933 and 1939, the Nazi regime had brought radical social, economic and communal change to the German Jewish community. Over that six-year period, the Germans had disenfranchised the German Jewish citizens so that by 1939 fewer than 15% of the breadwinners in Jewish families were even allowed to work. Somehow Ivan's father had used one of his many connections to get much of his savings and his son smuggled out of Germany.

Soon after Ivan arrived in the United States, his father and mother were sent to the concentration camps and both were eventually killed.

According to Ivan's wife Erma, Ivan was haunted by these past events, even though he had no actual memory of the events of that time because he was too young. Erma often told their friends that Ivan used every spare moment of his time gathering information about the time period before and during the Second World War in order to make some sense of his parents' history. As a Jew, Ivan was very concerned about the events that were taking place in Israel and the surrounding Middle East. He was convinced from his studies that there would be another World War during his lifetime. His wife Erma thought he was actually obsessed by that belief and the resulting feelings of suspicion and distrust of everyone that Ivan often demonstrated. Erma eventually became fed up with Ivan's obsessions. Between his work and his studies, they never spent any time together. Ivan had warned her years ago when they were first married that his work was his true love and that she had to live with that fact, which she did for several years. Now her son Michael was growing up, and she felt that Ivan needed to devote time to him and to her. Her objections seemed to fall on deaf ears, and she decided to move out and file for divorce, taking her son Michael with her. In the spring of 1974 Ivan received a call from Edward Mullen, Calbro's Vice President of Security, informing him that the government of Iran had made an agreement with the US Navy to purchase 80 F-14 aircraft under a foreign military exchange program. The work that Ivan had been doing for the US government was eventually applied to the Hughes AIM-54 missiles that were carried on the F-14. The Iranian air force, working through US government procedures, was offering a lucrative service contract worth millions of dollars, to send a systems expert to Iran to help adapt of the missile system to Iranian needs. Calbro's management believed that Ivan was the only choice for this assignment, since he was the single-handed developer of Calbro's input to the AIM-54 system.

Ivan remained silent for a long time after Mullen's comments, providing a hint that he was reluctant to accept it. "There are a lot of things connected to this offer Ivan so I think you should come in a talk to me about it tomorrow. Obviously, we cannot talk about any details over the phone because of the classified nature of the work. A face-to-face meeting seems justified."

Ivan agreed, but his agreement was more from curiosity of what the other things were, that were connected to the offer. This had all come as a shock to Ivan, who had for years avoided involvement with any of the politics associated with Calbro's company operations.

The next morning Ivan was in Mullen's office bright and early, even earlier that Mullen usually arrived. He was graciously welcomed by Mullen's secretary and provided coffee and a bun.

When Mullen arrived, he was a little surprised to see Ivan there that early based on his previous work records, but he politely welcomed him, asking him to wait just a minute so he could open the SCIF. Ivan knew that a SCIF, a Sensitive Compartmented Information Facility, was a special room that was constructed for top-secret briefings of the highest security level. These rooms were constructed from special materials that shielded the inside of the room from any possible outside interference. The rooms were swept electronically every day to ensure that no bugs or other recording devices have been placed there. Mullen had to call in special technicians to open and electronically sweep the room.

As he walked in, he was reminded that his briefcase had to remain outside, and he could not take any notes while inside. Once the room was cleared, they both entered, and the door closed.

To Ivan and most other Calbro employees, Mullin was sort of a creepy guy. He was slightly on the tall side with a skinny build. He always wore a sports jacket that never matched the pants that he wore. The jacket was there to cover an ever-present shoulder holster. Mullen always made sure that the holster was partially visible to impress people with his importance. The type of security work that existed at Calbro certainly didn't necessitate carrying a gun, but it did provide a justification for Mullen to make himself look more important that he really was.

As soon as they were seated, Mullen began what was obviously a well-rehearsed speech. "Ivan, I am required to remind you that there are certain rules attached to briefings in this room. You cannot take notes, nor can you discuss what is discussed here with anyone outside of this room. The Foreign Espionage Act dictates that if you violate these rules, you are subject to imprisonment without a trial. If you understand these requirements and want to continue this briefing, you are required to sign this acknowledgment." The paper was handed to Ivan, and he carefully read it and reluctantly signed it.

"Perhaps to permit you to start this meeting with open ears and an open mind, let me tell you that is a multi-year, multi-million-dollar opportunity for Calbro and for you. We will be getting paid twenty million dollars each year that you are assigned to the project. You personally will receive two million dollars each year. You will be required to work in Iran, in housing that they will provide, and that housing may be in a confined and protected area. Your residence will be supplied with care and maintenance services so that you will have your meals cooked, the facility cleaned so that you will have no need to leave the confines of the area. When you arrive in Iran, they will provide you with a document containing their rules of operation. If you do not accept those rules, you will be returned to the United States and the contract will be canceled. If you are returned because of non-compliance with the rules, you will also be terminated from Calbro after you are completely debriefed by US government security officials.

The work that you will be doing will be advertised as systems integration associated with the AIM-54 missile system, but you will also be spending a great deal of time on another project, not associated with the AIM-54 project. You will be paid by direct deposit into an American bank account, in a bank of your choice. All of your expenses in Iran will be covered by a separate account in Iran. Do you understand what you have just been told?"

By this time Ivan was in a state of shock. He wasn't sure if he had really heard anything after the two-million-dollar-a-year salary offer. "This sounds like I will be going to prison. I'll have little or no freedom and the job seems like a twenty-four seven job. Will I have an American contact to communicate with? How long will I be required to stay in Iran before I can come home without penalty? The last time I checked, even with the new rules and laws being put in place by the Shah, although bringing the country into current times but also creating turmoil among certain segment of the Iranian population and religious clerics, what happens to me if there is some sort of uprising?" "All good questions," Mullen responded. "Your contact will be a CIA operative and his or her identity will be provided to you by the CIA when you are on your way to Iran. Transportation to Iran will be provided by that same organization. Under normal circumstances you will stay in Iran until the project is completed, and that decision will be made by our government. Under any circumstances of government turmoil, your extraction will be coordinated by your CIA contact." Ivan paused for a long time, but this time he was thinking. *If Calbro is getting twenty million dollars a year for this project and they are doing absolutely nothing but sending me to Iran, why are they getting the biggest share of the money? They will not even have to pay my salary during the time that I am there. I'm being ripped off, and I believe there's more here than meets the eye.*

"Here's my initial response," Ivan quietly spoke. "I want ten million dollars each year, and Calbro can also get ten million. I am the value added to this deal and not Calbro. This company is contributing nothing to the deal and taking most of the reward with no risk. Also, my regular

Calbro salary of two hundred thousand a year must be placed in a trust account. My Calbro salary will be tax-free when withdrawn as will all of the monies paid into the special US account for my services in Iran. I will require a two million dollar cash advance bonus, not included in the ten million, which will be tax-free. There will be a time limit of three years maximum in Iran, regardless of project progress, unless I decide to extend the contract, and if I do, I will re-negotiate it at that time. When I return from Iran and I am assured that all of the funds have been properly put in place, my employment with Calbro will be terminated and all records of my ever being employed for this company will be destroyed. Also, I will need a guarantee from the director of the IRS before starting this assignment, that any and all earnings for the rest of my life will be tax-free. Since I am not sure of the specific contents of this assignment, I will also need a signed agreement from the Justice Department that I will never be tried or convicted for anything that I do related to this assignment in Iran, and I will need these assurances before I depart for Iran. Essentially, I want my identity completely eliminated. I may also require my name to be changed, since Iranians are not in love with people of Jewish heritage. Mr. Mullen, if the United States government, the Iranian government, and the management of Calbro agree to each and every one of these conditions, without further negotiation I will probably accept your offer. I may have other conditions as I think more about this." Now, it appeared that Mullen had been taken aback by Ivan's counteroffer. He'd never expected this mild-mannered Ph.D. to be so astute that he would recognize all of the risks associated with this assignment. "Obviously, Ivan, I cannot myself give you those assurances, but I will pass your offer along to the proper people and I will get back to you as soon as possible."

As they walked out of the room Ivan stopped, turned to Mullen and said, "One more thing Mr. Mullen: my offer expires in three days."

As Ivan left the Calbro facility, he was amazed at himself for his aggressive behavior. He had never before acted that way. He thought that maybe the offer seemed so ridiculous to him that he never expected his demands to be accepted, so his confusing behavior took over. Whatever the reason, Ivan felt proud of himself for this sudden aggressiveness.

CHAPTER 3

W HEN IVAN RETURNED home from meeting with Mullen at Calbro, his mood was one of a combination of depression, confusion and joy. He apparently was being rewarded for his years of work at Calbro which had given him international recognition, but the complication of the arrangements with this Iranian program seemed almost too risky, even though the financial reward was more than he could ever have imagined.

Ivan had never trusted Mullen, and he also had doubts about several other members of Calbro management team, even though they had rarely crossed paths. It was the rumors that were always circulating in the background that Mullen and some of the top management of the company was involved in shady contracts with our own government and a few foreign governments.

These "black programs," as they were called, seemed to funnel large sums of money into the company without much justification or oversight. Somehow the US Congress would take this money from programs that were publicly authorized and dump that money into "black programs" that had no oversight. The names of a few congressmen and senators would pop up periodically as rumors of paybacks and corruption within the US government hit the news media. Somehow these rumors were never investigated, and the discussion was always abruptly stopped because of the security levels involved.

What seemed to confuse Ivan more than anything else was the sudden aggression that he demonstrated in the meeting with Mullen. He had rattled off his demands as if he were a seasoned negotiator. He had never been that aggressive before under any circumstance that he could remember. He couldn't get this off his mind. Perhaps, he thought, he so disliked the idea of the offer that he threw out demands that he knew could never be accepted. But ten million a year, he thought, what he could do with that kind of money.

He would be able to realize all of his lifetime dreams.

Ivan was not a drinker, but that day as he arrived home, he decided that the bottle of bourbon that he got as a gift several years ago was about to be opened. When Ivan was first employed by Calbro, he was required to have a complete physical examination as part of Calbro's insurance program. He passed all of the tests, but he was told by the doctor never to use alcohol in times of heavy stress. There was some minor flaw in his heartbeat that gave the doctor cause for concern. Ivan remembered the doctor's comments, but he had not consumed any alcohol in years, so he poured himself a three-finger drink, went to his desk and removed a small envelope that was yellow from age. He sat in his favorite recliner, took a couple of sips of the bourbon, and took a wrinkled letter from that envelope.

When Ivan arrived in the United States from Germany to live with his aunt, she found this letter sewn into his clothes. Every so often, usually during times of stress or confusion, Ivan would read the letter. It seemed to give him a sense of confidence and calm. The letter also reminded him of who he really was.

The letter read:

My dear son, Ivan,

Sending you away to a strange country is the hardest thing that your mother and I have ever had to do, but we know it is for your own safety. Germany is no longer a place where Jews can live peacefully. I was born here, educated here, and ran a successful business here in Germany, but that has all been taken away from me now.

In the early years of this war, we worked with the Reich Association of Jews in Germany, an organization that initially worked to encourage Jewish immigration into this country.

In 1939, just before you were born, the German government imposed a strict curfew on Jews here. Jews were prevented from traveling to many German cities, our food supplies were rationed, and we were even told the times that we could buy food. These times were often stretched so far that we had no food at all to eat. Then the German authorities demanded that the Jews relinquish any property that we owned that was useful to the war effort. I lost my business and nearly everything that we possessed that was of any value. In 1942, the year after you were born, the Germans started to deport thousands of Jews who they felt did not fit the Greater German Reich. At that point your mother and I saw the opportunity to send you to America, away from what we felt was coming—the elimination of all Jews from Germany.

I had worked hard for many years for the country that I thought was my homeland. After all of that loyalty, we are now being thrown aside.

While sending you to America to live with your aunt, I have also sent your aunt money to care for you and ensure that you get a good education. I believe that in America you will have the opportunity to succeed in an environment of freedom.

If I were to give you one small bit of advice, it would be to work very hard to achieve success. Never doubt your own capabilities and your own objectives, but always be suspicious of others who might have motives that are different from yours. These suspicions will keep you alert.

Your mother and I wish you great success in your new world. Please live your life knowing that we did not abandon you, and you will remain always in our hearts.

Your Loving Mother and Father

Ivan was aware that less than one year after that letter was written, both his parents were killed in German concentration camps. Although he had read this letter many times during his life, the advice that he had been given by his father always stuck in his head and he believed that he was honoring his father's advice by having suspicions about all of the activities of others around him. He felt that those suspicions always kept his mind in a position to think carefully before he acted.

The bourbon was starting to have an effect. Ivan had become an expert on brain functions, and he knew very well that alcohol would affect his rational thinking.

He really didn't have a decision to make, since he had already given Mullen and Calbro his decision, or at least his proposal. Can they possibly accept this proposal he thought. *If they do, will I have an opportunity to still back out? Maybe I should have asked for more, he pondered. No, I suspect that would be acting a little greedy. This deal will make me a multi-millionaire; how will I handle that much wealth? Well, I guess most people would consider that a good problem to have*, he thought, and he did still have his dream for the future.

As he finished the bourbon that he had poured and laid the glass on the table next to his recliner, his senses were getting dull, a feeling that Ivan rarely felt. Having no capability to fight the effects of the bourbon, Ivan closed his eyes and fell into a deep sleep.

CHAPTER 4

DURING THE HOURS since Ivan was given the offer by Calbro, he didn't get much real sleep. As the hours passed, he kept re-thinking what his future might be like if this Iran assignment were successful.

On the other hand, what were the consequences if things went bad? His scientific background demanded that he try to keep everything in some logical form of order, and he was trying to mentally prepare a plan and alternatives. Unfortunately, there were too many unknowns involved here for any rational plan to emerge. Ivan's brain was quite able to deal with complicated scientific facts but dealing with life's complications was not his strength.

It was not unusual for brilliant scientific minds to pay little attention to the finances of their lives. Normally they were adequately compensated for their efforts sufficiently to provide a good life for them and their families. But now, there were millions of dollars involved, way beyond anything that an average scientist could ever imagine. Ivan knew that this wealth would permit him to live the remainder of his life any way he wished. With all of the options that Ivan was considering, there was one thing that he was sure of: when the Iran deal was finished, he would never return to Medfield, Massachusetts. It was too close to Calbro and he felt that he would never again want to have any dealings with that company.

When pondering his future, he began to think about his past, or at least his personal past. He realized that his dedication to his job resulted in the notoriety that he had received for his work, which was responsible for this latest opportunity. But building that success came with serious consequences. He had almost completely neglected his relationship with his wife Erma and his son Michael. For some reason that had never bothered him before, probably because he never allowed himself to think about it. This characteristic of spousal neglect was not uncommon among people with high intensity jobs. They were so dedicated to their work and their accomplishments that they forgot about compassion and the other senses that permitted them to offer any real feelings for their associates, even their families.

But now, there was sort of a pause to Ivan's career efforts. For the first time in many years, perhaps triggered by this recent offer, he was now beginning to think about many of his shortcomings, and his wife and family suddenly came to the surface.

When Ivan's wife Erma decided to divorce him, she took their ten-year-old son Michael and moved to Brookline, about ten miles north of Medfield. Even with that short distance, they had not seen each other or spoken since the divorce almost eight years ago. Ivan had no relationship at all with his son Michael.

But now, things were changing. Ivan suddenly was feeling guilty about the way they had parted and his total disconnection from his son. *Real people just don't act that way*, he thought. *I have to do something about that. I'm going to be thousands of miles away from the US, and I can't have this on my mind.* His mind was wandering because he believed that time was now not on his side. It was possible that he would be whisked away to Iran soon if his proposal was accepted, and he just did not want to leave his former wife and son with the hatred that they must be feeling for him. Perhaps instinct caused him to jump into his car and drive to Brookline.

He knew where Erma's sister once lived, but with the total disconnect that they had created, he was not sure if they were still there.

As he drove to the house that he had visited several times in the early years, he saw that nothing had changed. The trees were larger, the shrubs that decorated the front of the house were now overgrown, and the house clearly needed some maintenance.

As Ivan slowly drove up the short driveway, he could see someone peeking through the curtains at him. The image wasn't clear enough for him to recognize anyone, but there was definitely someone home.

Before driving to Brookline, Ivan didn't really think about how he was dressed. His motivation was to finally set things straight with Erma and Michael. He was clad in slightly dirty jeans that never really fit him correctly, his shirt was stained in several places, and he wore his comfortable slippers that looked like he was born wearing them. His hair was messed as it normally was, but those characteristics didn't bother him at this point. He just wanted to get this reunion done.

He rang the front doorbell and waited. There was no reaction. He knew someone was home, so he pushed the button again twice. There was still no answer, so he turned and began to walk back to his car. Just as he put his hand on the car door handle, he heard a voice coming from the house.

"What the hell are you doing here?" the female voice shouted. "You have no business here." Ivan turned to see Erma's sister Rose standing in the open door. He turned and started to walk toward the house and Rose shouted, "Don't come near this house. I don't want you here." Despite living most of her adult life in America, Rose always managed to maintain her Jewish-heritage characteristics in her voice inflections and the endings of her words. Rose looked exactly like Ivan remembered her, short and plump, with her hair pulled back into a bun.

Ivan returned the shout indicating that he just wanted to talk to Erma and Michael. "Things have changed in my life and I need to talk to Erma about a few things. I'm not going to harm anyone, and I'm not looking for anything except a chance to talk to her."

As Ivan was talking, he was edging closer to Rose. "Please, Rose, I really need to talk to Erma. I need to apologize to her and Michael for my behavior. I am going to be leaving the country, and there are things that I need to say to her before I go. Please let me see her."

"Well, she doesn't live here any longer. She got a job working for the City of Boston and she has an apartment there. I'm not sure I believe you, but I'll give you her phone number. You can call her and if she wants to see you, she can give you her address." Rose disappeared for a moment and returned with small piece of paper where she had written the number. She dropped the paper on the stoop and walked inside, closing the door behind her.

Ivan picked up the paper and slowly walked to his car. As he drove slowly around the village of Brookline, he was looking for a phone booth to call Erma. It was Saturday, and if Erma worked for the City of Boston, she would probably be home today, he thought.

He slowly pulled the car into a parking lot of a small drug store. There was a phone booth on the corner. He went into the drug store to get some change for the phone and quickly jogged to the phone booth.

He took out the paper and slowly dialed the number that Rose had given him. "Sixty cents, please," a voice from the phone spoke, in sort of a robotic voice. Ivan dropped in the sixty cents and waited as the number was acquired. The ringing seemed to take forever, but that was just Ivan's anxiety from the possibility of speaking to Erma for the first time in many years.

"Hello," came a voice, softly through the phone's receiver. It seemed like a strange voice, one that Ivan didn't immediately recognize.

"Hello, is this the residence of Erma Schwarz?" Ivan responded

There was instant silence on the other end. "Erma Schwarz?" the voice asked with a questioning tone. "This is the home of Erma Atwater."

Ivan suddenly remembered that Erma's maiden name was Atwater. "Yes, Erma Atwater," he stuttered. "I need to speak to Erma Atwater."

"This is Erma," the voice replied. Now the voice was beginning to sound familiar to Ivan. It had that tone of anger that he remembered was always present in Erma's voice.

"Erma, this is Ivan Schwarz." Ivan couldn't think of anything else to say because he was afraid that while he was talking, Erma would simply hang up the phone. He waited a few moments for a reply or the click of the hang up, but nothing came. "Erma, I really need to see you and talk to you, not over the phone but in person. I will be leaving the country soon, and there are things that I need to say to you and Michael, and they need to be said in person. I am in Brookline. Your sister gave me your number so you could decide if you wanted to see me. I'm not looking for anything from you, and I don't want to affect your life negatively any longer, but it's really important that I talk to you." "Ivan Schwarz, Ivan Schwarz," the hardened voice responded, louder each time she said the words. "How many years has it been, eight, nine? You weren't interested in me or your son for that long, and now it's urgent. I'm surprised that you took time off from your job long enough to drive up here to try to see us. You must be in some kind of trouble, or maybe you are going to die, and you want me to feel sorry for you. If either of those is true, forget about it, I don't need any problems from you." "It's nothing like that, Erma; there are major changes taking place in my life, and I need to make things right with you and Michael. I have to talk with you both."

"Well, Michael is not home today, he is traveling with his high school class on an educational field trip. Saturday was the only day that they could arrange it. I'll give you my address, but I assure you that if you cause me any trouble, I'll call in the police."

"That's fine with me, I'll get there as soon as I can." "Erma gave Ivan her Boston address and he quickly hung up the phone and headed for Boston. As Ivan drove toward Interstate 83 which would take him to Boston, he was reflecting back to his early years when he first met Erma. When he was brought to the United States by his aunt and uncle back in 1940, they all lived in St. Albans, Vermont. His uncle owned a large paper company in northern Vermont.

That was a very rural area back then. Many of the immigrants from Europe had settled in Vermont because there were jobs there. Lumber companies dotted the Vermont landscape, and there were plenty of job cutting and processing logs from the numerous mountain ranges of Northern Vermont. Erma's father worked for Ivan's uncle at the paper company, and they attended St. Albans High School together. There were very few Jews who moved to that area, and during those years, being a German Jew was not exactly popular with the local residents. Erma's family members were American citizens and they rarely talked of their Jewish heritage, but Erma and Ivan became close for exactly that reason. It was sort of like they needed each other for mutual survival. Ivan learned very early in their relationship that Erma's family had changed their name to Atwater to erase any trace of their Jewish heritage. Erma and Ivan dated all through high school. He was a very advanced student, not active in school social events and Erma was quiet and reserved. She had few friends and seemed to hang on to Ivan every chance she had. Ivan was offered scholarships to several colleges because of his academic status. Erma just wanted to be a secretary which was one of the few jobs readily available to women at that time. When Ivan completed his undergraduate work in college, they re-established their relationship, and by that time Ivan was already deeply involved with his work. Calbro had hired him before he finished his master's work at MIT and continued to support him while he pursued his doctorate. MIT had offered Ivan a full-time professor's job when he finished his doctorate, but Calbro was putting pressure on him indicating that they had stuck with him throughout his education, and he should acknowledge that by continuing his work with them. Being a little naive at that time, Ivan stayed on with Calbro, and between all of those studies he and Erma were married and had a child shortly thereafter.

Like many Jewish wives of that time, Erma was content staying at home, taking care of their son Michael and taking whatever role Ivan designed for her as his wife. She had not pursued any advanced education after high school, and she always considered herself very subservient to Ivan because of the huge difference in their education and intellect. She seemed happy with that arrangement and so did Ivan.

As Ivan got more and more involved and dedicated to his work, their activities together and their communication began to dwindle. Eventually they simply lived their lives in the same house but completely apart emotionally.

As for their son, Michael, he was kind of a mama's boy and always seemed to enjoy the coddling by his mother. After all, Michael was the only person to whom Erma could give to or receive any warmth.

When Michael got a little older and began to recognize that there was a problem with the family structure, Erma decided that she needed to take Michael away from this environment so he could grow up in a more stable and loving environment. That was when she and Ivan were divorced. She simply packed all of her personal belongings, along with Michael's, and moved in with her sister Rose in Brookline.

As Ivan approached the series of row houses that were so typical of the Boston area, he became more nervous, almost hesitant to stop and park his car. When he finally saw Erma's house number, he found the first available parking space and parked the car. He sat there for a while trying to get his thoughts together so he wouldn't sound like some bumbling idiot. When he finally rang the bell, Erma quickly opened it and welcomed him inside.

"Sit down, Ivan, but don't confuse my hospitality for any compassion. I have none for you. I'm glad that you are looking well. Would like something to drink?" Erma was holding what looked like a dish towel and as she spoke, her hands kept wringing out the towel, an apparent nervous gesture.

"No," Ivan replied as he looked around the room for any sign that was familiar to him. He found none.

"Look, Erma, without going into a long story that you probably won't believe anyway, I want to get right to the point. I wasn't a very good husband to you, and I was a bad father to Michael. I now know that, and I want you to understand that I am sincerely sorry. I have tentatively been offered a job outside the USA and that job will pay me a great deal of money, more than I could have ever imagined. I will probably never return to Medfield when I complete this assignment, so I won't be using the house. I want you to have it. You can use it or sell it. It will be yours free and clear. When this new deal is completed, I will also give you one million dollars to take care of you and educate Michael. That amount should ensure you a decent life as long as you live, and if properly invested, you should also not need to work any longer." Ivan stopped briefly, partially because he had said everything that he needed to say and also to try to judge Erma's reaction.

"One million dollars! Where the hell are you going to get that kind of money?" Erma shouted as she finally laid that towel on a chair.

"Don't you worry about that. I assure you that the money is legal, and I should be able to get it to you within a couple of weeks. Do with it whatever you like. I will have the house transferred to your name on Monday when I get back to Medfield. I may need you to sign something, but if I do, I will make it as convenient as possible for you. If possible, I would also like to see Michael one more time before I leave on this assignment, to let him know how I feel. You can call me when he is available, and I'll come back up here to talk to him." "Shouldn't we discuss this?" Erma muttered. Now her voice and her demeanor had softened significantly. Finding out that you were just offered a million dollars will do that to a person.

"There is nothing to discuss. This is simply something I want to do in partial penance for the way I treated you both for so many years. Let's just get this done my way, please, Erma."

Ivan wrote his telephone number on a piece of paper and headed for the door. "Please have Michael call me when he gets home. If you ask him or give him permission, he will obey you. Please do it as soon as possible."

"There's a lot about Michael that you don't know," Erma nervously muttered. "Boston has not been the best environment for him during these years when he is really developing. In his own way, he has kept up with your business activities as best he could, because he has never understood why you never thought enough of him to even call him. He has sort of fallen in with the wrong crowd in high school and he has been in and out of trouble for about two years now. He's a good boy, but he lacks the discipline that a father would have given him. I'm not trying to blame you for this. I only feel that you should know before you are surprised if and when you see him. I will ask him to call you, Ivan. I really will." Ivan made a gesture to shake her hand but pulled back, realizing that it would probably be inappropriate under these circumstances. He simply nodded, said, "Thank you, Erma," and started to leave the house.

"Wait," he said as he turned around and faced her again. "Do you remember my aunt and uncle that I lived with in St. Albans when we were young? Their name was Goldblatt. They owned the Mountain State Paper Company at that time. Have you ever heard of them from your family who also lived in that area? "Erma thought for a moment. "Of course, my parents both died, you knew that, so I don't really have any contacts back in St. Albans. But wait, I do remember seeing a newspaper article about one of their two sons who got into politics up there. Do you remember them having two sons?" "Of course, I do. They were slightly younger than I was, born after I arrived in America. One son was Samual and the other was Jonathan, if my memory serves me right. I'm sure the parents are dead, but I sure would like to get in contact with the sons. Erma replied, "I'll bet if you contact the St. Albans newspaper, they can tell you all about them, especially if one of the boys is in politics." "Good idea," Ivan said. "I'll do just that. Thanks a million, Erma, for that information, and please have Michael call me. Goodbye, Erma."

Ivan instinctively walked over and kissed her on the cheek. That was probably the longest conversation that they'd had in years without arguing, and Erma did not reject the kiss.

Ivan got into his car and drove back to Medfield. There seemed to be a million things going through Ivan's mind on the drive home. He should have been thinking about Michael and wondering if he would indeed call him, but instead he was thinking about the Goldblatt boys. He remembered that Ira Goldblatt, the owner of Mountain State Paper Company, had purchased a series of mountains that were located right along the Canadian border, some actually having a good deal of acreage that was actually in Canada. He remembered that there was a lot of controversy about the purchase of that land because some of it was in Canada. Back then, it was nearly impossible to buy land from the Canadian government, but in some way Ira made some kind of a deal to pay off some Canadian officials by paying them a percentage of the profits from the logs that were cut from the Canadian portion of the land. *It's funny how you remember things like that,* Ivan thought to himself. *I do remember there was a big scandal about that which was all over the news at that time. I'm going to have to try to make contact with the boys before I leave.*

With all of the things that Ivan would have to do if his proposal was approved, why was this so important? One of the things about a brilliant brain is that it can often handle several problems at one time, sort of like a computer. Since he was sent to the United States, Ivan had always believed that eventually there would be another big war, and this time it would not exclude America. He remembered the Goldblatt boys joking with him that if there was a war here, they would be safe because they would just go up to one of those mountains and hide on the Canadian side. No one would ever be interested in fighting over Canada they joked.

Ivan grew so intense on the idea of talking to the Goldblatt boys that he decided that the next morning he would drive up to St. Albans. It would be a Sunday, and it would take him most of the day to make the trip, but it would be easier to locate the Goldblatts if he was actually there rather than making several phone calls in search of some clue.

Ivan was actually expecting a call from Calbro on Monday, but he felt that they needed him more than he needed them. If he wasn't home to get the call, they would just have to call back. *Wow,* Ivan thought, *the thought of all that money is certainly making my mind wander in many directions at one time.*

CHAPTER 5

WHEN IVAN ARRIVED at St. Albans, it didn't take much detective work to find the Goldblatt's. He stopped at a local phone booth, opened the phone book and found the names of both Jonathan and Samual Goldblatt. He dialed the number of Samual only because he knew that he was the older of the two and probably the decision-maker in the business. Samual's wife answered the call and immediately put Samual on the phone. After the normal surprise greetings, Samual gave Ivan his home address and invited him to come to the house, and of course Ivan accepted immediately.

When Ivan drove up to the address that Samual had given him, he was more than a little surprised. The facility was quite a distance from the center of St. Albans, and it had a huge gated entrance, like some sort of enclosed compound. There was a call box on the gate, so Ivan pushed the red button on the gate box and waited for a response.

"Can we help you," muttered a voice from the box.

"Yes, this is Ivan Schwarz calling on Samual Goldblatt. I had made a previous appointment."

The gate opened automatically, and Ivan drove down a long, tree covered driveway to the sight of two enormous and beautiful log style homes. The grounds were carefully manicured, and everything just had the look of wealth. Which house should he try, he wondered to himself but then he saw two small brass signs pointing to the houses. One sign said "Samual family," and the other read "Jonathan family," so he headed toward the Samual house.

As he pulled up close to the front sidewalk which was paved with very unusual and beautiful granite stones, a stately middle-aged man came out the door.

"Ivy, is this really you?" shouted a strong, manly voice.

Ivan suddenly remembered that the Goldblatt boys always called him Ivy.

"Yes, it's me" Ivan shouted as they walked toward each other.

"Great seeing you again after all these years," Samual shouted. They shook hands and hugged for a long time.

"Come on in and relax a little," Samual said. "Can I get you something to eat or drink? You've had a long drive up here from the Boston area."

"I'll take something cold," Ivan responded, looking around in amazement at the interior décor of the house. "But nothing with alcohol, please."

"My wife is off shopping, and the two kids are with friends, so here we are, together after so many years," Samual said excitedly. "What the hell have you been doing with your life? I have seen your name mentioned in the paper a few times over the years, but it was always in reference to some highly technical thing you were doing." Ivan replied. "It would take me days to try to explain that to you but I have been working hard for a company named Calbro in the town of Medfield, just south of Boston. You know I married Erma Atwater, my high school sweetheart, and we have one son, Michael. She and I are now divorced. Conflict between job requirements and marriage, you know." "Yeah, I can understand that problem," Samual replied. "Jonathan and I have struggled with that problem for years, trying to keep the company going strong while at the same time trying to keep the family happy. We did find the solution, however—it's money. As long as the wives' pockets are kept full, the problems seem to just go away. What business brings you all the way up here to St. Albans?" "Without going into a great deal of history, I know that your father's company, Mountain State Paper, owned a huge mountain range adjacent to the Canadian border. Do you folks still own that mountain range?" Ivan asked.

Chuckling to himself, Samual responded. "That's a very long story, but I'll try to make it short. Yes, we do still own about 48,000 acres of mountain range, that's about 75 square miles of property. My father believed that to survive in the paper industry we had to own all of the property that would supply our pulp wood for the paper we produced. He also felt that the company needed to be completely vertically integrated before people even knew what that meant. It meant that he wanted to completely control the destiny of the company by owning and controlling the land, the trees, the cutting equipment, the pulp processing plants, and our paper mills.

"The mountain ranges that bordered Canada had some of the finest pine timber in the world, and that's what the company needed to make the high-quality paper we produced.

"The constant north winds on the Canadian side of those hills made the trees on that side of the mountain range grow with a much tighter grain, which made them much more valuable.

"Back in the thirties, when Dad had the business going strong, there were lots of complications for an American company that wanted to buy Canadian government land. As a matter of fact, it was considered impossible at the time.

"But Dad wanted those trees, so he cut some really creative deals with the Canadians, using payoffs to government officials and Canadian Land Management officers and he managed to buy the mountain range, or at least nearly fifty thousand acres of it. Our company paid the Canadian government a small fee for all of the wood that we cut and some of the officials a greater fee to make the deal happen. Back in those times, that's kind of how business was done, as long as no one got greedy and you didn't get caught.

"Our company took timber off those mountains for nearly fifty years, saving the younger trees and planting seedlings as we took out the bigger trees. When the Canadians were told that there was no longer any good timber left on the mountains, they sort of forgot about the whole deal and we stopped paying any of their people, many of whom had died or moved on. I'm not sure if the Canadian government even knows that a good portion of our mountains are on their side of the border. Why do those mountains interest you, Ivan?" "I have always had the desire to own a mountain, somewhere that I could spend my quiet retirement, all alone with my work if I desired to continue to pursue it. I am about to make a career change that might give me enough financial resources to do just that, and the first place I thought about was your land, right back near the place where I was welcomed into this country." Samual seemed a little confused, because he had always thought of Ivan as this brilliant scientist who would never really retire and certainly not on some mountaintop.

"Why a mountaintop?" Samual asked.

"Seclusion I suppose. I don't know, maybe just to do something different, sort of off the grid, so to speak." Ivan replied.

"Well, I have to tell you that my brother Jonathan is the wheeler and dealer in our business. He's into politics and all that stuff and spends about half of his time in the business. He is on the board of the local bank and also on the board of several regional businesses. We have built this business into a giant in recent years as the demand for paper, especially high quality paper, was increasing. We still keep the vertical integration concept alive and we still own all of the resources that we need to survive, the raw materials, the equipment to secure it and to process it. We have total control of our own destiny, which is very unusual these days. My father wanted it that way and we kept it that way.

"You remember, back when we were kids, the company would move logs from one end of Lake Champlain to another. Hundreds of miles, it seemed, to get the timber to the pulp mills. We also had water to the west with the Missisquoi River, east of the mountain range, to move it south in that area. My father was creative that way. As technology advanced, he purchased all of the equipment needed to move all of the product that we needed wherever we needed them. I believe that total integration concept, although expensive, is the reason for our continued success when other paper companies are failing." Ivan seemed deep in thought about this whole story of the company's success. "Do you think you could talk to Jonathan about the idea of selling me a mountain some day?"

I'll talk to him, but I can almost assure you that it will not be a sale, perhaps a lifetime lease. I know we wouldn't do it for anyone else, but you are really family, long-lost, but still family. Since my father did so many illegal things to get that land, I'm sure that we will not want to do anything that would go into the public records which would be required if any sale was completed, especially on the Canadian portion of the land.

"What's your timing on all of this, Ivan? Is it something that has any urgency attached to it? I know that Jonathan will not get involved in anything that he can't carefully work out, especially if it crosses borders."

"No rush, Samual. I still have to complete my negotiations for my new assignment overseas. I just wanted to see if there was any possibility that I could make such a deal in the future. If so, we can find a way to communicate on the issue in the near future. I'm not sure how much longer I'll be in Medfield but if you agree, I can call you or even Jonathan before I leave town, maybe in a few days." "I tell you what I'll do, Ivan. I'll talk to Jonathan about this tomorrow. Here's his business card with his office number. You can call him in a few days to discuss it with him. Whatever you and he agree on, I'll support."

"Great" Ivan responded. "I have much to do in the next few days, so I must get back home, or we could stay here and compare old times all night. I wish I could have met your wife and kids. Maybe someday, if things work out, I will be able to do that. Thanks for your time and your cooperation on this matter, Samual. I certainly appreciate it." With a handshake and a slight hug, Ivan left the house for his drive back to Medfield. His thoughts were very positive. Maybe, he thought, I can make my long-standing plan come together. Samual and Jonathan certainly have all of the resources that I would need to complete the project.

CHAPTER 6

WHEN IVAN ARRIVED home late that evening, he felt a feeling of relief having finally confronted his former wife. He never even realized the extent of the guilt that he was carrying around for the way he had treated her and Michael over the years. But he still needed to talk to Michael.

The sudden trip to St. Albans had eaten up his entire Sunday but he also felt that it was productive, putting him back in touch with his family and providing him a little hope that the Goldblatts could help him realize his dream. There was something about Samual, however, that made him uneasy. He wasn't sure what it was, but there was this nagging suspicion that Samual was putting on a show for him. For the time being he was going to put that suspicion aside.

He felt like time was closing in on him, and he was making it worse by wanting to do so much in what he perceived as such a short time. He remembered how the three fingers of bourbon relaxed him the other day, so he poured himself another glass and relaxed in his recliner. Within minutes, he fell sound asleep.

He was suddenly awakened by the ringing of the phone. It seemed like he had been sleeping for hours. It was late at night as he shook the cobwebs from his mind and got up to answer the phone.

"Hello, this is Schwarz," he said softly into the phone, as though still half-asleep.

An excited voice on the other end shouted, "Dad, this is Michael."

Ivan was still not totally awake, and he hesitated a moment to gain all of his senses back.

"Michael, I'm so glad you called," Ivan responded, with the same sort of excitement that Michael had exhibited.

"Man, I was so excited when Mom said that you visited her yesterday and wanted me to call you. She indicated that you wanted to meet with me to talk about things. I'm bummed out that I missed you, but my senior class had scheduled a field trip to a museum and Saturday was the only day that it could be arranged. I have been trying to call you all day with no success." "No need to apologize, Son, I do need to get together and talk to you as soon as possible." That was the first time he had called Michael "Son" in years, possibly ever.

"Dad, I know we have been out of touch for years, but you probably don't know that I have been checking out your technical activities whenever possible. Much of your work is secret, but I have actually read a couple of your early papers that were published. Remember, I said that I read the papers—that doesn't mean that I understood a word of what was printed. You also don't know this, but I actually attended one of your lectures at MIT two years ago. I skipped school to attend, and Mom was furious because I didn't tell her where I was. I figured the lecture I would get from her for skipping school that day was less damaging than the one I would have gotten from her if I told her that I went to hear you talk. I knew that you had become sort of famous in your technical circles and I have always been proud of that. My friends never understood why I had an interest in that technical stuff, because Mom had changed our name to Atwater, so my friends never made the connection." Ivan was so excited to hear these words that he interrupted Michael. "Great to hear those words, Son. I have some important business to attend to tomorrow, but if we can get together tomorrow, I'll change all my plans."

"I'll make arrangements with my school to make up the work, so that I can be here at the apartment all day tomorrow. What time do you expect to arrive?"

"Let's make it around ten tomorrow morning. Your Mom will probably be working, and it will be better if we talk when she is not there. But I think you had better tell her that you are taking time off school to meet with me." Ivan instructed.

"I agree," Michael replied. "She'll throw a fit if I don't come clean with her, so I'll talk to her tonight. She will probably respect my wished more than yours. Everything she says about you seems always to be in anger, although I will admit when she told me you were here, she seemed to be different, no anger and no frustration. That actually confused me a little." "Did she tell you anything about our discussion?" Ivan asked. "Nope," Michael replied, "just that you were here and wanted to speak to me"

"Okay then, I'll see you at ten tomorrow morning."

There was no sleeping that night for Ivan. He had years of non-discussion to make up for, so he had to plan out exactly what he was going to say to Michael the next morning. The truth, it seemed would be the best plan, but where to start?

The drive back to Boston the next morning seemed to take forever even though the Monday morning traffic seemed lighter than usual. Ivan kept going over in his mind the things that he had to say to his son after all of these years. Should he be apologetic for his absence, when deep down inside he really didn't feel guilty? Should he be firm in his resolve and simply lay out his plan? Should he use this meeting to offer Michael advice? How could he do that, when he had never set a good example himself. Most of all, he wanted to make sure that in the end, they might get a new start, at least emotionally.

When Ivan's car pulled into the driveway slightly before ten, Michael was waiting on the front stoop. As soon as Ivan was out of the car, Michael was right there and took the initiative to grab hold of him and they both hugged for a long time.

Ivan was a little shocked at the sight of Michael. He was about six feet tall and very well-built, almost like an athlete. He seemed strong and when they broke their hug Michael offered his hand for a handshake, which was very firm. Ivan kind of expected some kind of a wimpy kid, as he remembered Michael at a younger age. Obviously, Michael was now a man, and Ivan suddenly realized that he had to talk to him as a man and not a child, as he had planned.

"Let's go, inside, Dad," Michael suggested. "I told Mom about our meeting, and would you believe she wasn't even mad about me taking time off school? We will be alone, and we can feel free to talk without fearing that she was listening from the other room."

"That was very perceptive of you, Michael."

They sat at the kitchen table where they could talk face to face.

Just as Ivan was about to start the conversation, Michael put his hand up to stop him. "Dad, there is a great deal that needs to be said here today, and part of that is my responsibility. Before you start your story, I want to tell you mine, very briefly. I'm 18 years old now and just about to finish high school. Ever since I can remember, Mom has coddled me with the excuse that she was protecting me from your neglect. I never really felt neglected by you. I knew that you were a very brilliant man with a very important job and that job came before everything else in your life. I overheard you and Mom arguing about that many times when we were together, and as I got older, I understood and accepted it.

"When Mom took me to Aunt Rose's house to live, I hated it there and I let her know that, but she just thought that I was just striking back at her because I was angry at you. That was never the case at all. When Mom finally decided to get a job in Boston and we moved there, I needed some space from her, and I got involved with a tough Irish gang in the neighborhood. These weren't really bad guys; they just wanted to look tough. We hung around a gym in a bad neighborhood and worked out a lot, never really getting into any serious trouble. We might smoke a joint or steal cigarettes from the local deli, but that was about it. We did get dragged into the local station house a few times, but never for anything serious. Mom felt like that was an embarrassment to the family. I have never been arrested, and there is nothing on my record that will ever hurt me in the future.

"Mom keeps hounding me to start thinking about college, but I don't give a damn about college. I want to join the military and find myself there. I need the freedom from coddling, and I need someplace where I can develop into someone special, like you, Dad, someone special like you."

Ivan had tears in his eyes, and he found it very hard to respond to Michael's words. "Michael, I am so very proud of you. You just took away just about everything that I wanted to say to you. I am so very proud of you. I'm sure you know that people like me, who have very high-pressure jobs, often get caught up in those jobs and forget about some of the more important things in life. I did that, Michael, and I am extremely sorry for that. I am so happy to hear that your plan is success-oriented because without that kind of drive, you will never truly be successful." "Dad, you can mark my words, or for that matter you can bet your ass that someday you will be proud of me for my achievements."

"Son, you have already made me proud of you."

Michael pointed to Ivan and said, "Now it's your turn. What's your story that is so important?"

"Michael, you just reached into my brain and pulled all of the words out that are important to me, other than to say that if I have in any way damaged you with my behavior, I am very sorry. It is important to me that you understand that, but I also need to tell you of some future plans of mine which might take me away from you again. I have been offered a very important job outside of the country. I can't tell you where and the details of my work are involved with the US government and a foreign government and of course that makes the job a security issue. You understand that, because I have always had that type of work where I could never discuss my work outside of Calbro." Michael nodded as though he completely understood.

"This job is going to carry with it a lot of risk being away in another country, but the job also will pay me a great deal of money, more money that I could ever have wished for. When the job is finished, which may take several years, I might not be returning to Medfield, so I have told your mother that I am signing the house over to her free and clear. I am also giving your mom a great deal of money, which should be sufficient to educate you if you wish, and she should be able to live comfortably for the rest of her life without working. I suppose that she feels like this is guilt money, but nevertheless I want to do this for you both." "There are a couple of cultural things that are also associated with this assignment. I may be required to change my name. The area of the world that I will be working in might not be too friendly to a person of Jewish heritage. I have also established several criteria to my acceptance of the assignment that will help us all live a better life when I return, whenever and wherever that is." "Somehow I will try to find a way to keep you informed of my situation to help reduce the mystery but that might be very hard. When I was sent from Germany by my parents, who were later killed by the Nazis, they sewed a letter into my pants which was later discovered by my aunt. I want you to have that letter, because it provides some excellent advice. My father instructed me to use all of my strength to be the best at whatever I attempted. He also instructed me to always be confident in myself and never have any doubts about my own strengths, which were in my genes. He also warned me that even without self-doubt, I should always be suspicious of those who offered me the easy way out. I have always taken those words very much to heart because I understand that my father was a very smart person and had great vision of the ways of the world. Even in this new assignment, I have serious suspicions about the motives of Calbro and even my own government, so I think I have taken the necessary steps to protect myself from the things that might damage me or my family. You know, Michael, that I have always told you and your mother that I have this terrible feeling that sometime during my lifetime there will be another very large war, probably a world war. That thought eats away at me constantly as I see what is happening in the world. People are having a lot of trouble getting along with each other, especially in the Middle East where our heritage lies. I hope that my fears never come true, but I will be on a constant alert to ensure that I and my family are protected should this type of catastrophe happen. At some point in the future, I will discuss this with you further as my plan develops further. Let us both pray that my fears never are realized." Michael was stunned by Ivan's revelations. "Will I be able to communicate with you?" he asked.

"I'm not sure, but I will develop a plan for that as things become clearer to me. As long as I am in this country, I will keep you informed. When I get settled, I will try to figure out a method of communications. You will be graduating in June, and again I will apologize in advance for not being able to attend that event, but rest assured that I will be thinking about you and wishing you the greatest success in whatever you choose to be. Whatever it is, just be great at it." They both knew that whatever had to be said was now said and it was time for them to part. They hugged and gave each other kisses on the cheeks. Both had tears in their eyes that they were trying to hide from the other.

"I love you, Michael."

"I love you, Dad. Be careful and thank you very much for your kindness to me and Mom."

CHAPTER 7

AFTER A VERY long but rewarding day, Ivan slept in a very deep sleep that night, but was suddenly awakened by the ringing of his phone. This could be the call from Calbro, he thought. He had given them a week and today is only the third day. With the weekend in between, he thought maybe they couldn't get to the right people to make a decision on his offer but when he answered the phone it was indeed Edward Mullen.

The voice on the other end, after the normal hello, said, "Ivan this is Mullen at Calbro. I have worked out many of the requests that you made, and I think we can now move forward. There are a few things remaining that we need to talk about, so you will need to come back in at your convenience to discuss them in an appropriate environment. There will be two other gentlemen present representing our government, so please dress appropriately. When can we expect your arrival here?" "I'll be there in two hours," Ivan answered. He seemed to feel that Mullen's tone of voice was much more congenial than it ever had been. *Was this good or bad?* he thought. He really didn't know but he would shower and put on some appropriate clothes and soon find out. There were moments when he felt joy at the thought of all that money, and then there were thoughts of fear of the dangers that may lie ahead of him. Also, now, another element had entered the equation: he would miss his son, a feeling that he'd rarely felt before.

When Ivan arrived at Calbro, his welcome was like none that he had ever received before. He was actually met in the parking lot by Mullen who shook his hand vigorously like he was an old friend, long lost.

"There are some other people here today to brief you on the assignment. You will get more detail and a final opportunity for you to change your mind if you prefer that. We hope you don't change your mind but when you get these details you will know more about your work and the government's expectations of you," Mullen exclaimed.

In a way, Ivan felt relief that he still had a chance to turn the project down, but in his heart, he knew that possibility was very distant since his plans and dreams were already being put into place for his future.

They went inside and again entered the SCIF where Ivan was initially briefed by Mullen. This time there were two other men there. They introduced themselves by name but with no identification of their affiliation. Based upon their dress and first appearances, Ivan assumed they were CIA. He had seen those types before but never dealt directly with them.

Mullen started the meeting with the normal briefing warnings and indicated that the remainder of the briefing would be conducted by the two strangers.

The one who looked like the more senior of the two introduced himself only by his first name, Thomas.

"Ivan, the assignment that you have been selected to carry out is extremely important to the United States government. You are obviously aware that it is a top-secret program, and you understand that these types of programs carry with them high levels of risk. This assignment carries with it a national security implication, which means that it's important and has far-reaching effects on the future of our country.

"Whatever is spoken or published about your presence in Iran will be related to the integration of the AWG 9 system into the F-14s that Iran recently purchased from the US Navy. You will indeed be working on that project when needed.

"That's not the important part of the assignment it's only a front for your real assignment and an excuse to get you into the country legitimately. A small group of Russian and German scientists have been working on another project that we have also been cooperating with. The group is developing a new powerful series of drugs that, when properly administered, can be mind-altering. These drugs can apparently have a powerful effect on certain selected nervous system elements that, when passed on to the brain, can render a person or an entire community useless to themselves or others. The drugs can alter a man's will to fight or even to live under some circumstances. The drugs are not designed to kill, only to alter behavior. The overall objective of this development is to be able to fight a war without any casualties. A person given these drugs loses all memory of his actions and for the most part, as we understand it, the drugs are un-detectable in the body after a short period of time. There is more work going on with the research to refine the different applications that it might be used for.

"We have had two American scientists working with the group, but their specific skill specialty was not appropriate for the assignment, and we felt their principles may have been compromised, and they have been removed.

"The group may have done a fair amount of human experimentation with the drugs before our arrival and of course the US government has no connection to that experimentation.

"We have been informed that the project has come to somewhat of a halt because they cannot figure out exactly how to get certain body nerves to carry the drug to the portions of the brain that control selected body functions. Also, in order for the drugs to be operationally useful, there will have to be some very specific methods developed for their introduction into the body. This is why they specifically requested your presence on the project. You have established an international reputation in the field of neural networks, specifically how to develop a computer that will duplicate all of the functions of the human brain. The group feels that you have the answers that they need to bring this series of drugs to the operational stage. Are you with me so far, Ivan?" Thomas asked.

"So far so good," Ivan replied, "but my normally suspicious nature tells me that there is more here than meets the eye."

"That's certainly perceptive of you, Ivan. Perhaps that why you were selected by our top people to go along with the program. The real issue here is that we do not want this drug to get operationally into the hands of the Russians, the Germans, or more importantly the Chinese. It has been a very strange alliance that has been established here, Ivan, but it is a house of cards. We believe that each of the participating countries has the same motive, to steal the results and deprive the other participants of the benefits. Everyone gives the impression of working together, but we know that everyone is holding back from everyone else.

We want you to do your part to bring the project to its completion, but we also want you to build in sort of a kill switch, to hold back just enough to render the final results useless to the other participants. Do not share your work with anyone unless that makes them suspicious of you. If you sense that happening, give them just enough to feel comfortable but never reveal the final keys to success." "Do you think that I am smart enough to fool those brilliant scientists?" Ivan responded. "I'm sure that they were selected to work on this project because they also have a very high degree of intellect."

"We have reviewed several candidates who were recommended by the team in Iran, and we feel that your motives and your goals in life best suit this assignment. You have no family attachments, so that will never affect your work. You let nothing interfere with your work. You have proven that to Calbro. We also know that you want to carry on your work on networks eventually, and the financial reward that you will receive will permit you to do that on your own when you complete this assignment.

There are two elements of your proposal that we cannot accept. One is your demand that the program end in three years. Only you will be able to determine that, when you get integrated into the program in Iran. This will all be for nothing if we don't succeed in sabotaging the program results for the other participants. That will take as long as it takes. The second demand involves changing your name. You were requested for this project by others that are already on the team. Your former work and your reputation in your field put you in that position. Changing your name at this point would therefore not be prudent and would possibly signal the wrong intent on the part of our government. Except for the short time that you are being transporting through the country prior to your arrival at your final destination, you will have little or no contact with the Iranian government, so your concern about your Jewish heritage is probably not of great importance." Ivan went deep into thought and then replied, "Okay, I'm in. I guess by the terms that you folks use, I am now officially a spy."

"We don't like to use that terminology, Ivan," Thomas responded. "Call it whatever you like in this room, but outside you are just an eccentric, brilliant scientist doing a specialized job."

"I do have a slight modification of my original demands," Ivan said. "After the two million dollar advance is paid to me before I leave for Iran, I want my remaining salary deposited as gold in a place that I will pick, probably a US bank. I'm now not exactly sure who is making these payments, but I assume that it is the US government and not Calbro. The amount of gold deposited into my account will be a function of the price of gold at the beginning of this assignment. If the market price of gold changes, this factor will remain constant. In other words, if the price of gold increases significantly, my reward will be greater. If gold drops below the starting value, I will lose. Seems fair to me, since I am taking all the risk. Any problems with that, Thomas?" Thomas seemed a little annoyed at this added complication. "I don't think it's a problem, but it's above my pay grade. I'll take care of it for you."

"Deal's done, then," Ivan responded. "When and where do we start?"

"Probably two weeks, but we will call you with the exact instructions. Get your affairs in order and plan for two weeks."

"By the way," Thomas interrupted before they left the room, "you had once asked about having a contact point close by that you could use if necessary. There will be an operative stationed in the United Arab Emirates, right across the Gulf of Oman from where you will be stationed. You will stop there before entering Iran, and he will brief you in more detail about some of the local issues." "Sounds fine to me," Ivan stated. And they all shook hands and departed the SCIF.

CHAPTER 8

DESPITE THE FACT that Ivan might have appeared all in on this assignment when he left this latest briefing at Calbro, he couldn't help having the feeling that he was being used as some sort of a pawn in an international chess game. His father had given him that warning to be suspicious of anyone whom he didn't completely trust. These government guys, and also Mullen of Calbro, just increased his level of suspicion about the whole program. But the financial reward was certainly large enough to outweigh the risks, or at least it seemed that way to Ivan. After all, where else would a middle-aged scientist find a legal way to earn several million dollars in just a few years?

Now that he had some better schedules and more details about his work, he thought it would be a good idea to go back to St. Albans to meet with his other cousin, Jonathan Goldblatt. Things were happening fast, and Ivan felt that he needed to firm up his relationship with Jonathan. Much was yet to be done to firm up his business relationship with Jonathan so that everything would be in place to enact his future plans while he was out of the country. According to Samual Goldblatt, Jonathan was the wheeler-dealer in the family and very astute about politics and other ways of the world. He still needed to get a firm answer on his request to acquire a mountain from Mountain State Paper Company and according to Samual, Jonathan was the person he had to deal with and perhaps he could also provide some advice without actually requiring Ivan to provide any details of his new assignment.

When Ivan returned home, he called Jonathan to arrange a meeting. He wasn't able to talk directly to Jonathan on the phone, but his secretary arranged a meeting for the following day in Jonathan's St. Albans office. When Ivan arrived in St. Albans the next day, finding Jonathan's office building on Congress Street wasn't difficult. It was the tallest building in that area, but it contained no identification of Mountain State Paper Company.

The receptionist directed Ivan to the 10th floor office marked Jonathan Goldblatt. When he entered the reception area on that floor, he was astounded by the surroundings. It had all the signs of wealth. There was beautiful art on the walls, comfortable seating and worktables for waiting guests, and the prettiest receptionist that Ivan had ever seen.

"Good morning, Mr. Schwarz," the secretary muttered in a voice that was almost seductive. "Mr. Goldblatt is expecting you. Please follow me."

When Ivan entered Jonathan's office, it also had the atmosphere of very exclusive surroundings. It was what Ivan had imagined that the Oval Office of the President might look like. The desk and associated furniture were cluttered with books and papers and somewhat out of context with all of the other aspects of this facility.

Jonathan entered the office from a small adjoining room and quickly hugged Ivan as if seeing a long-lost friend, just as Samual had done when he first met Ivan. Jonathan was shorter than Samual, perhaps about five foot ten. His hair was thinning, but his overall appearance was stately and businesslike.

"Let's get comfortable," Jonathan said, "1 understand we have a lot of important stuff talk about. My brother told me about your request to do some business with us regarding one of our mountains up near the Canadian border. Why would a brilliant guy like you want to be off in that Godforsaken wilderness? You are a scientist who has dedicated his life to serving your passion with science. What's going on, Ivan?" Ivan had thought a lot about what form this conversation would take. He couldn't reveal any of the facts of his Iranian assignment to Jonathan, but he wanted to get to feel that he could trust him. He had to try to condense his story, so it made sense, but he didn't have all week to do it. So, he started slowly.

"Jonathan, I have always believed that sometime during my lifetime, considering the events of the last few years around the world, there is going to be a third world war and that war will come to America. I have been obsessed with that thought, and I have been so dedicated to my work that I wanted to find a place where I could get off the grid to finish the work that I started. Your mountains border Canada, as I understand it, and some of them actually take in a good deal of Canadian land. If a war happens, I don't believe that it will involve Canada; they are constantly moving toward a politically neutral country. I want to build an underground facility in that area that is undetectable but will provide me all of the comfort and tranquility that I will need to do my work. I have mentally designed that facility in my head, but I could never figure out how I could get it built without a lot of people knowing about it. I believe that your organization has all of the capability that would be needed to accomplish my goals." Jonathan stopped Ivan abruptly. "Ivan, you are talking about a great deal of money to accomplish a feat like that. You don't have that kind of money."

Ivan interrupted this time. "I only told you part of my story, Jonathan. The rest of it might have to remain somewhat vague because it involves the United States government. I have accepted an assignment outside the United States. I can't get into the details of the assignment, but it will make me a very rich man if it all goes well."

"How rich?" Jonathan interrupted.

"Could be fifty to one hundred million by my simple calculations, if it takes as long as I think it might. That would be about five years or so."

When that number was mentioned, Jonathan got up, walked over to the windows, and nervously closed the blinds. They were on the tenth floor, but it seemed like Jonathan was concerned that someone might be listening in.

"That was just a nervous reaction," Jonathan said. "You are talking about something very big here, Ivan. Are you sure of what you are getting into?"

"For the most part, yes," Ivan responded, "but since I am dealing with the US government, I really don't trust any of the people involved. I have arranged a contract that I think will protect me legally if I do my job right, but I am certainly suspicious of the government people involved. I have demanded that my salary for this assignment be guaranteed by the government and paid in gold. I have protected myself from gold price variations by insisting that my salary payments be based on the price of gold at the time of the contract signing. If gold prices drop, I am protected. If prices rise, I make out. I would also like you to manage the banking and transaction aspects of that part. I supposedly have written guarantees from the IRS that all of this money will be tax-free, and the Justice Department has assured me that I will be free from any prosecution for anything that might be illegal in this assignment. I have also demanded that if I desire, my entire existence will be erased from the records when I complete the assignment. All of this will be in writing and guaranteed by the highest sources in the United State government." Jonathan was now slowly pacing the office floor and appeared to be deep in thought. His whole demeanor had changed when he heard about the gold, especially when Ivan indicated that he wanted him to handle the financial arrangements while he was out of the country. All of a sudden, Jonathan was a different person. His whole personality seemed to change and become more thoughtful and cooperative.

"Ivan, I am shocked and amazed. I consider myself an astute businessman and somewhat of a wheeler-dealer, but I cannot imagine that I could ever negotiate a deal like that, especially with the US government. Who the hell is powerful enough in our government with enough longevity to provide those guarantees? Even the President might not be around long enough to offer that assurance. Ivan, you must be careful about this." "I know that Jonathan and I would like your help here. You have great political connections but not in these areas. I know that you have enough experience and connections to handle the gold transactions for me and make sure that the conversions and deposits are made when required. Of course, I will compensate you in any way you wish. When I find out more about what political connections are woven through this deal, I'll keep you informed about that, also. I'm on strange ground with the politics of all of this, but on the surface, there are no politicians involved here yet." Jonathan jumped in. "Don't be naive, Ivan. A deal of this magnitude, involving so much unidentified money, definitely has some political payoff somewhere very high up in Washington. Look, Ivan, I cannot sell you any of the land that you desire but I can make an arrangement to lease it to you. I have paid off so many Canadian officials to alter their records that I am not going to take a chance of disturbing that. Any sale that I make will have to be recorded, and that's a time bomb. You can understand that. A lease can be arranged, and we can keep it all in the family. Much of the 185,000 acres that we own was cut many years ago. Our conservation efforts and plantings have resulted in a regrowth of those forests to the point that we will soon be cutting there again so I can probably handle the construction that you asked for but I will certainly need more details of what you want. We can deal with that later, but I think you understand that a project like that will be very expensive. I'll provide you with a bank account number and the necessary information for safe and secure deposits without any IRS reporting. You may have IRS guarantees, but my bank doesn't; but we do have workarounds.

"You would be surprised, but when you line a few pockets with some money, you can get all sorts of protections."

Ivan was feeling pretty good about the progress of this meeting. Most important to him was that Jonathan made him feel comfortable and gave him a feeling of confidence that he could be trusted in these dealings, a feeling that Ivan rarely had about anyone lately.

"I'm not sure what the method of communications will be with you, Jonathan, once I am on station out of the United States. I suspect it will be though a government operative, but I will let you know as soon as I know. Jonathan, I can't tell you what a relief this meeting has created for me. I really feel that I can trust you on this, one of very few people whom I have ever trusted in my entire life.

Jonathan replied, "L'fum tzara agra," Ivan had not heard that expression since he was young. Jonathan's father always used it to define success. It loosely means, "Your reward will be proportional to your hard work."

"Let's hope so, Jonathan. Let's hope so."

When Ivan left Jonathan's office, he felt a sense of relief that this aspect of his life was now being put into place, especially with the possible construction of his dream facility. But something deep inside him was troubled. As soon as he left the office, he started to feel that perhaps things went too well with Jonathan. He seemed much too willing to take on this major task especially the task of managing the gold transactions and Ivan's other financial business. It seemed that Jonathan's whole demeanor changed when the extent of the money transactions was discussed. Up to that point, Jonathan seemed like he was simply being polite, sort of stringing him along. But when Jonathan realized the extent of the financials, he suddenly became very positive about everything.

When Ivan was in Jonathan's office, he'd felt as if a big load had been taken off his back, but suddenly Ivan was overtaken by the feelings of suspicion that were part of his personality since reading that letter from his father, written many years ago. *This is family*, Ivan thought. *If I can't trust family, what is left for me?*

CHAPTER 9

WITHIN DAYS AFTER reaching agreement with Calbro and the US government, Ivan received his salary advance that was part of that agreement. He was shocked that any deal involving the US government could be finalized that quickly, especially one that seemed very complex. He was even more surprised at how difficult it would be to deal with a bank when he walked in with a two million dollar check. He did manage to deposit one million dollars to an account in the name of his former wife, Erma. He also completed the necessary paper work needed to transfer the house to her as he had promised, and he sent legal papers to Jonathan Goldblatt giving him power of attorney over his financial affairs and signatory authority for the new one million dollar account that he had established in a bank that Jonathan had recommended. Along with the financial papers, he sent Jonathan a series of drawings and sketches he had made over the years, plans of the facility he wanted Jonathan to construct, promising Jonathan that he would provide much more information as a later date. Despite the rapid pace at which everything seemed to move in the beginning, all of a sudden everything seemed to slow down. Ivan really didn't mind this slowdown because it gave him more time to provide Jonathan more details on the proposed facility and to clean up all of the other matters in a manner that better satisfied him that it was all done properly.

Finally, the day had arrived for Ivan to start his new assignment. A courier arrived at his home with a message containing his final instructions.

He was to go to Hanscom Air Force Base in Bedford, Massachusetts, not far from where he lived. He would be shuttled from Hanscom to Andrews Air Base in Washington, DC. where he would board an Air Force C-130 which would fly him to Al Dhafra Air Base in the United Arab Emirates. He would then be shuttled to a Special Ops Command facility close by. There he would then meet his CIA contact operative who would provide him his final papers and answer any detailed questions that he had that might not have been previously answered.

After all of that, he would then be flown about 1000 miles north to Tehran, the capitol of Iran, for briefings and "conditioning" by an Iranian contact. Following that he would fly south by Iranian transport to Khatami Air Base in central Iran where the F-14s were stationed. He would meet with American technicians working on the integration of the AIM-54A to establish his cover with that project. The extent of the integration project would be determined by Ivan. Whatever the time frame when that work was completed, he would be flown to the town of Bandar Abbas which is located on the shores of the Gulf of Oman in the Arabian Sea. That would be his final destination for his work in Iran. He would live and work at that location.

He would be assigned an English-speaking assistant to help with his integration with the rest of the scientific team, many of whom spoke only their native Russian or German.

The instructions also made it very clear that he would be met at every stop by a special guide who would take him directly to his next meeting point, and that he should never leave the side of that guide while in any public environment in Iran.

When he left the UAE for Iran, he would be provided with Iranian Rials which was their currency. The conversion rate was about 10 million Rials to $550 American dollars. He would have little need for money while on the assignment because everything would be provided for him, so a few hundred dollars should be sufficient.

Ivan studied this communication over and over again to ensure that he understood all of the many details that it contained. He now realized that as soon as he boarded that Air Force airplane, he was no longer in control of his own destiny. Everything seemed to be well mapped out down to the smallest detail.

The next day he took a taxi to Hanscom Field, as directed, and was met at the gate by a smartly dressed female Air Force captain. He was provided a short briefing about the helicopter trip and introduced to the flight crew, and they departed for Washington. Ivan didn't realize that this would be a helicopter trip. He had never flown in a helicopter and was a little nervous. Was it really the helicopter that made him nervous, or the thought of leaving his home state possibly never to return again?

They arrived at Andrews about an hour later, after an uneventful trip. As he exited the helicopter, he felt his body still shaking from the aircraft's vibrations. It was a very strange sensation that soon wore off.

He was escorted to a briefing room at Andrews and provided covering flight gear for the next phase of the trip to the United Arab Emirates. This was not a commercial flight by any means. There were three of four other military personnel aboard that appeared to have nothing to do with his assignment. The seats were only mildly padded, and Ivan couldn't imagine spending 12 hours in this type of seating arrangement, but what choice did he have?

When the plane landed in Abu Dhabi, Ivan was exhausted. He was driven to the Special Operations facility where he was provided a small room with a shower and bed to spend the night. He showered and immediately sat on the bed. He wasn't sure if his body was experiencing day or night. He simply felt a very high level of fatigue, like he had never felt before.

He had been flown halfway around the earth since he last slept, and the only desire he had was to sleep. He reclined on the bed and fell immediately into a deep sleep.

Ivan slept soundly through the night and was awakened by a knock on his bedroom door. He opened the door to welcome another stranger who introduced himself as Peter Welch.

"I will be your CIA intermediate contact for this operation" Welch began. "I will not be located in Iran, but you will be provided with a method of contacting me if you need assistance while you are in the country. I must mention that once your assignment begins, your contact with me should be kept to a minimum, usually only under extreme situations. In your living quarters we have installed a small satellite communication signal device. Triggering that device will set off a series of events that will get you in contact with me. We are not confident that this system is always secure, so hopefully any contact with me will rarely be necessary.

"Let me tell you about the key people and organizations involved with this project. You are aware that the cover project that brings you to Iran involves the integration of the missile system into the Iranian F-14 aircraft. The political situation in Iran is very unstable, and their future relationship with the United States is also very unstable. If things turn hostile between the two countries, we may not want them to have use of these aircraft. Your purpose is to anticipate that situation and to find a way to sabotage that effort, to render that weapon system useless to the Iranians. I believe you have been briefed on that assignment. You also know that the F-14 effort is only a cover to get you into the country legally.

"The real purpose of your work here involves the development of a program using externally applied drugs that will render the subject useless for combat operations. Your expertise with neural networks makes you the leading expert in this external application problem, which the group has not been able to solve. You will work diligently on that problem, which if solved will permit the completion of this top-secret tri-country effort. While working on this project, however, your real intent will be to steal the technology of the entire project, bringing it home to our government while rendering it useless to the other two nations. We leave it up to your ingenuity to decide how to do that.

"Let me brief you about the other key participants in this project and the organizations that are backing them.

"The Russian connection of course is the KGB, publicly called the Committee for State Security. This organization reports to the Council of Ministers on paper, but on certain projects like this one, it reports right to the top brass. Time magazine recently defined the KGB as the most effective data-gathering agency in the world. They place their operatives in Russian embassies around the world so that they can claim diplomatic immunity when it is convenient.

"The German group is sponsored by their MAD organization which is the Military Counter Intelligence Service. This organization deals with matters of military significance.

"The leader of the Russian team is Dr. Alyusha Topolski. He is a graduate of the Military Engineering-Technical Institute located in St. Petersburg, Russia. He has deep KGB connections.

"The German team is led by Dr. Elias Beckert who is a graduate of the University of Rostock. He is a chemist who has specialized in lethal chemicals and drugs.

"The team has been working on this project for about two years. The United States, to date, has provided financial support for the project and we previously had two of our scientists assigned but they apparently had the wrong technical skills and were recently taken off the project. Associated with that initial is an administrative effort led by a lady named Anastasia Meinkoff. She is a graduate of Goddard College in Plainfield, Vermont." "Let me stop you, Peter, at this point," Ivan interrupted. "I live and work in New England, and I am familiar with Goddard College. That is a very strange school that doesn't offer any credible technical program. The school has been faulted for having very liberal, almost socialist leanings. Students design their own learning program, so why is Ms. Meinkoff qualified to manage the US input to this program?" Peter Welch replied, "This is where it gets a little complicated, Ivan. The US input to this program is being conducted under the sponsorship of the Central Intelligence Agency, as you are aware. The United States was initially willing to offer only relatively low-level technical support and administrative support to the project, and significant funding. We knew that at some point, if the project was a success, we might have to take the steps that we are now taking to grab hold of the results. Ms. Meinkoff was enlisted as an operative by the CIA immediately upon her graduation from Goddard because of her unusual political beliefs, which the CIA believed it could alter for this assignment. She is very young, and I might say, very attractive, and her liberal beliefs also cross over to her very loose sexual ideals. We have been able to use this behavior to gain much useful information throughout the term of the program so far.

"Unfortunately, our initial vetting of her background left a lot to be desired. We subsequently discovered that her father, Alexei Meinkoff, is an active figure with the Russian KGB. We have very strong indications that she is actually a double agent for both the United States and Russia. She will be your assistant and interface with others on the team when necessary. Obviously, you will have to take great care with what you tell her from this point on with the project. She is not aware of our intentions to sabotage the project at its completion. Her primary benefit to you will be her ability to speak perfect English, and she also is fluent in German and Russian. Her CIA contact has been another agent so he and I can compare reports to confirm our suspicions of her split loyalties." "Split loyalties?" Ivan replied. "She doesn't have split loyalties; she is a Russian, her loyalties lie with the Russians. How the hell can you believe anything that she tells you? You have put me in a very difficult position here, Peter. I'm just a loyal American scientist. I didn't take this assignment because I wanted to serve my country. I took it because of the large amount of money that I am being paid to do the job. Now I find out that I not only have to perform scientifically with the hidden goal of stealing the program results, but I have to operate in an environment where my assistant will be trying to steal everything that I learn, even by sexual enticement if necessary. Wow, I know a lot of men who would love this opportunity, but I don't think I am one of them. But I made a commitment and I will honor that commitment."

CHAPTER 10

AFTER HIS DISCUSSION with Peter Welch, Ivan was given time to have a small breakfast and shower and then boarded an Iranian airplane for the three-hour flight to Tehran.

He was met at the aircraft by a young man of Iranian decent named Farhad Ahmani, who indicated that he would be Ivan's guide throughout his stay in Iran. They boarded the plane, and during the flight Farhad assured Ivan that he would not get in the way of any of his activities and that his duties were simply to make sure that Ivan followed all of the many sometimes-strange Iranian rules and customs. Farhad spoke English that was quite good even having a slight Australian accent. Farhad was aware of Ivan's entire schedule and seemed quite comfortable with his assignment. Based upon all of the recent surprises facing Ivan, he was naturally suspicious of Farhad's motives, but he felt comfortable with him. The flight to Tehran was uneventful and seemed shorter that Ivan had expected. Upon landing, Ivan was driven by a government vehicle to a building that had mosque-like features, but it was a government building of some sort. Ivan was escorted inside by Farhad, and they proceeded to a room appearing somewhat like a comfortable lounge. Almost immediately after taking a seat, an old man wearing a military-like uniform came into the room and welcomed Ivan without introducing himself by name. He only mentioned that he was a member of the National Police Force.

"I will be as brief as possible since I know that you still have a long day ahead of you. First let me welcome you to Iran, but I will not make it a warm welcome, because for the most part the Iranian government does not want or need you here. We understand that you are part of a program authorized by a multi-nation agreement to carry out a number of services that may or may not benefit the Iranian government. We will not debate that issue here. The fact that the United States has chosen to send you, a Jew, to Iran, we consider an act of insult considering the current state of affairs between Iran and Israel." "Let me interrupt you, sir." Iva angrily shot back. "My presence here was requested by that multi-nation group because I had a technical capability that they could not find anywhere else in the world, including your blessed Iran, sir. So I suggest that you find a way to avoid your hateful insults about my Jewish heritage unless it has a direct bearing on the briefing that you are required to give me." Ivan wasn't quite sure how he had mustered the nerve to react with such an aggressive nature, since his personality had always permitted him to let comments like that to simply bounce off him.

Without comment the briefer continued. "I want to spend a brief time explaining to you some of the important laws, customs, and history of this great country. Many of our laws are very strict and noncompliance with our laws will result in immediate expulsion from our country without a hearing or a trial.

"About 50% of the people of Iran speak the Persian language. The rest speak a variety of languages, depending on the region of their origin. We are a young country, with more than 75% of our people under the age of thirty years. Our people love the outdoors, even though most of the country is covered by desert. As a result, the people bring the outdoors inside their homes with courts and gardens. Our homes are traditionally different from those in your country. Our rooms are multi-functional. We may set out a table spread for meals, then remove it and bring in bedding for our sleep.

"Men and women have very different relationships in Iran than those that you may be used to. Men are not allowed to sit on an area that is still warm from a woman who previously sat there. Women have a strong role in Iranian life, but it is not a public role; it remains within the home. Women are required to wear modest dress. Hair is considered erotic in Iran, and women must cover their hair in public. They therefore wear chadors which wrap around their bodies and cover their heads and arms.

The general rule for women's dress is that it must be modest so as not to inflame carnal desire.

"Women are not permitted to be alone in the same room as a man unless they are spouse. Women cannot wear makeup of any kind. Men must also dress modestly, wearing no tight pants, shorts, short-sleeved shirts, or open-collared shirts. Men are encouraged to be emotionally sensitive and women are encouraged to be emotionally distant without seeming unfeminine. Open weeping is encouraged for men and women and kissing and hugging between people of same sexes is encouraged as long as it is not erotic. Many marriages in Iran are between men and women of the same family, although it is always encouraged to marry upward in status. Sex before marriage is explicitly prohibited.

"Our food is generally a mixture of Greek and Indian culture. Our breakfasts are simple, usually some unleavened bread and tea. The midday meal usually has some meat and a variety of salads. The evening meal is usually left over from the noon meal.

"Alcoholic beverages are strictly forbidden in Iran, although some still partake of vodka. Restaurants are uncommon, although there are many tea houses where you can get food. 80% of our industry is run or governed by the government. Islamic Sharia law is the foundation of our legal system. Freedom of the press and assembly is a Constitutional guarantee, as long as it does not conflict with Islamic law.

"I have covered many subjects very fast only to inform you that we have laws that are very different from yours. You are in our country, and you must comply with our laws or customs or you will be evicted from Iran, or if serious enough, you might be jailed or even shot.

"Farhad Ahmani will be your guide as long as you are in Iran. He will always be close by to ensure that you do nothing that gets you into trouble while you are here. If you break our laws, Farhad will be treated as a violator and punished accordingly. Do you understand what I have spoken to you? If so, you will be required to sign a few papers, I will provide you with a visitor's pass, which you must keep with you at all times while in public. I am finished, and you are released when you have signed the papers." After Ivan signed the papers, the man left the room, and Ivan was escorted out by Farhad. They got back into the government vehicle for the trip to the airport for the next trip by helicopter to Khatami Air Base where the F-14s were stationed.

Ivan couldn't help thinking to himself, *Visitor, hell. I'm really a prisoner in this strange country.*

When their vehicle arrived at Khatami, it pulled up beside a helicopter and to Ivan's surprise he was welcomed cordially by the helicopter pilot who introduced himself as Captain Javar. The Captain spoke almost perfect English.

"Welcome to Iran," the captain started. "You may be surprised that I welcome you with honor rather than with the hostility that you probably received from the police. Most combat-oriented pilots in this area of Iran feel a degree of respect for Americans because of the many months of training that we received from your American pilots after the F-14s arrived here in Iran. Some pilots were sent to America and others were trained here by American pilots that were sent here.

"We will shortly depart for Khatami Air Base which was built expressly for the F-14s that were purchased from the US government by the Shah Mohammad Reza Pahlavi before he was overthrown. Iran received 80F-14s so we could prevent the Soviet built Mig-25s from threatening our borders. The F-14 was clearly superior to that Russian aircraft.

"By 1979, more than 120 pilots and radar interceptor officers had been trained both in Iran and in the United States. Several US companies had hundreds of their people stationed here for some time, including US Navy pilots and civilian experts from Grumman, Hughes, and Pratt & Whitney. Of course, when the revolution started, all Americans were quickly removed from Iran to protect their safety.

"You will find that most educated military pilots still have a high regard for their American trainers, in contrast to the attitudes of all other government personnel, who are forced to fall in line with their new leaders if they want to continue to live here. In a public forum, our pilots may appear to fall in line with the hatred, but privately they will respect you as an American.

"Let's climb aboard and get started for our trip to Khatami Air Base." Captain Javar shook Ivan's hand and gave him the traditional hug offered between friends in this country. They strapped themselves into the helicopter and started off to Khatami. This was the first time in days that Ivan felt any comfort that he wasn't a prisoner in this most interesting country.

By the time the helicopter arrived at Khatami Air Base, Ivan felt that he should check to see if he still had all of his teeth. Even after exiting the helicopter, Ivan felt that everything around him was still shaking. This actually created a feeling of unbalance even when standing still on solid ground. Of course, he had felt this feeling before.

As soon as the helicopter rotors stopped and were strapped down, Ivan and Farhad were put into a jeep and driven to the main building of the airport. There they were greeted by Colonel Brazzi, again a very cordial and respectful greeting. They were escorted inside where they were led into a fairly large briefing room. Farhad was asked to remain outside the room and the door was closed. The sound of the door closing and the soft silent atmosphere in the room gave Ivan the feeling that this was a special room, probably well insulated from the rest of the facility.

"Can I get you some tea?" the Colonel asked.

"No, thank you," Ivan responded. "But I could use some water if possible."

"The water here is not good for strangers not accustomed to it," the Colonel responded, "but we do have a bottled flavored drink if you wish."

"I'll pass on that," Ivan replied.

"Okay then, let me get started. I understand one of your missions here in Iran is to help our technicians with the integration of the Hughes AIM-54 Missile system into the F-14s here at Khatami. Well, recent events have changed that plan significantly. There are no longer any F-14s here at Khatami. When the Americans left Iran, many of the missile systems were sabotaged by Hughes technicians, or at least that is the official word from the military higher-ups. Actually, that is probably not true. The real problem is the lack of capability of the Iranian radar intercept officers. With the very few capable RIOs that we have, we are very capable of hitting our targets with the system, but in most cases the RIOs are incompetent. Hughes delivered 284 missiles, most of which are tucked safely away in underground facilities here at Khatami. We choose not to waste expensive missiles by trying to fire them using untrained officers. "As for the F-14s, the few that are flying are doing border patrols due to escalating skirmishes with Iraq. Because of some recent escalations with Iraq and intelligence information that we have received, most of the operational F-14s have been moved to other facilities within Iran. Even I do not know where they are located.

"Although this changing situation will significantly alter your plans and may be a disappointment to you, I can tell you that the F-14 with the AIM-54 is a deadly system. During training, I personally flew a training mission where I tracked an AIM-54 at mach 4 and 15 miles before it scored a direct hit on a drone target."

"I will have you accommodated in our officer's quarters this evening as we await further directions. I believe you have other business here in Iran that will require transportation but this change in plans will require a little time to get that transportation approved.

Ivan and Farhad were taken to the office's quarters where they were each given a small room with a cot. *What the hell happens now?* Ivan pondered. *Surely the CIA knew of these changing circumstances. Hopefully I will get some new directions tomorrow. This is my first effort that was supposed to be coordinated by the CIA, and it sure looks like they screwed it up. I hope that this is not representative of the competence of that organization here in Iran. If it is, this assignment will be hell for me.*

CHAPTER 11

IVAN SLEPT VERY soundly that night, perhaps feeling some relief due to the friendly treatment that he received from the Iranian pilots. But this new turn of events still had him worried. A soft knock on his door brought Ivan to his other new friend, Farhad. Ivan couldn't help wondering about Farhad. He was fairly young, about 25 years old, but he seemed to be very aware of everything that was happening and very much in charge when necessary. Was he an Iranian operative or part of the CIA in-country operation? Either way, he was told never to go anywhere without his guide, and Farhad was apparently his guide. After listening to that miserable old man from the National Police Force, Ivan thought he was better served to stay close to Farhad.

"Have you received any new directions?" Ivan asked Farhad.

"Yes, sir," Farhad responded, "we have a small plane that will pick us up in two hours to take us to your final destination in Bandar Abbas. We are going to make a couple of diversion stops along the way. Officially you are leaving the country, and we will make it look like that has happened. Officially your technical mission has been scrubbed. Your real mission is still in place, but we will have to slightly alter your travel plans. The colonel suggested that we have a light breakfast and then prepare for the flight."

"Okay, Farhad, I'll follow your lead."

"What does that mean, sir?" Farhad asked.

"It means that you seem to know what's happening, so I'll do whatever you want."

They were provided a light breakfast of bread and fruit, and Ivan managed to find a facility that gave him an Iranian-type shower. *These military soldiers are not accustomed to bathing every day as we are*, Ivan thought to himself, so when he found a faucet about six feet off the floor in the bathroom area, he used it as a shower.

At about 10:00 a.m. a small Beach Baron taxied close to their quarters for the trip south.

"The Bandar Abbas area does not have a large airport," Farhad indicated, "so we will be transported by this twin-engine airplane. We will first land in Tehran, where you will be seen boarding a plane out of Iran. But of course, it won't be you; it will be another operative." "That's fine with me," Ivan responded. "Let's get moving"

They packed the little that they had into the Baron and took off to make the trip to Bandar Abbas.

Ivan realized immediately that this pilot was not military. He did not welcome them and didn't utter a word during the entire four-hour flight including the short stop in Tehran for the fake transfer to a larger plane. When they landed at a small dirt airstrip north of the town of Bandar Abbas, the pilot unloaded their gear and immediately took off again, never uttering a word to either man.

There was a vehicle waiting to transport them to the facility where Ivan was to live and work for the remainder of his stay here in Iran.

When the vehicle stopped at a small, somewhat indiscreet building, Ivan was confused. The building was on a hillside facing the Sea of Oman. The view was spectacular, but could this be where he was to work on such an important project? It appeared to be so very small.

They entered the building which contained only an elevator and a small desk with no chair. Farhad pushed a small button near the front door and announced in a speaker that Ivan had arrived. He punched a short code into a keypad at the elevator and the elevator door opened. There was only one direction and that was down.

The elevator stopped, and when the door opened, it was like Ivan had entered a new world. The view of the Sea of Oman was even more beautiful than it had appeared from above. The facilities that surrounded him gave every hint of luxury.

Within seconds of the elevator door opening, Ivan and Farhad were welcomed by beautiful and well-dressed women. "Welcome aboard Ivan," she said. "I am Anastasia Meinkoff," she softly muttered. "You surely have been briefed of my duties," she added in perfect English.

Ivan had been briefed about this woman, but he was still struck by her demeanor. Her facial expressions, look, clothing, everything about her was seductive.

"Yes, Ms. Meinkoff," Ivan responded.

"Let's not be so formal, Ivan. Call me Anna. We will be working very closely together for the duration of your stay, so let us become more informal."

"I'm game for that," Ivan replied, because he was lost for words. Anna was stunningly beautiful. Her shoulder-length blond hair was unevenly cut so that when she moved her head from side to side, her hair brushed teasingly across her full bustline "Let me take you to the lounge," Anna suggested. "Your belongings have been delivered, and they are already in your quarters. Let's relax for a few minutes and let me tell you about this facility."

As they sat in very comfortable couches, Farhad dismissed himself and disappeared into another area.

Anna immediate changed her demeanor. Her voice had now softened. She discretely pulled her skirt high above her knee and managed to loosen the top button of her blouse. She moved closer to Ivan, maintaining just enough distance to keep it businesslike.

"About this facility," she started. "During the times of the early rulers of Iran, this facility was constructed as a luxurious fortress where the government leaders cold safely take refuge in case of disturbances. During the reign of the Shah, he modernized the facility and further strengthened its security, also offering it as a luxurious vacation retreat for those whom he favored. As you apparently observed as you approached the facility, it is built on more than one hundred acres of vacant land, and the main facility is nearly completely underground and not visible from the mainland. From the Sea, some portions of the facility are visible, but even that is made to look rustic and beaten, almost like a ruin.

"The facility contains more than 50,000 square feet of internal area which now houses several living suites and dozens of fully equipped laboratories. The facility is completely self-sufficient. It has its own water purification and waste system, and power is provided by state-of-the-art miniature nuclear generators that can be found nowhere else in the world. The facility is completely shielded against electronic penetration and any communications with the outside world require special arrangements. We can discuss exceptions to that factor later.

"Food and other necessities are brought in as needed by special couriers and all meals are prepared by resident cooks. Our personal facilities are cared for by a team of specially selected women who live on the bottom floor.

"You have been provided a very spacious laboratory space, the latest state-of-the-art computers, and whatever else you need will be supplied as needed. I have requested equipment that I knew you would need, but I'm sure there are specialty items that I am not aware of.

"In other words, there will never be a need for you to leave this facility until your work is completed. Everything you will need to live in comfort and work efficiently is available to you here. The environment has been designed so that all of the scientists here can produce their best work under ideal working and living conditions." As Anna was speaking and describing the amazing facility, Ivan's mind slipped back to his plan to build an underground facility to shield him from any future world wars and provide him with an ideal facility to do his research and live peacefully for the remainder of his life. This facility reminded him of his dream facility. But first, he had to complete his work here so he would have the resources to live out his dream. He was also acutely aware that this beautiful woman would be working at his side, with all of the temptations that her behavior would certainly provide.

"Let me show you to your living quarters, and then you can rest before you view your work facilities. You must be somewhat overwhelmed by this time.

"There are five levels to this facility. The top or first floor that we are on is just a reception and meditation area. There are workout facilities and a small swimming pool and several places to simply relax and think. The next floor, which is numbered floor 4, houses the living quarters for the scientists and some of the senior technicians. Floor number 3 contains the working laboratories. Each of the scientists has his own set of laboratory facilities. Each is isolated from the other.

"Floor number 2 contains some living areas and medical facilities where some testing is done. This floor is completely isolated from all other floors and requires special permission to enter."

Ivan interrupted, "Permission from whom?"

"We can get into that at a later time," Anna replied.

"Let me finish with the building summary. The first floor contains all of the infrastructure equipment for the facility like the water system, electric generators and general maintenance equipment. This floor is split into two general sections. The front part of the floor offers exits to a very private beach area that can be used with prior scheduling. This beach area is very secure and military patrols are constantly protecting the beach from any water entrance. The rear section of the bottom floor contains some shower and bathing facilities and living quarters and headquarters for the building security personnel, and some other staff.

"There are many more details that you should know, but I would prefer providing them in a more comfortable surrounding so let us move on to your quarters."

Ivan suspected that Anna had other things in mind based on her general demeanor, but at this point he decided to simply follow her lead. When the elevator reached the fourth floor and the door opened, Anna signaled to Ivan not to talk. She handed him a small note indicating that they should not have further talks until they were safely in his quarters. When they reached a door marked suite #3, Anna slid her key card into the lock and the lock snapped open. Anna motioned Ivan to enter the room first. She immediately grabbed his arm and led him to what appeared to be the bathroom. She closed the door behind them and quickly turned on the shower.

"What the hell is going on here?" Ivan snapped.

She motioned for him to join her on a small seat close to the shower. "You must assume that everywhere you go in this facility you are being monitored. I don't think the bathrooms are bugged, and it's probably safe to talk here. This program is supposed to be a cooperative program between our country, Russia, and Germany but we would have to be foolish and naive to believe that no one has this facility bugged in all areas, perhaps in cooperation with the Russians. We should never trust anyone here with sensitive information. In some instances, I have made it a point to put false information out there to see if there is any reaction, and there has been, so let's be very careful about having sensitive conversations in open areas of your suite." "That won't be hard for me," Ivan responded. "I'm suspicious of everyone and everything all of the time. It's just my nature."

"That's good," Anna softly replied. "No one here, especially the Russians, are to be trusted."

"Speaking of trust," Ivan started, "you have a key to my suite. I'm not comfortable with that."

"Oh, yes," Anna replied as she gave that key to Ivan. "I took the liberty of having your key made for you and it is now yours to keep. There are other key cards that you will get tomorrow when you are read-in to this project. You will also be given information on where you badge pass permits you to go." "This is supposed to be a free interchange of information" Ivan responded, "How can it be free if everyone is keeping secrets?'

"Everyone will seem to be very polite and cooperative, but you must assume differently for your own good." Anna replied.

"Well, I'll just have to see how that goes" Ivan snapped back.

"I assume that you are working for the same people that I am," Ivan asked, "what about Farhad my guide, where do his loyalties reside."

"I have had no previous dealings with Farhad. He arrived here with you, and I have not seen him here before. He does, however, seem to know his way around, so we'll just have to wait and see on him. Meanwhile, we will be on guard with him. I have been assigned my own interface with our superiors, much as you have with Farhad." "I am confused about you?" Ivan asked. "You have been here as an American representative for some time, but you have no related technical background, as I understand it. Why do you seem to have free run of the place?"

"I came here nearly two year ago when this program started. The US sponsors sent over two chemists and a technician, and I was simply their administrative interface because I spoke Russian and German fluently. The technical capability of the US chemists didn't seem to fit the direction of the program, and they returned home. One of my benefits to the program is that I am rather free with my free time and quite frankly with my body, so the two team leaders didn't want to see me leave. Most important, our superiors understood and encouraged my activities because it keeps me informed of things that others do not know. I assume you understand what that means?" "I have been divorced for many years, Anna, but I'm not stupid. Of course, I understand."

"Just so we understand each other, Ivan, I am here to satisfy any and all of your needs. Do you also understand that?" As she spoke, she gently rubbed Ivan's back.

"I certainly understand." Ivan laughed. "And we can deal with that also later, but for the time being, I need to get adjusted to the task ahead."

"Just what do you understand your job to be with this team?", Anna asked. Ivan suddenly felt that this was the start of Anna's information gathering, and he had to be careful.

"I was apparently selected because I have done a great deal of work with neural networks and have become well-known in that area. The team apparently has developed the drugs that they were after, and they need my expertise in the human nervous system to figure out how to externally apply the drugs under different situations without any invasive procedure." "Is that your only task?' Anna inquired, as though seeking to find out if he had other motives.

"Yes, that's it," Ivan responded. He didn't even bring up the F-14 integration diversion. He would test her knowledge of that.

"Where are your quarters?" Ivan inquired "And how do I get to you if I need you?"

"My quarters are right across the hall from yours. I will provide you a pager later today, and I also will try to determine the situation with Farhad for you. Would you like me to help you unpack and get your quarters in order, Ivan?"

"No thanks, Anna. I think I need some time alone to digest everything. Also, if anyone is listening in, they probably think that I take very long showers."

They both laughed as Anna turned off the shower and left the room. Ivan thought to himself that perhaps his easiest job would be in the laboratory. Perhaps it would be harder resisting Anna. For years Ivan had been divorced and rarely thought about woman. Even when he was married, sex was never a significant part of his life. Now, he realized, he could be aroused by Anna in a way he had not experienced in years, if ever. This might indeed be a challenge for him.

When Anna finally left Ivan, he looked around his quarters somewhat in amazement. This place looked like a very upscale American hotel that was somewhat lavishly furnished. It was actually a suite consisting of a huge bedroom, a separate lounge area, and what looked to be a computer room, completely outfitted with very up-to-date equipment.

Ivan carefully inspected the room in an effort to find any bugs or video cameras that had been hidden. At first glance, he didn't see any but remembered what Anna had told him. They were somewhere but probably very expertly hidden.

Ivan recalled also that Anna wore some very different-looking jewelry that could easily have contained recording equipment. He had to be very careful with her because she was a very seductive person with everything that she did or said. He needed to be very cautious about that, but he also knew that eventually he would probably yield to it.

From his lounge area he had a breathtaking view of the ocean below, but no exit to any balcony, which would normally be expected in a suite like this.

His belongings had been delivered as promised, so he unpacked and began the process of getting set up for a long stay. How long, he had no idea.

Ivan was used to living alone since he had buried himself in his work for many years, so this type of seclusion appealed to him. It seemed the ideal environment for conducting research, except that he still had the uneasy feeling that he would be living like a prisoner here. Everything about this assignment seemed to have a great deal of mystery about it, that's probably why it was paying him so well.

From the building description that Anna had provided him, Ivan was intrigued that much of it was what he had envisioned for years as his dream underground living and working facility that he was going to have built on that mountain in Vermont. He could most certainly learn some things from this building about the freshwater system, heating and cooling system, and most important and intriguing, the miniature nuclear generators that powered the building.

In the computer room there was a phone connected to a box with five buttons. Four of the buttons were marked, one for housekeeping services and another for reaching Anna. She would also provide him with a pager. A third button was labeled Lab, and there was no label on the last button. He didn't need to explore that now; there would be plenty of time to carefully investigate that later. There were several speakers spread around the room which would normally have been assumed to be for music, but Ivan knew that music was probably not in the plan here. Probably an intercom or alarm system of some kind he reasoned.

As he sat on the bed, Ivan realized that he had never felt this alone in the world before. He had no idea how to contact anyone. He surely didn't have the ability to walk around and explore the building. Every door required a key card and he was to receive those when he was to be read-in tomorrow. He remembered his briefing from his CIA contact who indicated that Ivan would have a capability to contact him but never told him how to initiate that contact. Oh well he felt, he would learn all of these things in time, so he decided to just try to relax and wait for things to become clearer.

As he reclined on the bed, he realized that he didn't even know what day of the week it was. Since he didn't see one sole since he entered the building except for Anna, perhaps it is a weekend, but it seems that people in this building never leave the building so what difference would the week end make. Why worry he thought, he was being very well paid for whatever he was to face. With that thought he fell off to sleep.

CHAPTER 12

MICHAEL ATWATER HAD finished high school, and the events of the past few weeks with his father had changed his whole relationship with his mother. His father's behavior toward the family was driven by his love for his work, and he always understood that, but he now realized that his mother was not free of fault in all of this. She had coddled him since they left his father, but now, based on what he had learned, he had developed a great deal of resentment toward her for her contribution to the family's problems.

He had never wished to attend college, always feeling that his future was with the military, where he could train and become something special. His mother never told him that his father had given her a great deal of money to secure her future, and he never let on that he knew about that.

They had moved back into the house in Medfield where she had to travel a greater distance to work in Boston, but she always told Michael that she convinced his father, against his will, to give her the house since he was going to be out of the country. He also knew that was a lie that she told to make his father look like he really didn't care. She told her friends that she was taking Michael away from Boston to get him farther away from the bad people that he was hanging around with there. Michael didn't believe that his friends were bad people; they were just a little rowdy.

Immediately after graduation, Michael decided to join the Army. He took a number of special tests having informed the Army recruiter that he wanted to accomplish something special during his time in the Army. The results of his tests were very impressive to the folks in the Army recruiting office. They suggested that after his basic training he be assigned to an Army Ranger Battalion or possibly a Green Beret training team. They discussed both options with Michael, and he indicated that whichever of those options was the most difficult, he would choose that one. They suggested the Rangers.

He decided that to achieve his objective of becoming a special type of soldier, he should free his mind of all things personal. Fortunately, he had not established any relationship with girls in school, and he was more than willing to walk away from his mother's grasp. Although his father remained in his mind, that was more of an incentive to excel at his job as his father had done.

Michaels attended boot camp at Fort Benning in Georgia, and he drew the attention of all of the training officers because of his motivation and his fearlessness. He became the leader of every exercise that was presented to him. He immediately had the respect of all of his comrades because he was willing to demonstrate to them how important it was to have the will to succeed.

After completing boot camp and airborne school at Fort Benning, he was transferred to Fort Bragg in North Carolina where he successfully completed several Special Forces qualification courses. He was later given his "silver wings" and became a full member of the Green Berets. He was designated a Weapons Sergeant. Michael was now fully trained and ready for whatever action came his way.

During this period in the late 1970s, there wasn't all that much going on around the world that demanded military action. There was unrest and many hot spots that threatened to explode at any time, but no active war action that involved American soldiers.

The Shah of Iran had recently been overthrown and President Jimmy Carter agreed to permit the Shah to come to the United States to get medical attention. Carter was not very astute with international affairs, and he didn't realize that a simple act of kindness such as permitting the Shah to come to America could cause trouble.

Iran had been in a state of disruption for months and the Ayatollah Khomeini, the new revolutionary leader, hated interference that he felt the American politician had imposed on Iran during the reign of the Shah. As unrest and hatred for the United States increased, tensions rose to a new height in Iran.

In November of 1979, a group of Iranian students stormed the US embassy in Tehran, taking more than 60 hostages, mostly diplomats and embassy employees.

The United States tried several diplomatic maneuvers to free the hostages, but they all failed to materialize.

In April of 1980, while he was in the middle of a special language training program, Michael and his group of Green Berets were alerted that they were about to embark to a special CIA camp in central Iran. The orders came in a somewhat unorganized manner. It didn't seem as though the officers of the Green Beret team had been properly briefed, more like the whole thing was just thrown together.

When their C-130 landed in Iran, the team was moved in a truck convoy at night to a location then called Desert One, a CIA compound that was established during the times of friendship with the Shah.

Michael was the team leader of his group and still had no real facts as to their mission. For the first time in many months, he recalled his father's words about not trusting people when he didn't know their motives.

Michael addressed his men: "Hopefully we will get briefed soon, but this does not feel right to me. I have a sense that some kind of a mission has been thrown together with little or no planning, and we know what those type of missions provide—a bad ending." "Attention!" Michael snapped, as Captain Willard Meadows entered the room.

"At ease," the captain snapped back.

"I am Captain Meadows, head of the Tehran CIA Special Activities Division. We are all now part of an activity known as Operation Eagle Claw. This is a combined activity of the Army Delta Force, the Rangers, and the Green Berets along with the CIA Air Force and Navy. Our mission is to rescue the hostages that have been held in the US embassy in Tehran. This will be a two-night operation. On the first night. we will bring in helicopters and fuel for other STOL aircraft and prepare all of the ground and air activities for the rescue the next night. These activities will take place at Desert Two, a CIA location just south of Tehran.

Michael interrupted, "Excuse me, sir, you're telling us that the troops and equipment will stay at Desert Two all day, in the open, and we expect no one to get suspicious of this activity. These people don't trust their brothers and sisters. Don't you think someone will notice aircraft and troops gathering in this remote complex?" "Stand down, sergeant," the captain angrily whipped. "This has been carefully planned and coordinated across many different organizations. There will be distractions that will draw attention away from the Desert Two installation."

"What kind of distractions?" Michael asked.

"A group of Army Signal Corps specialists will disable the electrical power in the area which will disrupt ground and air communications and slow any response by the Iranian Military.

"Sergeant Atwater, your team will move to Mazariych Air Base about 60 miles south of Tehran and you will secure that base, which is large enough to accommodate several C-141s which will arrive there for the airlift of the hostages to friendly territory."

"Do we have any intel on the number of Iranian soldiers that are housed at Mazariych Air Base?"

"We are securing that intel as we speak, but we believe that there's security force of less than 24 men, poorly equipped and not very well-trained," the captain responded.

Michael was starting to get a little worried. "Sir, with all due respect, are we authorized to eliminate the troops at Mazariych, or do we have to play some politically correct game with them?"

"Once the operation starts, sergeant, it's full combat rules. No games," the captain replied.

"Sergeant, your men will also be required to place infrared lights along the runway so the C-141s can land safely."

"Roger," Michael replied. "What is the status of the hostages at this point, sir?"

"There were 66 hostages seized initially. Thirteen hostages were already released. They were mostly women, African-Americans, and people who were citizens of a country other than the United States. A fourteenth hostage became very ill and was also released. That leaves 52 hostages that remain at the embassy." "What about air support in case of failure or unexpected events, which always happen?" Michael asked.

The captain replied., "Air support protection will be provided by Carrier Air Wing 8 operating from the Aircraft Carrier Nimitz, and Air

Wing 14 operating from the Carrier Coral Sea. These units will include Marine F-4s and Navy A-7s and A-6s and a whole group of helicopters."

Maybe this is better coordinated than I assumed, Michael thought to himself, and he prepared his team for their mission, collecting their arms, ammunition, supplies, and the infrared lights that they were to use to light the runway.

As soon as the darkness had set in, Michael's team of Rangers set out to complete their mission. Loaded in four jeeps, they proceeded quietly to Mazariych Air Base. The base seemed quiet and somewhat inoperable but there was one building lit with no guards visible.

The Air Base had no control tower. and it wasn't immediately obvious that there had been any air activity on this base for some time.

Michael established two groups of Rangers. One group was to quickly check the unlit buildings to ensure that there were no occupants. Once that was determined, the entire team would concentrate on those individuals in the one building that was lit. There were two specific actions necessary. One group was assigned to take out any communications equipment that could be used to alert outsiders to the operation. They would then all concentrate on taking out all of the soldiers that were in the building. The one direction that Michael had yet to give was the method to be used to eliminate the soldiers.

Michael pondered that decision. Even though the hostage crisis had become a massive public issue, our government had not taken any drastic steps to free them and as of this date, no one had been killed. There would certainly be shooting when the troops stormed the embassy, and lives would be lost. But should this team of Rangers be the first to take lives?

Michael questioned his options. When they took control of this Air Base, they would have to hold it for nearly two days. If they simply took the soldiers prisoner, they would have to guard them for that period and not be available for any other action. If they killed the soldiers, it would be the first act of war in this crisis and it could escalate to something far more serious.

He decided that if there were more than six soldiers in the building, they would have to kill them all as quickly and quietly as possible. If there were less than six, his team would take them prisoner. In either case, if the Iranian soldiers fired first, they would all be eliminated.

Michael briefed his men on the plan, and they surrounded the building, finding three entrances. Michael would give the signal and they would enter all entrances at once.

As soon as the first door was opened there was a shot fired by one of the Iranian soldiers and the rest of the activity was as scripted. All ten of the soldiers were quickly killed and all communications equipment destroyed. The team swept the building to ensure that there were no other soldiers hiding.

Two Rangers stayed behind in the building in case additional soldiers arrived, while the rest moved out to the runway to place the infrared lights.

Michael noticed, while running across the runway, that there seemed to be some soft spots in the pavement. He couldn't inspect the entire runway, but he was concerned that the runway might not be capable of supporting a fully loaded C-141.

When all of the lights were in place, Michael ordered two Rangers to enter each of the other buildings on the Base to destroy any operational communications equipment that might have been left there.

Michael then notified Captain Meadows by radio that the Air Base had been secured. He also notified the captain that he had some doubts that the runway could handle a fully loaded C-141, but at that point the plan could not be changed.

Michael was ordered to continue to secure the Air Base until all of the equipment supplies and troops had landed.

Within minutes, things began to happen. Six helicopters arrived and began to unload the Delta Force rescue troops. The sound of the C-141 was overhead, but their first approach was aborted because the infrared lights were invisible to the pilots of the aircraft. After three additional missed approaches, the C-141 finally landed, but the runway was so badly maintained that the aircraft damaged a wingtip upon landing.

Now it was to be a waiting game until the next night.

Michael was concerned about the ten dead soldiers back in that building. It would be at least 18 hours until the rest of the mission was completed. He felt that the nature of the activities of these soldiers was such that there was probably no command structure that even knew that the men were actually there. He decided to put all of the bodies in their jeeps to be taken back to the CIA compound. *We'll let the CIA take care of their disposal*, he thought. *They are experts at that kind of thing.*

It seemed that the first day's activities had gone well, except that only six of the planned twelve helicopters had arrived at the Air Base. The rest of the choppers suffered from hydraulic problems and were left behind.

On the second and critical day of the operation, a strong sandstorm hit the area. The storm, known as a haboob, blew fine particles of sand suspended in a milky consistency into all of the aircraft and equipment. One light aircraft was actually blown into a larger troop carrier aircraft damaging both vehicles. The helicopters that were to carry the rescue troops to the embassy were damaged or had additional hydraulic problems, and the entire mission was threatened with failure. The final straw that killed the mission was a fuel truck being blown into an operating aircraft, exploding both vehicles and killing eight soldiers. At that point, the mission was canceled. All troops were extracted, leaving all of the vehicles and equipment behind, most engulfed in flames by fires set by the exiting troops.

The debacle of Operation Eagle Claw spread through the ranks of the entire military. Most members of the military were convinced that President Carter had no grasp on military affairs from the beginning of the hostage crisis, but combat operations were still being directed from Washington. The American hostages had been captive for 444 days with no apparent Presidential action. Then, one day before Carter's anticipated reelection, the one planned action failed miserably.

The American election was held the day after the Eagle Claw debacle. When the Iranian government realized that American politics would likely change to a hard-line conservative being elected, they almost immediately changed their own hard line with the hostages. Ronald Reagan was elected President and the next day, even before his inauguration, all hostages were released by the Iranian government.

* * * *

Hank Farber was a part of a military family all his life. By the time he was ready for college, it was already ordained that he would attend the US Naval Academy. His dad was a vice admiral at the time so that the process of obtaining a political appointment appeared to be routine. The admiral was assigned as senior military advisor to the Senate Armed Services Committee and the chairman of that powerful committee was the senator from his home state of Maryland.

Hank went through the extensive application process, took all of the necessary tests, sailed through the interview with the senator's aid, and of course received the appointment.

Hank's father had laid out a complete plan for Hank, detailing the specific courses that he should take, activities that he should get involved with, sports that he should play, and even clubs that he should join or avoid. Of course, things had progressed at the academy since Hank's father attended, but the internal academic structure and cultural development activities had held firm.

Hank was raised with always having the objective of living up to his father's expectations. Within the military structure of the family, that was never questioned, so Hank simply followed the plan, with one exception. Hank's dad had hoped for his son to follow in his footsteps moving up the ranks in Naval Sea Command. Hank never intended to take that route; he wanted to become a naval aviator.

When graduation time arrived, Hank decided to take his route and took a Marine 2nd lieutenant's rank rather than a Naval ensign's rank and moved on to Marine Aviation School at Pensacola Florida.

Of course, Admiral Farber was a little disappointed, but understood Hank's wishes and, at least outwardly, supported his decision. When Ronald Reagan was elected President in 1981 and administrative changes swept clean through all of the committee chairmanships in the Congress and Hank's dad decided to retire from the Navy. He was almost immediately given a high-level position in the CIA by President Reagan because he had established a reputation of opposing almost every military plan of President Carter but having been overruled at every turn by Carter's ultra-liberal policies.

Hank Farber was progressing nicely through his flight training at Pensacola and was later assigned to Carrier Air Wing Four in Corpus

Christi, Texas, where he was designated to fly the Grumman A-6, all-weather light attack aircraft. Hank was thrilled to get this assignment because the A-6 Intruder was known as a very reliable fighting machine that could fly at speeds of over 550 knots and could carry more than 20,000 pounds of ordinance. The aircraft was used for missions that other attack aircraft could not fly due to its all-weather capability.

Having completed all of the necessary aircraft carrier training, Hank was assigned to the aircraft carrier *USS Enterprise* which was on duty in the Middle East.

Morale within the military was almost immediately increased after the Reagan election. There were many skirmishes throughout the Middle East that most Americans never heard about during the early Reagan years. He had put out the word throughout that region that American interests in the region would be completely protected at any cost.

In late 1981, the Iranian government was hinting that it was going to use its Air Force to attack forces outside Iran. President Reagan issued the order to have all of the Iranian F-14s destroyed or rendered inoperable.

Most of the Iranian F-14s were stationed at Khatami Air Base, a giant Air Base built just to handle the aircraft that had been purchased from the United States. The Air Base was located just outside Isfahan, and that meant that any aircraft from the carrier *Enterprise* capable of carrying out the assignment would have to refuel in Dubai either going in or coming out. The *USS Enterprise* could move closer in the Sea of Oman, but it would still be outside the range of American attack aircraft.

The A-6 attack squadron was selected for the mission. Six aircraft would leave the *Enterprise* and refuel in Dubai during daylight hours. When darkness set in, the squadron would fly into Iran and carpet bomb the entire Air Base. It was to be a closely coordinated attack. Each of the six A-6 aircraft had a specific segment of the Air Base designated as their targets. CIA intelligence indicated that some of the F-14s had been moved to an air base closer to Tehran, but the numbers were only a dozen or so and were not considered important at this time.

The six A-6 aircraft left Dubai at midnight and systematically destroyed most of the F-14s and several of the other aircraft based close to the F-14s. The attack run took less than five minutes and the Air Base was left ablaze in fire and explosions.

Hank's aircraft made the final run of the attack to verify that the mission had been a success. The fires had lit up the entire facility for Hank's last run. As his radar operator activated the on-board infrared cameras to get a record of the devastation, he commented that the aircraft that were burning did not look like F-14s to him. They all looked like single engine jet aircraft.

As Hank pulled up the A-6 and climbed toward 30,000 feet for the return trip to the enterprise, all hell suddenly broke loose. All of the anti-weapons equipment was blaring warnings. The instrument panel was lit with red lights.

"What the hell is going on," the radar operator shouted.

"We've been targeted," Hank replied as he immediately rolled the aircraft into an evasive maneuver.

No sooner had the plane turned when the rear of the aircraft exploded in a blinding flash.

"Eject!" Hank hollered. He looked to his right to ensure that the radar operator had ejected safely before he reached up and pulled his ejection handle. Hank's seat blasted him out of the burning aircraft into the blackness of the night. The initial shock of the ejection made Hank black out for a second or two, but as he regained his senses, he could see that he was falling into complete blackness—no lights of a village, a road or even a single residence. Hank considered this a good sign, because it would give him time to stabilize his situation and plan for his survival. His first task would be to try to locate his radar operator, Steve Mitchell, who had ejected a few seconds earlier.

Hank's ejection seat hit the ground with a gentle thump. He released himself from the ejection apparatus and immediately gathered up the parachute. Reaching into his flight vest, he took out his small radio device. This device had two functions, one of which was to trigger a signaling device to help define his location for eventual rescuers. The more important function at this point was one to try to contact Steve Mitchell. Together, they would have a better chance of survival than either would have individually.

"Stevo, this is Hank." He quietly spoke into the mike. No response, only silence from the low-level static of the radio receiver. "Stevo, this is Hank," Hank again called. Again, no response.

Hank was immersed in complete blackness. The bombing had been scheduled for that night because there was to be no moonlight and a heavy overcast. That was great for the mission, but it provided Hank with a situation where he would have to wait till sunrise to try to put together a plan for his escape. He knew that there would be a search for he and Steve since their aircraft was shot down by enemy fire. The Iranian soldiers would love to find them and use them as political fodder.

Hank concluded that his ejection seat had landed in an open area, since there seemed to be no trees or other growth to tangle his chute. His eyes were adjusting to the darkness, but he could not make out any landmarks. If his equipment was out in the open, he wanted to drag it into cover, but he could not determine where that cover might be. Any change in position would have to wait until there was enough light. That would at least three hours so he might as well rest and get his thoughts together.

As Hank thought about his situation, he began to realize the seriousness of this situation. The initial plan was to try to fool the Iranians into thinking that the destruction of the F-14s was the responsibility of the Iraqi government. The two countries had been in some form of border war for years. When Iran leaked that it was considering escalating that war to include its Air Force, it would be a normal conclusion that the Iraqis would make a preemptive strike on their aircraft.

The CIA could manage that information campaign, but once the Iranians found the crashed A-6, they would immediately know that the United States was involved. This could escalate into a major international incident.

CHAPTER 13

AT THE CIA Headquarters in Langley Virginia, Vice Admiral Farber, senior executive director for Middle East Intelligence had just arrived for an action status briefing about the Iran situation. He had been informed by the Navy that his son Hank had been shot down following the attack on Khatami Air Base, and he was only vaguely familiar with the purpose of that operation.

"Let's start from the beginning," Admiral Farber started.

"I have heard rumors that our intelligence about the F-14s being at Khatami were incorrect. Is that true?"

The briefer responded, "Yes, sir, our satellite photos taken this morning showed that there were no operational F-14s at Khatami on the night of the attack. Other intelligence reports indicated that the Iranians had moved all of the operational aircraft to Mashhad, close to the eastern border of Iran, as far away from the Iraqi border as possible. When the Hughes technicians were rushed out of Iran, it was rumored that they had sabotaged all of the AIM-54 systems, including the 284 Phoenix Missiles. The F-14s were moved to Mashhad where an elite team of Iranian technicians has been assembled to attempt the integration of the Aim-54 system into the aircraft. Our experts say that it is highly unlikely that these technicians are skilled enough to do that job.

"It was also rumored that an intelligence leak had occurred, indicating that the Khatami Air Base was going to be attacked by the Iraqis to cripple the Iranian air capability. The Iranians had therefore moved all of the operational F-14s to Mashhad. There were four F-14s left at Khatami, but most of the aircraft destroyed by the Navy attack were old non-operational MIG 23s purchased from the Russians and some French Dassault F1EQ's. The non-operational F-14s which had been used for spare parts were staged at each end of the line of aircraft to create the appearance of the whole group being F-14s." "So, these fucking Iranians, who are not intelligent enough to learn to fly the F-14s, are smart enough to determine that there was likely to be an attack on the aircraft at Khatami.?" Admiral Farber angrily shouted.

"It gets a little worse than that, Admiral," continued the briefer.

"How can that possible be?" the admiral responded.

"The leak most likely came from our own operatives in Pakistan and Saudi Arabia."

"How the hell did that happen?!" shouted the Admiral.

"When the attack on Khatami was planned, we wanted to create a diversion plan to draw blame toward the Iraqis. There had been border skirmishes for years, and things had been escalating between the two countries. We believed that by leaking the rumor of an Iraqi attack, it would almost surely direct initial blame on the Iraqis. Our planners even altered the route of the A-6 aircraft that carried out the attack, to establish a radar track that came from southeast Iraq." Admiral Farber now looked a little confused, and it was obvious that he was very angry.

"So, we took the risk of violating both the Iraqi air space and Iranian air space?"

"Yes, sir" replied the briefer. "But we felt that under the situation of suspicions by both countries, it was a workable plan."

"Have we received any communications from the Iranians yet?" the admiral commented.

"No, sir, not as of the beginning of this briefing"

Do we have any intelligence reports on the location of the downed A-6 or any hint about the two pilots?" the admiral asked.

"Our infrared satellite photos show a possible burning image on the ground in a remote area south of Nurabad. That location would make sense, considering the flight path planned for the returning A-6s. There has been no reported radio contact from either crewman, but we had a report just as this meeting was starting that our operatives in Kuwait might have picked up a weak locator beacon signal. We have asked to tighten the satellite focus in an attempt to verify that information."

"Aren't our A-6s equipped with a transponder beacon to signal their location for instances just like this?" the admiral asked.

"Normally, yes, sir, but because of the deception that we were trying to create for this mission, those beacons were disabled," the briefer indicated. "So, with all of our technology and expert planning, we are shit out of luck locating the pilots or even having any knowledge if they survived the crash?" "You might put it that way, sir," the briefer replied, "but we believe that by intensifying our electronics surveillance, we should have a location on the pilots very soon. When that happens, we can deploy a rescue team to extract them." The admiral rose from his chair, somewhat violently throwing the chair aside, and shouted, "Yes, and we can hope that this will all happen fast enough to get to the men before the fucking Iranians do. I'm sure that you all know by now that the pilot of that A-6 was my son Hank. The shit is really going to hit the fan in this agency if we cannot get to him before the Iranians do, so no more leaks, no more alternative plans, just use all of the capabilities of this organization to get this job done." The admiral then stormed out of the briefing room.

When Admiral Farber arrived at the Pentagon after his Langley briefing, he was immediately taken to the Situation Room. He was not pleased with his recent outburst about the recovery of his son. He had to control these emotions because his son was to be treated no different from any other soldier. As he entered the room, he noticed that the teleconference that was in progress included President Reagan. "This is really serious stuff," he thought, "if the President is in on the planning." President Regan was speaking. "Gentlemen," the President started, "the day before I was elected, I called the Ayatollah Khomeini, whom I assumed was in charge of things in Iran at that time. The American people were so enraged with the way President Carter was handling the hostage crisis that I knew I would be elected the next day.

"I told Khomeini that I expected to be elected America's President the next day, and I wanted to alert him of things to come. I told him that if the American hostages were not released by the time of my inauguration in January, I would have the American military forces destroy every Iranian military installation and every live body that was residing on those installations. Apparently, he knew of my seriousness because he released the hostages the next day.

"Obviously we have a situation here that will blow up in our faces when the Iranians find out that it was American aircraft that bombed Khatami Air Base. They will find the wrecked A-6 but hopefully we can extract the two pilots before they capture them and we have a prisoner incident and all of the political showmanship that will follow.

"You are directed to take whatever measures you feel necessary to find and extract those two pilots. If we can accomplish that, my staff will have a series of recommended actions on my part to defuse the situation, but that can only happen if we recover the pilots. Do you all understand that?" the President asked.

General Bachwirth, who was in charge of the meeting in the Situation Room, responded to the President, "Yes, sir, Mr. President, we completely understand that, sir."

The secure video link was cut off and General Bachwirth faced his group of officers and said, "Gentlemen, I'll listen to your suggestions and we will have the appropriate discussions, but we will not leave this room until we have a workable plan, a back-up plan, and your assurance that there will be no more leaks. I noticed that Admiral Farber has joined us. Would you like to address this group, Admiral?" "Thank you, General Bachwirth. There is one point that I would like to make very clear. There are two pilots stranded out there in Iran. One of them happens to be my son Hank. For purposes of your planning, that fact has no bearing. He is simply a Marine lieutenant. He is no more or no less important than any other soldier finding himself in the same circumstances. Please do not let his identity influence your decisions in any way. Please carry on with your plans." General Bachwirth pointed to the Army's Chief of Tactical Operations, General Tracy, and asked, "Where is your nearest special operations team at this time?"

General Tracy replied, "We have two Ranger Green Beret groups staged in Oman. They are at full strength and can be deployed immediately if required."

General Bachwirth responded, "What the hell are they doing staged in Oman General?"

General Tracy hesitantly responded, "They were involved in the debacle of Operation Eagle Claw, several weeks ago. They successfully got their job done, but the mission was called off when a severe sandstorm prevented air operations from being carried out. They are staged in Oman doing some special language training for future regional operations. They are located in a secluded CIA compound in northern Oman. This is a young group, but they are among the best of the best we have." "Does the CIA have air capability in Oman to drop them into the region?" General Bachwirth asked.

"They do, but a direct air drop might not be the best way to enter Iran. Nurabad, the area where the A-6 went down, is about 50 miles from the northern shore of the Persian Gulf. It might be easier to put the team on a Kuwaiti oil tanker that sails very near that coastline and send them in by small boat under cover of night. We can plan for both possibilities, watching the weather and any local border skirmishes and set final plans as the date of the operation approaches. Once we locate the missing pilots, their extraction will of course be by helicopter." General Bachwirth permitted a short discussion of this plan, with everyone agreeing that it appeared to be the best solution. "Contact your lead officers in Oman, General Tracy. Inform them of Operation Intruder and set things in motion for action within 24 hours." "Admiral Farber, will you coordinate CIA operation in Oman to ensure their complete cooperation?"

"Yes, sir," the admiral replied, "they will be completely on board."

"You are all dismissed," General Bachwirth abruptly said. "I will brief the President's Chief of Staff on our plan. Folks, make this work, and good luck."

They all left the room in silence.

CHAPTER 14

THE CIA COMPOUND in Oman was buzzing that morning as Michael Atwater awoke and started out for breakfast in the mess room. Life had been relatively easy for his Green Beret team since the Eagle Claw debacle. They had made a few relatively simple destruction missions into Iraq, blowing up small weapon installations along the Iraqi border and making it look like Iranian operatives were responsible.

Since it looked like this region of the world was going to be their base of operations for some time, Sergeant Atwater requested that his team try to learn the local language. The problem he found out was that there was not one single local language in this region, but several languages influenced by the nearest population. These were not only dialect differences; they were actual language differences. The most common language was Persian but every area also has people that spoke Kurdish, Arabic Baloshi, and Tati. He simply let his men pick whatever language they preferred, so they could get by wherever they were involved.

Sergeant Atwater made sure that despite the relatively easy life that the men were experiencing, they trained relentlessly to stay in physical shape for their future assignments.

Now, it appeared that something was up. He was called to the briefing room at 0800 hours and was given the following assignment.

"Two A-6 pilots were missing in Iran after their aircraft apparently received ground fire after their mission was completed in Iran. The A-6 was lost. Both pilots ejected, but intelligence indicated that only one of the beacons from the pilots had been detected south of the village of Nurabab. Satellite photos indicate that the area where the beacon is located has only light cover with only small growth, so it will be hard for the pilot to hide safely. Because the mission that the A-6 had completed was very intense, the Iranians would certainly be on a search for the pilots. If the pilots are captured, it will set of a major international incident with Iran. The US hopes to avoid that situation.

"The plan that has been put into effect will involve taking a small group of Six Green Berets to Kuwait. There they will be outfitted and provided the latest location information on the pilots. They will be put on a small patrol boat large enough to carry a helicopter and carried across the Persian Gulf to Iran, where they will launch and be dropped in the general area where the beacon was detected. The team will be in satellite communications with the CIA team in Oman that will be in continuous contact with the Pentagon in Washington. This should indicate the importance of this mission. President Reagan is being kept abreast of every step of the activity." Sergeant Atwater didn't think much of the plan that was in place, and he felt it was necessary to comment especially because of his former experience with CIA planning. "If time is so critical, and it surely is, why are we wasting time using boats and helicopters to get to the pilots? Why not depart right from Oman, fully equipped, and make a high-altitude parachute drop into the area? That would save us at least a day, maybe two. If the weather is cooperative, we should be able to make such a jump with decent accuracy. While the mission is in progress, they can stage helicopters in Kuwait to extract us when needed." Atwater's plan was presented to the CIA area chief, who accepted it immediately because all of the assets needed for the mission were there and available to them. All that was needed was agreement from the authorities in Kuwait to have the helicopters ready. The CIA area chief decided to initiate the plan immediately, rather than waiting for any other approvals.

A C-130 would be fueled and ready as soon as the troops were prepared. Sergeant Atwater requested HALO parachutes, which were specifically designed for high-altitude, low-opening situations. The troops did not like to jump from heights greater than 10,000 feet due to the possible high-altitude effects. The flight would take about three hours, mostly over the open waters of the Persian Gulf. The flight would certainly be monitored by radar installation both in Iraq and Iran. The CIA would register the mission as a cargo shipment from Oman to Kuwait to avoid additional suspicion. Once the aircraft turned inland, it would become immediately obvious to the Iranians that it had violated their air space. The Iranian reaction was hard to predict. There were so many border incursions every day between Iraq and Iran, that it was even possible that this one would simply be considered routine, as many were.

Atwater had one last request before they boarded the C-130. He requested a small amount of cash from the CIA. Locals in Iran would turn on their brothers for American cash, and Atwater felt that there were a number of situations that might occur that could be turned in his favor for cash. His request was of course honored immediately.

Atwater picked five of his most experienced comrades for the mission, men who were well-conditioned and seemed to have acquired a fair grasp of the language of the locals.

The C-130 departed Oman at about 2100. Each of the men was given a beacon receiver tuned to the appropriate frequency used by the Navy pilots. The weather presented no obstacle for the mission so it should be possible for the team to make a very controlled jump. Each team member was given maps of the general area where the pilot's beacon was originally detected. Navy pilots were usually instructed to stay in the general area of their landing once they ejected from their aircraft. They would normally seek some form of shelter and stay put awaiting their rescue. The maps also contained the markings of the general area where satellite photos had shown smoke from a possible aircraft fire.

Atwater knew that normal rescue protocol dictated that since only one beacon had been detected, it could be reliably assumed that the other pilot was either dead or severely wounded from the landing. Of course, it was also possible that the beacon itself had failed to operate but these beacons are notoriously reliable and rarely fail. Even with these possibilities, Green Beret rules required that both men be retrieved, living or dead. Each of the team members also carried his own location beacon which would identify his specific location so as not to get separated from the other team members. They would also be in continuous radio contact with each other. Sergeant Atwater was equipped with communications equipment that would keep him in contact with the central headquarters coordinating this mission.

The C-130 pilot turned on the red light at about 2415 or 12.15 indicating that the aircraft was approaching the drop zone. The team knew that timing was critical at a high altitude since it was possible to miss the target by a long distance if the jump was not efficiently completed. At the red-light signal, the team completed all of its pre-jump checks and readied themselves for the final exit from the plane.

Immediately upon the change to the green light, Atwater gave the "jump" command and they systematically exited the aircraft.

The night sky was so dark that it was very difficult for each jumper to maintain visual contact with all of the other jumpers, especially during the free-fall segment. The team planned to free fall for the first 6000 feet before permitting the HALO chutes to open. With arms and legs extended, each of the team members would free fall at a rate of about 150 feet per second, so the first 6000 feet would take less than one minute.

As the parachutes opened, each of the Green Berets switched on their beacon locators in an attempt to steer their chutes toward the area of the beacon. This was still a very inaccurate method of descent navigation, but it was likely to keep each of the team in fairly close proximity to each other.

One by one the soldiers landed safely, picked up their chutes, stowed them and started to regroup.

"Central, this is Intruder One, on the ground" Atwater quietly whispered into his radio.

Through a soft static the response came. "Roger, Intruder One."

It had been decided to keep the radio chatter to a minimum until the last phase of the rescue.

All six rescue troops landed safely without incident or injury. There were no lights spotted during the descent, so it was assumed that the landing area was uninhabited, but the team still attempted to hide their parachute equipment.

They were each equipped with night vision goggles which made it easier for them to spot each other and regroup.

"Anyone injured by the descent?" Sergeant Atwater asked. No one replied, but that was a good response.

"Let's all coordinate the beacon indications to see if they are all in agreement," Atwater suggested.

Four of the six indicators reflected the same general direction. The other two seemed intermittent or were receiving a very weak signal.

"Okay," Atwater ordered. "We are going to assume that the two inconsistent receivers might be detecting the beacon transmitter of the second pilot. There is a thirty-degree difference in the indicated direction, so we will split into two teams. Alpha team"—he signaled three of the team—"you will head in the general direction of those weaker beacons. Spread out but stay within sight of each other through the goggles. When it starts to get lighter, you can increase your spread, but don't lose contact with each other. Keep your radio chatter down to a minimum. Check in with me every few minutes." "My beta team will head in the direction of the stronger beacon with the same instructions. Move very slowly while complete darkness remains. As the light begins to appear you can increase your pace but don't get separated any great distances from each other. Look for any evidence of the downed aircraft and certainly any evidence of the pilots." "Time check," Atwater ordered as he looked at his watch. "It's 01:34; mark that time. It should get lighter by 0500. We will do a brief radio check at that time, unless you find something earlier. Okay, team, let's get those pilots."

Hank Farber did not have the benefit of night goggles, so it was necessary for him to feel around to find something that would represent a solid object that he could at least sit and lean against. Even in the total darkness, he felt that it was unusual that his eyes could not make any adjustment to the darkness. He remembered many times when he had been in dark rooms and his eyes gradually adjusted to the darkness to the point where he could make out the outlines of large objects. There was no such adjustment here.

Having no other alternatives, Farber decided to permit himself to drop off until the sunrise when he would formulate a plan.

Farber's sleep was sound but not very long. When he awoke, he knew that the sun had risen because he cold vaguely see light through his eyes, but everything was very hazy and blurred. There was no pain in his eyes, and he could feel no moisture around his face that might indicate blood.

The most encouraging thing that was obvious to Farber was that he was surrounded by complete silence. He considered this a positive sign that he was not necessarily near any village or road and more important, there was no sound of any Iranian troops that might be searching for him. For a second he thought that he might have also lost his hearing, but he tapped on his helmet and could hear that sound clearly.

Farber reached for his radio transmitter in his vest pocket. His mind seemed a little confused because he couldn't remember his pilot code name which was always used in place of using actual names. Rather than risking his location and identity, he simply started keying the radio with an SOS signal every few minutes.

He felt that the best thing he could do was to take inventory of his equipment and weapons. Instinct caused him to reach down to his leg holster to see if he still had his 45-caliber pistol. It was there where it has always been

In one of his vest pockets he found the small flare gun that pilots always carried. Other findings were his medical kit, a survival knife, and a pack of chewing gum that he always carried.

At this point, the best thing that Farber could wish for was for the time to pass quickly into the nightfall so he would not be visible. If he could wait out another day, perhaps his eyesight would improve. He also decided that he would make short periodic calls to Steve Mitchell, his radar operator in an attempt to locate him.

"Stevo, this is Hank. Do you read me?" Hank muttered into the transmitter. He listened hard, but there was still no response.

Hank began to think about the time of ejection from the wounded A-6 aircraft. The plane was still upright and in relatively level flight, so the ejection would have been straight up for both pilots. The time difference of the two ejections was only seconds. Pilots always ensured that their crewmates were safely ejected before they punched out. Under those conditions, Steve Mitchell the radar operator should have landed fairly close to the place that Hank landed.

Hank knew that the back end of the Intruder had been shot off by the missile that hit it, so the aircraft would probably not stay in level flight for very long before it nosed over and crashed. At the speed of the aircraft, it could also have traveled 40 to 50 miles before crashing. There was really no way to tell. Hank remembered that he had passed out immediately after ejection, which is not unusual, but he did not remember seeing any indication that the A-6 had crashed into the ground. The Persian Gulf was more than 70 miles from where the plane was hit so it probably could not have gone that far before crashing. These things kept going through Hank's head, probably because he was trying to make sure that it was only his eyes that were damaged and not damage to his brain.

As darkness arrived that day, Hank felt a slight relief. He knew that any rescue attempt would not take place during the daylight hours, and if there was to be a rescue attempt, it would probably come tonight.

All of the thoughts of a rescue suddenly faded when Hank heard voices in the distance, accompanied by the sound of several vehicles. Hank wasn't sure if he was hidden or in the open, so the only thing he could do was stay as still as possible. His pilot outfit would keep him somewhat camouflaged, but if these men found his ejection seat, they would surely know that he was close by. All he could do was wait and listen.

It seemed like hours had passed since Hank heard all the commotion and activity. The noise has subsided and there were no longer vehicle sounds but there were repeated unusual noises that were strange to Hank's ears. "Maybe when you lose the sense of sight," Hank thought, "other senses kick in. What the hell are those noises?" he wondered.

Hank tried to concentrate on remembering his initial examination of the terrain map that he had studied before making the flight. Most of the southeastern region of Iran was uneven, with a mixture of hills and valleys with some farming areas in the valleys. He wasn't running into trees or bushes and the terrain seemed flat as far as he had traveled. "I must be close to a meadow of some type," Hank thought.

Still trying to keep his mind active, Hank recalled the beginning of the mission. After they crossed the coastline of the Persian Gulf, the Automatic Terrain Following equipment was turned on. He remembered that after setting the equipment at 500 feet, the aircraft was navigated through altitude ranges of nearly 1000 feet. This would indicate that a significant portion of the trip was made over rolling hills and valleys with the peaks of the hills ranging up to 1500 feet above sea level.

"We went down in farm country," he thought. "*Who the hell fires a missile capable of hitting us in farm country?*" he thought. "*For the most part, these local people have no bone to pick with Americans. Many Americans came to Iran as the Shah began his program of social modernization, and I believe the local population got along fine with them. The NAJA were the police force throughout the country but they were primarily concerned with watching people who broke the rules, no matter how vague those rules might have been. The people were generally suspicious of the NAJA, and they could usually get out of trouble with them with a slight money pay-off. The NAJA definitely didn't have access to any missiles that could down a high-speed aircraft."*

It suddenly dawned on Hank that his A-6 must have been shot down by an aircraft. But if it was an Iranian aircraft, they would have immediately known the position of the downed aircraft and alerted the military.

"It has been nearly 24 hours since our plane went down," Hank pondered. *"There should have been a lot of military activity in this area, not just a few vehicles and some fairly calm voices. There is something very unusual going on here,"* he thought.

CHAPTER 15

AT 0500 NEITHER the Alpha or Beta teams had made any significant progress with their search. Now, with daylight approaching, they could rely on their own eyesight and not simply the night vision goggles to get around.

The terrain surrounding them was of no concern. The landscape was gently rolling hills and a few distant mountains. The trees were in full bloom and the undergrowth was not difficult to navigate through.

Sergeant Atwater triggered his transmitter mike and called out, "Alpha team, what is your status?"

"We should be at 312 degrees from your position and at the slow pace that we had to proceed last night, we should be about 300 yards from you" was the reply. "We are still receiving the weak beacon response. There has been no increase or decrease on signal strength. That puzzles me, because even with the relatively short distance that we traveled last night, there should be some change in signal strength." "Roger that," Atwater replied. "Our signal indicates the target is at 340 degrees from our current position and the signal is fairly strong. Keep heading for your beacon and we will continue this course." "Roger," was the response.

Suddenly there was a weak burst of static coming from Atwater' radio, as though someone was attempting to speak.

Keying his mike, Atwater spoke loudly into the mike. "This is Rescue One, anyone there?"

"Farber here," was the excited response.

"What's your status?" sergeant Atwater responded.

"Holding firm, eyesight damaged, can't see much. Other than that, I'm kokay," Farber responded.

"Can you hear any identifying sounds?", Atwater asked.

"I heard people and vehicles last night and strange noises but it's quiet as a mouse today."

"Roger," Atwater responded. "Stay put, and we'll continue in our current direction and contact you soon."

"Will do," Farber responded.

"Alpha team, did you hear that conversation?", Atwater asked. "Roger, your voice was much clearer than his," was the response.

"Keep heading for your beacon and keep the mike open," Atwater ordered.

"Roger," was the response.

After about twenty minutes of continuing their current direction, Atwater again keyed his mike. "How's this signal, Farber?"

"Getting stronger," Farber responded.

"Do you have any instruments that can make noise?" Atwater asked. "I can bang on my ejection seat. That's metal and should make noise," Farber excitedly responded.

Atwater's team was silent waiting for some noise. None was heard. Then, after a minute or so, there was a banging sound at equal intervals.

"Okay, Farber, we have that. Stay put. It sounds like you are about 100 meters directly ahead of us. Stop banging until I tell you to start."

"Roger," Farber answered.

Atwater's team started running in the direction of the banging sound. "There he is," hollered one of the team members. All three men rushed to Farber's side.

"Thank God," Farber shouted, "Sitting here blind was a scary feeling."

Suddenly the radio blasted, "Beta team, this is Alpha team." the voice was not excited.

"Go ahead," Atwater responded.

"We found the other pilot, sir, but he didn't make it. He was still buckled into his ejection seat. It looks kind of like his neck is broken. Did you find your target?"

"Roger. He has a sight problem but is otherwise okay. We have Farber the pilot; you have the RO. Cut him loose and head toward our position. I'll look for a clearing and call for a taxi," Atwater ordered.

"Roger, we are on our way. Whoa, just a minute," the voice hollered. "Stand by one minute."

"Sir, I think you should head this way. I think we discovered a hidden surface-to-air missile installation. This is the strangest thing I have seen in a long time. It's camouflaged and partially underground." "We're on our way," Atwater responded.

The beta team helped Farber move forward with them. He couldn't run at full speed, but the excitement of his rescue gave him the energy he needed to keep up.

In a few minutes, the Alpha team was in sight. Sergeant Atwater was alerted in the direction of the partially hidden missile installation. He walked around the area, carefully observing all of the details. This was probably the weapon that shot down his aircraft. There was a switching system that pulled away the covering. Atwater activated the system and a series of small motors started pulling off the camouflage.

"That's the noise I heard last night," Farber shouted"

Atwater was very puzzled. He had gone through many weapons training programs during his Green Beret training, and this didn't match any Iranian missiles. They really didn't have an effective surface-to-air weapon. He carefully examined all of the markings and remarked with surprise, "This is a Russian Scud missile system, guys, and that's not the real shocker. The Iranians don't have any Russian systems; they stopped buying from the Russians when the Shah was in command. But! The Iraqis do still have the Scuds that are operational. This is an Iraqi missile installation, but what the hell is it doing here in Iran?" "The one piece of equipment that we are not equipped with is a camera, so let's all look this system over and make notes of as much as you can absorb."

"Should we set it up for destruction, sir?" one of the men asked.

Atwater thought a moment. "No, we'll leave it, maybe the CIA can make hay of it and use it to our advantage regarding the attack on the F-14 installation. If the Iraqis have one of these installations, they probably have more along the coastline. These two countries have been arguing about the border for a long time. Who knows what the Iraqi strategy regarding these missiles is?" "Okay, guys, let's move to the center of that clearing and get a good set of coordinates, and I'll call in the helicopters."

"Switching to the Command Center frequency, Sergeant Atwater called out. "Center, this is Intruder Rescue. How do you read me?" Atwater called out.

"Loud and clear, Intruder. Where have you been? We're waiting."

"Recovered pilot Farber, Mitchell dead. Recovery coordinates are Latitude 30.4999002, Longitude 54.0661608. You have a clear area for chopper landing. No apparent civilian or military in area. Provide ETA please," Atwater answered.

"Two choppers from the carrier are in the air as we speak, based on your coordinates, they should arrive in about two hours."

"Roger," Atwater responded. "Can you give me a secure channel to the Company? I have important information for them."

"Not possible at this time, but I'll call you back on emergency channel in a few minutes, with a secure frequency."

"Roger, sir. I'll be waiting.

It was nearly an hour before Atwater's radio signaled an incoming call. During that time, he had cut all of the apparent power cables to the missile system in order to prevent it from detecting and destroying his rescue helicopters. He wasn't sure what the detection mechanism was in this old missile system, but it apparently was able to detect and destroy a high-speed aircraft, outbound from Iran. The system had what looked like two high-frequency antennae, and his men disabled both of them.

"Rescue this is Command One. Do you read?" That was the call that Atwater was awaiting.

"Go ahead with code clearance," Atwater responded.

"Frequency channel as previously stated, input code 18559 Charlie" was the order.

"Roger. Changing channels." Atwater spoke.

The response on the other end was loud and clear. "Rescue, state your information."

"We have rescued the pilot, Farber. RO deceased. We discovered a partially hidden Scud ground-to-air missile installation at the coordinates provided. It apparently was responsible for the shoot-down of an intruder outbound from mission. Since Scuds are the old Russian system, I was suspicious that the Iranians would not possess such a system. I checked all of the markings, and it appears that it is an Iraqi system installed as part of their border disputes. But why this far inland? I assume, if there is one, there are probably more inside Iran that the Iranians don't know about. I have disabled this system so it will not bother the incoming choppers. Thought you might be able to use this to create a distraction from the F-14 bombings. Over." There was a fairly long period before Atwater received a response. Then came a response. "Bombing mission was a failure. All aircraft on the field were either old F-14s or old MiG 23s. The mission must have been leaked and the F-14s moved to a safe haven." Atwater slammed the radio to the ground in disgust. "Son of a bitch!" he yelled. "Goddammed son of a bitch. I can't believe it. That's two missions coordinated by the CIA that were failures, and I was in the middle of both of them. We lost ten men the first time and another pilot on this mission. What the hell is going on in Washington? Why the hell can't those bastards get it right? We had the politicians managing both Korea and Vietnam, and the CIA running things today, and we are as fucked up today as we ever were, and the only ones that get punished are the good guys who lost their lives." "Cool it, Sergeant," Lieutenant Farber interrupted. "Let's keep our wits about us until we get back and get more details."

Atwater replied, "I don't have a lot of rank, but I am going to raise hell about this and try to make sure that heads roll for these screwups. I want a Congressional hearing, and I want the heads of those who caused the deaths of eleven good men. American soldiers defeated armies of millions of men and women over the years and today we have better training, better equipment, more dedicated soldiers and we come to this part of the world that is less than third world and we can't succeed on two relatively simple missions. What the hell are we doing wrong?" Atwater dropped his head into his hands as though in defeat.

Recovering quickly, Atwater directed his men to find anything light or colored that they had on them and start making a mark in the clearing. "Use your first aid stuff, handkerchiefs, bandages, underwear, anything that will stand out, and mark the pick-up spot for the choppers. Based on everything else that has happened, the GPS equipment on the choppers will probably be inoperable when they get here, and they will be unable to locate the clearing." The men followed orders and when they'd completed making the marker, they all sat on the ground to rest, waiting for the incoming helicopters.

The rescue team waited for about two hours after making whatever markings they could in the area of the most convenient helicopter landing site. They spent this time gathering all of their equipment and belongings that would leave any clue as to their specific identity.

In the discussions between the men in the group, there was some concern and even confusion that the A-6 crash and the recovery activities had not resulted in some form of Iranian military activity in the area. Atwater had mentioned some human sounds that he had heard the day before and the assumption now was that the noise involved personnel resetting the scud system. Again with the assumption that the missile system was not Iranian but more likely Iraqi, the people involved were not likely to be Iranian but more likely Iraqi sympathizers. All of this of course was mere speculation, but what more did the men have to do but speculate while they waited for their rescue.

Then there was the sound of a helicopter suddenly audible. All the men got up, gathered their equipment, and prepared for the rescue. Suddenly two SH-3 helicopters made their rapid descent.

Sergeant Atwater shouted to the helicopter pilot, "Why two ships? We could easily fit the entire group in one ship."

The helicopter pilot responded that they sent a second ship to fly over the area of the missile site to take photo and film of the site. "Have your men load the dead pilot and all of the men in the other helicopter and have one of the rescue team board the first chopper to quickly direct that vehicle to that site." "I'll go with you to the site but wait a few minutes until I am sure that all the men and equipment are safely loaded in the other chopper. I also want to ensure that the two ejection seats are also loaded with their parachutes to help reduce anything left behind that could be used to identify the men or equipment. This would include any of the marking objects that were placed to help the choppers locate the group. Much of that material has been scattered around by the blade backwash, but we should get as much as we can."

As soon as Atwater was convinced that everything was in order, he gave the signal for the first chopper to take off and he boarded the second chopper.

The pilot gave Atwater a headset so they could talk more easily as they slowly left the ground. "Fly a course of about 280 degrees. The missile installation is only about 200 yards in that direction. It won't be hard to locate." The chopper circled the missile installation for a couple of minutes with the co-pilot taking both still and video pictures. When he felt that he had sufficient photos, he signaled the pilot with a thumbs-up signal and off they went, leaving the area behind them.

"What's our destination?" Atwater asked the pilot.

"We are going to the US Naval Base in Kuwait. Our government has excellent relations with Kuwait because our military provides them significant financial resources and some shipping protection around the Persian Gulf. We also have a fine hospital there, where your lieutenant can be treated. With the little that I know about your mission in Iran, I'm sure you will be thoroughly debriefed by the local CIA to make sure that your story and theirs are in agreement." Atwater responded. "I'm not exactly pleased with the CIA at this point. I've had two important missions with them, and in both cases their intel has been bad enough to cause several of our troops to die. I intend to raise some hell about that when I get the chance." "I'd be a little careful about that, Sergeant," the pilot cautioned. "The father of your wounded pilot is very high up in the CIA, and he has already put big-time pressure on this particular incident. There are two congressional committees that have threatened hearings on this incident if things turn sour with either Iran or Iraq. The slightest misstep here could cause some big turmoil politically." "Thanks for the heads up, sir. That's good to know. I didn't know about Farber's father."

"Yeah," the pilot muttered, "his father was a vice admiral in the Navy and he really was out of phase with President Carter's policies, especially during the Iranian hostage crisis, so he retired from service. When President Reagan took office, he recognized the admiral's capability and he brought him back to help boost the country's intelligence capability that Carter had all but destroyed. He is number two or three in the CIA at this time, but rumor has it that he eventually will get the top CIA spot." "Wow!" Atwater responded. "I'm going to have to get closer to Farber. He may be able to get me some good ears on these screw-ups."

As the two helicopters landed in Kuwait, they were welcomed by a medical team that took charge of the dead pilot' s body and also showed unusual care for Lieutenant Farber who had still not regained his eyesight. The remainder of the rescue team was also debriefed and given medical exams, which was routine on missions such as this.

CHAPTER 16

LIEUTENANT FARBER WAS anxious as he entered the review room where he was to receive the doctor's first evaluation of his eyesight problem. It had been three days since his sight became blurred and although he had no medical experience, he knew that time must not be on his side.

Doctor Cambre entered the room and as doctors usually are, he was cordial and pleasant, but Lieutenant Farber immediately felt that meant that the news was not good. He could not see the expression on the doctor's face but from the tone of his initial words, he just assumed the worst.

"Lieutenant Farber," the doctor started, "because you are an aviator, I am very concerned about your injury. I have not made a definite diagnosis because we need to consult an ophthalmologist before we start any treatment. There are three possibilities that we are investigating but I assure you that all three are very treatable.

"I believe you must have obtained some form of head trauma when you ejected from your aircraft causing you to become unconscious for a short period. My first reaction is that you caused a traumatic reaction to the occipital lobe of your brain. I'm looking in this direction because both of your eyes have been affected. Other possibilities normally will affect only one eye.

"A large portion of the neocortex of the human brain is the machinery that affects our eyesight. This portion is called the occipital lobe. Because your period of unconsciousness was very short, I will need to get MRI results to determine if there has been significant damage. Regardless of the results, most conditions in this category are treatable and vision can be restored.

"Another possibility would be some form of retinal detachment. The retina works with other parts of the eye and also your brain to produce normal vision. Depending on the degree of detachment, this problem is also treatable.

"The third possibility is what is called *amaurosis fugax*. This sounds scary, but it sounds worse than it is. There are blood vessels on either side of your neck that carry blood from your heart to your brain. If that blood flow is cut off for a period of time, it can cause blindness. In most cases if this is the cause, the blindness is very temporary, only a few minutes or maybe a little more. That's why I'm kind of ruling that only a slight possibility. I'm only looking at it because you were harnessed into an ejection seat, and you could have had significant pressure applied to your neck.

"We will do an MRI today and then consult a specialist with these conditions before we start any treatment protocol. Meanwhile, I want to keep you in the hospital for complete rest."

Because two aviators had been negatively affected by aircraft ejections, the Navy Fight Safety Command had some questions that needed answers regarding Lieutenant Farber's incident.

While he was still in active stages of his medical evaluations, Lieutenant Farber was somewhat surprised when he was visited by Lieutenant Commander Ramsey, a Human Factors specialist from the Flight Safety Command.

"You might think this is a little early for another debriefing," the Commander started, but since both you and your radar operator were seriously damaged in an ejection incident, we consider that very uncommon, especially with the Martin Baker Mark 7 ejection seat. We want to get to the bottom of this incident as fast as possible to avoid possible future problems of a similar nature. If you don't mind, I have a few questions to ask, if you feel up to discussing the situation with me." "I'll give you what I know," Lieutenant Farber replied.

"How soon after you determined that your aircraft had been hit did you give Steve Mitchell the command to eject?"

"It couldn't have been more than a second or two. I realized that I had no altitude control of the aircraft, indicating to me that the tail section had been damaged," Farber replied.

"Did you see Mitchell's position in the seat when he pulled down the face shield that activated the ejection?" Ramsey asked.

"No, I wasn't looking at him. I did hear the canopy blow out, and of course I knew that he had ejected the aircraft."

"So, you are fairly sure that the canopy blew as it was supposed to do?" Ramsey asked.

"Absolutely sure," Farber replied.

"These new Mark 7 seats have the ability to recline slightly for added comfort in long flights. Are you aware if Mitchell's seat might have been reclined?"

"I have no way of knowing that, sir, but we were in a combat mode, so I assume that his seat was completely upright," Farber answered.

"Do you think that Mitchell might have been twisted in his seat looking back to observe any damage to the aircraft."

"Hold on now, doc. I'm getting a little annoyed at these questions," Farber responded. "It seems like you are trying to imply that Mitchell caused his neck to break during the ejection."

"I'm certainly not trying to imply that, Lieutenant Farber," Ramsey responded. "You are aware that occupants of these seats are supposed to be seated securely, facing forward when the seats are blasted out. Mitchell was found with a broken neck. I'm simply trying to determine if that was caused by the ejection or resulted from the fall to the ground. The men who recovered Mitchell's body indicated that the chutes appeared to have deployed properly, which would indicate that his injuries might have happened as he left the aircraft. Considering that you also were injured from the ejection and your chutes opened properly, I have to assume that the ejection itself caused the damage in both cases and I want to determine what the cause might have been. You can certainly understand that."

"Sorry, sir," Farber replied, "I'm just a little frustrated that my eyesight problems are still not solved, and eyesight reduction could seriously affect my flying future."

"I completely understand that," Ramsey responded, "but my determinations here might also help the flight surgeon with his evaluations of your situation. Let's get into that a little more. Let's go over your flight conditions when the aircraft was hit. Give me as much detail as you can remember." "Certainly," Farber began. "We were accelerating our speed to exit the area. I was climbing toward 30,000 feet and we were probably at about 4000 feet altitude. Everything happened very fast. The countermeasures indicator began to blare that we had been acquired by an enemy missile. Within a second or two I felt the shock of the strike and realized that I had no rudder or elevator control. The engines were still operating, so I naturally assumed that the tail section of the aircraft had been seriously damaged and that there would be no recovery from this situation. That is when I gave Mitchell the order to eject. I did a quick evaluation of the instrument panel and tried to put the aircraft into a stable flight situation, but I had little success with that. I think I was somewhat successful getting the aircraft into a level flight situation but that was the only control that I managed to apply. I suppose that in those few seconds I thought that if I could level the aircraft, I could possibly get enough distance to reach the water, but that was probably only a flash thought. I remember pulling down my face shield that activated the ejection seat, and I guess I passed out at that point, because the next thing I remember was waking up just before the seat landed." "Do you remember feeling any pain before you passed out?" Ramsey asked.

"I have no memory of any pain," Farber replied.

"Do you remember feeling any shock as the seat blasted through the canopy?"

"Can't remember that either," Farber replied.

"Was your helmet securely in place during your exit from the area?" Ramsey asked.

There was a long hesitation as Farber thought about that question. "You know," Farber replied, "if I think about that a little, I remember Mitchell telling me that as we made our last pass over the site, he didn't think that the airplanes that we bombed were F-14s. I remember twisting my head and body around to try to get a glimpse of the situation on the ground. I think that I did feel that my helmet was a little loose or maybe that I had twisted my body too fast for my head to follow. That is a possibility," Farber responded.

"You also indicated in one of your discussions with the accident investigation people that when you realized that your aircraft had been acquired by a missile, you made a quick standard avoidance maneuver. How radical was that maneuver? Could it have been radical enough to twist you in your seat? This could be important because the doctor is trying to determine how you may have gotten enough pressure on your neck to affect your eyesight." Farber thought for a moment. "The standard maneuver is to climb and turn hard right. I couldn't climb much once we were hit, but I was able to roll right. I don't remember that maneuver causing a very radical movement of the aircraft that would have thrown me off balance in the seat, but I suppose it is possible." Commander Ramsey closed his notebook and said, "That's all for today, Lieutenant Farber, I may get back to you later if I need more information but you have been very cooperative and the information that you gave me will be very useful in coming to some conclusion about the events that took place here."

CHAPTER 17

AFTER A GREAT night's sleep, Ivan was awakened by a man's voice coming through one of the many speakers in his room. "Mr. Schwarz, could you come to the lobby area at 0900 to start your security briefing?"

Ivan showered and dressed and for the first time he was going to leave his private living quarters. He walked to the elevator and pressed the button for the lobby floor. He wasn't sure that he could actually get access to any other area without any key cards, but since the elevator opened, he assumed that somehow, he had been given access.

He was greeted by a pleasant-looking middle-aged man, nicely dressed, with his hand out to welcome Ivan.

"I am Albert Brokow. I am in charge of just about everything except the scientific work in this facility. Let's go to the cafeteria area and have some breakfast, I know you have had some hectic times and little to eat in several days."

They walked through a large door at the rear of the lobby area into a very spacious cafeteria-like room. "This is where you will take all of your meals and get any snacks between meals that you might desire. There is someone here at all hours of the day or night to serve you. Many of the scientific people work through the night and often need a break and some refreshments. This is where you will come for that. You will get used to this room on your own, but I will tell you that this is one of the few places in Iran where you can get alcohol. The rear area of the room, as you can see, has a lounge-like arrangement. The scientists often meet here to discuss their work over a relaxing beverage, if you know what I mean." "I certainly do," Ivan replied. There was something about Albert that made him very likable. Unlike everyone else that he had met, it didn't seem like Albert was all about business. It was like he had become an instant friend, but Ivan immediately became suspicious as he always was. Be careful, he thought, and don't trust anyone.

They sat at a small table and they were soon approached by a friendly-looking young lady dressed in black attire. "What can I get you gentlemen?" the lady asked.

"I'll have some tea, a roll, and some fruit," Albert responded. "I'll have the same, except make mine coffee," Ivan commented. The young lady politely nodded and left the room.

"Okay," Albert started, "let me assure you that I am not like many of the other people you will meet here. I don't give a shit about anything that is going on in the laboratories, and I couldn't care less about the politics of the countries that are working here. I got this job because of the good standing of my family back in Russia. I am in charge of the facility and the security of the building. I have worked here for nearly twenty years, and I like what I do, and I want to keep doing it for many more years. If you understand that, you can deal with me in any manner that you like, as long as you do not jeopardize my tenure here." "I certainly understand that," Ivan replied. "If I may ask, what is the history of this facility, it seems to have a very different standing with the government of Iran, its kind of like it off limits to most Iranians. Am I reading that correctly?"

"That is very perceptive of you, Ivan," Albert responded, "and a good way to start this meeting."

Albert was interrupted by the young woman who had brought them their breakfast. She politely placed each order in the proper place and left the room. The two men immediately started eating.

Albert started his history lesson. "You may be shocked by some of what I am about to tell you. The genesis of this building started back in the early 1900s. The Iranian rulers who were considered royalty at that time built the main structure sort of like a fortress, but one that contained luxurious living conditions. Back in those days there were many ruling families throughout the Persian territories. The leaders of Iran wanted a place that they could safely bring those leaders together for meetings and also to offer them a place to vacation in luxury with their families. It was not difficult in those times for the Iranian leaders to claim the entire area off-limits to all but the most elite Persian leaders.

"In the middle of World War Two, Nazi Germany began Operation Barbarossa and invaded the Soviet Union, breaking a long-standing treaty that had been in place. Because Iran had previously been dealing with both Germany and the Soviets, it declared its neutrality in that conflict. Later in that year, British and Soviet forces occupied Iran in a military invasion forcing then Shaw Reza to abdicate. Iran soon became a conduit for British and American aid to flow through Iran to Russia. This effort became known as the Persian Corridor.

"During those hectic wartime days, this facility was used as a secret meeting place for the allied leaders of the US, British and Russian military, it then took on a very secretive identity. When the war ended, the Soviet Union purchased this facility from Iran in a very rare treaty that identified the facility as part of the Soviet holdings, completely separate from any Iranian laws.

"As the war came to an end the Russians used this facility to house dozens of German scientists that they claimed from Germany. The Americans took some of those scientists who were rocket experts, while the Russians wanted the ones that specialized in chemical warfare. The Russians began converting the facility into laboratories and living facilities for the German scientists and also as a place to accommodate many German top political leaders as they fled from Germany to other countries to avoid prosecution for war crimes.

"I was sent here by the Soviets in 1958 as a young Russian officer. My job was to continue to modernize the facility and keep it in good condition for activities such as those that are conducted here today. I no longer have any military status in the Soviet Union. They simply pay me to continue to do my job here. I suppose I am still a Russian citizen, but I have been here for more than 20 years, never once returning to Russia." "If I may interrupt you, Albert," Ivan asked, "there must have been something special about you as a young officer that singled you out for this type of service. Am I wrong?"

"Again, you are quite perceptive, Mr. Schwarz," Albert replied. "My father was a general in the Soviet Army. I'm sure that he carried the necessary weight to get me this appointment. He was killed in 1960 in what was described as non-combat military activities. I believe he was assassinated by the KGB, because he was never a strong believer in the Communist doctrine and that eventually caught up with him." "I'm sorry to hear that, Albert," Ivan sadly responded.

"Thank you, but condolences are not necessary," Albert replied, "I have only loyalties to myself now. Russia is my employer, no more and no less than that."

Ivan felt a very strong attachment to Albert. He felt that this man could indeed be his friend, but he would have to develop that friendship slowly and carefully, always with suspicion.

"Now about your place here," Albert started. "I have three key cards for you, and I believe that you already have a fourth, that one for your quarters. Is that correct?"

"Yes, Anna gave me the key to my quarters," Ivan answered.

"About Anna," Albert softly whispered. "Be very careful with her. I'm not sure exactly what her position is here. She has gained full access to the facility and all of the scientists, but her skill seems only to be her sexual freedom, and she has offered and accommodated every one of the men here with that freedom, except of course me. I have no interest in her. You do what you want with her offerings, but just be very cautious with her." "Where do you think her real loyalties lie?" Ivan asked

"Supposedly with you Americans. They sent her here originally with the other American scientists, but as they left, she simply remained," Albert answered.

"Why did the other American scientists leave?" Ivan asked.

"I can only speculate about that," Albert answered. "The complete team worked together for several months on the project. They were apparently at a point in their work where they needed human verification and testing. That meant bringing in men and women to test their product. I believe that those that were brought into the medical facility for this testing were Iranian political prisoners, many of whom left the facility in body bags. That's when the American scientists left. I assumed that the Americans just did not want to be involved with using these human test subjects." "How many people were killed by these tests?" Ivan asked.

"Since I had the job of removing them, I can tell you: exactly six men and three women. They were removed by helicopter without any fanfare," Albert answered.

"And that's when the Americans stopped their work here?"

"Yes, and it seemed that the entire project came to a halt at that point or changed its direction. Dr. Topolski is the technical head of the project and he might be able to give you more on that. He will brief you later today, after I give you a facility tour and show you around," Albert answered.

"I'm ready for that tour right now," Ivan noted.

"First let me explain the key card system that we have," Albert instructed. "The card marked with the number 5 will permit you to enter any of the rooms on the 5th or top floor where we are at this time. The reason this floor is secure is that only the scientists and their staff members are permitted into these facilities including the kitchen and serve staff.

"The card marked with the number 4 you already have in your possession. That card will allow you entry only to your specific living quarters but no others on that floor.

"The card marked number 3 permits entry into laboratory floor but only access to your specific laboratory and one other conference lounge that serves all the scientists.

"The card marked number 2 allows entry into the medical facility. This floor also contains the living quarters for all the supporting staff members for the facility.

"The bottom floor, or floor number one, permits no access except by my personal permission. That floor contains the infrastructure for the building and a small lounge that permits exit to a very private beach area. There are occasions when a group of scientists will hold a friendly meeting on this floor but that is rare and only entering with my key. Okay, let's start the tour." As Ivan and Albert entered the elevator, Ivan asked, "Albert, you speak nearly perfect English. How did you learn our language so well?"

Albert glanced around the elevator nervously as he pushed the "stop" button and the elevator came to a halt. Albert started in a soft voice, "When I was sent here many years ago, I knew I was going to be dealing with people of several countries. I asked my superiors in the Soviet Union if I could be given speech lessons to learn several languages. They provided me with a series of tapes that covered English and German and some Persian. I concentrated on the English and when the American scientists were here, they helped me with the dialect and pronunciation. I kind of leaned to the English, thinking that if I was even forced to leave here, I would try to get to America. No one else knows that, sir, so let's keep it between us." Ivan felt good about that answer because he knew that Albert had leanings toward America as a possible future home. That could come in handy in the future.

The elevator was restarted, and the door opened to the third floor where the labs were located. "You will notice that there are three doors on this floor marked "no entry room 1, 2 and 3". Door number three is your laboratory, and your key card is marked 3-3, meaning third floor, room number 3." Ivan slipped his key card into the lock and the door snapped open. Ivan's eyes nearly popped out of his head as he got the first glance at his new laboratory. "Wow!" Ivan exclaimed, "This facility is to die for. Excuse the pun, of course."

"I was told that your lab was needed several computers and much of the best associated electronics and recording equipment. All of the text material that was forwarded by your associates is included in this lab. Each of the computers is independent to all others but each has the capability to be interlinked not only with your computers but also with those of the other scientists, with their agreement of course.

"The laboratory is completely shielded from outside electronic interference and of course has its own self-contained fire prevention protection system. The door to your left has toilet and shower facilities and a small, comfortable lounge area. The door to your right is storage and contains much of the supporting equipment that you might need for your work. You will notice three television monitors. One connects you to a camera in the medical facility. The big screen is an interconnected video conferencing system so you can connect with the other scientists without leaving your facility. The third system is empty and can be developed as you proceed with your work. There are two voice recording systems for your dictation if you need that, and of course each computer has printing capability. If there is any other equipment that you need, I can have that delivered to you within days of your request. Of course, you will need time to get this all set up to your liking, but I am here to assist you in that regard if you need help. Let's move on to the next area." The elevator door opened at floor number two, and there were two locked doors immediately in front of the elevator. "The door on the right has no entry for you, Ivan. That door enters the living quarters of all of the other technical staff. The door on the left marked "MeD 1 can be entered with your key card similarly marked." Ivan slipped his key into the lock and again the lock snapped open. The room that was exposed looked similar to a well-established emergency room at any American hospital. There were a few men and women doing what looked to be somewhat menial tasks but no real medical treatment taking place.

"This facility has a full-time doctor and two registered nurses and several medical technicians. The facility is equipped to handle almost any medical situation. It also houses a complete operating room."

"Is this the area where the experimentation was done on the Iranians?" Ivan asked.

"Yes, this is the area" Albert responded, "but the staff here did not participate in that work. Only the scientific staff did that work," Albert answered.

They left the medical facility and moved down to the bottom floor. Ivan had no key access to this floor, so Albert used his key card to open the facility.

Albert started. "The rear of this floor contains all the infrastructure for this building including the water filtering system, the heating and air conditioning equipment, electric generating system and waste treatment system. We will not enter that area now, since there is no need for you to know about the systems." Ivan interrupted, "Are you expert on all of the systems in this facility?"

"I am indeed," Albert proudly responded, "on every last volt of electricity and degree of heat."

"The front area that we are in leads to the beach, as you can see. There are two lounge areas here and a small gym facility that is rarely used, and its use is limited to the scientific people who are here. If you have any reason to gain access to this floor, you will need to gain access through me. The reason that this floor is so secure is that it the only other way for ingress or egress to the facility. We are mostly concerned about invasion from the beach area since that area can be approached from the Sea. I live in the rear of this floor and I have electronic monitoring of the waters adjacent to the facility with alarms that have been strategically placed around the perimeter of the beach area." "Have there even been attempts to enter this facility from the sea?" Ivan asked.

"Not that I am aware of" Albert replied. If you were to look at this facility from the sea, it simply looks like some sort of broken-down old fort of some sort. No one has ever seemed interested in exploring it."

Ivan interrupted. "This may not be the right time to ask you this question, but we do seem to be expressing opinions about people. What is the story with my guide, Farhad Ahmani? Is he an Iranian, and who does he work for? Does he live here? He seems to have relative freedom throughout the country." Albert was a little cautious in his reply to this question, saying, "The Iranian government has no actual jurisdiction over this facility since it is owned and completely controlled by the Russians. The original agreement between the two governments, however required that each country had to establish a guide for their people who resided here, and those guides were to be Iranians. Any activities outside this facility carried on by our technical people always had to be accompanied by their guide, to ensure that all of the government's rules were always known and obeyed. They are sort of your bodyguard in reverse to keep you under control when on Iranian soil. I believe they are paid by your government, but they are Iranian citizens. You can probably assume that they are spies for Iran although they have very little access to areas within this compound. The unusual aspect of the four that are here is that they are all relatively young and very well-educated, a strange set of credentials for this type of job." "Okay, Ivan," Albert stated, "I'm going to leave you alone now. I'm sure you want some time to explore your lab and perhaps rest for a few minutes in preparation for your briefing by Dr. Topolski. You can grab some lunch around noon, and you are scheduled to meet with Topolski at about 1300. He will probably meet you in the lunch area and go to the lobby for his briefing. It is possible that he will brief you with the other top scientist on the lab conference area but that will be his decision. He is hard to predict, somewhat of a pain in the ass in my opinion but apparently a brilliant scientist. By the way, how come you seem so nice a fellow Ivan, I'm told that you are the guy at the top of your field. Why haven't you turned into a pain in the ass like the others?" "I suppose if you asked my ex-wife that question, she might tell you that I am the worlds worse pain in the ass, but that's why she is my ex-wife." Ivan laughed "We're going to get along just fine, you and I" Albert quipped, "Just fine."

When Ivan returned to his room after the briefing and tour from Albert, He had some time to meditate on all that he had heard so far today. If he was to be successful in his assignment, he was going to have to develop relationships with a few people that he could actually trust. Albert certainly seemed his most important ally although he could not jump to that conclusion too fast. Albert could certainly give him valuable data that he needed for his planned facility in Vermont. Although Albert is Russian, he certainly has American leanings, Ivan would have to nurture those leanings, always exercising his suspicious nature.

As for Farhad, his guide, this was a little more challenging. He was obviously an Iranian in good standing with the government, but he was now employed by the US government. At this point, he was Ivan's only connection with the outside world. He would play that relationship very carefully, but Farhad was certainly someone that Ivan wanted on his side in the future.

As for Anna, she was Ivan's mystery woman. He would treat her with great suspicion until he understood more of her motives. He decided to turn that relationship into somewhat of a game until he was able to better understand exactly where her loyalties lay. If the CIA had suspicions that she might be a double agent, he would take that position for the time being. His most difficult task with Anna was going to be resisting her sexual advances, if they were offered. Ivan had been celibate for many years, but he was still a man and knew that he might have weaknesses in this area. But this might be a game that he would enjoy playing.

Although Ivan had not yet met any of the other scientists, he felt that he would most certainly be considered the "new kid on the block" by the other team leaders. The project had apparently come to a halt and the team needed his input; this should place him in a more important position than might be expected. Ivan felt that to establish himself as an equal on the team, he would probably need to exert himself more than he was accustomed to doing. He recalled how powerful he felt when he responded to the Iranian briefer about his being a Jew. That experience made him feel powerful. For most of his career he had always stayed away getting into controversial discussions which made him look like the scientist wimp. This would not work here. He had to establish himself as the strength on this team of scientists. That strength would automatically give him some degree of power over the others on the team.

The problem here was that Ivan really didn't know if he had it in him to change his stripes at this point in his life, but he believed that his eventual survival might depend on a change in his reaction and interaction with people.

Above all, Ivan knew that if he was going to be successful with this assignment, he needed to develop a plan. Things would change as time went on and he learned more about the personalities involved and his plan would have to be flexible, but if he hoped to get through this period of his life with the kind of wealth that this assignment would provide, so as to live the remainder of his life as he had dreamed for, he would need a great deal of discipline and a well-thought-out plan. The plan was going to be as important as any of the future work that he would do here.

As Ivan entered the eating area, he noticed two other gentlemen sitting together having a light lunch. Both men immediately got up and beckoned him to join them, introducing themselves as Aylusha Topolski and Elias Bechert.

"Please join us Dr. Schwarz," Dr. Topolski pleasantly requested. "We have a meeting at 1300 in the laboratory conference room but perhaps we can use these few moments to get acquainted."

"Thank you," Ivan replied as he pulled up a chair and slowly sat. "We have heard a great deal about you, Dr. Schwarz. You have achieved quite a well-deserved reputation in your field. We have both read much of your published material dealing with neural networks and we are quite impressed. That is why we requested your presence here, to help our team move the project forward. We won't discuss the work here, of course; that type of discussion should always be limited to the secured conference room in our work area." Ivan respectfully replied, "Thank you for your kind words, Dr. Topolski. It may take me a while to adapt to the rules here, but I assure you that I understand the importance of the work being done here."

"We really do not look upon our procedures as rules, Dr. Schwarz, but in this strange setting, we never know who is watching or listening," Topolski replied.

"I certainly understand that," Ivan softly responded.

They continued their idle conversation over lunch and agreed to move down to the Laboratory area for more detailed discussions.

Arriving at the conference room, Ivan was amazed at the surroundings in the room. The walls were cluttered with charts and data related to the project. DR Topolski took his place at the front of the room as if in charge as Dr. Bechert simply sat beside Ivan. Bechert had said very little since they met, seemingly very willing to let Topolski do the talking.

Topolski started. "Most of the scientists working on this project are under the supervision of Dr. Bechert. His team is made up of specialized offspring of many of Germany's greatest scientists who moved here after the war. Your government inherited scientists skilled in rocket technology, the Soviet government welcomed scientists skilled in other area such as chemical sciences.

"I am the technical leader of the team here, and we have been working for more than two years developing a series of chemicals and drugs that are intended to be used for peaceful purposes, not for the creation of warfare. As we understand it, the results are to be shared equally by the three governments in a cooperative treaty-like arrangement. We have no interest or concern about the political aspects of that arrangement. We are simply scientists who are getting paid well to complete this project.

"To date, we have successfully developed drugs effecting human reaction in four areas: aggressiveness, passion, depression, and discipline. Singly or in combination, these drugs can render a human being useless for aggressive combat and we believe that in very short periods these drugs are undetectable to outside analysis. We know the drugs work effectively when taken internally, but the objective is to gain the same effectiveness when applied externally through the skin.

"That is why we asked for your assistance. You know the human nervous system completely, and we hope that you should be able to move the project toward completion for us.

"We have done an exceptional amount of work on this project already to get the drugs developed. We don't expect any interference from you as this effort continues to refine the work already done. We want your expertise to solve the problem of external application, and we expect that you work will be limited to that area.

"Many on the team consider you an outsider, and you may feel treated that way by most of the other scientists and sometimes even Dr Bechert and I. We hope that you will understand that situation, but that is the way it is."

"If I may interrupt you, Dr. Topolski," Ivan responded, somewhat annoyed. Ivan stood up as if in a slight motion to leave the room. "Let's be completely clear on my standing here. Your project has come to a complete halt because you don't have the problem of external application solved. I may be able to solve that problem for you, and without my help all the work you have completed to date is useless to your governments. In order to be effective in my work, it may indeed be necessary to alter some aspects of these drugs, so I will need to be completely familiar with all of the work you have done to date.

"The way I see it, I am now the most important member of this team, because without me you have no chance of success. If the entire team cannot accept that status for my work, then I may as well pack up and leave right now. I expect you and Dr. Bechert to make sure your people all understand that. Have I made myself clear to both of you?" Both Topolski and Bechert nodded their reluctant agreement.

Ivan continued, "Beginning tomorrow, I will want to meet in detail with each of your area specialists in their laboratories to be brought up to date on their work. I hope that I don't sense any hostility on any of their part toward my presence or my importance on this team. If at any time I discover that I have not been provided the correct and up-to-date information, I will expect that either of you will respond accordingly. If we agree, let's start to work. I will be spending a few days getting my laboratory set up, but you should start scheduling the briefings immediately. I consider myself to be able to handle multitasking, so I can handle the lab and the briefings at the same time." Ivan stood up and started to the door. "Good day, gentlemen," he said with a smile." Tomorrow starts a new era with this project." Ivan left the room alone, not looking back to see the expressions on the faces of the two scientists. He had performed in a manner that he was not accustomed to. He was forceful and took charge of things. This was the first time in his life that he had exhibited these characteristics, and he felt very good about it.

CHAPTER 18

A S IVAN LEFT the briefing room for his laboratory, he felt a feeling of great relief. Never in his life had he taken such a strong and aggressive stand on anything. He remembered the briefing by the Iranian military officer where for the first time he took a positive and aggressive stand. He had thought about his role in this project and decided that as the newcomer he didn't want to become the second-class member. He realized that the project needed him more than he needed the others. Also, if he was to accomplish his entire mission, he needed to have access to everything that had been done to date. He believed that by taking the stand that he did, he could demand detailed briefings without feeling that key information was being withheld from him. He would have to test that theory as time passed.

There were two other tasks that Ivan knew he had to complete. He had to try to develop a relationship with Anna to make his own determination of which side she was on. He preferred to start that relationship in the laboratory rather than in the bedroom, but he knew that at some point he would cave to her beauty and sexual aggressiveness.

His second task was to better understand the role of Farhad Ahmani, his so-called guide. Where was he supposed to guide Ivan since he was going to be confined to this facility for most of his stay here. Farhad seemed to have a good grasp of the English language, and Ivan couldn't sense any loyalty to Iran in any of his dealing with them so far. Farhad was apparently able to come and go as he pleased within the community, so whatever his relationship was with the Iranians, it apparently gave him freedom of access. This seemed to be a strange set of relationships that didn't entirely make sense to Ivan.

Ivan also had an overriding challenge, which was to find a way to have open discussions with these two people without any fear of being overheard. Anna seemed confident in her belief that his room was bugged so he could also assume that his laboratory and conference space were also bugged.

For a scientist like Ivan, the solution seemed rather simple. He would build white noise generators that he could install in his private facilities and in his laboratory. He would simply include the parts needed to build the generators in the material list that he would give to Albert Brokow, who seemed to be in charge of everything in the facility. Ivan also felt that he could develop a strong relationship with Brokow. It seemed that Brokow had strong pro-American feelings. Perhaps Ivan could develop a deal over time that would be helpful to him when it was time to complete his assignment and return to the United States.

If Ivan was successful building these generators, it would also be a tool to see who was with him and who was against him. He wouldn't tell anyone about the white noise. Whoever started to get inquisitive about the sound blackout would be giving away the little secret that they heard about it from someone. Rather clever, Ivan thought. This spy stuff might even get interesting.

Ivan also decided to impose his newfound aggressive attitude on Albert Brokow.

That control panel in his room … he would direct Albert to arrange to have it signal Farhad, Anna, Dr. Topolski, Dr. Bechert, and him, Albert Brokow, so he could beckon them or talk to them whenever he desired. That would be a good test of his newly established power in the facility.

Anna would be his first step in this plan. She was supposed to be his assistant, so he had to test her first. When he returned to his room, he approached her suite and knocked on her door. When she answered, she was certainly not dressed for work, wearing a very seductive and tight-fitting outfit.

"Come in, Ivan. What a pleasant surprise." Anna spoke softly. "Come in and sit down and make yourself comfortable."

"Comfort is not high on my list, Anna," Ivan started. "You are supposed to be my assistant, so I would like to start our arrangement by establishing a mutual understanding of exactly what your duties are. As I understand it, you have no technical background at all based on your education. I understand that when the American scientists left the program, the government left you here to kind of honor their commitment to be part of the program. Now that I am here, I am committed to honor our country's commitment to finish the project, and I expect that all of your efforts will be directed toward assisting me in that endeavor. As my assistant, you will carry out whatever tasks I ask of you without question. Do you understand that, Anna?' Anna was somewhat taken back by Ivan's sudden aggressiveness, and she responded, "Yes, sir, I understand."

Ivan continued. "I also want you to understand that if your extracurricular activities with the others in this facility in any way jeopardize my efforts or threaten the program in any way, I will have you removed immediately. I know that you are sexually active with some of the men in the facility and that has earned you somewhat free access to them. If I get any hint that you are playing sides against each other, I will take immediate action with our government. Do you understand what I just said, Anna?" "I certainly do, Ivan," Anna tersely responded.

Ivan gave Anna instructions on his desire to have Albert Brokow connect his communications panel to the people he desired, and he directed her to get that accomplished as soon as possible. "Getting things done for me is your primary job, so you can start with this task. Also, have Farhad come to my room." "I'll get it done," Anna replied, as Ivan left her room.

As Ivan sat in his room, he let his mind wander for the first time in a while. He couldn't help but notice the stark contrast between his suite and that of Anna. He realized that she had been in that facility for a long time, but her rooms were somewhat lavishly furnished. The walls were well-decorated and in very good taste. She certainly must be using her sexual attractiveness in her favor, he thought. What is she giving up for these favors, other than her body? Based on what he was told in his CIA briefings, Ivan didn't think that the former American scientists had made much of a contribution to the project, so she could not have revealed any valuable information to the others. It was just that her mere presence here made no sense to him. If the CIA had suspicions about her loyalty, why would they leave her here? He would certainly have to keep his eye on her to see if he could answer some of his concerns.

Within a few minutes, there was a knock on the door. Farhad had apparently gotten the message from Anna, and he was at the door. Ivan let Farhad in and whispered to him softly, "Do you think that this area is bugged, and our conversations can be overheard?"

Farhad nodded his head in silence. Ivan then invited Farhad to the bath area, where he turned on the water. "I believe for the time being we can talk in here but even with the water running, we should talk softly.

"Farhad, I need to know a little more about you. I feel very alone here, not knowing who to trust and who to suspect. What the hell is your role here? You have been defined as my guide; what does that mean? There is no place for me to go, so where are the places that you will guide me? These questions make me suspicious that there is another role that you are playing in this operation." Farhad raised his hand as to signal Ivan to stop talking. He handed Ivan a small device that looked very much like a pager. He whispered, "Use this when you need me. I will be very close by most of the time." He handed Ivan a small notebook and said, "Read this, and it might make things clearer to you. When you finish it, please destroy it. If it gets into the wrong hands, our whole operation will be jeopardized." Those words made Ivan feel a little better. Apparently, Farhad was on his side, but he didn't want to talk about it here.

Ivan responded, "Within days, I will create a situation where we can talk openly. I'll read your notebook and get back to you."

They each got up, as though knowing the next move, and Farhad walked straight to the door and left. Ivan turned off the water and returned to his lounge area to read the notebook.

After opening the small notebook, he kicked off his shoes and started reading.

> *Farhad Ahmani is my real name. I am an Iranian-born American. I was educated in the United States, and that is where my loyalty lies. My parents left Iran many years ago, when things were not as dangerous as they are today.*
>
> *After college, I was recruited by the CIA as an operative in this country. I have been in that role for several years. Through my family connections, I have been given certain privileges in Iran that are unusual. There may come a time*

when the current rulers catch on to me and those privileges will be taken away.

In the meantime, I am your resident contact operative. I have the ability to get information in and out of the country for you. I hold diplomatic status and have established a communications link for you to the USA. This link is to be used for important information only.

Each of the other two lead scientists also has similar operatives but by agreement we have little or no interaction with each other. Anna also has a similar connection whom I do not know. You are probably aware that the Russians purchased this facility many years ago and used it to smuggle high-level German leaders and scientists out of Germany to avoid their prosecution as war criminals. The Germans and Russians have a completely different relationship with the current Iranian government, since they continue to supply them with weapons and other unusual materials for their nuclear programs.

I believe that the system that the CIA has established for us is very secure and we can rest easy that whatever you give me will not get into any other hands. You should also know that if anything happens and it becomes urgent to get you out of this facility to a safer location, we have a plan in place to also accomplish that.

There are two computers in your residence. One of those computers has encryption capability, so if you choose you can use that machine to document very sensitive information. I'm sure you can figure out how to use that equipment.

I assure you that you can have complete trust in my loyalty to our country. I would also advise you that you should not assume the same for Anastasia Meinkoff. I believe you have already received that advice.

I am at your service. Please do not hesitate to call upon me whenever you need help.

Signed, Farhad Ahmani.

Ivan felt as if a huge load had just been lifted from him. He finally had a friend here, one whom he could trust, but even with this assurance, Ivan would continue to have his suspicions about everyone, including Farhad. After all, he needed to carry out the wishes of his father not to trust anyone who offers him friendship or help.

Ivan had several plans that he needed to put into place other than those involving Brokow, Anna, and Farhad. He needed to get started finalizing the plans for the facility in Vermont that his cousin is going to have built for him. The first gold deposit representing his salary should have already been delivered and he probably wants to get started before winter sets in. It is unlikely that any work can get done during the winter months in Vermont.

He also needed to start thinking about how he was going to accomplish his two-phased plan here in Iran. First, he needed to get his job done to help complete the project, and he also needed a plan to ensure that the other two countries are not able to use the results. The first step would probably be fairly simple considering his career background. The later plan might be more difficult since he was not experienced in that aspect of being a CIA operative.

He felt confident that he had established himself as a strong-willed member of the team, but he would have to continue that position with his everyday actions. This might be more difficult since it kind of went against his normal personality. His first task was to get his laboratory set up, his white noise generators built and become integrally involved with the team on all aspects of the project.

Ivan kept having an uneasy feeling about Albert Brokow. Even with his inherently suspicious nature, Ivan felt warmth toward Albert. He remembered that he had mentioned a long-standing desire to eventually move to America. but he was very content with the job that the Russian government had given him here in Iran. Brokow held all of the secrets of this facility, and there was some of that knowledge that Ivan wanted for himself, especially the knowledge of the design of the miniature nuclear generators that provided all the power for this facility. Wouldn't it be nice, Ivan thought, if Brokow could get him the specifications for that generator for use in his Vermont facility? Not only did he want to get better acquainted with Albert Brokow, he wanted those design specs for himself.

Ivan decided to go down to Brooke's work area and have a discussion with him about a few important items that would eventually affect his work. Ivan took the elevator down to Albert's level not knowing if Albert was actually there at that time. Ivan decided not to notify Albert of his coming. After all, Ivan was trying to make his tour here more pleasant and feeling at home wandering around the building would be part of that effort. Less formality seemed appropriate in this instance.

"Hello? Anyone home?" Ivan shouted.

"I'm here in my office," Albert replied. "What a nice surprise, having you pop in on me like this. I like the rare casual surprises."

Ivan pulled up a stool that was in the corner of the office and sat facing Albert, who was still at his desk.

"I thought this was as good a place to talk as any other," Ivan started. "I have started my preliminary discussions with Dr. Topolski and Dr. Bechert. Nothing detailed, just laying down some of the ground rules that I intend to operate under."

Albert interrupted, chuckling a little. "Yes, I heard about that casual meeting. I expect that both men were set back a notch or two."

Ivan was a little surprised that Albert knew about that discussion, since he believed that those two scientists had little interface with him. He would simply put this point in his memory bank for future reference.

Albert started, "What brings you here, Ivan?"

Ivan responded, "I think you and I kind of hit it off the other day, like a couple of regular guys, you know. I like to get to know the people who surround me in my work. You never know when you might need a favor from one of them."

"I agree with that," Albert muttered.

"Let's get right to the point, Albert," Ivan started, leaning over the desk toward Albert. "Why the hell are my facilities bugged, and who and where are the listening stations?"

"Wow," Albert replied, "It didn't take you long to get right to that one, Ivan. Well, all three scientists and others that work here have their facilities bugged. The Russians own this building and they want a record of everything that goes on here. They have been paranoid about that for years. All of the pickups are wired to a central recorder and the tapes are always rolling. My job is simply to change the discs when they are full and file them away by date." "Does anyone ever ask to see those discs?" Ivan asked

"Not to my knowledge," Albert responded.

"Is it possible for someone to see them without you knowing about it?" Ivan asked.

"I suppose so. They are simply filed, not locked very securely away," Albert responded.

"If these recording devices are always on, there must be a million recordings," Ivan commented.

"Well, not really," Albert responded. "The recording devices are only triggered by sound. If there is no sound coming into the recorders, there are no recordings made. Otherwise, most of the recording space would be blank and a waste of time and equipment."

"How far back does this system date?" Ivan asked.

Albert responded, "I'm not really sure. It was here when I got here. Some technicians came in a year ago and changed from the old analog recorders to new digital units. The old units used tapes, and there are boxes of old recordings stored in the back room. I'm not sure what condition they are in, because no precautions have been taken to preserve them." Ivan whispered somewhat jokingly, "Do you suppose we are being recorded right now?"

"Not a chance," Albert replied. "When the technicians came in to convert the system to a digital technology, I studied the wiring plans from the files and found that all of the pickup sensors were originally wired in a parallel pattern, so simply cutting one of the connecting wires actually cut all of them off on that circuit. I simply made one small cut and there was no more pickup from my area." "No alarms on the system alerting anyone to your action?" Ivan asked.

"Nope," Albert responded.

"Let's get off of the bugging now, Albert," Ivan said. "I have sensed that you have no real interest in the actual work that is going on here. You are paid well and left alone by your Russian bosses. But you must have opinions about the others that are working here. Would you care to tell me about them?" Albert suddenly got less talkative. "Not really," he responded, as he started toward the door, seemingly to escort Ivan out of the room.

Ivan jumped up as to try to stop Albert, saying, "I'm sorry, Albert. I didn't want to put you in a bad position with that question. To be successful, I feel that I need to know a little about the people that I am working with. If you don't want to talk about that, it's okay with me."

"It's not that you are putting me in any bad position, Ivan. It's just that I don't really get involved with those people, and although I have strong feelings about them, it's possible that my feelings are just that—feelings that have no substance. I think you should develop your own opinion about them, and perhaps at a later date we can compare notes. Is that okay with you, Ivan?" "Certainly," Ivan replied. He shook hands with Albert and returned to his room.

It was obvious that Ivan needed to continue to nurture his relationship with Albert Brokow, but for now, his job was to make steady progress with his assignment. Based upon Albert's information about the bugging system, Ivan disabled the system in his quarters, but he still proceeded to build a white noise generator as he had planned.

Ivan was spending most of his time in his laboratory getting it set up as needed to do productive work. He wasn't moving particularly fast with this lab development, because he had not sensed any great urgency from other areas. During the days that led to weeks of laboratory setup, he had neglected the other members of the team except to deal with them during meals and chance meetings. He had prepared an action plan, and thought it was time to present that plan to his other team members.

The intercom system in his room had been set up as he had ordered. This was the first assignment that he had given Anna, and she had apparently completed it without any additional input or assistance from him. Over a period of the next few weeks, he would do some testing to assure that this new system wasn't just another facility bug. In the meantime, he used the system to have brief talks with others who were connected to the system. Using the intercom system, Ivan asked Topolski and Bechert to schedule a time that was convenient to them so he could present them with his operating plan for his portion of the project.

At the agreed to date and time, all three men proceeded to the conference area adjacent to their laboratories. They entered the room and gave each other their normal cordial handshake. Ivan knew that there was no real meaning to these handshakes, but he would continue to insist that they use them even if only as a sign of respect.

When both Dr. Topolski and Dr. Bechert were comfortably seated, Ivan began his first informational presentation. He had decided that he would continue his somewhat aggressive behavior by taking a positive and seemingly cooperative position on the interchange of information. After all, these men had been working on this project for many months and were apparently at a point where they needed Ivan's help. For Ivan to successfully carry out his assignment, he would also need access to all of the work that the two scientists had done to date. They apparently had already developed a series of drugs that would accomplish their behavioral goals, but they couldn't figure out how to make the drugs work as desired, without serious consequences.

Ivan started. "Gentlemen, I have done a great deal of thinking about our mutual goals in this project. I sincerely believe that we collectively have the knowledge to accomplish these goals but to do so we will have to be very cooperative in our efforts. I decided to start off this sharing process in order to break the ice, so to speak. In order for me to provide the help needed, I will need the same degree of cooperation from both you brilliant scientists as we proceed.

"The danger as I start these briefings is that I may be talking beneath your level of intellect at times. I will apologize for this in advance. I have always found that starting from the beginning with a complicated subject provides the best understand in the long run, so please indulge me as I proceed.

"The objective of neuroscientists like me is to create a computer that can think and reason just as we humans do. Therefore, my many years of study involve a very comprehensive understanding of the human brain and the nervous system that feeds the brain. The human body is constantly sending out millions of tiny signals, all of which are sent to and processed by the brain. The central computer of the brain is the neocortex, which I'm sure you know. The neocortex processes the signals necessary for the higher function of the human body, such as perceptions, spatial reasoning, development of motor commands, conscious thought reasoning, and much more.

"One of the biggest problems that we scientists have, when attempting to move forward with our work, is that there is a tremendous difference between this central computer of the human body and that which is present in animals and other non-human species. In us humans, the neocortex is made up and many grooves and ridges which create a great deal of surface area to process all the incoming information. In non-humans, these grooves and ridges do not exist, and the neocortex has a smooth, flat surface providing much less capability to process these functions. For a similar-size skull, humans can process more than twice the information compared to a non-human skull. In small animals where the skull size is much smaller than the human skull, that difference is even greater. So! When we want to test out theories in this area, we cannot use animals for the tests. We need to do the tests on humans. From what I understand, you both have already realized that, and that fact will have a very great effect on future progress.

"Knowledge of the neocortex of the brain is the one area of science that much more study is needed. In my field, IBM has made that problem a little easier. They developed a computational model of the human brain that simulated the electrochemistry of the neocortex. They built a supercomputer named the Blue Brain Project in order to better understand the processes of perception, learning and memory. Fortunately for our project, I was I involved in that development and I have all of the algorithms in my computers. That will save us a great deal of time.

"I will need to know everything about the drugs that you have developed, because of the objective to apply these drugs to the human body transdermally. Very little work has been done with transdermal drug delivery, as a replacement for delivery of drugs orally or by hypodermic injections. The use of microneedles and thermal ablation has progressed in recent years and there are some areas where transdermal drug delivery has been successful, namely with drugs to help control balance. This has helped people who suffer from air and sea sickness. I see the transdermal application process as our most serious obstacle to success in this project. It's not that we won't be able to make the concept work it's a problem of quantity. We will have to very carefully control the area of application and the quantity of the drug that is applied. If we put too much in the wrong area, we can do irreversible damage to the brain. One of our objectives as I understand it is to make the drug undetectable. This will be our greatest challenge. The dissipation rate of most drugs is too long to be undetectable and if we use too little of that drug, it will not have the desired effect. This can only be determined through testing, and I'm not yet sure how to get around that problem. We will really have to work together on that one.

"I'm going to concentrate my efforts on three areas of the human body for transdermal application, the arms and hand area, the head and neck area and the chest and upper back. These are the areas of the human body that are most likely to be exposed for transdermal application and also the areas that contain literally millions of neuron transmitters that send the important signals to the brain.

"The hand and arm have more than 200,000 neurons that send very rapid signals to the brain. There are five major nerves that send important signals from the arm and hand. These are critical nerves for getting large amounts of information to the brain quickly.

"The nerves of the neck and head carry some of the most vital information about the important organs of the nervous system. These nerves work together to control every part of the body. The brain weighs about three pounds, but these are the most important pounds in the body. About 100 billion neurons in the brain control almost all of the body's activity and most of this information passes up to the brain though the neck area.

"The chest and upper back are critical because most sensory information from the bodies various areas is passed through this region on the way to the brain. The spinal cord is the vital link between the body and the brain. The spinal cord is only about one inch in diameter, but it carries nervous signals and processes many reflexes to support the structures of the body.

"One area where we will have to work very closely together is a complete understanding of the content of the drugs that you have developed. Some drugs quickly become addictive to the body because their chemical structure mimics that of the natural neuron transmitter. This permits the drug to attach to and activate a neuron. This leads to abnormal messages being transmitted to the brain, and with very little repetition, they become addictive.

"I believe that when I complete my laboratory set-up, I will be able to input all of the substances contained in the drugs you have and make a preliminary determination of their effect on the body functions and reactions. If we continually repeat these computer iterations, I believe we can achieve 95% assurance of the final results. The remaining 5% can only be determined by human tests, and we must have very serious discussions about using human test specimens.

"Gentlemen, this has been a very cursory summary of my operating plan for my input to this project. If either of you have any questions or concerns about my plan, we must discuss those concerns very soon. I will share all of my results with you both and expect that you will reciprocate." All three men sat in silence for a few moments. Once again, Ivan had laid down the law about how he intended to operate. He fully expected that the other two scientists probably did not agree or would not honor his plan. They would certainly talk it over before they respond to Ivan. Once again, they all shook hands as they exited the conference room.

CHAPTER 19

SEVERAL MONTHS HAD passed since Sergeant Atwater and his team had successfully completed the rescue of Lieutenant Farber and the recovery of the body of his Radar Operator Steve Mitchell. Since the rescue, Atwater had been retained in Kuwait in a training status, but it seemed to him like he was in a perpetual state of inquiry and testimony to various specialists from the JAG (Judge Advocate Group) lawyers, CIA specialists, even FBI investigators.

Atwater was beginning to get nervous about the apparent motives of his interviewers. The initial questioning emphasized details of both the botched programs directed at rescuing the hostages and the performance of his team with the rescue of Lieutenant Farber. As time progressed, the questioning seemed to be shifting toward a more hostile direction, even to the point where he felt he was being forced to justify his actions when he was ordered to secure the airport in Iran in preparation for the hostage rescue. More specifically, he was being hammered about how and why he killed the people that were guarding that airport.

He was also questioned about the high-altitude jump that he had recommended, intended to speed up the rescue of Lieutenant Farber. It seemed that emphasis of this questioning was centering on his recommendation for a direct flight into Iran rather than a two-day small boat ride along the Iranian border. To him, the logic of his recommendation was obvious. The high-altitude jump, although more dangerous for him and his men, would cut two days off the rescue attempt, greatly reducing the chances of the two aviators being captured by the Iranians. Besides, both of these highly dangerous missions had been approved by officers of much higher rank that him.

The incident that really aroused his suspicions was one interview where two staff members of the Senate Armed Services Committee were present. They did not participate in the questioning, but they did take very detailed notes. Atwater believed that political involvement in these two incidents could only mean one thing: somewhere there were politicians who were taking steps to cover their asses regarding the two missions.

There had been a suspicious silence from Iran about either incident. If diplomatic complaints had been filed, he would have heard something, if not officially, at least through the military rumor system.

Sergeant Atwater was starting to smell a setup and he thought it was time to have a private discussion with Lieutenant Farber. Farber's father certainly would know what was brewing in Washington. Whether he had discussed that with Lieutenant Farber was not known, but it seemed a good move to have this meeting with Farber.

Lieutenant Farber had been retained in the Kuwait military hospital as his eyesight injury was corrected, so it would be relatively easy to get to talk to him. Atwater made a couple of phone calls and was soon on his way to the hospital to talk to Farber.

Upon entering Lieutenant Farber's room, Atwater was somewhat taken back by the apparent situation with Farber. He had apparently regained his sight, but he seemed very depressed, almost unwilling to discuss the mission with Atwater. The two men had talked before, when they returned from the rescue mission, and Atwater had visited him once before about a week after they returned to Kuwait. At that time, he seemed in good spirits. What, Atwater wondered, had happened to bring on this new attitude of Lieutenant Farber?

Farber was no longer confined to bed. It seemed that his current treatment was something other than purely medical. After a quick salute by Atwater and a handshake between the two soldiers, Farber closed the door and they both sat facing each other.

"Mike—can I drop the formalities and call you Mike?" Farber asked.

"Certainly, buddy," Atwater responded.

"Mike, I feel like I am getting totally fucked by the government. The damage to my eyesight was apparently not permanent, but there are still some potential problems that may recur. The investigators are implying that it was something that I did incorrectly before ejecting from my aircraft, that caused my injury. Whatever that was, it apparently put tremendous pressure on the blood flow to both sides of my brain, causing my extended blindness.

"There is a formal flight surgeon inquiry scheduled for next week to further investigate my qualifications to continue to fly. Every time I am questioned about this incident, I feel that the military is building a case against me for this accident.

"The doctors have already informed me that they will probably not be able to approve me to fly jets any longer. That was my life, Mike. When I graduated from the Naval Academy, I wanted to break away from my father's Navy, so I went to the Marines because I had a better chance to do combat flying. I was one of the top A-6 pilots in term of my performance ratings by my superiors. Now, for some unknown reason, they are taking all of that away from me, and I don't understand why." "Have you talked to your dad about this?" Atwater asked.

"No, I haven't. I have always tried to keep him out of my military business. If I was going to succeed in the military, I wanted to do it on my own, not with any pressure from him."

"Well, Hank," Atwater responded, "it might be time to have that discussion. That's why I came to see you today. I have been hammered for the past few weeks about my last two missions. I have been interviewed by everyone and anyone that seems interested. I have even had political staff present which makes me very suspicious of the government's motives in my case. The more they interview me, the more they seem to be trying to place guilt on me. I really don't understand the government's motives here. Now that I hear your problem, I am more suspicious that there is something bigger than the two of us going on here.

"From what I have learned about your mission into Iran, it seems to me that it was the result of a serious CIA intelligence failure. They had bad information about the location of the F-14s, and they sent you into a bad situation. In my case, they seem to be blaming me for killing civilians at the airport that I was ordered to secure as part of the rescue attempt of the hostages. That mission was a massive fuck-up and again a failure of intelligence. They are also questioning my recommendation to make a high-altitude parachute drop onto Iran to rescue you and your RO. Why the hell would anyone question our motives, unless some international incident has been created and made public and for some reason we are at the bottom of the pile in terms of rank, and we are being made the scapegoats?" "Wow," Farber responded, "I thought I had problems, but if your suspicions are even remotely true, we could be drawn into some big international incident and made the fall guys. I think a message to my father is certainly in order."

Two weeks had passed since Atwater and Farber discussed their mutual concerns about what seemed to be happening to them. Sergeant Atwater believed that in the time that had passed, Farber must have made contact with his father about their concerns. Why had Farber not gotten back to him, he wondered. Concerned about this lack of communication, Atwater decided to visit the hospital to see what was happening.

When he arrived at the hospital, he was shocked to learn that Lieutenant Farber was no longer there but had been transferred to the Naval Hospital in Okinawa, Japan, for further medical evaluation. *This was strange*, Atwater thought. *Why would the Navy suddenly move him without providing him enough time to get back to me?*

Atwater wouldn't have to wait long for the answer to that question. While the team was getting ongoing language training in Kuwait, he received orders from his commanding officer that a special CIA order had been received to transfer his team to (of all places) Okinawa, Japan. No explanation was given as to the purpose of this transfer, but that was not unusual for the Special Forces missions. They were trained to move at an instant's notice to respond to crises anywhere in the world. So, they packed their gear and off to Japan they went.

When they landed in Okinawa, there was a jeep waiting for Sergeant Atwater while his men were taken to their quarters.

The jeep stopped in front of an official looking building and Atwater proceeded immediately to enter the building. To his amazement, he was greeted at the entrance by Lieutenant Farber. "Come on inside," Farber suggested, and as they entered another larger room, Atwater saw another man sitting at a conference table. The man stood and welcomed Atwater.

"Glad to meet you, Sergeant Atwater. I'm Stanton Farber, Mikes father." Wow, Atwater thought, things are moving fast. He snapped a salute to the admiral.

Admiral Farber continued.

"Hank has briefed me on the concerns that you both have, and I thought that the best way to get to the bottom of your concerns was to hear them from both of you in person and in a secure environment. I arranged for a CIA special meeting here in Okinawa, so we could have this meeting. "To put the situation in better perspective for you, President Reagan as you know, replaced President Carter. During the Carter Administration, international affairs came totally apart within our government system. The intelligence community was nearly destroyed by Carter and his liberal advisors. I was asked to join the CIA to help repair that situation.

"I retired from the Navy because I could no longer go along with the Carter doctrine. When President Reagan found out how bad things really were in the CIA, he asked me to help clean them up."

When President Reagan was elected, the Republicans took over the Senate. That was the first time in more than 20 years that the Republicans won any chamber of Congress. The House is still run by the Democrats, so there is a great deal of Carter philosophy that still exists in Washington." "Middle Eastern oil has been a huge economic driver around the world, and many of the ranking Democrats in the House have filled their pockets for many years with oil money to preserve the financial interests of the Middle Eastern royalty.

"With the Iranian revolution that has taken place and the continued border conflicts between Iran and Iraq, the Middle East is now playing a much more important role in the American economy. These same politicians are getting nervous that they may no longer be able to exert the power to keep oil prices high. More important, if the liberal political power base is neutralized by Reagan policies, there could be many congressional asses that are hanging out in the wind, so a cover-up mentality is beginning to show in Washington.

"The intended F-14 bombings and your previous work with the Carter boondoggle with the hostage rescue effort was fortunately at a time when these same political powers were able to keep the incidents quiet through those same diplomatic channels that were funneling the big money into

Congressional pockets. Through my work with the Senate Intelligence Committee over the last few months, we have surfaced many of the massive CIA screw-ups that resulted from congressional directions to the leaders of the CIA. I suspect that somewhere in the system, both of your young military heroes might be getting set up as the scapegoats for bad CIA leadership and bad orders that were authorized by the top brass.

"I want both of you to go over every detail of your missions with me so I can be in a position to ensure that blame if necessary is directed to the proper people. Unfortunately, there is a downside to all of this. I may be in a very powerful position in Washington, but I am only one guy fighting a long-standing political power base. Things take enormous amounts of time in Washington. One investigation can take a year or more to complete, because the real facts often get buried by the desire of politicians to get re-elected.

"Even within the CIA, there are going to be massive shake-ups, so I will be dealing with a great deal of ass-saving in my own organization. I still have not determined who is loyal to me and who is not."

I can only ask that you both keep focused on your individual jobs with the hope that I can make the right things happen in Washington. I hope you both understand that." Both men nodded their heads in agreement.

"There is one thing I would like to ask of you, Admiral Farber, before we start our discussions."

"Go ahead," replied the admiral.

"My father, Ivan Schwarz, is on some sort of special assignment from the US government somewhere in the world. He is getting paid a great deal of money for his work, so I assume it must be on some black ops assignment under the control of the CIA. He was an employee of Calbro Corporation, out of the Boston area. If you could find out exactly where he is, it would set my mind at ease." "I'll see what I can do," the admiral replied.

At that point they then began detail briefings of their specific missions to the admiral.

Over the period of the next several months, Atwater and Farber crossed paths several times.

Lieutenant Farber had lost much of his interest in continuing his military service, because he was found to be unfit for pilot duties flying combat jets and had been relegated to flying helicopters for rescue missions.

His moral was at an all-time low but he had more time left in his service commitment resulting from his Naval Academy education. He could however opt out based on his medical condition.

Sergeant Atwater and his team of Special Ops soldiers was sent to several different parts of the world for short interdiction activities. In 1981, his team served as military advisors in El Salvador after a gorilla offensive was performed against the government.

He next went to Lebanon to support a multinational force to assist in extracting members of the Palestine Liberation Force from Beirut.

While in Beirut, Atwater was approached by a gentleman named Tommy Wilkenson, representing a company named Grey Skies Service Corporation. Wilkenson was having discussions with several Special Forces soldiers, trying to enlist them to become part of his military assistance company. Wilkenson had invited a group of soldiers to a meeting in a local restaurant in Beirut. There were about ten men and women assembled as Wilkenson took center stage.

"Gentlemen and ladies," he started. "My name is Tommy Wilkenson. I am the president of the Grey Skies Service Corporation, with headquarters in North Carolina.

"Everyone in this room has undergone highly specialized training in the US military and you all have some very special capability. Most of you are reaching the end of your committed tour of duty, and we at Grey Skies believe that it would be a shame if all of that training went to waste.

"There are many hot spots in the world today that are requiring quick strike capability. The United States Military is rapidly rebuilding its capabilities after the disastrous period of reductions under President Carter. But the military objectives are changing, and President Reagan knows that. The real, important soldering is going to be done by small 'Special Forces' type military units.

"Military leaders also know that liberal congressional leaders have redefined the rules of war, seriously limiting the rules of engagement that we operate by. Politicians are becoming more concerned about their reelection than they are about protecting the security of Americans around the world. As a result, a new term is evolving called "Political Correctness." Politicians want to fight wars while inflicting no casualties, which of course means that we will engage in battle, but we can never truly win.

The smarter people in Washington know that this is impossible if we are to remain the military power base in the world.

"The CIA is being rebuilt rapidly, and they are gaining war fighting capability. CIA installations throughout the world are re-establishing our intelligence capability, but they are also being asked to put out fires that flare up in their regions. The CIA is going to operate under a different set of rules than they have in the past. Much of their combat capability is going to be purchased from organizations such as Grey Skies Services. We already have several established small groups of former military specialists in our employ that have been assigned to CIA outposts around the world. These groups may be defined as security forces for the outposts, but in fact they are combat soldiers." "Our marketing strength lies in the fact that we are using well-trained former Special Forces people to do the job. The US government paid for the training of these people and we are preventing that training from going to waste.

"Because of our status as independent security forces, we can do things that are outside the box of political correctness and we have the cover of secrecy of the CIA. Under these new rules, we can operate with a wide range of flexibility without the fear of prosecution, just like the CIA has done for years. This is going to be an important part of the new military.

"The Secretary of Defense has had very detailed discussions with the Justice Department and has worked with the Senate Intelligence Committee to place these activities under the cover of the Black Ops Programs. These programs have little or no oversight by congress so they can be carried out with direction from true military leaders and not politicians.

"My company understands the rigor of the training that each of you has received. You voluntarily underwent that training because you individually wanted to be the best of the best. I know this because I served six years as a Navy SEAL.

"The current structure of our organization is set up to offer an attractive salary structure for each one of our employees. Our non-combat pay will be around $75,000 per year. If you are subjected to actual combat, that salary will increase to $100,000 a year. The government has agreed to provide us a program that will provide a $50,000 life insurance package for each employee. Each participant will be given a command rank at least one level higher than your current military rank. Rank is important in order to have an effective command structure.

"I know that I have dumped a great deal of information on you at this briefing, and I don't expect that you will jump to this opportunity immediately. As you leave you will receive a brief information package with my personal telephone number and other contact data. Each of you has already been reviewed by my senior staff, so your acceptance is now automatic if you decide to take me up on the offer.

"Also, if you have friends and associates who may be qualified for our program, please feel free to refer them to me for review. I will take a few questions, but I have made this briefing very detailed in order to answer most of your questions."

Sergeant Atwater got up to ask a question. "How secret will our assignments be, and will we have a somewhat permanent station?"

"There will be no need for secrecy regarding your employment with our company," Wilkenson replied., "Your permanent address will be our headquarters in North Carolina. As for the specific assignments, each one will take on whatever degree of secrecy is required by the circumstances, just as it does in the military." After the meeting, Sergeant Atwater felt it was important to contact Lieutenant Farber to inform him of this new development. Both of these soldiers were getting increasingly fed up with their current military assignments. Perhaps this was an opportunity for them to use their real training and capability. Atwater was actually excited about what he had heard from Wilkenson.

Atwater made a few calls to determine the whereabouts of Lieutenant Farber. When he finally located the lieutenant, he went to his company headquarters to make the call.

"Lieutenant Farber, this is Mike Atwater. I have some things to talk to you about that are very important. I don't feel that the material can be discussed over an open line, especially considering my current location. As an officer, you might be able to get a secure line or find a way to talk openly, but we should talk very soon." "Sounds important, Mike. Give me your contact information and I will work on a secure line of communication. There is one thing, however, that I need to tell you. You remember the favor that you asked my Dad to do for you?" Lieutenant Farber questioned.

"Sure do," Mike replied.

"The answer is Iran," Farber replied.

"No more than that."

"Holy shit," Atwater replied, "I can't believe that."

"Enough said on that subject," Farber concluded. "I'll get back to you on your request to talk."

Atwater was shocked by the news that his father's assignment had taken him to Iran. All kinds of things were going through his mind. Because of his father's experience of having his parents killed by the Nazi's because they were Jews, Iran seems like the last place on earth that he would go. Iran has outwardly and publicly stated that they are anti-Jewish. *I know that whatever he is doing on this project, it is paying him a great deal of money, but risking your life isn't worth any sum of money*, Michael thought.

Michael had been taking classes to learn various Middle Eastern languages and during those classes he was made aware of some of the recent history of Middle Eastern Countries. When the Shah was overthrown and replaced by Ayatollah Khomeini. The previous autocratic monarchy was replaced by an Islamic Republic based on the principle of rule by Islamic jurists, where the clerics serve as head of state and in many powerful government roles.

Iran's former pro-American foreign policy was exchanged for one that rested on three pillars of justice, including mandatory veils for women and opposition to the United States and Israel. The third pillar was the replacement of the rapidly modernizing capitalist economy with a populist and Islamic economic culture.

These new methods of governing created massive instability throughout the country. The country's economy and governing apparatus had collapsed, and military and security forces were in serious disarray. Khomeini and his supporters were attempting to crush all of the rival factions in order to consolidate power.

There was no doubt that in this unstable environment, any Jew who was anywhere near Iran was in serious jeopardy. It was obvious that as the unrest continued, Michael's father would be in greater and greater danger. Michael felt that it was important that he try to find out more about his father's situation. Lieutenant Farber's father was obviously the person that could provide that information but even he might not be in a position to disclose it, even to Michael. He would therefore try to keep abreast of Iran's situation as he continued to try to get more informed.

Two days later, Sergeant Atwater received a message from the office of his commanding officer that he was needed at company headquarters to participate in a secure communication. Atwater knew that this was the secure communication he was waiting for from Lieutenant Farber. Lieutenant Farber started by welcoming Atwater with a slight warning. "This line is supposed to be secure, Mike, but in this part of the world, we never know, so let's be cautious." "Okay," Mike responded. "We have both become increasingly unhappy with the way we have been treated, and we both have been having different thoughts about our future in the military, right, Hank?"

"So far you are on track," Farber responded.

"I'm going to give you the contact information for a fellow named Tommy Wilkenson. He heads a company named Grey Skies Service Corporation. This group hires out its services to the US government and possibly other governments to do jobs that the regular forces are not always equipped to do. Most of their employees are former 'Special Forces' people who have had all of that specialized training. Their concept is not to have the US government lose all of that training when individual duty tours end. They have a great salary structure, and it sounds really interesting. I am about 90% sure that I am going to sign up when my tour ends.

"There is one very interesting sidebar to this job. We start our job with a series of briefings in North Carolina, where the company is headquartered. This will provide us the opportunity to have some real in-person conversations with your father in the United States, where we can be free and open with things. I'm still a little suspicious about the possibility of you and me being set up to cover the asses of some CIA guys who screwed up our missions. Your father has at least temporarily squashed that, but I'm still nervous about it. We need to have a good strategy session with your dad, and it has to be completely private. Being in the US is the only way we can get that done. What do you think, Hank?' "Wow! That's a lot of shocking information, Mike, but I am definitely interested, especially if I can make use of the flying experience that I have. I'll contact Mr. Wilkenson and get back to you as soon as I can."

"Thanks, Hank. I'll wait for your call. No need to go out of your way to make the call secure, just a yes or no and possibly a date will do."

"Wilco, Mike. Have a safe day."

Mike's mind was just about made up. It probably would not make any difference what Hank's answer was, he was just about sure he wanted to do this. If Hank joined him, it would just cast it in concrete because it would give him the direct access to information about his father that Mike really wanted. It would possibly also provide him with a way to contact his father since he was also apparently associated with the CIA. Mike was having these growing suspicions that his father was going to need help from him to get out of Iran. These were only suspicions, but Hank had grown to know that there is usually some basis for unusual feeling like these.

Hank Farber had developed a close relationship with Mike Atwater over the past year as the doctors were trying to determine the cause and treatment protocol for his eyesight problem. Their relationship was, of course, greatly influenced by the fact that Mike had pulled off his rescue from within a very hostile Iran. That was Mike's job as a Special Forces soldier, but the conditions surrounding this particular rescue were certainly way beyond what might normally be expected, with the political situation in Iran as complicated as it was at the time and still is.

Mike Atwater's abilities as a soldier were reflected in his rapid rise through the ranks. His enlistment period was four years, and in that time he was at the top of his sergeant rank and as high in rank as a non-commissioned officer could go. Mike knew that Hank was a career soldier, so things that were happening to him must have been very serious to cause him to lose faith in the US military.

During his more than three years as a Marine pilot, Hank also became a decorated pilot. He had been advanced in rank to first Lieutenant which was very common for his MOS and his time in rank, nothing really special about that progress. But his medical situation really frustrated him.

The doctors were never really able to determine exactly why he had lost his eyesight. There had been very detailed investigations of the ejection seat, even to the extent that the Navy went back to Grumman, builder of the A-6, to review all of their initial ejection seat test data. The investigations also included the Martin Baker Company in London, England, the world's largest supplier of aircraft ejection seats. There was nothing in any of the test records that shed any light on Hank's injuries that pointed to a mechanical problem with the seat itself or the aircraft canopy, through which an emergency ejection takes place.

The doctors had concluded that the loss of blood flow through both sides of Hank's neck to his brain had caused the problem and that condition has been seen before. But the length of time that Hank had been without his sight remained puzzling to the doctors. Throughout the final stages of the medical evaluations, the doctors were increasingly critical of Hank's behavior just before ejection. They believed that he must have twisted his body to some unusual position that was abnormal for an ejection. Hank knew that things had happened very fast, as would be expected in that type of emergency situation and he had indeed passed out for a short period of time. With all of that turmoil, Hank was confident that his training had provided him the instinct to properly locate himself in the seat before ejecting.

His eyesight had recovered, but it was not considered a full recovery. The doctors recommended that Hank no longer be allowed to fly jets. He could retain his pilot's status but was reassigned to fly helicopters. To a combat jet pilot, flying helicopters is like trying to drive a Volkswagen Beetle in a NASCAR race.

Despite his appeals, that was the decision of the Marines, and Hank had no choice but to comply. He hated his assignments, but more than that, he had lost his desire to make the Marines his career choice. Why, he thought, would he spend the best part of his adult life doing something that he hated.

Unfortunately, he knew that he would have to deal with his father on this issue. As a lifetime Naval Officer, Hank's father was going to be extremely disappointed with him if he dropped out of the military. There was no doubt in Hank's mind that this would be the case.

Hank decided to write his father a letter, informing him of his concern about his career with the Marines. He sent the letter, and within days he receives a call from his father. Rather than receiving the third degree from his dad, he found him very understanding of Hank's situation. After a quick hello, how are you doing, the admiral spoke.

"Hank, as disappointed as I may be at this instant, I truly understand your feelings. I served the last part of my thirty-year career under a

Commander-in-Chief that I despised. The Navy's hands were tied at every turn by a political situation in Washington that turned every day into arguments and frustrations. I simply couldn't take that any longer and I retired.

"Of course, I was fortunate that I was in a position to get out under those conditions. That's quite different from your situation. Since working under the Reagan Administration, my whole life has turned around. I have the most challenging job I ever had, and I love going to work every day. I'm getting old but I have been re-inspired. If you can make that happen in your life, then I support whatever decision you make, son." Hank was brought to tears by his father's words. He quietly responded. "Thank you very much for understanding my feelings, Dad. My friend, Mike Atwater, you know, the Green Beret that rescued me from Iran, we might have an opportunity to join a company named Grey Skies Services. Hank's four-year tour of duty is nearly over, but mine was for six years, and I have a lot more to complete. Under the circumstances of my demotion to fly helicopters, I should be able to request an early termination based on medical limitations. I'd like your opinion about that, Dad, not now but whenever you get a chance to review the situation." Admiral Farber responded. "Before you fellows make a commitment, why don't you take some leave together and come back to the US and we can talk about the whole situation. Put in for stateside leave, but do not process any papers until we take the time to discuss it. Meanwhile, I'll do some checking on Grey Skies so our discussions might have more substance." "Sounds like a plan," Hank replied.

In the next two weeks, both he and Mike Atwater made the appropriate requests for a stateside leave. Both were approved.

CHAPTER 20

A S ATWATER AND Farber drove toward Admiral Farber's home in suburban Arlington, Virginia, they couldn't help but wonder what it must be like to have a job that would permit you to live in an area like this. For the last few years both men had lived in or around in a combat zone of one type or another. They were accustomed to seeing broken down shacks or half bombed out residence or sometimes Middle Eastern-like religious structures. Here in Arlington the lawns were nicely manicured, the flower gardens were in full bloom, and as they approached Admiral Farber's house, they could actually see across the river with several monuments of Washington clearly visible.

Farber commented, "Before I attended Annapolis, we never really had what normal people would call a real home. We lived in military housing most of my life, often moving from one country to another. I can't believe that my dad can actually live in one place without getting antsy. Goes to show you how we humans can change our ways."

"Roger that," Atwater replied. "I had a couple of permanent homes in suburban Boston, but it was never like this. I'm not sure that I could live like this. I need excitement and activity. I would go crazy here."

Admiral Farber welcomed the two soldiers at the door, first with a handshake and then giving his son a big hug. "Haven't seen you in some time, son," he exclaimed.

"Yes, it has been a while," Farber replied.

"Come in and relax, I'm sure you don't hear that too often lately," the admiral said.

Atwater replied, "No, sir, not for some time now."

"Your mother is out for the afternoon, I thought it would be better to have her out of the house as we talked. She will return in time for dinner and we can all talk then."

"Sounds fine with us," Atwater replied.

Admiral Farber led them into his study, which was lined with awards and other military memorabilia. They were seated around a large round coffee table with four comfortable chairs surrounding it. This was a perfect place to talk because everyone was facing each other.

"There are so many things we need to talk about," Admiral Farber started, "and I'm not sure we can get it all accomplished this afternoon. First let me tell you a little about your father's assignment in Iran, Michael. He is currently fine. He has been in that country for nearly two years now under contract with the CIA. He has a CIA handler named Farhad Ahmani, who is a young Iranian who was educated in the United States. Ahmani actually works for the Iranian police but he had been recruited by us while he was being schooled here. He provides your father direct communication with one of our agents in that area. Your father has sent many messages and packages to his cousin in Vermont who is managing his money for him and a project while he is out of the country. We can get into his assignment later if necessary but first we should discuss what has been going on with both of you fellows.

"Michael, you were the victim of a couple of massive CIA screwups. Your assignment with the Eagle Claw mission, which you successfully completed, created some diplomatic difficulties between Iran and the United States. At the time of the failed mission the Iranian government was in a state of disarray. The Shah had been overthrown and the clerics were taking over the government. Their military was in really bad shape and they were actually paying civilians to do much of their security work. The ten people that you killed that night were civilians, and it took some time for all of that mess to sink in with the new government.

"Months later, when the events of that night were brought to the attention of the new powers in place, they filed a formal complaint with our government about the killing of innocent civilians. Your superiors and the CIA agents in charge claimed that your team had gone rogue, killing the civilians against their orders. The Army was going to have a court martial to use you and your men as pawns for the CIA screwup. "When President Reagan was briefed on the situation, he told the Secretary of Defense that no soldier in his Army was going to take the fall for the Carter administration's screwup. There was so much made of this by the CIA and the Army that Reagan ordered a secret investigation of the events leading up to the boondoggle. The result was that the CIA agent in charge and Captain Meadows the Army officer in charge were both reduced in rank for attempting to place blame on you and your men. President Reagan had one of his top aides go to Iran and settle their complaint quietly by threatening to expose the fact that they were using civilians to do their military chores. Because of the tough stand that President Reagan took with the hostage crisis, everything just went away quietly.

"Unfortunately, however, I don't think you are completely free of future Congressional interference. Even though a new administration is now in power, the national embarrassment that took place as President Carter completely failed with the hostage crisis ... Congress will probably still open hearing on that situation to ensure that this country never acts in that manner again. If that happens, you will certainly be called to testify about your role in that activity. You need to understand that if and when that happens, the hearing will simply place Republicans against Democrats with the true facts of the situation taking a back seat. The Republicans will be attempting to blame the previous administration and the Democrats will be looking for as many scapegoats as they can find. If you are called to testify, I would suggest that you contact me, so I can give you some advice about the political winds that are blowing at that time, so you don't get trapped.

"After the hostage crisis came, the next CIA screwup with the F-14 bombings. There was really no excuse for that mess. The CIA actually leaked the fact that we were going to sabotage those airplanes. The Iranians wanted to make us look stupid, so they let that mission take place. The Iranian government was a little more organized at this point, and they again filed a complaint about our actions. I got into that situation because Hank was involved. Here, again, I started to see people covering their asses to protect themselves from bad decisions. The CIA was trying to divert blame for their bad planning and once again things were getting complicated. The Iraq missile installation that your team spotted was the solution to that crisis. We played the Iranians against the Iraqis here and helped Iran locate five additional installations that Iraq had installed within Iran along their border. There had been growing tension between the two countries and playing one country against the other was kind of fun and it made the bombing screw-up go away as an international incident. The CIA leak source was determined, and two agents were fired. One may actually stand trial if President Reagan doesn't interfere.

"Now let's talk about the question that you asked me, Hank. The Grey Skies organization is real, and it has legal standing with the US government. The war planning strategy of the Defense Department is going through a massive change. The Middle East situation is very explosive. Internal radical groups in several countries are causing great internal hostility that is likely to spill over into other more civilized countries, even the United States.

"Much of the world's economy is driven by oil and there is so much money involved in and around the oil industry that economic chaos can easily be created. Our military is not currently trained to fight this new kind of battle. The Muslim culture that prevails through the Middle East seems to have little value for human life, and we need to combat that new attitude is different ways. Unfortunately, the political environment in the US has been moving toward more politically correct solutions where the hands of the military are often tied by new rules of engagement.

"The result of all of this is that the new and re-designed CIA is playing a much bigger role in international affairs. Protecting our embassies is now being turned over to the CIA. The CIA operates with a slightly different set of rules and they can accomplish things that the military is unable to do. We have been using the Grey Skies organization to help us with the security of many of our embassies and also to help staff the growing number of CIA outposts throughout the world." Most of the people who work for Grey Skies are former Special Forces men and women whom we spent a lot of money training. Like you two, these top of the line soldiers are getting increasingly fed up with their hands being tied by political involvement. Frankly, I can probably say the same thing for myself except that I have been given complete authority by the President to make changes in our organization and that has been challenging for me although I'm not making many political friends these days. That brings me to my last subject, political corruption. Normally that subject gets thrown to the FBI but for years there has been so much money floating around Washington, that the FBI itself has internal problems. You might have guessed by now that I have great difficulty determining who can be loyal to me in my investigations and who is on the take from some oil lobbyist.

"With the increasing hostility that exists around the world, specifically the Middle East, oil is now the base of much of the world's economy, and as such, of much of the real power in the world. Most of the Middle East countries that produce most of the world's oil are run by people who do not have to account for much of what they do or what they spend. The oil lobby in Washington plays with billions of dollars of uncontrolled money every year that is funneled into the United States legally but used for illegal purposes. Much of this money eventually finds its way into the pockets of our politicians who make sure that our laws and regulations continue to keep that money coming. Between illegal oil money and drug money there seems to be an unending source of financing for political corruption.

"A good example of this is the oil supply. The United States has enough oil and gas resources under our land to eliminate our dependence on foreign oil. Payoffs to a few well-placed politicians have prevented us from getting to that resource.

"Drug money is the other corruption source. Our southern borders have been left relatively open to the drug cartels in Mexico and other South American countries. Even though the drug problem in this country has been growing for many years and our government has spent untold billions on the War on drugs, the problem has simply gotten worse. The flow of drug money into the pockets of a few well-placed politicians is a little harder to locate but believe me it is happening.

"The problem is that so many politicians have been in office so long that they have gained such political seniority and the associated power that comes with that seniority, that the problematic system is hard to change. Every time we have national elections, whether for the House, Senate, or even the President, we see new people trying to get into office that say that they are going to change the way Washington works. The fact is that they can't change it and they know it. New representatives have so little power that the system almost immediately swallows them up. It's like trying to swim upstream in a flooded river in the rain—the faster you swim, the stronger the current gets, and you stay in one place or even go backward.

"I'm not trying to discourage you guys, only trying to paint the real picture for you of what's going on in your country. I know that you both want to be the best that you can be at what you do. I never thought that you would hear me say this, but I can understand why you no longer think a military career is the way to accomplish your goals. I tend to agree with you, and that's why I support your apparent decisions to join Grey Skies Corporation. That company will continue to grow and hopefully you both can grow with them. I know they pay reasonably well, certainly better that the military can pay you. The benefits may not be as good, but the rewards should be there if they are successful. I do have a selfish motive, of course. Much of the Grey Skies work is contracted in areas of our organization that I control so I can have visibility of what you guys are doing and where you are doing it. We should occasionally have the occasion to communicate with each other if that's what you want." Lieutenant Farber jumped in. "Dad, I don't want you pulling any strings for either of us. It has to be just like the military, no favors.

"Wait a minute, Hank," Atwater responded with a slight laugh, "speak for yourself in that regard. I don't mind a favor or two now and then if needed."

"I'll only speak for myself then, Mike," Farber joked.

"I was only kidding," Atwater responded. "I'm my own man and I can take care of myself."

Admiral Farber seriously responded. "Then it will only be favors in life or death situations."

"We'll both buy that," both men responded.

"I think we should go no further until we have a relaxing drink," the admiral said while nodding as in approval of everything that had been discussed.

"That's fine, sir," Atwater commented, "but I do want to talk more about my father."

"We can certainly do that, but we'll have to do it before the boss gets home, which should be soon. There are aspects of that assignment that I can't even discuss with you in this environment. So, let's have a drink and some small talk and do more talking later," the admiral commented as he moved toward the bar to fix some drinks.

After a long and pleasant dinner including the admiral's wife Maryann, the admiral suggested that Hank and his mom move to the den so that he and Mike could talk some about Mike's father Ivan. Mike accompanied the admiral back to his study for those discussions.

Once they were comfortably seated, the admiral started. "Mike, there is a lot going on with your father, much of which I cannot tell you about. The fact that I did tell you about Farhad Ahmani was a mistake on my part. That is something that is not openly known and probably very classified, so please never mention that name to anyone. If that information were to leak out, it might jeopardize his life and perhaps even your father's.

"I'm not going to tell you much about his actual assignment in Iran. That is classified at a very high level. Since I'm not totally sure what is classified and how deep that classification goes, I'm going to stay away from many of the details.

"First, let's talk some about the conditions of his assignment. You are probably aware that he is being paid a great deal of money for his work there. That is because his specific knowledge was critical to the success of the project and he is probably the only person in the world that can provide the input that the project needed.

"I suggest that while you are here in the United States, you talk to Jonathan Goldblatt up in St. Albans, Vermont. He is your father's cousin who is handling all of his financial and other affairs surrounding you father's future plans. From what I understand, there is nothing illegal happening, just some very strange goings-on there.

"Let me tell you a little about where your dad is located, because I'm sure you would never have guessed that he would end up in that country. After the Second World War, when the United States and the Soviet Union were dividing up the spoils from Germany, so to speak, the Russians had some hidden motives. Despite treaties and agreements, they were deep into the research on chemical warfare and had assembled a group of noted scientists who had been working in that arena. Of course, when the war ended, that work was supposed to be terminated but the Russians knew that the Germans also had many experts in that field and they wanted to latch on to that experience as we did with the rocket scientists. They knew that they could not openly continue that work so they cut a deal with Iran, in return for some weapons expertise, to buy a section of land in Southern Iran that contained a hidden building on the shores of the Sea of Oman. This property was formally cut off from Iranian jurisdiction so Iran could never get access to the facility. The Russians completely modernized the facility, making it a very secure building.

"That facility also became a convenient place for the Russians to hide many of the top German leaders, who were trying to escape the country to avoid prosecution for war crimes. Many of these German leaders stayed in that facility for years, while others used it as a stopping-over place on the way to other countries.

"A few years ago, we discovered that the Germans and the Russians were working on a project that could put some of their chemical knowledge into a project to develop a drug that had the potential as a weapon of war, without causing any casualties. There seemed nothing that the United States could do to stop that work since it was not violating and treaties or laws, so the Carter Administration decided to join forces with the Russians and Germans, so we could at least be aware of what they were up to.

"We had two scientists and one assistant assigned to the project which was already well under way. Because of the nature of the work being done, it was assigned to the CIA as a black project, as many of the advanced weapon projects were. Three years ago, our people reported that they were planning to use Iranian prisoners for human test subjects and most of our technical people asked to be removed from the project. We did leave one female technical assistant there on the project, since she had been recruited by the CIA as an operative. Her name is Anastasia Meinkoff. She is an American-schooled Russian who took on American citizenship after college. We have a strong suspicion that she is working both sides, since her father is in the higher levels of the Russian intelligence circles. Her value to us is that she is very sexually free and very active in that arena with both the Russian leaders on the project and the German leaders.

"She is not aware of the objectives of the United States on this project, which are aimed at sabotaging the project and stealing the material for our own use. Your father is hoping to provide the expertise needed to complete the project, but also to bring it home to the United States. From what he has told us to date through his CIA contacts, he expects that the project will be completed in one or maybe two more years. We currently know nothing of his plans to steal the material or sabotage the project. Obviously that aspect of the program will be very risky on his part, but we will provide whatever he needs to pull it off when necessary." Mike Atwater interrupted. "Admiral, didn't my father go to Iran under a cover program having to do with the F-14s that were sold to Iran?"

"Yes, he did, Mike," the admiral replied. "That's why I'm even telling you much of this. You got involved in that fiasco indirectly so I thought you should know the background. When the Shah's administration fell apart and he left the country, the Iranian military started coming apart. Most of the American technicians from Grumman and Hughes were extracted from the country before the program was completely integrated. The weapon system had not been completely integrated into the aircraft, so the planes were not useful for the mission for which they were intended. Your father had some experience with the development of the integration of the software for the missile system and his cover was an agreement between Iran and the United States to quietly complete that integration. Of course, this was another agreement that showed the foreign policy ignorance of the Carter Administration.

"There were many people around Washington that were running around trying to put plans into place that would take those aircraft out of operation. The Hughes technicians had actually already left the program in a mess. In essence, they had already sabotaged the missile system before they left the country. The bombing mission that Hank was sent on was just supposed to be the finale of F-14 sabotage program so by the time your father got to Iran, all of these plans were already ready to be implemented. Unfortunately, there was terrible planning coordination between the CIA and the military, and some stupid people in the CIA had leaked our plans to a source that got it back to the Iranians, and the planes were moved to a safe location, making the United States look very bad. It would have been much worse if President Reagan hadn't been so tough with the Iranian leaders about the hostage crisis. The Ayatollah Khomeini was so frightened of Reagan that he didn't initially make a big issue of the bombing and the circumstances surrounding it that you and Hank got involved in. Iran did eventually make some noise about your people killing those civilians. You would be surprised how many people in Washington were trying to protect their asses when that problem came to the surface. "Anything that happens in the Middle East these days has political ramifications in this country. There are a couple of liberal Congressmen and Senators that have gotten themselves in very deeply with the oil cartel in the Middle East. They have taken millions of dollars to take whatever action is necessary to keep the oil prices as high as possible. That's why there has been very little effort for the United States to start getting our own oil from under our own land. There are several low-key investigations going on as we speak to get the goods on these politicians but that's another story for another day." Mike questioned, "How is my father communicating with the outside world, and what steps have been taken to get him out quickly if need be."

Admiral Farber responded. "We've established a series of our operatives in several places within the Middle East that get information from your father and use diplomatic channels to get it to the United States. He has had many packages of information sent to his cousin in Vermont for a project that they planned before he left the United States. He also communicates regularly and sends us technical data from the project through that network and his local operative Farhad Ahmani. Again, Mike, that name does not leave this room, understand?" "Yes, sir, I understand. I'm glad that you went out of your way to get all of this information and very appreciative that you choose to pass some of it along to me. Please keep me informed whenever you can, especially if things start to get serious about bringing my father home."

"I'll do what I can, Mike," the admiral replied, they shook hands and re-joined Hank and his mother.

CHAPTER 21

MIKE ATWATER RECALLED that his father had mentioned to him that his cousin Jonathan Goldblatt was looking after some of his affairs while he was out of the country, so when Admiral Farber suggested talking to him, Mike was curious how the admiral even knew about that contact. That curiosity coupled with the tendency to be suspicious of new people in his father's life, created some urgency for Mike to go to Vermont while he was in the United States.

St. Albans didn't have an airport of any size, so Mike was required to fly to Burlington, Vermont, about 30 miles from St. Albans. He rented a car and as he drove the short distance to St. Albans, he went over a number of things in his mind that he needed to determine. What were his father's interests this far north in this somewhat Godforsaken Place? Why this new interest in his cousins who he had not contacted in years? He would soon find out as he pulled into a parking lot adjacent to the address that he had determined was the office of Jonathan Goldblatt. There was no sign on the building on Congress Street, just the street number in very large gold letters. The sign in the lobby indicated that Jonathan's office was on the tenth floor, and when he entered the reception area, he was shocked by the expensive layout and furnishings of the facility. His visit was not prearranged, so he was taking a chance that Jonathan Goldblatt would even be present that day, let alone make time for him.

Mike approached the receptionist and put out his hand in a gesture to greet the beautiful young lady. "Hello, ma'am," he said softly. My name is Michael Atwater, and if possible, I would like to see Jonathan Goldblatt. I know that I didn't make an appointment, but I am the son of Ivan Schwarz, and I know that Mr. Goldblatt is familiar with my father and that they do business together. I'm on leave from the Army and didn't have time left to make an advance appointment with Mr. Goldblatt. I hope he is here, and if so, perhaps he can make some time to see me." The receptionist politely responded that Mr Goldblatt was in a conference at that time but she would give him the message. She entered the office and returned shortly after, saying, "Mr. Goldblatt must have certainly remembered your father, because he directed me to cancel the rest of his meetings today to make time for you. He will be with you as soon as he can break free." "Thank you very much," Michael replied, as he sat in one of the comfortable chairs to wait his turn.

As he waited, he couldn't help but stare in amazement at the surroundings. The paintings on the wall of the waiting room probably cost more than the Army paid Mike in a year. The furnishings were obviously selected with no concern for cost but great concern for luxury and comfort. The place simply reeked of money and wealth.

The main office door soon opened, and three well-dressed men came out and left the facility. Mike stood as Jonathan approached him. "So, you are Ivy's son, Michael. I'm Jonathan Goldblatt, your father's cousin. I suppose that makes us distant cousins. Michael, come on into my office and relax." "What brings you up to this neck of the woods, Mike?" Goldblatt started.

"I really don't know where to start, sir. I am completing my tour in the Army and about to possibly make a career change. A well-placed Admiral recently suggested that I meet with you to get brought up to date on your relationship with my father. The last couple of years have been a complete mystery with regards to my father's activities and I know that before he left the country he made business arrangements with you, so you must be able to give me more information than I currently have about him.

"I know that he has been put into a very dangerous situation by the US government and that there might be a need in the near future to get him out of that danger. I want to be prepared to ensure that whatever is needed will be provided when that time comes."

Jonathan interrupted. "You and I are in somewhat the same situation regarding Ivy's work assignment. He never really went into detail about that with me. I can tell you that it must be extremely important because he is making a great deal of money from the assignment. That's where I come into the picture. He asked me to manage his income and take care of some of his plans for the future, which have been very interesting for me. "Before he left the country, he was very thorough with his legal matters. I am handling his affairs, but he has assigned you as his benefactor, and I even have his signed power of attorney permitting you to eventually handle everything should you desire." "What the hell is he planning to do with all of that money, Jonathan?"

Jonathan replied, "That answer could take me a very long time to explain, Mike, but I'll try a short version. All of your father's salary is being paid to him in gold. I have managed all of the transfers that were needed to accommodate that through my banking associations. Since he started earning that money, he has deposited more than 30 million dollars in gold value that I have managed to keep in different accounts. He made specific arrangement with the US government that all of this income was tax-free.

"That's only part of the story, Mike. You may know that your father was a very suspicious man. That was passed down to him from his father, who was betrayed by the Germans during the war. His father had accumulated some degree of wealth in Germany, but the Nazis took all of that from him before they killed him and your grandmother. Ivy lived with a great deal of suspicion of everyone at his father's suggestion. Those experiences and suspicions led him to become nearly paranoid about his future security. He believed that there would almost certainly be another world war during his lifetime, and he wanted to protect himself from any fallout from that war.

"Ivy was also very dedicated to his work. You are certainly aware of that. He told me that when he returned from this assignment, he wanted a place to work in complete privacy and solitude and he instructed me to build him an underground facility on a mountaintop close to here, where he could live out his life in privacy, continuing his scientific work in a facility that was free from any future enemy threat in case of war. During the past two years, he has been giving me instructions and plans to build that facility on land that he leased from me before he left. The land is in both the US and Canada. That gets complicated, so we won't go into that right now.

"Because our paper company has most of the resources needed to build the facility in relative secrecy, we have it nearly completed. All of the actual construction has been completed in accordance with your father's plans and directions, which he has sent to me over a period of time since he left. There are a few infrastructure items that are still to be completed. He has apparently come upon a design for a miniature nuclear generator that will power the facility. That is the last item that we are awaiting to complete the facility. He has spent nearly ten million dollars constructing this facility so that it was nearly invisible to the human eye. All public access to the facility has been cut off and getting there is a chore in itself, but that is the way he wanted it." "You never really had any connection with my father over the last few years as far as I knew. Why the hell did you do this for him?" Mike asked.

Jonathan replied, "It was a simple business deal. He paid my company a fair price for the land, and of course we paid all the workers much more than their normal wages to keep the work secret. He also paid my company a good fee to manage the project. It was just a good Jewish business deal, no more than that, Mike." Mike asked, "Is there any way that I can see this facility, Jonathan?" "If you have time to stay with us tonight, I can possibly arrange for our helicopter to fly us up there tomorrow," Jonathan stated

"I'll make time," Mike replied. "After coming all this way and hearing this fantastic story, how could I possibly refuse the offer? Thank you so much, Jonathan, this has been a life-changing meeting."

"I'll call my wife and make arrangements for you to stay with us tonight, and we can talk some more about what you have been up to, Mike," Jonathan said.

"Let's do it," Mike replied, and they left the office heading home to Jonathan's house.

Michael spent a nice night with Jonathan and his wife Rena at their beautiful home outside of St. Albans. Both Jonathan and his brother Samual had obviously continued the success of their father's paper business, even through a period where several paper companies had been forced to close. Both men attributed the success of their company to the quality of the paper that they produced from the unusually hardy Canadian pine.

Both men appeared to live in quiet luxury. They seemed to be very popular among the residents of St. Albans, if one were to believe their stories. They attributed their popularity to the fact that they created and maintained hundreds of jobs in the community by running a company that was nearly totally vertically integrated. They owned and operated all of the resources that were necessary to plant the trees, harvest and process the pulp, and manufacture the paper. They indicated that they paid their employees a fair salary and contributed significantly to the community. This all added up to a great relationship between the company and the townsfolk.

Michael, however, was harboring this strange feeling that something was not quite right, especially with the financial arrangements with his father. Perhaps it was this feeling of suspicion of everyone that his father had pounded into his head during his early years. Perhaps it was being raised by his mother, who seemed always to be angry at Ivan, creating horrible stories about him and his family. These things seemed to never bother Michael before, but now, there was a terrible feeling of suspicion about the Goldblatt brothers that Michael could not shake.

Although Jonathan seemed open enough about the financial arrangements with Michael's father, he really didn't go into much detail about it and with the construction project and all the secrecy that must have been involved with that project, it must have been a major complex project to handle.

Also, when talking to Jonathan and Samual, Michael couldn't help but feel that they were both holding something back from him. They didn't want to talk much about the arrangements with their wives present, as though the women were not completely aware of all of the facts. Perhaps Michael was simply exercising the feeling of suspicion that he inherited from his father. He decided to try to put those feelings aside for this night and wait until the morning to have further discussions as they toured Michael's father's new facility.

It was a long might for Michael, as he continued to harbor those suspicious thoughts about the Goldblatt brothers. He remembered that his father had made a couple of trips to St. Albans before he left the country, but two shorts visits didn't seem adequate to resolve all of the legal affairs that must have been required to lease the land, establish the process of transferring money in large quantities, and have it all work smoothly when his father wasn't even able to talk to them after he left the US.

Sleep didn't come easily that night, and as the hours ticked away, Michael simply got more and more nervous about this whole arrangement, but he could not show his suspicious concerns to either Samual or Jonathan. If they had anything to hide, sensing Michael's concerns might just send them into a protective mode, and in that case, Michael would be able to get no real facts from either of them.

After a light breakfast, the company helicopter arrived on the front lawn of Jonathan's home. The three men boarded the aircraft and prior to lifting off, Jonathan handed Samual and Michael a headset so they could talk and hear each other during the 20-minute flight.

Jonathan did most of the talking. "The land that you father leased from us lies right along the border between the United States and Canada. We brought in all of the material and labor for this project straight in from the US side to avoid any suspicion by Canadian surveillance of the area. I thought they might get nosy if they regularly tracked aircraft traffic along their border. Ensuring that all traffic came up from the US side of the mountain avoided any problems of that type.

"We were cutting logs on the bottom of the US side of that mountain, so we cut a small road in for that access but that road ends about two miles from the site of the construction of your father's facility. You will notice that as we approach the site, the pilot will fly low over the trees from the bottom of the mountain and land in a field that is completely surrounded by large trees. The area was harvested more than 60 years ago by our father, but it was always his policy to re-plant for future use. We cleared enough growth to make that field.

"As we approach the site, you will see a small cabin at the edge of the field. You will also notice a large pond that we built to your father's specifications to provide water to be filtered for use in his facility. The pond water has several uses which we will see later. The cabin was built as a construction office while construction was in progress, but after completion we converted it to a nondescript hunting cabin. It also serves as a hidden entrance to the underground facility.

"As soon as we completed the superstructure of the facility, at your father's direction, we restored the surface area above the facility and planted trees and bushes. As we approach the area, all you will see is the cabin that I mentioned, and sure enough, there it is.

As they exited the helicopter, Michael noted, "Wow, one would never know that there was anything but an old cabin on this site."

Jonathan unlocked the cabin door and they entered slowly with Michael gazing around as if looking for some sign of an entrance to the underground facility. He could not immediately see any sign of such an entrance.

"Stand away from that rug in front of the fireplace," Jonathan indicated as he operated a small remote device that he was carrying. The rug folded back as two doors swung open from the floor and up through the opening came what looked like a small elevator. "We'll all fit in there," Jonathan said with a laugh, and all three men entered the elevator. Again, Jonathan triggered the remote device and the door closed and the elevator slowly began to descend. When the elevator stopped, a door at the rear of the machine opened into a well-lighted hallway that looked to be about 40 feet long. "You are now out of sight from the rest of the world," Jonathan said, still chuckling. When Jonathan opened the main door into the facility, it was like walking into a typical new house. There were no decorations on the walls, but the floor was carpeted, there were windows that appeared real and showed outside scenes which of course were painted. The walls were all painted white and the lighting was all hidden but very effective. In this main room, there was no hint that we were completely submersed underground." The only thing that has not been completed is the heat and air system. Your father is designing a small nuclear generator system to power the entire facility. He has not yet had that delivered to us. In the meantime, we are heating and cooling the place with electricity brought in underground from the base of the mountain. The lines are tied to one of our buildings down there to avoid suspicion." Jonathan pointed to several other doors that led to three bedrooms and a huge bath area complete with shower, tub, and hot tub. "We had to drill two wells to provide water for the pond that you saw, and that water is filtered and is the source for this facility."

Two other doors led to two large rooms that were again well-lit but had no windows. "These are the two rooms that you father will use as his laboratories. They have been provided with capability for separate power and shielding completely isolates these rooms from any outside electrical interference. Wiring and other capability have also been provided for future communications systems if your father requires that.

"There are two other small rooms off of these two laboratory rooms that will eventually be used as office and study areas. We were instructed to simply provide those rooms with heat and air and capabilities for several computers and other electronic equipment. We also provided ducting to all room for possible consideration for future television or other outside communication equipment. There wasn't much that you father left out of his planning, and he simply spared no expense to get exactly what he wanted." "How the hell much money did all of this cost?" Michael asked.

"To date, we have spent nearly twenty million dollars on the facility. An awful lot of that money was because of the secrecy that was necessary, and the problems associated with getting materials and equipment up the mountain without being seen."

At this point, Samual piped in. "And of course, there were all kinds of fees and transfer costs to get the gold properly registered and transferred to actual cash."

"How much did that amount to Samual?" Michael asked, "Close to a million dollars," Samual responded.

"You're shitting me, guys. Is there any money left when my father finally gets to use this facility?"

"Don't worry, Michael," Jonathan replied, "he'll be fine when he finally gets here,"

Michael replied, "If you both don't mind, I would like to go over his finances with you before I leave, so I can feel better about his future security. Living in solitude and away from the world is fine, but I want to make sure that he can actually live the life that he dreamed of. He still has to furnish this place and spend a lot of money outfitting it with the equipment that he needs. That highly technical equipment doesn't come cheap, you know." "Sounds like you're questioning what we have done for your father, Michael." Samual said.

"Jonathan, you told me that my father wanted me to be the beneficiary of his money so I simply want to take a look at what has been going on so I can be assured that my father will not have worked these several years for nothing. Did he even question how much this was all costing?" Michael asked.

Jonathan replied, "Not really, he just felt that he had enough money coming in to take care of everything. He instructed us to spare no cost to make it happen and that's what we did."

It was a very quiet trip back to the Goldblatt house. Everyone knew that there would be tense hours ahead going over all of the finances of Ivan's new facility. "I think I can stay another night if that's okay with you and your wife, Jonathan?' Michael said.

"Not a problem, Mike," Jonathan replied. "We should clear the air on all of this as soon as possible. Your father came to us because we were the only family of any sort that he has in this country. We would never do anything to disappoint him."

Michael replied somewhat sarcastically, "One exception to that, Jonathan. He has me."

Following a very nice dinner with Jonathan, Samual, and their wives, the men adjourned to the study to talk business. Jonathan immediately handed Michael a portfolio that was nearly six inches thick. The folder was packed full of papers dealing with all aspects of the financial arrangements and also dozens of construction records.

"It's all in here," Jonathan indicated, "the entire record of all of the transactions between your father and our organization. We can sit here and go through everything in detail if you choose, or you can take the material to your room and look everything over. Everything is filed in chronological order, from the agreement that your father had with the government to the final bills for work done on the facility. Everything in this package is a copy as you will immediately recognize. I keep all of the originals in the safe in my office in town." "This business about my father's salary being paid in gold—where is that gold stored?" Michael asked.

Jonathan replied, "I have rented two safes in two different banks in town that are designed specifically for people who deal in gold investments. The records of that storage are also contained in that package."

Michael observed a slight nervousness in both Goldblatt brothers when the subject of gold came up, but if all the records were intact, he thought maybe that was simply because there was so much money involved associated with that gold.

"Let me ask you something, Michael," Jonathan quietly murmured. "What the hell is your father doing for the government that's so valuable that it pays him that kind of money? My experience has always proved that when there is that much money involved, there are probably illegal activities associated with the money." Michael felt as though that question was designed to take the subject away from the money situation. He replied, "I have been assured that everything associated with my father's assignment is on the up-and-up. My source of that information is among the highest-level and most trusted executives in our government.

"My father had gained world-wide recognition for the scientific work that he did while he was at Calbro. His specialty was very narrow, and he was one of the only scientists I the world that had developed that skill, whatever it was. I suppose when you are in that position you can demand whatever you want when your skill is in demand. It's the old supply and demand concept of economics, I guess." "Can I get you a nightcap?" Samual asked?"

"No, thanks," Michael replied, "but I would like to use your phone. I need to call the airport in Burlington to arrange for my return flight to Washington. I have a special military fare that leaves the trip open-ended, and I need to confirm that there is a return flight available tomorrow." "There is a phone in your room. Feel free to use it. We can drive you to the airport tomorrow, if you would like, Michael," Jonathan noted.

"No thanks, Jonathan. I have a rental car that I have to turn in at the airport, so I suppose I'm set on transportation. I think I'll just go to my room, do some reading and turn in for the night."

"That's your call, Mike," Jonathan remarked, "as you wish."

The men shook hands, and Michael went off to his room for the night, taking the information package with him.

Michael didn't get much sleep that night. He spent most of the night studying the paperwork concerning his father's finances. Jonathan had done a good job keeping the records in good order, making it easier for Michael to run through the financial history. Most of the financial aspects of the actual construction project were well-documented. Although many of the expenses related to the project seemed very high, that could have been caused by the process itself and the secrecy that was attached to it.

The overall finances, however, gave Michael an uneasy feeling. He would need more time to digest a couple of aspects of those finances, and he needed to do a little more research with the details. He decided, however, that he wouldn't give the Goldblatt brothers any hint that he was concerned so they could simply go about their business as usual.

When Michael came down to the dining area, both Samual and Jonathan were already sitting at the table having coffee. Michael helped himself to a cup from the pot and put a small pastry into his plate.

"Did you sleep well?" Samual asked.

"Yes," Michael replied, "like a log. I actually fell asleep reading those boring papers. It looks like you have all of the material in good order Jonathan. I noticed you have a copy of my father's paper giving me power of attorney. That paper is of no use to you, so could I have a copy, or even better, the original of that document?" "No problem, Michael," Jonathan replied. "I can't imagine why your father didn't give the original to you. It was sent to us with several other documents shortly before he left the country. We always thought it was strange for us to have it, unless your father didn't trust you with it." "Why the hell wouldn't he trust me? He must have just forgotten about it and passed it along with the other papers," Michael replied. "Would it be possible for me to stop at your office today on my way to the airport and pick up the original? You said that you kept all the originals in your office safe." "Well, I won't be going into the office this morning. I have a board meeting out of town, but I will have my secretary take it out and give you the original, if that's okay?" Jonathan replied.

"Sounds good to me," Michael replied. "I'll be leaving as soon as I finish a second cup of coffee."

Both Samual and Jonathan seemed noticeably relieved that Michael had no other comments about the data package that he had studied. They seemed in a rush to help him along his way to the airport. Michael picked up on that fact.

Samual and Jonathan both gave Michael a copy of their business card and shook his hand as he prepared to leave.

"Feel free to call us at any time," Samual said. "Do you know your next assignment?"

Michael replied, "I don't know yet. My orders will be waiting for me in Washington when I return, but I'm sure I will be in some Godforsaken place on the other side of the world." This response was planned so neither man would expect any further threat of Michael's interference in his father's matters.

"Good luck and stay safe," Samual muttered and that statement was echoed by Jonathan.

"Same to both of you, and thanks for all your help," Michael replied. Michael's first stop was at Jonathan's office to pick up the original of the power of attorney. Jonathan's secretary had it ready for him as he entered the reception area.

Michael planned to spend a few hours in St. Albans before his flight which he scheduled for that evening. He drove around town looking for a barber shop. He knew that a small-town barber has more real information than the local newspaper. He found a small shop, parked his car and entered the small establishment. It was fairly early in the morning, so the shop was nearly empty, just right for some questioning.

"Come sit down," the barber invited. "Don't recognize you so you must be new in town." The barber's accent and voice tone gave away his identity as a real local New Englander. It was a Northern version of what Michael was used to hearing when he lived in Boston.

"I'm here for a short visit. I'm in the Army and my tour will soon end. I was offered a job with the Mountain State Paper Company and I'm in town for an interview."

"Thanks for your service," the barber commented, "but I'm surprised that the paper company is doing any hiring at this time."

"Why is that?" Michael asked.

"Well, they have been cutting back on workers over the past few months—nothing drastic, just a few workers now and then. They claim that automation of the plant is creating more efficiency and fewer people are required," the barber replied.

"It just hasn't been the same since old man Goldblatt died a few years ago. He would invent a job before he would let any of the townspeople go. But the boys ... when they took over the business, it just was never the same. It seemed that it was all about the money, and they appeared to be taking that money out of the business rather than investing in the future. Then, a couple of years ago, they got some big government contract for some project that was a mystery to all the townspeople. They brought in companies from out of state and in some cases out of the country to do the work. That really pissed off the local contractors, but the company said that the government required that they use these companies. I will say that they took care of many of the local contractors that didn't get the work by paying them a nice sum that would have represented their normal profit if they had gotten the work. This kept everything sort of quiet.

"You mean they were just throwing money around?" Michael asked.

"Kind of like that," the barber replied. "They must have been paid well by the government, because they all bought new expensive cars, their two kids got new cars, and they would take a family vacation out of the country every year."

"They must have hit it big," Michael commented.

"For a long time, we didn't hear or see much of Samual Goldblatt. He ran the paper company and Jonathan was pretty much here in town doing his political stuff, bank business and working for the several boards that he was on. The new contract that they got took them out of town together a lot and they always took a big limo from their homes to the airport which they never had done before. I guess money changes men, if you know what I mean," the barber said.

"You're probably right," Michael replied. "Was Jonathan ever actually in political office? I understand he is very well-connected politically."

"He never had any serious political position in town or in the state, but he has many politicians in his pocket and he always have. Many government agencies buy their high-quality paper from Mountain State. That company always claimed that the tight-grained Canadian pine made the highest quality paper. Jonathan has half of the Canadian forestry officials on his hidden payroll so he can continue to harvest that type of pulp. I have to admit it has kept them in business for a long time, and there are several hundred people in this town who depend on that company for their income, probably including me. I guess about four out of every six customers of mine work for Mountain State, and even more people work for businesses that depend on them for a living." "How are the Goldblatt brothers respected in the community?" Michael asked.

The barber replied in a softer tone of voice, "Not like the old man was respected. People loved him. When he and his family came to St. Albans, there were not many Jews living here, so people had to earn the respect of their neighbors. The Jewish population here is still not large, but old man Goldblatt laid down the carpet for them, and they integrated well into the community. The boys are respected simply because of their name. The way Jonathan operates, people seem to know that he always operates on the edge of legality, buying those whom he needs for survival. People kind of like Samual because he is sort of private. As long as he keeps the company going fairly strong, he'll be okay with the people. Would anyone come to their rescue if they were going to be hit by a bus? No." Michael replied, "Thanks for the nice haircut and all of the valuable information that you provided me."

The barber said, "Remember that if you take that job and move into this area. I'll do the same good job each time I cut your hair."

Michael came away from his visit to Vermont with far more concerns than he'd had before he'd gone there. He didn't give the Goldblatt brothers any hint that he was suspicious of their activities relative to his father's finances, but he had some really strong suspicions. Perhaps the nearly paranoid suspicions that his father had lived with all of his life had rubbed off on Michael, but he had never before felt nervous and distrustful about anyone in the same way that he now felt about the Goldblatts.

There were several voids in the records with which he was provided. The financial conditions of his contract with the CIA appeared to have been redacted or even retyped. His father's salary was to be paid in gold, but the records had no reference to any gold transactions. There was also no record of any authority that his father had given to the Goldblatts to convert his salary to cash needed to build the complex.

Outside the records themselves, the Goldblatt brothers just seemed very suspicious to Michael. They never discussed any details in the presence of their wives. Why not? Michael wondered.

Michael's suspicions were so strong that he decided to write a letter to Admiral Farber, asking for his help with these concerns. On his plane trip back to Washington Michael wrote to the admiral.

Dear Admiral Farber

At our recent meeting, you suggested that I meet with the Goldblatt brothers in Vermont to discuss my father's business relationship with them. I have just completed that trip and I came away with many very serious concerns about that relationship, particularly regarding the payment of my father's salary in gold. I could find no records of any sale or conversion of that gold to the currency needed to complete the work that my father had authorized. If I consider the significant increase in the price of gold in the period in question, there could be many millions of dollars that are not accounted for, perhaps even more than 100 million.

I know that my father's contract is with the CIA, possibly through the Calbro Company. As such I'm sure you can get access to that contract and perhaps also have someone investigate how and when that gold was sold or converted to cash. I know you are a very busy man, and I do not expect that you can immediately look into this issue but any help that you can give would be appreciated.

Of course, I also have serious concerns about the assignment that my father accepted. Perhaps these concerns are simply a result of my inbred suspicions of anyone and anything that looks too good to be true. If it looks too good, it probably is.

I am sending this letter to you at your residence since I know that you have your own suspicions about the loyalty of those surrounding you. I hope that this does not offend you in any way.

Thank you in advance for your help in this matter.

Signed, Michael Atwater

CHAPTER 22

VAN HAD BEEN working with the other scientists for many months. The times had not always been pleasant and cooperative especially when Ivan had to give them one of his lectures about who was more important than the others. Ivan knew his assigned tasks, and although he didn't share this fact with anyone, once he had gotten the IBM software working well with his computers, he believed that he could get his entire job done in weeks if he chose to. Much of what he was feeding the others was simple front-end stuff to see if they understood anything of what he was doing. They either were clueless, or they just didn't care, because they gave him the impression that they appreciated how much progress he was making. He was providing both men briefings on his work, but he knew that there should come a time when they would have to begin working closely together to integrate their work, but neither man seemed to be working toward that end. Actually, both Topolski and Bechert were, on the surface, exchanging progress reports, but Ivan didn't see any real scientific significance to the material that they were giving him. He felt that they were simply coasting, waiting for him to produce some significant results. If they are working hard he thought, it was not reflected in their progress reports. There were times when Ivan felt as if they were playing some sort of a game with him.

Many months had passed since that talk with Albert Brokow about his feelings about the two men. Perhaps it was time to broach that subject with him again.

A few days later, Ivan went to Albert Brokow's quarters. He knocked on the door and was graciously welcomed in by Albert.

Ivan started. "I have been working hard for many months now. I am making good progress but I do not believe that the rest of the team is working with the same degree of urgency as I am. Some months ago, we started a discussion about your feelings toward the other scientists and you indicated that I should develop my own opinions about them and not be influenced by any bias that you might have. Well, I think that time has come for us to compare notes."

Albert seemed a little relieved as he replied, "I didn't think it would take you this long to get back to me on that. I'm going to lock my door, so we won't be interrupted. Do you have time to do it right now, Ivan?"

"Now is fine with me," Ivan responded.

"For this conversation, I need to fill a glass with vodka and take a few swallows before I start. Can I get you a glass, Ivan?"

Ivan responded, "I'm not really a drinker, but to keep the conversation socially relaxing, I'll join you in a drink."

Albert poured two glasses of vodka and took a couple of big gulps while Ivan sipped a little from his glass.

Albert started. "I have been here for a long time associating with these two scientists. This is the first time I have been asked to voice my opinion about them, and I have a lot to say so please bear with me, Ivan."

"Certainly," Ivan responded. This was the breakthrough that Ivan was hoping for.

Albert took another gulp, refilled his glass and started. "These two guys are real assholes. They are apparently brilliant, but they are still assholes to me. Neither of them treats me with any respect, as though they are so far superior to me that I am simply ignored. The first time I talked to you Ivan, I realized that you were a real nice guy. So far you have treated me like a peer, and I appreciate that very much, more so because of the complete lack of any respect from the other two.

"Topolski is a real Communist Russian, but I believe that despite his apparent loyalty to the homeland, he would turn on them in an instant if there was enough money involved. His connections in Russia are falling into disfavor there and he knows that and acts accordingly. I'm not sure he gives a shit about this project that you are all working on. He has a family back home, but I think his main joy in life here has come from the service that has been provided him by Anastasia Mainkoff. He has been banging her regularly since she arrived here. I know she is supposed to be your assistant and maybe that is part of your country's plan for her, and if so, she is performing it very well. I don't believe Topolski ever plans to return to Russia. I think he and Anna plan to defect to Germany when this project is completed. I'm not sure, however, that her plans include that. I believe she is playing him for something, I'm not sure what it is but I don't think there is any love there on her part. As a matter of fact, I don't think that woman could love anyone but herself.

"As for Bechert, he is a different kind of asshole." Albert got up and refilled his glass again.

"Bechert is an offspring of one of the German officers that fled here after the war. I don't know where he was educated, probably South America. That is where many of those scientists went when they left here, to hide from prosecution. Bechert seems to exert a good deal of authority over Topolski. I'm not sure why that is. I suspect that Bechert has expertise and real-world experience with germ warfare and I think that hidden in his agenda here is research in that field. Many of the Germans mentally never accepted the fact that they lost the war and their offspring still support some of Germany's extremist policies. I believe that, on the side, Bechert is developing highly toxic chemicals and that is part of a germ warfare program that Germany still has active. I think he feeds a lot of material out of here that represents his work in that area. For that reason, I don't think he is interested in a rapid completion of this project. He is happy here and wants to do his research here. It's a safe place to do that type of work. There is no threat of interference from any government.

"Because of the authority that Bechert seems to exert over Topolski, I believe that Russia is also involved in Bechert's work and that they will be beneficiaries of the results."

Ivan interrupted, "Do you mean that you suspect that both men are involved in the development of germ warfare techniques and chemicals? That would mean that both Russia and Germany are violating the ban on such weapons."

Albert nodded and his words began to slur from the effects of the vodka. "Yep, I think that's the plan. I believe that the United States has been sucked into this program by both countries as a way to avoid being accused by the US government. Don't forget: the Germans still have a built-in culture of world domination, as do the Soviets. The Russians still have their wall dividing Germany in order to avoid any cohesion in that country. Both of those countries fully understood the incompetence of many of the high-level people in the Carter Administration. This project could be a contrived way to embarrass your country while developing a major new weapon." Ivan was stunned by Albert's allegations so stunned that he got up and poured himself another full glass of vodka and drank it down with two or three gulps. "Wow," Ivan responded, "your whole theory blows my mind. Do you have any concrete proof of your theory?"

Albert responded with slurred words, "No, not really, but I'll bet that those disks that I have stored contain some evidence. But right now, I think I have had too much vodka and we should end today's conversation."

"I'll drink to that," Ivan muttered as he emptied his glass, put it down and staggered to his room.

Ivan continued to work intently to give everyone the appearance that he was working diligently on his portion of the project. He kept an eye on the efforts of the others and he was never able to get the feeling that Topolski and Bechert were enthusiastic about the details of this project. More important, both of those two scientists seemed to work long hours at their tasks, but the results that they shared with Ivan were insignificant in his opinion, certainly not representative of the hours that they put in. He couldn't help but have regular flashbacks of that conversation with Albert Brokow and his suspicions that Topolski and Bechert were using this project as a cover for work that they were doing to develop new chemical warfare weapons.

Ivan thought it might be time to notify the CIA of his concerns and Brokow's theory. Ivan had been sending regular progress reports to his contacts at the CIA and he also provided the Goldblatt brothers with all of the design data that they needed to complete his underground facility. In all of the time that he had been in Iran, there had never been an occasion where he received any communication back from his American contacts. He wasn't sure if there was any significance to that fact, but he simply thought it to be strange that he was receiving so much money to perform a task that no one in the United States seemed to care about.

He didn't expect that there were too many other American scientists that would understand his specific work, but he had also been forwarding the information that he was receiving from Topolski and Bechert regarding the drugs that they had and were continuing to develop. Did that mean that no one really cared or could it have been that there was nothing out of line with the information he was forwarding. It just gave Ivan more cause to be suspicious.

Ivan was not a chemist and he paid little attention to the drug data so far into this assignment. He had been concentrating his work on the application system within the human body to see if he could find direct paths to the brain that would affect the four behavioral patterns of interest. Actually, in his mind he already knew the answers to those questions. At some point he would have to dig into the drug aspects when investigating how the drugs could be effective without being traceable. He actually thought that aspect of the studies was more the challenge of the other two scientists and that area would require very close corroboration, but he seemed to be the only one worried about that fact.

Ivan also often wondered what kind of reports Anna was transmitting back through her CIA source. She had been working fairly well with him doing bits and pieces of his work that seemed too trivial for him to waste his time on. Ivan believed that she was still working her sexual affair with Topolski, although that was never discussed between them. He assumed that was the connection from which the CIA was interested in having her derive information. She certainly wasn't giving our people information about his work; he was already doing that.

Since his early discussions with Anna, she had not made any significance advances toward him, although everything that she did had some sexual implications, from the clothes that she wore to her movements and comments. Ivan felt that if she was serving as a double agent, she should have been trying to get information from him to pass back to the Russians. She was certainly not making any advances in that direction. She had access to his work but not necessarily his results and even if she gained that access, she didn't have enough technical knowledge to know what she was looking at.

As for Albert Brokow, Ivan had a steady, good relationship with him. They had become good friends even though they had little or no occasion to cross paths technically. Albert had been very willing to give Ivan the design data on the miniature nuclear generators which Ivan had forwarded to the Goldblatt brothers. The only thing that Ivan was not able to determine from Albert was the source of the small amount of radioactive material needed for the operation of the system. Albert had hinted that it was a local source and it was purchased through his normal procurement channels, but he didn't know or didn't care where it came from. He was provided instructions for its use and destruction and he acted accordingly. Albert had a gravy-train job here and he knew it so he didn't want to make any waves that might jeopardize that position. Ivan had made a pact with Albert that when the project was over, he would make arrangements for Albert to come to the United States to live and possibly work with Ivan in his new facility. Of course, Ivan had no authority to make such a promise but it established a base for trust between the two men.

Ivan prepared a rather lengthy report to the CIA spelling out all of his concerns and suspicions, especially those concerning Topolski and Bechert's possibly working on some form of new chemical weapon. He believed that this information should be significant enough to draw some one's attention in Washington. If he didn't get a response, then he would really get more suspicious of the whole operation. So far Ivan felt no threat to himself in this project. He was running hundreds of iterations of neural patterns on his computers every day and no one seemed interested in interfering with him on that work. He was well-fed and had acquired no significant medical issues. From a technical point of view, he was in a technological heaven, doing his thing as he had always hoped to do, without any pressure or interference. What more could he desire?

He gave this detailed report to Farhad to be delivered as usual to his CIA contact. He could now only wait for a response.

Back in Washington, Admiral Farber had assembled a small cadre of people that he knew he could trust. There had been a major shake-up within the service and the admiral needed to be very careful who he used as trusted associates. Almost every day, internal investigations were resulting in the dismissal of key people from very sensitive positions. Most of these people had gotten their jobs through the political patronage system during the Carter Administration. The weed-out process was slow and painful. Complicating the organizational housecleaning were a significant number of fairly highly placed politicians who had been taking large sums of money from foreign organizations for many years. Previous investigations had gotten close to these politicians but pay-offs to agents clouded the collection of the data needed to prosecute these officials. Admiral Farber was having great difficulty trying to help clean up this messy situation.

Shortly after Ronald Reagan was elected President, he ordered several internal investigations of many government agencies in an attempt to root out much of the corruption that was rumored to be present. Unfortunately, he found that they were more than just rumors. One result of these investigations was action by congress passing the Intelligence Oversight act which created two committees to watch over all activities of the CIA. The senate oversight arm was through the Senate Select Committee on Intelligence (SSCI) and the House Permanent Select committee on Intelligence (HPSC). Unfortunately, some of the senators and congressmen who were assigned to these committees were also determined by internal CIA investigations to be taking pay-offs from foreign agents for a whole series of political favors. The result of all of this activity caused Admiral Farber to be very cautious of the people that he took into his inner circle. When the Admiral was received the letter from Michael Atwater, that letter triggered a series of questions from Admiral Farber across agency lines to answer Michael's concerns. These agencies included the IRS, State Department, FBI, Federal Reserve and several congressional committees. When Ivan's report came into the CIA, the implications of its contents were so significant that the report was immediately flagged and sent to Admiral Farber. His earlier inquiries about Ivan's contract terms with the CIA created a chain reaction of information that now was sent directly to the admiral. This latest information from Ivan immediately alerted him and some members of his staff to more serious issues. Michael's request and Ivan's letter suddenly brought the two subjects into the same office.

There had been rumors floating around the Middle East that there were shipments of a new poisonous gas being moved to different countries in the region. Iraq had already admitted to gassing thousands of its citizens that were considered enemies of the leadership, but those rumors had not led to any definite conclusions as to who was supplying the gaseous product. If Ivan's concerns had any real substance, this would be a very significant international event that would have to be brought to the attention of the President or his senior staff.

Before that could happen however, Admiral Farber needed to get more assurance in terms of solid evidence. Assignments previously given to both his son and Michael had gone bad due to major screwups within the CIA in that exact region. The admiral had not yet proven who was responsible for that mess within the agency. A couple military officers were held accountable but the CIA was much slower seeking out blame within their own organization so he could not afford to hand this assignment to any of those same operatives. He decided instead to ask Ivan to be alert for more concrete proof that the gasses were actually being made and transported from Iran by a German/Russian scientific team. He knew Ivan had absolutely no experience or training as an operative, but he felt that he was alert and intelligent enough to gather more evidence if it existed.

The subject was so sensitive that Admiral Farber wrote the report back to Ivan without any staff assistance and he had it encrypted prior to having it transmitted to Ivan. This was the first time that the CIA had sent any correspondence to Ivan since his arrival in Iran and the Admiral hoped that the encryption equipment provided to Ivan was in working condition. He wasn't even sure that Ivan would know that the information was coded but he had to assume that someone as smart as Ivan would soon figure that out.

CHAPTER 23

MORE THAN TWO years had passed since Ivan became a part of this rather unusual program. He had spent nearly six months of this time getting his computer network set up to accommodate the neural network evaluations that he was performing. After all, that was his specialty, and apparently the missing link in the work that had been done so far by the Russian-German technical team. A unique capability of Ivan's technical plan was the use of IBM software that he had managed to secure for his earlier work. It took a great deal of time adopting that software to the new computers that he was given but once operating, he could get a great amount of data output in a short period of time. In a typical day he might run hundreds of iterations on his computer to simulate nerve activity and brain reactions. This became a rather boring daily routine, but Ivan was accustomed to this routine, it was a price that he paid for success in his very specialized field of study.

He was briefing the two other scientists regularly on his work. They showed mild interest in the work but never seemed to make any connection to their real interests, which puzzled him until he thought about what Andrew Brokow had told him. Conversely, both Topolski and Bechert provided him data on their work on the various drugs that they were developing. Ivan was no expert on this subject, but he had enough knowledge to recognize that the work that was being presented to him was very basic. That inspired Ivan to begin his own research on various drug combinations, which further supported his suspicion that the material he was being shown was not representative of the capabilities of these two scientists.

Ivan was also intrigued by the performance of Anna, his assistant. As time passed, she seemed to improve her work practices, dedicating more and more time to her work with him in the laboratory. Her assignment did not include any detailed technical input, but she seemed to be slowly showing more interest in those aspects of his work, often running the computer iterations herself, a task that was in itself very basic. As his laboratory grew in effectiveness, there were fewer administrative tasks for Anna to perform. She seemed to be filling in the disappearing administrative time with assistance in Ivan's technical work. The nearly automatic result was that Anna and Ivan became very close working partners and often spent time together in the lab discussing different elements of Ivan's work. The fact that Ivan was kind of faking his progress would never be discovered by Anna, because she didn't know the first thing about the data that she was seeing.

Since their first few meetings several months ago, Anna had made no outward sexual advances toward Ivan. She seemed to accept his desire that their efforts together would be strictly work related. Ivan sometimes thought about this change, because he himself was feeling a degree of warmth and desire toward Anna. Ivan had been told of Anna's sexual involvement with Topolski and perhaps even Bechert, so he assumed that these men were satisfying Anna's sexual needs and there was no need for her to make any outward advances toward him. There was also the fact of the age difference between Ivan and Anna. Anna was at an age where her sexual motives would be directed toward a younger man. But, Ivan thought, neither Topolski nor Bechert were younger than him.

Ivan never thought of himself as a sexually active person, as a matter of fact his dedication to his work and career had been placed before any intimate emotional feelings or actions toward any woman, even his wife Erma. This fact was probably the major cause of their separation and divorce.

But Ivan had never been in a situation where he was so cloistered in an environment and separated from society for months at a time. The only woman that he had any contact with for two years was Anna, and as time passed, he found himself spending more time thinking about her, not as his work partner, but as a woman. Perhaps for the first time in his life, Ivan often found himself infatuated with thoughts of him and Anna in a sexual relationship. He usually dismissed these thoughts as outside the realm of possibility because of the very pointed statements that he had made to Anna when they first met. Now he seemed sorry that he had established that atmosphere. His emotional desire toward Anna was growing and he felt that the time had probably come for him to act on that desire. But how could he do that? He has no experience with women in this regard and he didn't want to do anything that would damage their working relationship or jeopardize their work.

Ivan knew that Anna lived outside the boundaries of the normal rules of this unusual facility where alcohol was forbidden, as least openly. He knew that Anna maintained her own stash of booze in her apartment and he thought that perhaps the suggestion of a social drink together might be an icebreaker. What damage could be done by a mild suggestion to that end, he thought?

Several days later, as they were closing the laboratory for the day, Ivan suggested that they might continue their discussion of the day's events over a drink. Ivan was expecting some surprise from Anna at his suggestion but there was none. As she always did, Anna simply responded politely that she would accommodate Ivan's request.

"I would be delighted to discuss our work over a drink. I expect that you have no alcohol in your apartment, so why not come to my place in about half an hour. That will give us both time to shower and get comfortable for whatever is destined to be," Anna replied.

Ivan was so excited by Anna's response that he was lost for words. His head was spinning as he searched for the appropriate words of response, but none came to mind. Ivan simply responded, "I'll be there in thirty."

Ivan tried to appear calm and routine as they walked together to the elevator that would carry them to their quarters, but his head seemed to be splitting with excitement from the thought of what might be ahead for him. Anna seemed to sense his anxiety as she commented. "Ivan, please be relaxed. We have been working together for many months now and we have never taken the opportunity to become friendly on a purely social basis. That time has now come, and we should make the most of it. I'll be your gracious host in my apartment. I just want you to relax, so we can both enjoy each other's company for the first time since we met." As the elevator door opened, she gave Ivan a quick kiss on the cheek and said, "See you in a bit, Ivan."

Ivan was now completely outside of his normal safety zone. He showered and was then left confused as to what to wear. He had no real lounging clothes, only a couple pairs of jeans and a sports shirt. That would have to do for now, he thought. He changed his clothes every night after work was complete, but he never gave much thought to what he was wearing, but this time was special. Would his appearance really make a difference to Anna? After all, they had worked together for many months his dress on this day should have no real meaning. He completed all of the tasks that he felt were necessary to make him presentable and proceeded to Anna's apartment.

The door to Anna's apartment was slightly ajar as though expecting Ivan's arrival. He knocked quietly, pushed the door open and entered Anna's suite shouting softly, "I'm here, Anna. Are you here?" What a stupid entry, Ivan thought. Of course, she knew it was him.

Ivan heard a slight voice from the other room respond, "I'll be ready in a minute. Make yourself comfortable." For some reason, Anna's voice was comforting to Ivan. What was he expecting, to be stormed by the Russian Mafia?

Ivan sat on the sofa and as he did, so Anna entered the room. She was dressed in a loose-fitting outfit that did a fine job of covering her and yet showing off her splendid curves. She proceeded to the kitchen area and returned with two glasses of bourbon. "I prefer bourbon when I'm relaxing. Is bourbon okay with you, Ivan?" she quietly asked.

"Bourbon's fine," Ivan replied. "I'm not a big drinker but I have enjoyed bourbon on a few occasions."

Anna seemed to move across the room with the ease of skilled figure skater. Ivan had never noticed her walk, but now her every move made her appear more desirable to him. As she handed him his glass, her breast seemed to burst from her clothes, not completely but just enough to add to the temptation and make it obvious that she was not wearing a bra. She sat gently next to Ivan, held up her glass to him and said, "To what shall we drink this toast, Ivan?" Ivan thought for an instant and replied, "To a new relationship for both of us." Ivan wasn't sure why that toast was appropriate, but it was the first thing that came to his mind. Well, it wasn't the first thing. He might have said, "To finally getting laid," but that would have seemed a bit forward. He had decided that he was going to let Anna be the aggressor on this occasion, not because that was the appropriate thing but because he had absolutely no idea how the hell to behave in this situation.

Anna moved closer to Ivan, took his hand in hers and asked, "Do we really want to discuss out work tonight or do we want to get better acquainted? We have worked closely together for two years now and each day we have grown closer, even though we may not have realized it. I know this situation is awkward for you Ivan, but I also feel that you have grown closer to me in a sexual way. I realize that your background and life experience has not provided you any degree of sexual experience and I am willing to deal with that. Let me take the lead tonight, Ivan, and I will try to make this a pleasant and exciting experience." As Anna spoke, she moved Ivan's hand up to her breast and put her glass down as she leaned forward to kiss him. As she made this move, she skillfully took his glass from him and also placed it on the table. Anna took Ivan's other hand and put it on her thigh. Ivan instinctively moved his had up her thigh and immediately realized that she wore no undergarments. His next move was obvious and signaled to Anna that the game was now on, but before this went further, she needed to clear some air.

"Ivan, I know that you have been told that my activities in this facility include performing sexual favors for some of the men. I will admit that to be somewhat true, but it was always with a motive. I knew from the beginning that I was not on a par intellectually with the scientists and many of the staff here. If I was to survive and enjoy the experience, I needed to establish some relationships that could give me some needed rewards, like the suite, alcohol, food, and freedom of movement. I have received those rewards, so I feel that my efforts were worth the rewards, and I feel no guilt. It has also been widely rumored that I have a continuing relationship with Alyusha Topolski. That is not true. I have been trying to keep a close eye on his activities as part of my assignment, but I will not discuss that now. My assigned task is to support you and your work here. I intend to dedicate all of my effort to the successful completion of that assignment. I believe that the closer we can be personally, the more successful we will be in our mutual assignments. Now that I have tried to clear that air, let us try to enjoy the remainder of the evening and begin to solidify our relationship. Please follow me to my bedroom, Ivan." Without hesitation, Ivan complied.

CHAPTER 24

LATER THAT EVENING, Ivan returned to his quarters feeling spent and exhausted from his hours with Anna. These were hours that Ivan had fantasized about for many weeks and had finally been realized. Unfortunately, the excitement of the anticipation, coupled with the bourbon that he had consumed and the rather high level of intensity of Anna's love making, had given him a splitting headache coupled with an apparent serious increase in his heart rate. These factors triggered Ivan's memory of the warning given him by the doctor way back when he took his entrance physical examination to start work for Calbro. Despite his heart pounding like a base drum, his mood was somber and for the first time in months, he felt a sense of relief that he and Anna had broken a barrier that had existed and the coming months would provide a much better relationship between the two of them. This feeling of relief overtook the other negative physical feelings that he was experiencing so he put those feelings out of his mind. The years of living with suspicions about everything and everyone were still driving his thought process. He realized that the sexual interaction with Anna was only about sexual satisfaction and had little to do with personal emotional or love. For Ivan, this was not particularly difficult to handle, since he had never before let his emotions drive his thinking. In the coming weeks, he would make sure that his interactions with Anna never took on any emotional component since that would be very detrimental to his work. Ivan believed that he could handle the emotional issues.

On his way to his bedroom, he passed his office area and noticed a light blinking on his computer. The light was a signal from Farhad that they needed to meet. Although it was very late, he responded to the signal requesting a meeting in his quarters first thing in the morning. Within seconds the meeting was confirmed.

When Farhad knocked on Ivan's door at 7:00 a.m. the next morning, he expected to find Ivan barely awake, but to the contrary Ivan opened the door quickly as if waiting patiently for Farhad's arrival.

"I'm surprised to find you so alert so early in the morning," Farhad commented.

"I couldn't sleep well last night, knowing that you had something important enough to request a meeting," Ivan responded.

As Ivan closed the door, Farhad handed him a pouch containing a coded letter.

"I knew that this must be very important, sir, because my sources tell me that it came directly from the office of Admiral Farber and needed to be delivered as soon as possible directly to you." Farhad commented.

"Thank you, Farhad," Ivan responded, "but I'm not familiar with Admiral Farber. What is the significance of his name?"

"Admiral Farber holds the position of Deputy Director of the CIA, sir. He was appointed by President Reagan to handle only the most urgent and serious situations within the agency," Farhad responded somewhat excitedly. "Have you familiarized yourself with the procedures of your secure computer, which you must use to translate this correspondence?" Ivan muttered, "I've played with the equipment, but this is the first time I have had the need to actually use it."

"I probably do not have a sufficient clearance to view the message, but I will stand by as you try to make the translations in case, I can assist you with the operation of the equipment," Farhad suggested.

"Thanks, Farhad," Ivan responded, "your clearance is probably higher than mine but let's see if we can work it out."

It took some time, but the two finally made the translation. Ivan didn't let Farhad read the entire message, which was possibly due to the nature of the decoding. When Ivan finally put the entire message together and started to read it, he immediately asked Farhad to leave and let him digest the contents. Actually, the digestion was not necessary since the message was very clear and read as follows:

The material that you recently forwarded describing your suspicions that Dr. Topolski and Dr. Bechert may be involved in the development and production of chemical weapon material is extremely important. There have been reports for some time that several Middle Eastern dictators have received such weapons from an unknown source. Your suggestion of that source has been unofficially confirmed but we need specific proof. There have been at least two instances where dictators have used extremely lethal gas to conduct their "ethnic cleansing" programs killing thousands of innocent citizens. The international significance of this information cannot be over emphasized.

Please take great care but do everything possible to secure unquestioned proof of your allegations. This subject is of such significance that your future contacts on this subject will be directly with my office. The correct coding for future correspondence is listed below. I will provide additional instructions as appropriate.

The letter was signed by Admiral Stanton Farber, Deputy Director, CIA. Ivan leaned back in his chair and slowly read the message again and again. "Holy crap," he thought aloud, "what the hell have I gotten myself into here? It sounds like I am now a full-fledged spy and I am not trained or equipped for that."

Ivan was now in a state of shock. His primary assignment seemed now to have taken a back seat to this new need for proof of Topolski and Bechert's activities producing lethal chemicals. He needed to think this out carefully, because he knew that even a small mistake on his part would most certainly mean his own life. He would need to move slowly and smartly at every step of the way. Suspicion would now have to take a back seat to facts, but he knew that his lifelong tendency to be suspicious of everyone would come in handy here to keep him from acting irrationally. He would have to continue to pursue his assigned tasks as part of the team without showing any signs of this new assignment but to do this he needed to alter his original plan. He needed to get closer to Topolski and Bechert and at the same time strengthen his alliance with both Albert Brokow and Anna.

Brokow knew more than he had revealed, and it was possible that those stored tapes contained much of the evidence that he needed to prove his case. Brokow had become his friend, but that friendship was always fueled by alcohol. He would use that fact to test Brokow's ties to Topolski and to his home country of Russia.

As for Anna, if Topolski was indeed this deep in the chemical weapons business, she would most likely have detected some strange behavior that gave her a clue to these activities. Anna had indicated in passing last night that part of her assignment was to keep an eye on Topolski. For whom was she working on that assignment, was it the CIA or the Russian government? There had been suspicions that Anna might be a double agent, but now it was more important to determine if that was indeed the case. This was a tricky situation with Anna. Ivan knew that he could not move too fast with her. They had gotten together sexually, but that didn't necessarily mean that they were closer together in terms of trust or even loyalty. His plan would have to include moving very slowly with Anna to create a situation where she might inadvertently reveal something of significance about Topolski.

Ivan had many options to consider but he knew that to avoid any behavioral characteristics that would point suspicion his way, he needed to act as though it was business as usual with the project and he would have to mentally adjust to that reality.

CHAPTER 25

AT THE WHITE House in Washington, Admiral Farber had just finished a private meeting with the President. There were certain subjects that had serious International significance that needed the attention of the President. In this case Admiral Farber had developed a plan regarding the events that were occurring in Iran and at home that needed the President's review and approval. Farber's plan had several unusual elements that could prove explosive and possibly might be considered by some to be unethical. He had received the qualified approval from the President with certain reservations and he was directed to coordinate his efforts with the FBI and the intelligence branch of the Defense Department. Farber had discussed his plan with his boss, the CIA director, and they agreed that the director should be excluded from the President's briefing to establish an avenue for plausible deniability if the plan did not work as designed. Even among the most trusted and honest people, simply operating in the Washington environment made everyone sensitive about covering their ass in critical situations. The Director, however, was in agreement with Farber's plan.

Waiting in Admiral Farber's office was Tommy Wilkenson, the president of Grey Skies Securities. Wilkenson had been invited to meet with Farber to discuss the role of his company in Farber's plan.

"Good afternoon, Mr. Wilkenson. My name is Stanton Farber and I am the Deputy Director of the CIA. I suppose you already know that considering the nature of your company's work with our intelligence organizations. I am aware of your security status and would therefore like to have our discussions in my SCIF. You are aware of the rules involved for this type of briefing, so I won't bother to repeat them. Needless to say, we will be discussing very sensitive material." "I understand," Wilkenson replied as the SCIF door was closed.

"I'm not going to reveal to you my entire plan since many aspects of the plan may change from time to time. I was invited to this position by the President immediately upon his inauguration. My reputation as a straight shooter in the Navy had preceded me and President Reagan knew of my many negative policy encounters with the Carter administration. There was a great deal of concern for corruption within this and other agencies throughout the government. The President gave me this job with all of the authority that I needed to get things cleaned up. The corruption was widespread throughout the entire government structure, including members of Congress, executive staff and even CIA field and operational personnel. This made my job more difficult because I had to assemble a staff that I could trust and that has become more difficult than I had assumed because there are still many carryover people holding important jobs from the previous administration. Many of these people still want to administer programs with the policies of the previous administration. Many of my closest operations personnel had to be brought in from outside the government's reach, and we are still trying to clean out the bad apples inside the government.

"I am aware of your company's activities in support of our war efforts and you of course are aware of the many unusual services that your people perform for us. This relationship will hopefully escape congressional interference and we can continue to operate effectively together.

"Now let's talk about the rather unusual part of my request. Your organization is about to hire two service men that are part of my plan. The first soldier is Mike Atwater, a special operations soldier that has gained significant experience in combat and has my upmost support and trust. The other is a naval aviator named Lieutenant Hank Farber. Yes, the name is familiar. Hank is my son. Having him as part of my plan is highly unorthodox and possibly unethical, but it is part of the trust issue.

I will certainly be severely criticized for having my son participate if the slightest thing goes astray. I am willing to take that chance."

Wilkenson interrupted. "Yes, sir. I know both men and I have spoken personally to both of them on several occasions. We are very anxious to make them part of our organization."

Admiral Farber continued, "I am forming a special task force to investigate and collect data and evidence on a number of illegal activities in several areas of the world. Some of these activities involve corruption in this country involving highly placed officials of our government. The FBI will be working with my task force on those activities.

"Activities in other countries, mostly in the Middle East, have serious international significance. These activities fall under our responsibility at the CIA. There will also be some Defense Department involvement where necessary and of course at some point the Justice Department will be brought in depending on our findings.

"My task force will be headed by Colonel Mark Overton who has a long record of outstanding combat service with our US Special Forces. I personally recruited him for the job based on my past experience with him in critical situations. His loyalty is unquestioned.

"The two men that I am asking you to hire will come under the command of Colonel Overton. They will be employees of your organization assigned full time to the task force. I will give you a training plan for these men which will be primarily concentrating on knowledge and awareness of specific Middle Eastern areas, habits, and culture so that they might move throughout that region more effectively. I expect that this initial training will take about three to four months. Depending on our progress I may ask you to hire one or two others as the program progresses and any additional people will operate under these same conditions.

"Once the men are assigned to us, they will be working under our command with little or no command communications back to your company. That might seem strange to you, but it will be necessary due to the very serious nature of the work that they will be doing. We will of course provide your company the legal assurances that you might need to hold you harmless for their activities.

"From this point on, your interface with the CIA regarding this project will be through Colonel Overton. He will be in contact with you shortly with all of the details that you will need. Do you understand what I am asking of you, Mr. Wilkenson?"

"Yes, sir, I understand completely, and I will await contact from Colonel Overton." The two men shook hands, and both left the SCIF.

CHAPTER 26

OVER THE NEXT few months since Ivan's first sexual experience with Anna, their relationship became more of a mixture of solid professionalism and intermittent private togetherness. In their now frequent talks that they held in both Anna's apartment and Ivan's quarters during the evening hours, they had both agreed that there would be little or no real emotional tie between them in spite of what was developing into a routine sexual pattern. Anna had never shown any real emotional warmth with Ivan even during their sometimes marathon sexual adventures. The word love was never used and they both instinctively knew that sexual activity was simply an expression of physical relief in this very different environment.

For Ivan, there was another motive to his relationship with Anna. He had to decide if she was loyal to the United States or still had serious ties with the Russian government. His one path to that determination was to continue to try to see if anyone else on the team had been made aware of their sexual escapades. If Anna was indeed still working for the Russians, she would certainly have leaked her relationship with Ivan to Topolski. During his many meeting with Topolski, Ivan had not gotten the slightest hint that he knew anything about the relationship however he also knew that Topolski was a pro at what he did and probably would be skilled enough to hide any knowledge of the relationship.

The team was making slow but steady progress with their work. This assignment to Ivan was barely a challenge in terms of his technical ability, so he decided to feed significant information to the rest of the team in small bursts just to keep them off-guard to his other interests which now involved the interface with the CIA on the chemical weapons issue. He was now a self-styled spy, which made him very nervous but also offered him a challenge that he had never before felt with his technical work. He needed to get solid evidence of Topolski and Bechert's role in developing this new lethal chemical.

A key element in this new role was to get his hands on those boxes of tapes that were stored in the room in Albert Brokow's facility. This would be his next challenge.

Ivan's relationship with Albert Brokow since his arrival had become warm and cordial but it had developed purely on the basis of a man to man friendship with little or no tie to the assignment that Ivan was here to complete. They had met often to sip vodka in Albert's apartment and their discussions were normally very casual. Ivan had told Albert about his plans to build a special facility in Vermont and had even hinted that he might want Albert to move there and manage that facility. Albert had shown some interest but had also indicated that he had a very good job here and seemed not interested in interrupting the security of this job. It was now time to further pursue his relationship with Albert Brokow.

Since his new relationship with Anna had developed, Ivan felt it necessary to modify the contents of his quarters and he had asked Farhad Ahmani to get him a few bottles of the best vodka that he could find in this strange country. Despite local customs that forbade the consumption of alcohol, the ruling class and political leaders had ready access to it. Farhad had indeed managed to obtain several bottles of the best that was available. Until now Ivan had shared that vodka only with Anna but now it was time to broaden that circle of users.

Ivan showed up at Albert Brokow's quarters with the vodka carefully concealed under his lab coat. It was Saturday evening and both men had finished their work for the day. Albert was a little surprised to see Ivan and even more pleasantly surprised to see the high-quality vodka that he was carrying. "Come in, Ivan," Albert said with a chuckle, "it looks like you have come bearing gifts." Ivan started, "This has been a very tiring week Albert and I just thought it might be nice to relax for a change and enjoy a drink or two with a friend. Friends are in short supply in this facility and sometimes a man just needs to kick back and relax with someone who he trusts."

"That would be me," Albert replied. "You and I have indeed developed that kind of a relationship."

Ivan knew that it would take several drinks before Albert would loosen up and he would have to try to keep up with Albert or at least make him think he was keeping up, for that to happen. That meant hat Ivan would have to control the pouring of the vodka.

Ivan went to the kitchen area and grabbed two glasses. He knew if he took that initiative, he would have a chance to control his consumption. He poured the drinks, handed one to Albert and sat in the soft easy chair opposite where Albert always sat. Albert quickly downed the first drink and Ivan quickly rose to get him another one, making like he had also finished his drink. After Ivan handed Albert his drink, they sat for an instant simply staring at each other.

Ivan decided to lead this conversation. "Albert, I have been troubled for some time about what might be going on in this facility. I believe that you are the only one that I can share my concerns with since at one point several months ago you also stated some concerns that you had. I'm getting the feeling that the work that I was sent here to do is not really the important work that is going on here. I am considered an expert in my field and because of that I'm astute enough to know that the rest of the team is not working with the same degree of passion about the work that I am. There has to be something else going on here and for my own safety, I need to know what it is." As he finished that sentence, Ivan moved to get Albert a refill of his drink. Albert gulped that third glass down quickly. He put the empty glass on the table next to his chair with a forceful thud and leaned a little forward toward Ivan. After a moment of thoughtful silence, he started.

"Ivan, since you have been here, I have developed a liking to you because you have treated me as a friend and not as a subordinate. Our friendship has grown for the same reason. We have discussed our different lives and our differing goals for the future. Some months ago, under conditions similar to this, I revealed to you some concerns that I had about this facility and we have not discussed that subject since that time, probably because of my desire not to pursue it further. I believe that you are referring to that subject, so I am going to be totally honest with you. Two years ago, I had developed a similar relationship with your predecessor on this assignment. As a fine gentleman, one of those scientists also made friends with me and we too talked about my concerns, but he took it a little further and started snooping around for more information. Within the next month, as the technical team was doing human testing, I saw him wheeled out in a body bag along with other human test specimens. Since that time, I have discussed my concerns with no one but you. This is a very sensitive subject and if you give any hint to anyone here that you are investigating other aspects of this facility, your life will be in great danger." As Albert spoke, tears began to roll down his cheeks.

Ivan needed to redirect this conversation because he sensed that Albert was about to shut down.

Ivan interrupted. "Albert, lets step back for a moment or two, I need to tell you a little about myself but to do that I need to refill my glass." Ivan rose and took both glasses to refill them. Albert made no attempt to stop him.

Albert now sipped his vodka, sat back in his chair, wiped the tears from his face and said, "Go on, Ivan."

This time Ivan gulped his drink and started. "Before I was born, my parents were considered an integral part of Germany's population as were millions of other Jews. My father had developed a good clothing business and was considered well-off by the standards of that time. As Hitler's power grew, he made it very clear that he intended to cleanse the country of those who were not pure Germans. When I was born, Hitler's cleansing process had already started. My parents were allowed to continue their lifestyle because they were required to use their business income to support Hitler's war causes. My father knew that he would be allowed to continue as long as he had the resources to continue this support but that was about to run its course. At that point he managed to make the proper connections to send me to the United States to live with my relatives there. Within weeks of my departure, the German military sent my parents and all of their relatives that remained in Germany to work camps and eventually when their usefulness was reduced, they were killed in the death camps. I understand better than most people the horrors of ethnic cleansing and more than most, I never want to see that happen to any group of humans again. If I am in a position to use my knowledge to prevent that from happening, I am willing to risk my own life to do it." Albert started responding with his words slightly slurred by the Vodka. "Many of the German scientists that Russia sent here after the war were experts in the development of various forms of lethal gas. They had carried out many experiments in the work camps in Germany that helped advance their work and the gasses that they developed killed thousands, perhaps millions of Jews. These same men remained loyal to their cause years after they arrived here and there work was carried out here under somewhat primitive conditions. When the Russians saw the value of their work, they modernized this facility and sent in several younger offspring of these knowledgeable scientists to advance the work. Topolski and Bechert were two of those scientists.

"They have always worked under extreme secrecy here and a couple of years ago this new alliance with your government was established. I never understood why the United States would get involved in lethal chemical program and I have now assumed that it is simply a cover to reduce international outcry if the project is ever discovered. The two projects, of course, have nothing to do with each other, but if enough time passes, that might be hard to explain away.

"I know that more than two years ago, Topolski and Bechert shipped several containers of liquid to Saudi Arabia and later to Iraq. I assume that this was the lethal gas that they have developed. I also believe that they have continued to improve on their original work to develop even more lethal versions of this gas. Of course, this activity is in direct violation of the Geneva Convention making it extremely sensitive." Ivan responded quietly. "Albert, what is your opinion about all of this?

Do you feel like you want to see this work continue?"

"No" Albert replied, "but I feel like I have been caught in this terrible web and never felt that there was a way out for me except to be carried out in a body bag."

"Are you willing to work with me if I can get you some assurance that you will exit alive?" Ivan asked.

"I'm not sure," Albert responded, "These are two very dangerous governments. They have their tentacles all over the world and their leaders still have the inherent desire for world dominance. I'm not sure there is any place on earth that would be safe for either me or you if this were exposed."

"Well," Ivan said, laughing, "I have the place that will be safe. I have developed it for circumstances quite like this. The facility that I am having built in Vermont will provide absolute safety because no one else in the world will even know that it exists. I can get you the immunity that you will need if you are willing to come with me to complete and eventually manage that facility." "I'm interested," Albert replied, "but do you have a plan that will permit it to happen?"

"I think so, Albert, but we will have to move very slowly and carefully," Ivan commented. "It starts with those tapes that are stored in your storage room. I believe that those tapes might contain the direct evidence that is needed to permit my plan to work. What we have to do is develop a plan to get those tapes out of this facility and into the hands of my contacts in the US. If my suspicions are right, we can make it happen very rapidly, but it all depends on what is on those tapes. We have to come up with a plan to get them out of here. Do you think that anyone actually still knows that the tapes exist?" "I'm not sure," Albert replied, "No one has ever mentioned the tapes since the system was upgraded. I'll have to think about this and see if I can develop a plan to perhaps remove a few boxes to see what, if anything happens."

Ivan replied, "Let's not do anything right now. As long as I know you are willing to cooperate with me on this, we can move forward together quietly and slowly, but I have to be sure that you are committed to our plan. Why don't you think about it for a while and we can talk more? Why don't you keep the rest of the vodka and we can sip it when we discuss our plan further? By the way, Albert, is there any way that you can determine the approximate dates that those shipments were made to Saudi Arabia and Iraq? I believe that information would permit more detailed investigations by my people that would be solid evidence and very useful to our cause." Albert thought for a minute and responded, "I'm not sure. When my head clears, I'll look through my files and think about that shipment. Most material that leaves here at some point goes through me but back then I'm not sure." Before Ivan moved forward any further, he needed to inform his bosses of what he had learned and what he needed to proceed. Without specific commitments from the government, he couldn't make the promises that were needed to Albert for his future safety.

Ivan transmitted all that he had learned back to the CIA as he was directed. He also asked if he could make a promise of immunity to Albert or even Anna if necessary, to get the needed solid evidence. He did not intend to go further with Albert unless he could make that promise.

Ivan was now convinced that this new track that he was on was of much greater important to his country than his original assignment, but he had to keep both in proper balance in order not to create and suspicion from the other players.

Ivan was very confused about the interactions that he should have with Anna. He felt that in this cloistered world that he was living in, he needed other allies, but could he really take the risk of bringing her into his confidence. He just wasn't sure, and he also didn't know how to proceed with her. For the time being he would not involve her in anything but his known assignment. He did however ask his CIA contact to do more investigation of her activities to see if she was playing both sides in this spy game.

Ivan also asked for an update on Farhad. To date, Ivan had not used Farhad extensively, only to carry diplomatic packages of information to be delivered for him. Ivan had not yet developed confidence in the encryption equipment that was attached to his computer, so he had been using Farhad's diplomatic standing to hand-deliver messages. He believed that Farhad could be a key player in his plans, but he needed assurance that he could be completely trusted. Now again, Ivan's inherent suspicious behavior was kicking in except that this time a bad judgment could be a life-or-death proposition.

CHAPTER 27

A T THE HEADQUARTERS of the CIA in Langley Virginia, Deputy Director Admiral Stanton Farber has assembled a small group of men in a secret briefing room and was about to initiate one of the most important activities of his relatively short career at the agency. Admiral Farber had made arrangements with the Grey Skies organization to hire and begin training of several former military veterans for this special mission or series of missions.

In the room was Colonel Mark Overton, a former Special Operations commander, Mike Atwater, a former Green Beret specialist, Hank Farber, a former marine pilot, Chris Jenkins, a seasoned FBI operative, and Ashem Povac, a CIA field agent. This group was to be the focal point for some very sensitive activities and Admiral Farber was expected to brief the man on some of their future assignment.

Admiral Farber had made arrangements with Tommy Wilkinson, president of Grey Skies Corporation, to hire each of these men with the understanding that they would be assigned to special units of the CIA but would have employment attachment with that company. Under contract with the CIA, the group would receive special training given by Grey Skies under a plan developed by Admiral Farber. Other than administrative association, the group would have no other relationships with Grey Skies except for this training. All mission direction and field operations were to be directed by Admiral Farber's office.

This type of arrangement had never before been executed by the US government, but the missions were so sensitive that the entire program was reviewed and approved by President Reagan himself. Organizational lines of communications within the CIA and several areas of the government were to be carefully managed to assure that there would be plausible deniability if the missions were not a success. Also, each member of this special team had received special immunity from legal prosecution for all activities conducted as part of this program.

The atmosphere was tense as Admiral Farber entered the room. He briefed all present on the rules associated with this room as a SCIF and began his briefing.

"Gentlemen, we are about to embark on a project that may have extreme international significance for years to come. Each of you has been hand-picked by me for this assignment because I needed to be absolutely sure that I had your complete confidence, trust and loyalty. In addition, I needed to be confident that each of you was physically and mentally capable of handling this type of work.

"The CIA in recent years has had very serious problems. Probably not surprising, when any organization does work that is so secret and sensitive, its activities get little or no oversight, things tend to get out of control. That is what has been happening within this organization. President Reagan brought me on board with the specific assignment to clean this problem up while also dealing with some serious issues.

"Because of this history, I found that I could not take any member of the current organization into my confidence, never knowing that they were innocent of any corruption and could be trusted with key assignments.

"Intelligence is the cornerstone of every military operation and it is unlikely that any military actions can be effectively planned and carried out without effective and correct intelligence. Some of you in this room have actually been involved with combat actions where intelligence was in error and that bad information caused serious loss of life and potential embarrassment to our country. That is why this team has been recruited for this program.

"I would like to introduce Colonel Mark Overton, seated at my right. He will be the commander of this group in all of its activities. Colonel Overton is known to some of you who have served or trained under his command with the Special Forces. From the time you leave this room, you will be completely under Colonel Overton's command.

"Within days, you will be flown to a small town in Saudi Arabia named Rafha. This town is located in relative proximity to many of the areas where your missions will be centered. We have established a safe facility there as the base of operations for your training and future operations.

"Saudi Arabia is on record as being a strong ally of the United States. Take that pledge with great suspicion, since there are many activities in that country that are contrary to our military or economic interests.

"Let me give you a summary of our concerns that will form the basis of some of your future activities.

"First, you are all aware of the variety of disruptive cultures throughout the Middle East. Because of the importance of oil throughout the world, this region has become the center of corruption in any activities that deal with the production of oil. The wealth that this oil has created throughout the region has also made money a commodity that is easily used for creating corrupt activities with anyone involved with production, transportation or even the politics of oil, This corruption has touched some members of the CIA field operations that have created channels for providing a great deal of money to Americans politicians for favors for oil subsidies and much more. We need to get solid proof of these avenues of monetary flow into our political and economic system.

"Second, when the Iranian government fell and was taken over by religious radicals, the United States imposed an arms embargo against Iran preventing any sale of weapons to that radical government. It has come to our attention that some high-ranking US officials may be facilitating the selling of arms to Iran against this embargo. We are not sure how our weapons are getting into the hands of the Iranians and we need to determine the specifics of how and who is involved in this activity.

"The third area of concern deals with several activities being carried out in Iran. The US government has been concerned for many years with the possible development of nuclear weapons and other weapons of mass destruction, throughout the Middle East. Many of these Middle Eastern countries have a culture and history of carrying out terrorist-like activities against their own people. We have hints of nuclear material being smuggled into the Middle East from several South American and African countries. We do not believe that any of these countries have the technology to process this material and product a nuclear weapon, but as time passes, that possibility grows.

"We have also recently received information that there is a German/Russian program being carried out in Iran that has developed and produced large quantities of a very lethal new poison gas that has been shipped to Iraq and a few other countries and may have already been used as part of ethnic cleansing programs in those countries. This information is very current, and we are working hard on a plan to verify the information.

"Gentlemen, these are four areas that you will be charged to investigate, to gain the needed evidence and solid proof of their existence.

"Mr. Povak has been added to this group because he is a skilled combat soldier but also speaks several of the Arabic dialects. He will assist in your language training in Saudi Arabia and will be an integral part of all mission operations. Mr. Jenkins was added because we believe that many of the corruption activities will lead back to criminal activity in this country and will require additional FBI investigations especially where the corruption ties to US politicians.

"This team will be supplied with every possible item of equipment and weapon that Colonel Overton deems necessary. All communications from and to this team will be through Colonel Overton and will come directly to my office. The rules of engagement for this operation are whatever is necessary to get the job done.

"You are all asked to clean up any and all issues that you have in the US and be prepared to fly to Saudi Arabia within three days."

Admiral Farber rose, saluted the group, and promptly left the room.

As the group walked out of the meeting, Mike Atwater was handed a message that he was requested to meet with Admiral Farber before he left the building. The receptionists showed him to a conference room where he waited patiently for the admiral.

Mike stood as the admiral entered the room, but the admiral quickly told him to be seated and relax.

"Several months ago, you drew my attention to your father's personal situation in Vermont. I asked an agent of the Treasury Department to conduct a low-key investigation into that situation and they are continuing that investigation. I received a preliminary report from the agent last week and as a result of that report I asked him to continue his work. I can tell you based on what we know right now that the Goldblatt brothers have and are continuing to commit significant crimes against your father. Your suspicions were valid.

"When your father signed his agreement with our government to take on his current assignment, he was, perhaps unknowingly, very smart in the way he asked to be paid. He is being paid in gold and his agreement required that his base salary each month be based on the price of gold at the time of the signing. As the price of gold has risen significantly since that time more than tripling in value, his salary has also risen in direct proportion to that price increase.

"When he left the country, he had an agreement with the Goldblatt brothers, specifically Jonathan Goldblatt who had deep political and banking connections, to manage his financial affairs. He also asked the brothers to take on a specific project for him building an underground facility in land that he had leased from them on the Canadian border. You are aware of that project, which is nearly complete at this time.

"We have absolute proof that both brothers have developed a scheme to embezzle millions of dollars from your father as a result of that rapid increase in the price of gold. They are booking the salary that they are receiving for your father at the original contract price, not fully taking into consideration the gold price rise. They have banked, in foreign banks, more than 20 million dollars of this money in accounts in the names of their spouse and children. In addition, they have significantly increased their lifestyle with additional money that was not banked.

"I have asked the agent to continue to follow this, digging as deep as possible in order to get solid evidence for future prosecution. If we get thorough data and properly record it for future prosecution, there should be no problem recovering most if not all of the money for your father when we finally move in and arrest the Goldblatts." "Wow," Mike replied. "I suspected that something was wrong when I made that quick examination of the files provided to me by the Goldblatts. My father was always a very suspicious man and he taught me to also always be suspicious of those who appear to be doing me favors. He also once told me that those who will hurt you most are your closest friends and family. This is certainly proof of that theory." The admiral responded, "Mike, there are no circumstances under which you should get involved in this issue. I have brought the FBI into the investigation and the Rutland Vermont field office is coordinating this case. Please do not contact any of the principals in the case, even if they attempt to contact you. We have the situation well in hand, do you understand?" "Yes, sir," Mike responded. He rose and saluted the admiral, but the admiral did not return his salute.

"There is no longer a military relationship between us, Mike. You are a civilian employee of the Grey Skies Corporation on temporary assignment to the CIA, that's it."

"Thank you, sir," Mike replied. "You have certainly gone out on a limb for me on this issue and I am truly appreciative of that, sir." The admiral and Mike left the room together and went their separate way.

CHAPTER 28

IVAN HAD COMPLETED a long day in his laboratory and when he returned to his quarters, he noticed that his computer was indicating that there was an encrypted message waiting for him. Since he now knew how to decrypt the messages, he proceeded to process it. The message was short and concise, but it did provide him with some information that he needed to proceed with his plan.

The message read: *You have approval to offer friend a new identity if he cooperates. Courier may be trusted completely. Assistant still in doubt, make your own judgment.*

The message did not answer all of Ivan's concerns but at least he had the approval to work with Albert and Farhad could get more involved if necessary. He would have to develop a plan for dealing with Anna but in the meantime, he would proceed with Albert since getting his hands on those tapes could be vital to determining the facts about the development of the lethal gas.

He didn't want to waste any time moving forward so he went to Albert's quarters to start that process in motion.

Albert welcomed Ivan warmly. They had by now developed a very close relationship.

Ivan started. "Albert, I have some important news for you. My government has offered you a clean slate and a new identity if you cooperate with me getting the information that is on those tapes. You can come and work with me in my new laboratory and living facilities in America."

Ivan waited nervously for Albert's response. They had discussed this possibility several times and Albert seemed amenable to the idea, but now it had become a possible reality.

Albert left the room without comment and Ivan was slightly confused, but when Albert returned, he was holding two glasses filled with his favorite vodka. He handed Ivan one glass, smiled and said, "To our new partnership, Ivan," and the two men hugged for an instant, then sat to devise their plan of action.

Ivan started. "I've given this a lot of thought, Albert. We don't actually know if the tapes contain the incriminating information that I need. I believe we should collect a sample of possibly 10 tapes from different time periods during the time that you suspect that they were working on the lethal gas. You were involved in the shipment of that gas to some extent so you can recall the time frame. If we randomly take the tapes from different days around that time period, I can have them studied for value. If my people tell me that they want more, they can return those tapes to me and we can look at 10 more. We can continue this process until we have gathered all of the data that those tapes contain. If I get the word that the tapes have no good content, we can simply stop the process and go about thinking up another avenue to get those two bastards. In this manner, we reduce the risk of anyone recognizing that the tapes are missing, and the 10 tapes will represent a small enough package that I can get it out without anyone getting suspicious." Albert responded, "That sounds really good to me, Ivan, I'll select ten tapes and have them ready for you tomorrow morning"

"I have another item that I need to talk to you about," Ivan started. "I need to make a decision about my assistant Anna. I'm not sure that I can place my compete trust in her. She has performed well for me in her assigned capacity as my lab assistant, and between you and me, she has also provided other favors for me, if you know what I mean. But her background and heritage suggest that her loyalties may lie somewhere else. What do you think, Albert?" Albert got up from his seat and wandered slowly around the room as though thinking carefully about his response. "Ivan, you know that Anna and I come from the same Russian culture. However, her background and family relationships are very different from mine. She was educated in the United States and has apparently stayed with your country, obtaining citizenship there. You know that her father has serious ties with the Soviet government. I don't know if she even maintains contact with her family or her father, but blood ties are very significant, especially with the Russian culture. If I were you, I would remain suspicious of her. Maybe you want to design some sort of a test to see how she performs; I just don't know." "I trust your judgment, Albert," Ivan replied. "I'll keep that in mind." Ivan returned to his quarters and the next day he summoned Farhad.

This was the first time that Ivan and Farhad had any real serious sit-down discussion. Ivan began, "Farhad, to date I have used you almost exclusively as a courier and we have not attempted to develop any sort of relationship. Now that situation has changed. I have discovered some very important information about the activities of some of the scientists in this building that would indicate a serious problem for US and world security. My contacts in Washington have approved some actions on my part to secure additional information in the form of proof of my suspicions. It may now be time for me to better understand and use the people around me that I can trust, to carry out my plans going forward. I know you work for the same people that I do, and they have informed me that you can be completely trusted so I may be depending on you for more activities as I go forward. Many of these activities might be dangerous and I hope I can trust you to perform in my behalf." Farhad replied, "You can be assured that I will support you in any manner that you choose. My duties with you are only a small part of my overall assignment with the company. As a matter of fact, your activities represent about ten percent of my activities. I am an active operative for this region of the world, and I am part of a widespread group of operatives that are confined mostly to Iran, although our activities often take us to other countries. All of the agents in this country were selected because of their background and heritage so that we can more easily operate in the country. If the time comes when we need to fight, we fight. At all other times we are collecting intelligence to help our country conduct its diplomatic and military activities. I believe that current records will show that I am still officially employed by the Iranian police although I have not associated with them since the fall of the Shah, nor have I received any compensation from them.

"Since President Reagan was elected, all of us in the intelligence business have become much more motivated and active, because President Carter downplayed the importance of intelligence, and many of the agents became demoralized and lost interest in risking their lives for the cause. Reagan has changed all of that. During that period before Reagan, some of the operatives kind of went rogue, taking great sums of money to act like double agents. They were not really spying for the other side, but they often gave information to the enemy that caused death and destruction to our friends and even our own military. Within a short time after President Reagan took office, all of that changed and most of those people disappeared from their duty stations. Our force is now fewer in numbers, but we are twice as effective because we are now motivated. I have your back, Ivan, and I am here for you, whatever the circumstances." "That's great news," Ivan replied. "What can you tell me about my assistant Anna? Do you know her, and can she be trusted?"

"Anna is a strange person," Farhad replied. "She apparently works for the same people we do but I have been given no duties in her regard. I don't even know if she has a contact although I cannot imagine that she does not."

"Inside your circles, is there any talk of her having any contacts with other outside our organization?" Ivan questioned.

"The rumor mill indicates that her only purpose is to use her sexual freedom and good looks to get information as an operative. If she does that, I have no knowledge of how she gets that information back to our people." Farhad commented, "She certainly does not go through my channels."

"That's very interesting," Ivan responded. "Stay tuned in to that situation and see if you can uncover anything else.

"I will have a package for you tomorrow that will need to get back to Washington. The package will contain several old recording tapes that need to go directly to the people listed here," Ivan handed Farhad a note with Admiral Farber's name and address on it. At some short time later, you will probably get that same package back to be returned to me in exchange for another similar package. This exchange will go on for some time until we come to some conclusions about the content of the tapes. Can that process be carried out okay, Farhad?" Ivan asked.

"No problem," Farhad replied.

"I'll call for you soon with the package, possibly tomorrow or the next day," Ivan said. "There is one more subject we should discuss. Is there any way you can check to determine if there has been shipping activity from this facility to another Middle Eastern country, possibly Saudi Arabia or Pakistan in the past two years or so. It probably would not have been a huge package but could have been small drums of liquid. I can't image that there is any way to find that information, but you guys can get and do things that would otherwise be impossible to most of us." "I'll check that out," Farhad replied, and he left the facility.

Ivan still had not gotten any positive response about Anna, so he decided to give her a series of tests on his own to try to determine which side she was really on.

The next couple of days were rather routine in the laboratory. Ivan received 10 tapes from Albert and passed them along to Farhad for delivery to Admiral Farber. For the remainder of the week Ivan acted a little warmer to Anna, sometimes getting into personal conversations with her as the beginning of his plan. As the week was coming to a close, Ivan suggested that he and Anna might want to get together again socially. Since their first sexual endeavor, they had used the term social evening to mean drinks and sex. It had been several weeks since they last spend an evening like that, and Anna responded very favorably.

"Let's have the evening in my quarters," Anna suggested. "This will permit me to prepare some snacks and we can enjoy the night together."

"Fine with me," Ivan replied.

When Anna opened the door to her quarters, Ivan was nearly lost for words at her appearance. She was outfitted in a beautiful, well-fitted dress that hung perfectly to her body. The outfit permitted her to project every part of her body that might interest Ivan. She was also perfectly made up in a manner that Ivan had never seen from her. It was fairly obvious that she was ready for more than small talk that night.

"I have the drinks ready, Ivan, but I thought that we should hold off on the snacks that I prepared, until a little later, perhaps after we have had a chance to work up an appetite," Anna seductively murmured.

Ivan may have lived a shielded married life, but he certainly knew what those words meant as he responded, "Your plan sounds like exactly what I was hoping you would say, that's what I was thinking also." They went into a very warm embrace and Anna took his hand and they walked directly to the bedroom, drinks in hand.

After a very pleasant round of sexual frolicking, they returned to the living area, sat close to each other, and enjoyed another drink.

Anna started the conversation by asking, "Ivan, I have had the feeling lately that there were things on your mind that you want to discuss with me. The last week or so you have become a little friendlier with me in the lab and after all these months, that seemed a little unusual to me. Am I correct in my assumption?" "You are right Anna," Ivan started. "I have had very complicated personnel life in the past years and being here alone in this solitude amplified several things to me that I think I need to address, but our situation here makes addressing them nearly impossible. My wife and I divorced many years ago and that has never bothered me except that having dedicated myself to my work, I completely neglected any relationship with my son. He is now in the military service and hopefully doing well but there are some things that I need to communicate to him. Part of my agreement when I accepted this assignment was that I could not attempt to have any contact outside the formal contacts with our government representative.

"This assignment will someday come to an end and I need to have my son start getting involved by ensuring that the plan that I left behind in the hands of others is being moved forward. The plan is a complicated one and someone needs to get me some assurance that it is proceeding as I had planned."

Ivan proceeded to lay out his entire future plan to Anna including his personal suspicions about nearly everything in life. He noticed that when he described the facility that he was having built outside the borders of the United States, Anna seemed particularly attentive and somewhat intrigued by the whole thing.

"I need to get some information to my son, but under the terms of this arrangement, I am forbidden from making outside contact. I assume there is a concern that if I tried to make outside contacts, someone would actually learn of my presence here.

"You have been here much longer than I, and I thought you might have established some method of getting personal communications out of this building and out of the country."

Anna seemed a little confused as she rose and went to the kitchen area to get the snacks that she had prepared. Perhaps this was a designed tactic that she used as a delay when she needed time to think before answering. When she returned to her seat, placing a plate of snacks on the table she responded, "What kind of communications are you planning?" "I need to send my son some detailed plans for the electrical system for my facility. This building is powered by very small nuclear generators. They are actually small nuclear reactors. The design would be perfect for my facility, but I will also possibly need to send him a few key components that I can obtain here that can never be purchased in the US. I have no way of getting a package of that size out of here and shipped to the US without our government finding out about it. I also need to pass some important information about my work here to my son as sort of an insurance policy on my future. I have been passing all of my work on to our people but there is some vital information that I am holding back, and I want my son to have it." "Can't your contact with the government get that done for you, Ivan?" Anna asked.

"I don't think so Anna. He seems to be a very loyal agent and he probably would never break the rules, I just cannot take the chance of asking him. You know your way around here much better than I and I thought you might be able to help me with this."

"Why, don't you think that I would report this to our employer, Ivan? Don't you think I am also loyal to our cause?" Anna claimed.

That response almost sounded to Ivan like a slight joke because she was smiling when she said it and she was rubbing her hand through Ivan's hair at the same time. She was also making other contact and gestures that were very suggestive and not indicative at all of someone that was annoyed that he had asked the question "I'm a suspicious man Anna. I told you that," Ivan returned. "But we seemed to have developed a relationship that we know how to control. During the few times that we have permitted ourselves to bond emotionally, I have developed an unusual sense that you can feel warmth and emotion despite your outward cold act. I simply have grown to trust you and believe that we have the ability to share some personal secrets. If you can't help me here, that's fine, but I just feel that you would not turn on me in this case." Anna hesitated for a moment and then looked at Ivan with a smile. "Perhaps we should move back into the bedroom to think about this Ivan, I usually can think clearer when I free my mind of all other thoughts so perhaps you could help me free my mind."

As soon as they had reached the bedroom and reclined together, Anna turned to Ivan and softly whispered to him, "Ivan, please tell me more about your secret hideaway. It sounds intriguing to me and like a place that two people could live their lives in complete comfort, free of all worldly concerns. What a beautiful life that would be, don't you think so?" "Absolutely," Ivan responded. "That is exactly why I selected Canada and a place deep in the mountains. With the world going in the direction that it is, I have always feared that there will be another world war in my lifetime. No matter if that war reached North America, no one would ever be interested in the mountains of Canada. One could live there without any worldly concerns, provided that they carefully planned their existence and ability to survive." "I would like to talk to you more about this facility, Ivan, but now, we must concentrate on clearing my mind of all things unpleasant." They turned to each other and began their warm exchanges.

CHAPTER 29

E VEN WITH ALL of Ivan's new challenges, he still managed to appear to work intently on his technical assignment. He felt that he could easily complete his work quickly, but he was stringing his efforts along to provide him time to work on the bigger plan. He was also hinting to the rest of the team that he had taken his portion of the project as far as he could without closer coordination with the work of the others on the team. Through his work, he had demonstrated several methods of altering the neuron behavior in the neocortex of the brain by transdermal delivery of the drug to nerve sensors in several normally exposed areas of the body. Up to this point in history, transdermal application of drugs had been limited to microneedles or thermal abrasion. The work that Ivan was doing had proved at least in theory that a controlled transdermal application could be made to work but it is a complicated process that requires very careful application. The team still needed to find a way to make the new drug disappear from detection in the body in a relatively short period after its application. That work would probably also involve developing an antidote for the drug. He had discussed both of these aspects of their work with Topolski and Bechert months earlier and they seemed to make light of the problem like it was simple to solve. Actually, Ivan had developed an external method of deactivating the drugs but his method involves rapid nerve ending manipulation like rapid trauma to the nerves or even the brain. He had also made progress with the idea of using emotional shock to reset the brain's memory system. He had no intention of sharing those findings with the team.

Still looming as a major problem, of course, was the subject of human trials. Ivan had run hundreds of thousands of iterations of his theory on his computer, and some work had been done with animal tests, but these tests were very preliminary. Even though this project was not subject to any formal medical testing, it certainly was a necessity to prove to the team itself that the drug would have the planned effect on humans. It was time now to discuss these subjects with Topolski and Bechert to see if they really were serious about completing this project.

At the next weekly meeting of the team leaders, Ivan introduced the subject. "Gentlemen, I believe we have made exceptional progress with our work here. With both of your expertise, you have developed the drug that we think will have the desired effects without causing permanent human harm. I believe I have developed the transdermal application technique that was needed to get the desired effect. To my knowledge we have yet to prove that the drug will be undetectable in a short period after application and I don't believe we have made any progress developing an antidote. For both of these areas we will almost certainly need human testing and that's where I begin to have a conflict of principle. If there is any possibility that you feel that human testing could be lethal, I cannot continue to participate. Since you have only tested the drug on rats and a couple of chimps, human testing seems to be a natural next step. Even in the animal testing, the drug was injected, and my application theories did not get tested and they may not apply to animals in the same way as in humans. I would like to hear your opinion on these subjects." Elias Bechert was the first to respond. "My friend, Dr Schwarz, you have been a valuable asset to this team. You have worked tirelessly in your laboratory, running thousands of computer iterations in an attempt to simulate the behavior of the human brain and its reaction to nerve ending stimulation. I believe that your work in this regard has opened new frontiers in neural networking that will be recognized around the world at some point in the future when and if your work here is published. Unfortunately, this program has not been authorized by any country's scientific community and therefore will possibly never be scrutinized by experts in any of our countries.

"We are not conducting this work under the rules of any government, therefore we are authorized to do what we see fit to accomplish our intended goals. Perhaps in your country, the development of a drug also requires the development of an antidote, but here those rules do not apply. This is not a poison that we are developing, and I see no need to develop an antidote. An antidote in the wrong hands could be considered a defensive mechanism against the desired effects of our drug.

"As for the short or long-term effects of the drug and its ability to be detected after application, this is not important to me, but I believe that future human testing will point us in the right direction on that subject. As for human testing, we certainly must do that regardless of the above concerns and that testing is likely to take place over a long period of time. Dr Topolski and I have already made arrangement with two other regional countries to conduct tests in their prisons and possibly in their hospitals. We will provide them the drugs and the criteria for application and measurement of results. We would also like to use the results of those tests to do further tests right here in our facilities. The tests here would serve to make those final small adjustments that we feel might be necessary." "Dr. Bechert, I must interrupt you here," Ivan shouted. "What you have just laid out is a complete alteration to nearly everything that we had agreed many months ago about the way this team would work together. You both agreed then that I would be apprised of all of your activities, just as I have kept you aware of all of mine. Under what authority have you made these decisions?"

Bechert replied, "There is no authority issue here, Dr. Schwarz. You have done the work that you agreed to do, and we have done as we see fit for the success of this project. If you object to our action, so be it, you are free to leave the project as your predecessors did."

Ivan was furious at this response and he nearly jumped across the table lunging at Bechert. "You son of a bitch, Bechert, this is 1980, not 1940 in Germany. You are acting like your leader back in that time period. There are rules these days and some of us have become civilized enough to operate by those rules. You are not Hitler, Bechert, and you are not Stalin, Topolski. When we have an agreement, we are all obliged to operate in accordance with that agreement.

"There are a few things that you forget. I have done the work that I agreed to do on this project, and you have seen the results of that work.

But I am smart enough that you don't have all of the algorithms and key software keys to use my information with any degree of success. Do you really believe that I would lay out all of my work to you without holding back the key triggers to its success? Transdermal application is a very tricky problem and if you make one small mistake with where you apply the drug, there will be very serious unwanted results. If that happens, the desire to produce a drug that will not permanently affect the person to which it is applied will not be accomplished. Or perhaps that is not what you were seeking right along. Perhaps you wanted a drug that would be destructive. By today's standards, that would be defined as a weapon of mass destruction. Is that what your desire is?" Topolski jumped in at that point. "Gentlemen, this is getting way off course. Perhaps there has been some misunderstanding among the three of us about certain aspects of this work, but I believe that if we approach each of these misunderstandings, we can come to some common ground. Dr. Schwarz, Dr Bechert and I have been working on projects in this facility for several years before you arrived. Those projects have little or no connection to the work that this team is doing, but in the past to be successful, we have worked in accordance with our own rules and procedures. Perhaps those old habits have caused some misunderstanding with this work. Let's take a deep breath and perhaps a break from these discussions for a while and think it over. Maybe when we re-convene, we can proceed without name-calling and insults." Ivan rose from his seat as if to leave the room and commented, "Let's meet here again tomorrow morning at 9:00 a.m." And he left the room without any other comment.

As that conversation was unfolding, Ivan realized that he had waited too long since he last exerted his authority with the two other scientists. When he first realized many months ago, that he was considered the weak one on the team, he took steps to put them in their place. But he now realized that by simply doing his job as part of the team, he didn't have that much daily opportunity to exert his authority with them. That, he felt, might have been a mistake.

On the other hand, Ivan felt that he had received some valuable information, especially from Toploski who had admitted that they had been working together on other projects long before Ivan arrived. One of those projects must have been the development of the lethal gas. When

Bechert admitted that they had arrangement with other countries in the region to do human testing, those were probably the same countries that received the lethal gas. Ivan felt that he now had to begin behaving in a way that he could get more information about those relationships in order to track down the shipping information that he needed as solid proof, hoping of course that the tapes would also be very incriminating.

It was interesting that it wasn't until Ivan mentioned the words weapons of mass destruction that Topolski jumped right in to change the subject. This was now getting very interesting and Ivan needed to be very careful how he proceeded from this point on. He knew that this assignment was probably a sham to in some way get the United States involved in the lethal gas controversy, if it ever became public knowledge. Or perhaps this program was actually a continuation of that same program and his activities would trap the US as a partner, ensuring to Russia and Germany that the project would never get exposed. Ivan's excitement level was at an all-time high now, he was in the middle of a major international conspiracy and he had a great deal of responsibility in that conspiracy. He had to make sure that his every move was planned carefully. Ivan wasn't accustomed to this type of secret stuff. Although it was a new and exciting experience, it was also one that could easily get him killed.

After thinking about what had happened in their last meeting, Ivan decided that he needed to change his strategy when dealing with the other scientists. He was now convinced that the specific assignment given him was a sham, or at least so, on the part of the other two scientists. In all of their interactive meetings over the last many months, Ivan had grown more suspicious that the motives of Bechert and Topolski were not directed at the specifics of this project but possibly the project was a cover for other more serious work that they were doing that was not being shared with him. If this was true, the US government had been duped into thinking that the effort would advance the cause of peace, when in reality it had sucked the United States into a program that was developing a weapon of mass destruction.

Ivan had known from early in his work that there was a very fine line between developing a drug that would play tricks on the human brain and one that would be extremely lethal if not properly controlled. This type of drug could easily be rendered lethal or could have tremendous disabling or even killing power. He now believed that it was the intent of Bechert and Topolski to eventually turn the drug into such a weapon.

When Bechert admitted, in the heat of the argument, that he was not interested in developing an antidote or gaining a better understanding of the short and long term effects of the drug, this was a strong hint that his real interests were in the lethal effects of the drug and nothing else.

Ivan had been passing along to his contacts in the CIA, every bit of technical data that he was receiving about the drug being developed. He assumed that the CIA scientists were taking a closer look at the drug for possible other effects. He was also confident that these US scientists were developing an antidote independently as the development process progressed although he had never given his contacts any hint that he was suspicious of the motives of the program. If the people responsible for the approval of this program were incompetent enough to not foresee this problem, perhaps it was time now to present that possibility to the members of the new administration.

This information was so sensitive that Ivan did not want to trust the secure communications line that was available to him but would prefer to write a report and have Farhad deliver it through diplomatic channels. So, he spent several hours preparing a very detailed description of his suspicions and summoned Farhad to his quarters.

When Farhad arrived, he seemed nervous and somewhat excited as if he was anxious to tell Ivan some new information, so Ivan permitted him to start the conversation.

Farhad started, "You asked me to check every possible information source to determine if there had been any regular shipments from this facility in the last year or two. Well, I have determined that there has been a shipment trail between here and a small outpost in Pakistan. That outpost is apparently not connected to either the Russians of the Germans but is secretly controlled by Iraqi militants. The people in this outpost move regularly between Iraq and Iran. About five months before you arrived here, there was a shipment of five large drums of liquid from this facility to that outpost. The shipment to the outpost was made over ground apparently to avoid detection. From that point, the shipment was split with half of the drums shipped by air to central Iran and the other half to a military installation in Iraq. I have not been able to determine the exact location in both countries, but I will continue to work on that." Ivan now understood why Farhad was so excited. This was very important information, especially if the exact locations could eventually be determined. This should be fairly easy for operatives in the two countries to determine, so he would ask Farhad to pass the information along to his CIA contact for immediate transmittal to Admiral Farber. He also asked Farhad to try to determine the exact date that the drums left this facility. If the drums came out of this building, it was definitely the work of Bechert and Topolski since there was no other authority to approve shipments out of here, except possibly through Albert Brokow, who would be his next contact.

Farhad also gave Ivan the tapes that had been returned to him from Admiral Farber. He had received no word from Farber as to the value of the content of the tapes, but they had agreed to a rapid exchange to avoid any suspicion. Ivan took the tapes and went immediately to Albert's quarters. Albert opened the door to welcome Ivan. 'This meeting is more than simply a tape exchange," Ivan commented. "I want to talk some about how material might leave this facility with or without your knowledge." Ivan didn't want to give Albert any specifics since there was still a small amount of suspicion that remained with Ivan regarding Albert.

Albert responded. "All materials that leave or arrive here must go through me. There is no way that I know of that anyone else can make or receive a shipment without my knowledge."

"Does that policy go back to the beginning of your tour here?" Ivan asked.

"Yes," Albert responded,

"What types of shipments have left here with your knowledge?" Ivan asked.

"Nearly nothing of significance has left here but I have had many equipment shipments received. Even your computers and laboratory equipment and also Bechert's and Topolski's have been incoming." Albert responded.

"What is done with any outdated equipment and even the old equipment removed when the facility was modernized a couple of years ago," Ivan asked.

"We had accumulated a large amount of scrap equipment a couple of years ago, before you arrived. Bechert and Topolski suggested that we dump that scrap into the sea at the waterfront."

"Did you leave it at the beach, or did you have a boat take it out and dump it?" Ivan asked.

"Now that you mention it, Topolski had arrangements made to have a barge come in and pick up the scrap equipment," Albert recalled somewhat puzzled. "That was the only time he ever got involved in anything that was not technical. As you know we keep access to the beach very well controlled and that was the last time that there had been any breach of that security, but we didn't consider it a breach at that time."

Ivan decided to take Albert into his confidence. "If someone wanted to have that scrap or a portion of it sent to Pakistan, could that be accomplished by water?"

"Not really," Albert responded. "The coastline along the Sea of Oman is very carefully monitored, but there is a small port just south of here where I suppose something could have been unloaded for ground shipment to Pakistan. The port is too small to be monitored so it would be easy to make a quick drop there. How does Pakistan come into the equation, Ivan?" Albert asked.

Ivan decided that if he was going to work with Albert, he needed to be honest with him. "I have information that some time before I arrived here several drums of liquid were sent to Pakistan from this facility. From Pakistan the drums were sent to central Iran and also to Iraq. I believe those drums contained the lethal gas that Bechert and Topolski had developed. There have been rumors that the Iraq leaders have been killing thousands of their people with lethal gas. The gas used might have been the gas developed here by Bechert and Topolski. If that is true, we need to get hard evidence of that theory. Albert, do you ever get access to the laboratories of Bechert and Topolski. If they developed that gas, they would certainly still have evidence of the gas in their labs, possibly some small test vials or maybe even additional drums for future shipment. If we could find that evidence, we could blow the whole scheme open." Albert responded, "I'll have to think about that. I suppose I could come up with a reason to enter the laboratory, but to have time to look around, I'm not sure. I will get back to you on this. Meanwhile, here is another group of tapes for you to send to your people. I will return the tapes that you have to their original spots. Have you heard anything about the original tapes?"

"No, I have not," Ivan responded. "I knew that it would take some time to wade through many tapes before something might pop up. The first few tapes were only a start."

CHAPTER 30

AT ANDREWS AIR Force Base in Washington, Colonel Overton had assembled his new team for a preliminary briefing prior to their departure for Saudi Arabia. The team appeared ready for their new and exciting assignments, wherever those assignments would take them.

Overton began his briefing. "Gentlemen, this assignment is a new experiment in Special Operations intelligence gathering and combat operations. We have tentatively been given a full plate of different assignments that will take a special type of soldier to complete successfully. That's why each of you has been selected for assignment to this special team, as is also the case with me. We each have proven our loyalty to the cause of freedom, we have served in a system that has in the past has been seriously restricted by politically correct decision and guidelines. Now we have been given rules of engagement that will permit us to do what is necessary for successful completion of our missions. This is new and exciting especially since we are really citizen soldiers, not restrained by long-standing politically developed rules.

"With these new rules comes an awesome responsibility to act smart at all times and not let our emotions get away from us or in the way of mission success. The entire strength of the United States government is behind us but even with that power, mistakes cannot be covered up. Every mission and every move that we make needs to be a no bullshit action with perfection at every turn.

"We are about to depart for a city named Jedda, in Saudi Arabia. Jedda is on the southwestern border of the country near the Red Sea. The CIA also has a safe installation in Ad-Dammam which is on the northeast border, near the Persian Gulf. These two locations were chosen for us because they will give us fairly easy access to Africa and the critical regions of the Middle East. The US has good diplomatic relations with Saudi Arabia but the country, although completely controlled by the royal family, has many different political factions in that family that are often at odds with each other. We operate with trust toward the country leaders, but always with suspicion and caution that trust of that type can change in an instant.

"Both of these cities have good airports. We will have ready access to a helicopter and also a small jet that can carry our entire team. Hank Farber, one of your first tasks will be to check out in both vehicles since you will most often be our pilot.

"The first days and possible weeks of our presence in Saudi Arabia you will be doing special training, mostly language and culture. I have initially divided the team into two segments based on what I know at this time. These segments will sometimes operate independently and sometimes together. Hank Farber and I will take on an effort dealing with the African nuclear program. Mike Atwater, Chris Jenkins and Ashiem Povac will work on the oil corruption and Iranian arms situation. We will train together at first so that we can easily assist each other if and when needed. "The CIA has reviewed the operatives at both of their sites that I mentioned. All hands are aware that we are coming, and we will be considered the senior combat operatives at each installation for purposes of specific assignments. The on-site agents will provide us with whatever information we need but they are not fully aware of our specific assignments and they are not to be made aware by us. Their purpose is to provide us with whatever we need to succeed.

"This initial trip will be a long one and you will each be given a rather detailed briefing package. The long flight will give you a leg up on reading the material. The package also contains details about each of you so that you can get to know each other's background and experience in advance. Once we board the aircraft gentlemen the real work starts, so let's start acting like a combat team.

When the team arrived at the Jeddah airport in Saudi Arabia, they were met by the senior CIA operative in that area and taken by truck to their new outpost outside of the city. As most compounds of this type, its external appearance was run down and it would appear to a passer-by that the building was unoccupied. The facility was off a very rough road that appeared to be rarely traveled. Inside, however, the living arrangements were comfortable, and all of the visible electronic and radar equipment was up to date and appeared to be functioning. Colonel Overton was detained at the Jeddah airport for an unexpected briefing before being transported to the compound. When he later arrived there, he called the team together for another, more detailed briefing.

"Gentlemen," he started, "there is already an alteration to our plans. You will have a couple of days to unpack and get settled and finish reading all of the material that you probably didn't finish on the plane. Instead of breaking the assignment into two pieces as originally planned, we will initially operate as one team and we will soon travel to South Africa. There have been some changes in the situation there that need our attention. These last-minute changes are probably going to be routine for us so we should get used to them.

"For many years, the South African government has been doing active research into weapons of mass destruction, including nuclear, biological and chemical. The country has been a signatory of the Biological Weapons Convention since 1975. Back in 1970, the US government established a program for the Peaceful Nuclear Explosions program (PNE). The South Africans joined that effort with the stated objective of using the technologies developed for their mining industry. These peaceful uses are always the published goals but usually lead to some form of weapons development." "It has been determined that the government's efforts have secretly grown beyond the original stated goals. A couple years ago the South African government started working with Israel, trading them 50 tons of South African uranium in return for 30 grams of tritium. Their apparent intent was to work with Israel on the development of a ballistic missile and word now has it that they have built at least six nuclear bombs that are being stored in an abandoned building in Beta-Beta a few miles North of Pretoria.

"They have also been working with nuclear experts from Pakistan on techniques for uranium enrichment.

"Our government has issues South Africa a stern warning about their nuclear development program and they continue to deny that their objectives include development of such a weapon. We now know however that their plans are moving forward.

"President Reagan has informed Israel that their cooperation with South Africa must be limited to peaceful use of nuclear power. Israel has indicated that they will cooperate. Most of our leaders in Washington believe that we can take the Israel government at their word.

"We understand that the six bombs that exist have not had their warheads activated but their uranium enrichment program is continuing despite our government's warnings. Our assignment is to see to it that there is a major accident at the enrichment facility that completely destroys it and also to destroy the six bombs that are in storage.

"Our government does not believe that the South African government has the money or the will to start over with this program so these two incidents will most likely result in the termination of their weapons programs.

"Our people in Pretoria will give us what they have on the two facilities, but we will have to gather the needed intelligence ourselves in order to develop our action plan.

"I have ordered satellite photos of both facilities so we can study them prior to going in-country. The Israeli's are also going to send us more detailed information that they have particularly on the enrichment facility and the process being used there. While doing our job, we really don't want to make a mistake and set off a major nuclear explosion.

"We will study whatever information we receive over the next few days and begin our planning process.

"The CIA leadership believes that it would be better all-around if there is no knowledge of this team's presence in the country so current plans are to enter South Africa through Mozambique. In that part of the world, money will get you all kinds of cooperation and those arrangements are being made now with elements of the Mozambique government.

"When our assignment has been completed, we want it to look like the carnage was caused by Angola rebels who have been outspoken about South Africa having nuclear weapons. We are arranging to have explosives known to be used by Angola's rebels and we will be sure to leave a good deal of evidence behind.

"As soon as I receive the intelligence from the sources cited, we can gather to formulate our plan. In the meantime, start getting prepared and do as much reading as you can.

What Colonel Overton did not tell the team was that this mission was to be a prototype of their future assignments which would involve getting into a country undetected, carrying out an important assignment and exiting quickly without leaving behind any incriminating evidence of American involvement. It would be important because of the make-up of this team that the existence of the team must never be made public. For each of their assignments, they would try to leave enough evidence behind that could point a finger at some other culprit. With all of the strife throughout the world, it seems that there are opposition groups to nearly every regime in power in every country. Some of these opposition groups are more violent than others.

Overton continued, "Rebels and radicals in the areas that we will be operating have no value for human life, either theirs or others. If any of us are captured, certain death will be a reality, probably by be-heading. That is the reality of our new world gentlemen, that why our rules of engagement must reflect the same principles. The only good opposition is a dead opposition so treat all enemies accordingly."

CHAPTER 31

I VAN WAS STARTING to think that maybe life was getting too complicated for him. He was faking his way through his assignment, continuing to run hundreds of computer iterations each day on the project, while at the same time significant information was being collected that could blow the whole program wide open. Meanwhile, he had still not yet received an answer from Anna about her ability to get a message out of the facility without the CIA becoming aware of it. That was his first test of her loyalty to him and possible connections that she had outside American channels. If she had resources that could get information out, then she probably could also have assisted in getting the lethal gas out of the facility or at least she may have known about those shipments. He felt that he could not wait any longer for her response. Now it was time for a second test of her loyalty. They met again that evening and Ivan requested that the meeting be in his quarters.

"Why are we meeting in your apartment?" Anna asked as she entered Ivan's quarters. "We usually have our personal conversations and activities in my apartment."

"Tonight, it's strictly business," Ivan started. "Some time ago, I asked you if you knew of any way that I could get a message to my son without our people becoming aware of it. I am not permitted any personal contacts and I need to communicate some important information to him."

"Yes, Ivan, I remember that," Anna answered. "I have found no such channel out of this place. I haven't talked to you about that because I continued thinking of other possibilities, but they all were dead ends."

This gave Ivan some degree of comfort. If she was still active with the Russians, she would certainly have had access to channels in that area, but if she was smart, she probably would not leak that to Ivan.

Now Ivan was about to take a giant step with Anna and approach an area that until now they had avoided.

"Can we talk about Topolski, and your relationship with him," Ivan asked.

Anna made no outward sign of annoyance when Topolski's name came up. She simply hesitated a long time before she answered.

"My personal activities are considered off limits in our relationship Ivan, "She responded. "But we, you and I, have developed a closeness that has probably changed that now. When I was sent here as part of the original American team, my role was to gather information by using whatever means were available to me. You know that my technical skills are limited, but my sexual skills are still sharp, are they not, Ivan?" She smiled when she mentioned her sexual abilities, referring to her sexual encounters with Ivan.

"I suppose I can vouch for that," Ivan responded, smiling.

"I played Toploski and at times Bechert through sexual experiences. Bechert was stone cold and there was nothing that I believed I could get from him, so I eventually cut that relationship off. Topolski was another matter. I actually grew fond of him, and I believed he returned that fondness. We had actually talked of plans to leave this facility together when his work was done and run off somewhere to live in peace. That possibility appealed to me. In all of this there was no political relationship.

When you arrived here, that relationship changed. Topolski grew cold to me and withdrew from any conversations of our future. Eventually I realized that he really didn't care about me in the same way I cared about him. Without saying a word to each other, we rapidly grew apart."

Ivan interrupted, "Did he ever talk at all about the work he did here before you arrived here, work that was not connected with this project?"

This time Anna reacted to that question. Her face got slightly red and she squirmed a little in her seat. In a breaking low voice Anna responded.

"He never really discussed the details, but I knew that he and Bechert had been working on something very big. Any time the conversation came close to that subject, he quickly changed the subject. I reported this to my contacts back home, but nothing ever came of it."

"You reported that to our people?" Ivan asked.

"Yes, I did, on several occasions," she answered. "No one back home seemed to think it was important I guess since they never asked me to dig any deeper, so I didn't dig at all, I just continued to get friendlier with Topolski. There was a great deal of corruption within the CIA in those times. Many of the in-place operatives were taking bribes from several sources at the same time to work both sides of the road, sometimes even three sides. This part of the world is very complicated and the Administration that was in place in the US at that time didn't have any oversight into CIA activities. Oil money flowed through this part of the world very freely and there was little accounting of it anywhere." The oil cartel was paying big money, often funneling it through the operatives to highly place politicians to keep American oil subsidies alive and well and to help keep the price of oil where the cartel wanted it." "Basically, what you are saying is that the Carter Administration didn't give a damn to try to find out what was going on?" Ivan responded.

"That's right, absolutely right," Anna replied.

"Getting back to Topolski," Ivan asked, "do you remember his ever talking about Pakistan and any dealings that he might have had with that government?"

"I don't remember Pakistan ever coming up in conversation," Anna replied. "Why the sudden interest in Topolski?"

This was the moment Ivan felt he had to take a leap of faith with Anna. He began, "I believe that Topolski and Bechert have developed a very highly lethal gas. I believe they perfected that weapon of mass destruction here in this facility and that they gave it to the Iranian and Iraqi governments. I believe the gas is being used or has been used to kill thousands of people in recent years as part of an ethnic cleansing program. I believe that they found a connection between that work and the drug that we were supposedly developing here and we were dragged here innocently to unknowingly get the United States involved in the whole mess if it ever became known that the Germans and Russians had developed such a weapon." Ivan watched the expression on Anna's face as he told her his theory. It was an expression of shock, but possibly not the shock that he expected. With a slight smile, Anna responded. "I think you are on the right track, Ivan. There were a few times when I was intimate with Topolski that he allowed me into his laboratory. He had collected many vials of liquid that he kept lined up near his desk as if they were a collection of his. They were all labeled with a number but the numbers were not in sequence so I took a couple of them, feeling that they would never be missed. Since the CIA people didn't seem interested, I never passed the vials on to them for analysis, but I still have them in safe keeping. Later, when the drug program was initiated, he started another collection of vials of the drug. I also collected a couple of those vials, feeling that I might someday use the vials to my own advantage." Ivan couldn't control his excitement. "Wow, Anna, you have what I need to blow this whole program open," Ivan shouted. "Can you give me one of each of the vials?"

Anna hesitated. "Not so fast, Ivan. Those vials are my security. I believed that someday they would be worth a lot of money in the right hands. I'm not sure I want to give up that security."

"If I promised you a new life, one that would permit you to live out your life in quiet solitude with me, would you consider giving me the vials?"

Ivan proceeded to tell Anna the whole story about his secluded complex in Canada that was nearly ready for his occupancy. He told her about his plan with Albert and he now included her in his future plans. He still had that lingering suspicion about her, but it was now worth the risk.

"I even have the antidote for the drug," Ivan excitedly responded. "I had the information for that antidote sent to my Canadian facility when I sent them the information about the small nuclear power generators. With the right plan we can have this whole program destroyed. We can pass the evidence along to our people and live a very comfortable life together. I wanted to make sure my son knew where that critical information was in case something happened to me." Ivan had never thought of a future with Anna but if that could give his plan a better chance of success, why not, he thought.

"This is so big that you will understand why I need some time to think about it. I will certainly give you one of each vial. The rest of the plan needs some thought on my part. I hope you understand, Ivan," Anna concluded as she made some very seductive motions toward Ivan.

"Not tonight, Anna." Ivan ended the conversation. "Not tonight." He opened the door to let her out of his apartment.

He quickly sat and wrote it all in a report. If Anna provided him the vials, he would call Farhad the next day to transmit the report and the vials of evidence. He also would tell Albert that he no longer needed him to find a way into Topolski's laboratory. Once this was all accomplished, he would have to simply continue his work as if nothing had happened until he received a response from Admiral Farber with further instructions. There was however one open item on Ivan's list, he needed to have another meeting with Topolski and Bechert to settle their little spat about the future of the program. If Ivan was right, there would be no future for the program but until he received a plan from Admiral Farber, he would have to act as if the program would be carried on to its conclusion. Actually, this would be his big chance to let loose on the two scientists again. Each time he had done it before, he felt this surge in self-satisfactions that he had rarely felt in his life.

When Ivan finished his rather lengthy report to Admiral Farber, he sat back and thought for a long time about the events of the last few days. He might have been a brilliant scientist, but never in his career did he have to deal with so many potentially important and dangerous situations at one time. Logic, facts, and data were always the important factors that would lead his to a conclusion as a scientist. Now he was confronted with a situation where his inherent suspicions were confusing his ability to put all of the facts together, leading him to a rational decision. Advice from Washington was very slow and gave him little clue as to the direction to follow. The more he thought about all of this, the more concerned he became Complicating all of this, Ivan was still not completely sure that he could trust anyone around him. He had taken Farhad, Anna, and Albert Brokow into his confidence and all of their actions were pointing to loyalty on their part. But Ivan was never able to find a way to shake those words that his father left him with, not to trust those who befriended him but to always suspect their motives.

Farhad was his most recent ally and he recently provided him with very important information about the shipment of materials out of the facility. But there was still an awful lot about Farhad that Ivan was not sure about. What were his activities during the long periods when he was not called to service by Ivan? Why did he have such apparent freedom outside the facility within the surrounding Iranian community?

As for Albert Brokow, Ivan felt that he had worked smartly on that relationship, letting it grow slowly over time. But Albert was still a Russian and being paid by the Russians to manage this secret facility. Ivan kept remembering that Albert had told him that he was very happy with this assignment and was looking forward to continuing that work for a long time in the future. Now he had agreed to jump to Ivan's team with what seemed to be very little convincing.

As for Anna, Ivan felt that she was his most dangerous ally. She was Russian born and American educated and her father was once very well-placed within the Communist establishment. The CIA had recruited her for this assignment but even that agency was not sure that she was not acting as a double agent. His relationship with Anna had taken a new twist over the past months, driven mostly by their sexual involvement. The emotions of that relationship were new to Ivan and that made him even more suspicious of her motives. He was much older than Anna and did not consider himself the kind of personality that would be attractive to a person like Anna. The only time that Ivan lost his suspicions of Anna were during their sexual exploits and he realized that those times might simply be temporary distractions for both of them. Ivan had rationalized that Anna, being younger and very attractive, had emotional desires that needed to be fulfilled and at this point in this remote setting, he was able to fulfill those desires. But could he really trust her. He had recently told her some very important information about his suspicions about the work of Topolski and Bechert. He was now feeling that may have been a mistake. But she had also shared some valuable information with him and provided him with two vials from Topolski's laboratory which he had forwarded to Washington for evaluation. Those vials could break the case wide open for him if they contained samples of the gas that was being developed.

But were they as valuable as he expected them to be? He had not received any response from Washington about the vials, so it was too early to tell.

Ivan decided to slow everything down a bit. He had provided his apparent new allies with a great deal of information about his suspicions. Perhaps if he just backed away from his suspicions for a while and appeared to simply do his job, he might see some reactions that would help him with his concerns.

That's exactly what Ivan did. He decided to hold off for a while with his planned confrontation of Topolski and Bechert and watch them a little more closely to see if they might suspect him in any way. If any of the three associates that Ivan now considered his allies were actually his enemies, there would be some noticeable reaction from the other two scientists. This would simply be another test of Ivan's three trusted associate and it would be worth a little more time to watch individual reactions.

CHAPTER 32

BACK IN SAUDI Arabia, the tactical team began dividing up specific information that was needed to prepare an effective plan of attack on this assignment. Hank Farber selected a small airport at Limpopo located on the South West border of Mozambique, only a stone's throw from the South African border. The airport was only manned when specific government activities were planned, and the runway was long enough to accommodate the jet that the team would be using. The trip from Jedda to Limpopo was nearly 3500 miles and the plane could carry enough fuel to get them there but not enough to get them back. He would have to figure a way to re-fuel for the return trip.

Farber determined that the US had a CIA outpost in Botswana and if he could have them arrange for fuel on the way into Mozambique, he could make a slight detour north on the way into Mozambique and pass through Angola. Although this stop was out of the way, it would give him enough fuel for the round trip and possibly permit the team to create a trail through Angola, further supporting the plan to leave evidence of Angola involvement in the plan.

Meanwhile, Mike Atwater was planning the ground operation. He had received the satellite photos of the two facilities near Beta Beta and he was convinced that the sparsely populated area would permit fairly easy access, especially if the operation was conducted at night. He also contacted the agents at Botswana and made arrangements for them to supply some Angola rebel clothing and as many explosives as possible with Angola markings. Since he didn't exactly trust the reliability of these Angola weapons, he also ordered an adequate supply of more reliable Israeli explosives. Almost anything but US identity would be sufficient. Colonel Overton along with other team members was making arrangement to have two vehicles with Angola markings waiting at the airport in Limpopo.

The plan was to make the strike a coordinated event, destroying both the bomb storage facility and the enrichment facility at the same time. The problem that remained in the plan was the security that was present at the enrichment facility. That problem was yet to be solved. The team needed more detailed intel about the movements in and around the enrichment facility to complete their plan so they needed to use the operatives in Pretoria to provide that information. Colonel Overton decided to kick that problem back to Washington to avoid any local leaks of the plans that were being developed. The team would continue to sharpen their plans but would also now be in a waiting mode for information from Washington.

In the detailed planning that the team was doing, it was obvious that the operation would have to span at least two days and possibly three because of the distances involved and also because nearly every activity would have to be conducted at night.

To help avoid detection, the team decided that the explosives would have to be triggered by long duration timing devices, possible as long as 12 hours. This would give the team time to plant the explosives and possibly be out of the country when the explosives were triggered. If that timing could be achieved, it would significantly reduce the risk of detection.

As the team leaders continued their planning, both Chris Jenkins and Ashiem Povac continued reviewing the satellite photos that they had been provided. They decided to time sequence the photos to see if there were any routine occurrences that became obvious that might help with the security problem. That effort soon paid dividends because they determined that every day at 0630 a truck arrived at the security gate bringing in relief workers for those workers who had worked the previous shift. The truck was routinely admitted without a search. The workers would depart the truck and as the shift workers changed, those who had worked were loaded on to the truck and taken out of the facility, again without any search. This seemed to offer an opportunity to get someone in and out of the facility but to use this plan, that person would have to remain inside the facility for a 12-hour period without detection. Since there are not a lot of people working in the building, they would also likely know each other, making this type plan very risky, but it was a possibility.

Jenkins decided to open up the area of view of the satellite photos in an attempt to see if he could determine the point of origin of the truck and sure enough, he determined that the truck originated at a garage area at the outskirts of Pretoria. It appeared that there was only one driver who arrived at that area a few minutes before the departure time. The driver appeared to have no contact with the passengers who were lined up ready to board the truck. There also seemed to be little or no contact with the truck driver. He simple moved the truck to the pickup area, loaded the workers, and drove off. The truck driver was the vulnerable person in this operation, and it appeared possible to develop a plan to disable the driver for a long enough period to substitute two team members in the cab of the truck. The driver would be visible, and the passenger would be hidden. Since there was no search of the truck, it should be easy to place two team members in the cab, possibly leaving one behind to plant the explosives. That member would have to remain undetected in the plant until the truck returned 12 hours later.

The driver of the pick-up truck would have to be the same team driver so two drivers would have to be disabled long enough pull off the swap.

The team had gathered to compare their individual ideas and Chris Jenkins asked the first and most critical question. "Colonel Overton, what are the rules of engagement here? The plan Ashien and I are developing required that we disable two Africans. Also, if our plan is used, there will probably be at least ten workers in the facility when the explosives are set off meaning that they will likely all be killed. Do we disable the two drivers permanently and do we try to save any of the workers?" Colonel Overton thought for a moment. Not because he didn't know the answer but because he wanted to use the right words. "Gentlemen, as Americans, we always try to avoid the deaths of innocent men and women. But remember, this is supposed to look like an Angolan rebel attack. Those people are terrorists and they have little or no value for life. If we are to make the whole plan work, there is to be no evidence of hesitant to prevent loss of life. That would be the first hint that Americans were involved. We will do whatever is required to protect all aspects of the mission. Is that clear to all of you?"

The group answered in unison, "Yes, sir!." Colonel Overton continued. "We will need a few more days to pull all aspects of this operation together. In the meantime, I want all of us to brush up on Dutch, Afrikaans, and Portuguese. It might be helpful to be able to use a few phrases in those languages in case you are overheard. The Dutch Afrikaans is a dialect of many South Africans and Portuguese in one of many languages spoken by Angolans. Just a few common phrases will do to help with the deception.

"Farber, the only passenger type jet that Angola has is an Embraer CRT 135. That is a much larger airplane that we will be using but you should try to have the markings make the plane look as much like the Embraer as possible. Get the identifier of that aircraft in case you get picked up on someone's radar and are required to report. Create a flight plan for yourself that takes in all possibilities of detection. I'm sure I don't have to tell you about flying but be sure you are familiar with the terrain at all points because you may have to do a lot of low altitude flying. Your A-6 Intruder flying experience should help you in that regard, since that aircraft was an all-weather low altitude night attack aircraft." Farber responded. "By the time we deploy, I will have our aircraft down pat. I have been waiting a long time to strap a jet aircraft around me again sir, this will be a piece of cake I assure you."

After several days of planning, Colonel Overton's team was ready for their first test as a Special Operation civilian team. They had each mentally rehearsed their individual jobs based on all of the intelligence information provided them by various CIA operatives in several countries. Hank Farber had honed his qualification in the jet that they would use, and he had developed several alternate flight plans to cover many circumstances that might develop.

All of the ground operations had been well rehearsed and all of the material and supplies that they would need were in place. Even though this mission was the first for this newly created team, they all felt confident that they could pull it off without a hitch.

They had prepared all of the explosives and timing devices that would be used and nearly everything that they took with them could be identified as Angola rebel material, right down to the shirts and stockings that they would wear.

The trip from Jedda to Limpopo was uneventful including the refueling stop in Botswana. Most of Hank Farber's previous flying was done under strict navigation control procedures so he was a little surprised how little air traffic control was present in the areas that they would cross. That made his job much easier.

They landed at Limpopo just before dark as planned and the two vehicles that they needed were there for them as planned. The trip to Beta Beta would require that they drive all night under road conditions that were less than optimal but they made do. They arrived at the garage area near Pretoria at 0500 so they had plenty of time to make last minute preparations.

Mike Atwater and Chris Jenkins would handle the enrichment facility which required the most critical timing. Colonel Overton and Ashiem Povac would handle the bomb storage facility. Their efforts would need to be delayed nearly 12 hours to ensure that the explosions would be carried out at the same time.

Chris Jenkins was to be the truck driver and Mike Atwater would enter the enrichment facility and set the explosives. He would them have to remain hidden for 12 hours until the truck returned for him. Both explosives were to be delayed another 12 hours so that the entire team would be back out of the country and on their way back to Saudi Arabia when the blasts took place.

The first leg of the plan went off smoothly. Atwater disabled the truck driver and the worker pick up and drop off went smoothly. Atwater entered the enrichment facility with no interruptions and quickly found the areas where he had planned to plant the explosives. He then found a storage closet and hid there until the 1800 planned pickup which also went smoothly. Colonel Overton and Ashiem Povac found the bomb storage facility empty of any guards, just as their intel had indicated. Overton made an unplanned check to ensure that the bombs had not been activated. The team certainly did not want to set off an unplanned nuclear event. As expected, the bombs were in a storage mode of operation.

At 1830 both teams met at their planned assembly point. They left a few items behind for Angola identity and drove the seven hours back to their aircraft and departed the region just as planned.

By the time they got back to their quarters at Jetta, the news was already well broadcast that Angolan rebels had blown up a storage facility and the enrichment facility at Beta Beta. The Angola government of course denied that claim, but with all the internal strife throughout Africa, neither announcement created much of a stir internationally.

In Washington however, Admiral Farber was pleased with this first experiment with the new special operations team. They had performed exactly as planned and left no trail behind that would implicate the United States in any way in those events. Admiral Farber personally briefed President Reagan's Chief of Staff on the events so as to create a situation of plausible deniability for the president.

This was a fine success for Admiral Farber's new team, but it paled in comparison to the news that he was receiving from his team in Iran.

The CIA analysts had found some very incriminating information on the recent series of tapes sent to them by Ivan Schwarz. Ivan's most recent report concerning the shipment of barrels through Pakistan to Iran and Iraq was also a bombshell. The vials that Ivan had sent contained only colored water and that puzzled Admiral Farber, but he had to let Ivan know what he had learned and he had the information sent to Ivan through the encrypted system, asking Ivan to continue probing for more definitive data. Admiral Farber's message also cautioned Ivan to proceed with greater caution now. Just a little more solid evidence would be all that was needed to proceed with action against the Russians and the Germans.

CHAPTER 33

ALTHOUGH IVAN HAD decided to slow things down with his personal investigations outside the primary assignment, it wasn't obvious that anything had slowed down with others that were involved. Ivan got an unscheduled visit from Farhad late one afternoon. Farhad told Ivan that he had been contacted and questioned by operatives elsewhere in Iran about the information that he had gathered concerning the shipment of those drums from Pakistan to Iran and Iraq. The reports that Ivan had been sending to Washington had apparently triggered several parallel investigations about these drums.

Farhad was a little confused about these events. "I'm not exactly sure who to trust in this country," Farhad started. "Several CIA agents have been working both sides here in Iran for many years and they have become very wealthy playing that role. I told them only what I told you but I do have additional information about the drums that you can pass along to your sources.

"Independent militants made two shipments of the drums from a small port on the Pakistan border very near Iran on the Gulf of Oman. On both occasions they moved the drums by land vehicles to Yazd, a small airport in the central Iranian desert where they remained for some time. On several different occasions, a small aircraft with Russian markings would take a drum and depart eastward toward Iraq. From what I have determined, some of the drums may still be at Yazd. Rumor has it that the Russians have made an arrangement with some faction within Iran, probably not the government, to sell the material to whomever would pledge their allegiance to the new Russian cause, whatever that is. There are dozens of militant groups throughout the Middle East that would pay big money to get their hands on WMD material, and as you know, money in this part of the world flows like water.

"As I said, I did not pass this information along to those who contacted me because I know that your Washington connections are trustworthy. I trust that you will pass the information along to them for action."

Ivan actually hugged Farhad as he answered him. "This is extremely important news, Farhad, I think you know that. I also appreciate that you have enough trust in me to use my channels of communication. I do have one question. Do you know the names or other identities of those agents who questioned you? Perhaps it's time to start finding out who is really on our side in this forsaken country." Farhad handed Ivan a note containing two names. "I thought you would ask me that so I wrote their names here so I wouldn't make any mistake about that. They also gave me a contact number to reach them if I had additional information. I also wrote that number here. I will make no contact unless I hear from you to do it."

Ivan was now fairly confident that Farhad could be completely trusted. This was the first time that he felt a sense of confidence that he had at least one ally to depend on.

As soon as Farhad left, Ivan prepared another report that he sent to Washington via his secure link. He was sure that this new information would trigger a rapid response. He could do nothing but wait for that response.

Ivan tried to establish some degree of normalcy with his activities, but it appeared that the odds were against him in that regard. He received a message from Albert Brokow indicating that they needed a meeting as soon as possible. Was this an important discovery by Albert or some other problem that had arisen?

When Ivan entered Albert's quarters, something was different. The place seemed messy and disorganized and Albert looked like he hadn't slept in days.

"What's up, Albert?" Ivan asked.

When Albert responded, it was obvious that he had been drinking. His words seemed broken with emotion and he was obviously very upset. "Ivan, we need to have a very serious discussion about your suspicions about Topolski and Bechert. I believe from what you have shared with me that this whole mess is about to explode and if and when it does, you are going to find that I have not been entirely honest with you about what I know and what I have experienced." Tears began to flow down Albert's cheeks.

"My Russian upbringing causes me to be very distant with most people with whom I associate. Perhaps that's why I got this job. But in your case, it has been different. You showed me a friendship that I had not previously experienced and I believed that your actions were very sincere, and I accepted that friendship willingly.

"When you took me into your confidence about your suspicions about Topolski and Beckert, I didn't know how to handle my response and I found myself misleading you about what I knew and what I had done. You offered me a way out of this place that showed me your sincerity and I responded as though I would support you in your efforts. That was misleading on my part and if this whole thing blows up, I will eventually be implicated in some of the activities of the two scientists.

"I knew exactly what those scientists were doing when they first arrived here. I processed all of the materials that they needed, and it wasn't difficult to determine their motives and goals. A year or two after their arrival, they indicated to me that they had completed the first phase of their program and they needed to ship several containers of their product out of the facility, but that shipment had to be handled with great secrecy. I arranged for the shipment by barge as part of the disposal of the computer equipment when the upgrade was completed.

"But my knowledge goes further back than that. Before they announced that the first phase of their work was complete, they told me that they were bringing in a few prisoners from Russia and that they would be testing some of the material on these men and women. Ten men and three women were smuggled in from the ocean side of the facility. Within two weeks, all thirteen were dead and their bodies dumped into the Persian Gulf. Before their disposal they were all processed in such a way that they would never be recovered or identified. It was a horrible series of events that has given me nightmares ever since.

"At that point I knew that I never again would be permitted to leave this facility and I was assured by my government that in fact that was the case. I simply conditioned myself to those events and that reality. In effect, I was a prisoner here and I would remain a prisoner for the remainder of my life.

"When you came along, I was confused. The Americans who were here before you stayed only a short time. They seemed to be under the false narrative that they were part of some cooperative effort to development a peaceful weapon. I don't know why they left only that their departure was sudden, but they left that woman behind. That confused me until I realized that she was here simply to gather information on the activities of the two scientists.

"I was told that you were assigned to this activity as part of a three-country team that was researching possible uses of a drug that would be used for peaceful purposes. I had been around these people long enough to realize that you were only a pawn to establish an American role in the illegal activities if those activities were ever revealed to the world.

"Every time you and I grew closer, I became more ashamed of how I was misleading you. Now I can no longer carry this secret. You have obviously figured out what has been going on here. I'm sure that the organizers of this scheme thought that you were simply another egg head nerd scientist who was too innocent to discover the truth. But you proved to be something quite different from that. Your suspicion of everything and everyone has permitted you to reveal the truth. I believe that you will soon break this operation wide open and when that happens, those of us who knowingly participated will all be killed to prevent us from disclosing needed information. Ivan I am sorry for what I have done to you and I will forever regret that. I will not ask you to forgive me, only to try to understand my position in this whole scheme." As Ivan listened to Albert's story, he noticed a revolver sitting on the table in the kitchen area. Next to the gun was a half-full bottle of vodka. He knew that Albert was the final key to information that the government needs to close this case. He could not let Albert get away from him.

Ivan took Albert's hand, looked him straight in the eye and spoke softly. "Albert, I understand everything that you have told me, and I know that it took a lot of guts for you to come clean with me on this. The information that you gave me is the most important evidence that my government needs to close this case properly. I see from looking into the kitchen, what you are planning and I beg you not to take that route. Your knowledge is so valuable to the United States that I am sure that I can make a deal for you that will assure you your freedom in our country. Please give me a day or two to get that assurance and we can both come away from this place with a clear conscience. Can you do that, Albert?

"Only for your sake will I cooperate. I know if I make a foolish move it will put your life in danger and that's the last thing that I want to happen. Tell me what you want me to do and then we will move forward."

Ivan took the gun, poured two glasses of vodka, and they clicked their glasses in agreement.

Ivan rushed to get to his quarters to send this latest information to Washington. He knew that Albert's testimony was the key evidence needed to prove beyond any doubt what the Russians and Germans were up to. In his report, he indicated that timing was critical here. If Albert took some foolish action and killed himself out of guilt, there would be little chance to ever get this type of evidence again. Ivan thought of asking Albert to record his confession but believed that it would have much less value than his personal appearance.

Ivan nervously finished his report and clicked it off to Washington. He wanted to stand by his computer and wait for a response, but he realized that it was impossible for decisions to be made that rapidly in Washington due to the severity of the situation.

As he lay in his bed that night, sleep was an impossibility. About midnight, he heard the computer go on and he leaped from bed to see what was coming in.

The message, once decrypted, read: *Prepare yourself for extraction. Requested immunity approved. Action could come within days. Do not alert associate but ensure that she can be extracted.*

CHAPTER 34

AFTER THE SUCCESSFUL completion of their first assignment in South Africa, Colonel Overton had split his team into two parts as originally planned. Mike Atwater and Chris Jenkins were in Israel attempting to get intelligence on the illegal weapon sale to Iran. Ashiem Povac and Hank Farber had already been sent to Iran to investigate a facility in Yazd where some tanks of lethal gas may have been sent. Both of these assignments were for data gathering only and no combat encounters were expected. The plan was to regroup in Ad Dammam in three days to plan additional action. Colonel Overton received an unexpected urgent message to return to Washington immediately for classified briefings. He boarded the first available military transport and left within hours of the message.

When he arrived the CIA headquarters at Langley Va. as directed, he was greeted by Admiral Farber himself and taken to a nearby SCIF.

Inside the SCIF were two people, the Chief of Staff to President Reagan, and the Senior National Security Advisor to the President. Colonel Mark Overton was introduced to both men as a special projects' coordinator for the Director of the CIA, reporting to Admiral Farber.

"Mark," the admiral started, "these two men have been part of a special task force that I established right after President Reagan was elected. There was so much internal corruption throughout the government at that time that I needed a few people that I could trust to carry out some very sensitive assignments that I was given.

"We have been following a special project in Iran that the United States joined under the Carter administration that has now developed into one of the most explosive projects that the CIA has even encountered. President Reagan has a different approach to diplomatic dealings with other important heads of government. He likes to negotiate from a position of strength and power and that power often comes when he has specific information about those governments that they would not like to have made public.

"In this case, the Russian and the German governments have conspired to develop a facility in Iran that has long-standing history. After the Second World War, Russia made a strange deal with Iran to buy a facility on the Persian Gulf that was diplomatically cut away from Iranian territory. Initially the facility was used as a safe haven for many of the important German scientists and political leaders as they fled Germany. Over time many of these scientists and their families remained in this facility to carry our special projects for the Russians and Germans that were not exactly in line with international law. Now some of the offspring of those scientists are still performing this work which is shared by both governments.

"We have determined that in the last few years, two scientists that reside in this facility have developed a very lethal new chemical that in its gaseous state becomes a weapon of mass destruction. There is a good deal of evidence that this gas has been used several times in the Middle East as an ethnic cleansing weapon.

"Chemical warfare, of course, has been outlawed since the end of the First World War but there have been several occasions where it is suspected that it has been used since that time.

"Three years ago, the Carter administration agreed to participate in a cooperative program with the Germans and Russians to develop a drug that could be used as a peaceful weapon to render troops useless in combat. It was thought that in many skirmishes that pop up around the world, this type of drug, if applied properly, could help deter warfare without incurring casualties. The United States naively agreed to participate in this program. What the Russians and Germans were really doing is attempting to drag the United States into a situation where if it was discovered that a WMD was being developed, the US would be implicated and information regarding the whole project would simply disappear from public attention.

"Fortunately for us, the scientist that we sent there to participate was a very suspicious fellow who didn't trust anyone and as time went on, he realized that things were not as they should be with that project.

"At that point my people who were reading his reports brought the situation to my attention and I personally took charge of the program, requiring that all of his reports be sent directly to me after they were decrypted.

"We now are at the point where we have all of the solid proof that we need to pull our people out, hopefully also capturing the two scientists. There is also a female American operative working with our scientist. We suspect that she may be a double agent, but we want her extracted. Our scientist has also converted a Russian man who knows a great deal of factual information about the development of the WMD. He is being given immunity for his cooperation, so he is a very important person to be extracted. I suspect that if there is the slightest hint inside the facility that we are on to the scheme, this man will be killed because of what he knows. We have been evaluating tapes of recordings made over a period of several years. Some of these tapes provide supporting data confirming our beliefs but these tapes pale in comparison to the personal knowledge of the Russian. Second only to our scientist, this Russian is critical to a successful extraction.

"We believe that the poison gas developed by the Russians and the Germans was shipped to a facility in Iran and one or more of the containers may still be there. Colonel Overton, your people are already gathering intel on that location although you did not know that it was connected to this program.

"Mark, now for the shocking news for you and your team, the name of the American scientist that broke this case wide open is Ivan Schwarz. That name might not mean anything to you but is certainly will mean something to one of your teammates. Ivan Schwarz is the father of Mike Atwater, one of your operatives. Mike is aware that his father is somewhere in Iran, but he has no clue that he has been working for us on this project. There are other aspects of Ivan Schwarz' life that are important to us but not related to this assignment. The FBI has been working on that aspect, and you might be read in on it at a later date since it has no connection to the facts of this operation.

"Schwarz has been notified to be prepared for extraction within days. The only other person that is aware of the extraction is the Russian that Schwarz converted. He will provide you with everything we know about the facility including the location of the living quarters and laboratories of the German and Russian scientist. It is not necessary to destroy this facility and others that work there are probably innocent workers who know nothing of the internal goings-on. Once the extractions are made successfully, we will send in a SEAL team to recover the computers of the two scientists before the other residents are aware of what has transpired. We suspect that the Russian government will eventually destroy the facility quietly. What they do with the other workers is their problem, but we suspect that those activities will not be pleasant but are of no concern to us. You will be provided with location information in detail before you return, Mark. The facility is at water's edge on the Persian Gulf so I expect that your planning will involve a water ingress and egress. We will provide you contact information for our operatives in Saudi Arabia, Bahrain, Qatar, the UAE and Oman. They will assist you if you need their help. I will also provide you with detailed satellite photos of the facility and the surrounding area for purposes of your planning.

"One other item, Mark: there is one CIA operative that has been in constant contact with Schwarz as his contact to the outside world. When you decide the exact time of your planned extraction, I will have him notified. We are very concerned about several of the operatives that have been in Iran for a long period of time. We know that some of them are working both sides for the large sums of money that are available to them. That's why we are very cautious of who we keep informed of sensitive operations like this. It's a sad situation, but the previous administration provided little oversight to field operatives as they cut back on security operations. Without oversight and with all the money that flows through the Middle East with no accountability, you can expect that nearly everyone who has been there for a long period of time has taken some of that money. We are trying to make appropriate re assignments, but it is taking a long time to get that job done. Colonel Overton, do you have any questions?" "Only one, sir. Are our rules of engagement different here than on our other assignments?"

"Same rules, Mark. Do what has to be done for a successful mission. Mark, I have a couple more administrative items to go over with you so please come to my office for a few minutes before you leave."

"Yes, sir," Colonel Overton replied as he followed Admiral Farber to his office.

CHAPTER 35

IVAN COULD HARDLY control his excitement after he read the message from Washington. He had gotten the approval for immunity for Albert and there would soon be an extraction. He was not permitted to tell Anna of the planned extraction so the CIA must still have some doubts about her loyalty, and they don't want her tipping anyone off about the extraction. Ivan wanted to share his excitement with Albert who seemed to be waiting in his quarters for some word from Ivan. As Ivan entered Albert's quarters, Albert was waiting nervously for him.

"Great news Albert," Ivan shouted. "They have approved your immunity and a new identity for you and more important our extraction will be coming very soon, perhaps within days."

Albert got up and hugged Ivan. With tears rolling down his cheeks he murmured, "Thank you, Ivan. I am so relieved."

"Just understand," Ivan replied, "you will have to go through a period of intense questioning when you are rescued, but it will be well worth it for you in a long run. You can live the rest of your life without that guilt hanging over you.

"Let's talk a bit about the extraction," Ivan started. "I don't have any details except that we are to be ready at any time now. It could be today or tomorrow; I don't know and I probably won't know until it happens.

"I assume, because of my knowledge of this building and its location that the entry for the extraction will be from the sea. That means that you should make easy entry possible. You have control of that security, don't you?" "Yes, I do, and I can easily kill the security system without anyone knowing it."

"Since I have seen no weapons of any kind in the facility, I don't think that there will be any gun fire. Are there any weapons hidden that I am not aware of, Albert?"

"Not that I am aware of except the pistol that you took from me." "The extraction team will not know who you are and possibly not even recognize me. I assume they will be given a photo of me but not you, so we will have to quickly let them know who we are, and more importantly, where they can find Topolski and Beckert. You can give the leader the room numbers of both men. The extraction will likely be at night so both men will probably be asleep. Better yet maybe I should provide my Washington contact that information too and also the location of our rooms and Anna's. She knows nothing about this, and I have been instructed not to inform her. They apparently are still not completely sure about her loyalty and they don't want to take a chance of her leaking this extraction.

"I think we should travel light. Take only what you really need with you. It might not be a bad idea for both of us to take a few more tapes with us if that does not create a problem.

"It's possible that I may receive another message with specifics about the timing. Maybe when I forward the info about the room locations, I will get more specifics.

"I'm excited, Albert, probably more excited for you and the possibility of a new life for you."

"Again, I thank you, Ivan," Albert responded. "Let's hope this all comes off effectively and none of us is hurt or even killed."

"I second that, Albert." They both parted very excited.

CHAPTER 36

IN AD DAMMAM, Colonel Overton's team had re-assembled for what they thought was a briefing of their findings in their recent travels to Israel and Iran. That was not the case. There was an excitement about Colonel Overton's entry into the briefing room. He quickly asked the team to gather around the table as he spread out a series of charts and photos. "Gentlemen, as usual, things have changed for us, which seems like a regular occurrence. This time our assignment is big, I mean really big, and for one of you it may be the biggest thing you will ever do for the rest of your life.

"Mike, you are aware that your father has been on an assignment somewhere in this part of the world. You were never told what he was doing and where exactly he was located. I can now tell you that he is in Iran and he has performed some of the most important work for our country that he could ever have dreamed of. In the process of doing his job, he stumbled upon information that has very significant international significance.

'His initial work has been prematurely terminated and it is now time for him to leave Iran. Sounds simple doesn't it but it's not that simple. He and two of his associates need to be extracted rapidly and without warning. The facility that he is in also houses two other scientists, one from Germany and the other one from Russia. These two are not friendly's and will not come easily but they are extremely important to us. They are to be considered foreign combatants, but we need them alive. It is possible that they will even try to take their own lives rather than be captured so keeping them alive may be our main challenge.

"These two men should be thoroughly searched to find any kill pills or other apparatus that they may use to take their own lives.

"The building is located here," he said, pointing to a map. The name of the town is Bandar Abbas, but the facility is not legally considered part of Iran. That's a strange situation that is not important to this operation. We will approach the building from the sea in three separate low detection boats that will be launched from a freighter passing south in the Persian Gulf. The Iranians have sloppy radar coverage of this area so detection should not be a problem but for insurance we have arranged for an airborne distraction about 100 miles north of the extraction point to detract any attention from our mission.

"We will make the extraction during the early morning hours when most of the resident will be asleep. Our friendly's will be notified of our arrival in advance but the others will not so you will be given the room numbers of all of the people to be extracted. You may be welcomed into the building by Mike's father. This is the last known photo of him that we have. He will certainly identify himself. The other friendly is named Albert Brokow. He is a Russian but speaks good English. He is completely familiar with the building and can give any directions needed.

"There is also a woman friendly to be extracted. We are not sure of her loyalty, but we are to assume that she is on our side. But be cautious of her. "The two enemy scientists are Dr. Topolski and Dr. Beckert. Both speak and understand English.

"Keep the talking and noise to a minimum. There are other innocent workers in the building who will likely be sleeping. These people are of no interest to us but if they provide any significant resistance to your operation you are to take whatever action is necessary for a successful mission.

"The people we take out will be taken in three different directions to three different locations.

"I will take Ivan Schwarz. That might be confusing to you, Mike, but that's the way it will be handled. Mike and Chris, you will take Brokow and the woman. Hank, you and Ashiem will take the two combatants. All three groups will meet their pickup ship at different points. Here are the coordinates for each of your pickup points. Your pickup will also be a freighter or tanker that will use the coded signal light system for your notification using the standard Alpha Alpha signal. You will respond with Zebra Zebra, so brush up on your Morse code. The three segments of our team will possibly not meet again until we are back in the United States.

"I want you all to study this material immediately because the current plan is to depart tomorrow night for the extraction. We are not aware of any weapons that will be encountered but you will all carry light arms just in case.

"There is one more very important fact. These two unfriendly scientists have been secretly developing a very lethal liquid that in gaseous form is an instant killer. Try to stay away from any liquids during this operation and make sure the two scientists are also kept clear of liquids. "Mike, I want to talk to you privately for a few minutes. The rest of you start getting smart.

"There is actually another aspect of your father's situation that you are partially aware of since you alerted the FBI to the situation. They have gone over your father's money transfers very carefully and his cousins have been committing very serious crimes against him with his money management. They have not been accounting for the rapidly increasing value of gold during the three-year period that they have been managing his money. They are doing the accounting based on the price of gold at the time of the contract signing and they never escalated it to reflect its true value. Because the price of gold has more than tripled during the three-year period, they have embezzled millions of dollars from your father over that period. The FBI has them dead to rights and they are just waiting for your father's return to arrest them. They have committed a very serious crime and they will be put in jail for that, but our people feel that you father should have the opportunity to come face to face with them on this subject. Because of his inherent suspicion of everything and everyone, this is possibly the first time that he ever let his guard down and placed complete trust in family members, thinking that family could always be trusted. The only question is how much money your father will be able to recover from them since they have established a very fancy lifestyle. I suspect that if he wanted, he could get the entire paper business from them as payment for their crimes. That's another subject that he and you can discuss at the right time. I think you know, Mike, that under normal military rules, I would have to exclude you from this operation because of your father's involvement. But we are not military, and our rules permit me to use judgment in this regard. I trust you and believe that you will act accordingly put the mission objectives first and foremost in your mind.' "Yes, sir," Mike replied. "You can depend on me for that."

CHAPTER 37

W HEN IVAN RETURNED to his quarters, he noticed that there was a message indicator on his secure computer. His excitement level, which was already high, rose even further and he found himself fumbling to enter the proper codes to unscramble the information. When he finally was able to read the message, he nearly blacked out with excitement. It read: *System will shut down at 2:00 a.m. tomorrow. Make the proper provisions for this shutdown.*

Ivan knew exactly what this meant. He was being taken out that night at 2:00 a.m. in the morning. He responded,

Understand. Other scientists' room numbers on 4th floor, suites 5 and 6.

Ivan had no idea of the plan for taking him out, but he assumed that they would also want Topolski and Bechert and those were their suite numbers. He would also notify Albert of the timing and his last dilemma was Anna. What the hell should he do about Anna? He had always remained suspicious about her but as time went by, she had gained his trust.

He could simply tell Albert to meet him on the lower floor before 2:00 a.m., but what about Anna? If he told her about this and she wasn't as loyal as he thought, she could warn the others and cause all kinds of problems with the rescue operation. If on the other hand he kept her in the dark, she might be left behind, and he didn't believe that should happen. He had never made her a key factor in any of his reports back to Washington and they might not consider her important enough to save, especially if

Washington had information that conflicted with Ivans feelings about her loyalty. He felt that it would make the rescue easier if he and Albert were waiting on the bottom floor near the beach. He thought, wouldn't it make the plan work better if Anna was also with them. What should he do?

He needed some time to think this out, so he went back to Albert's quarters to notify him of the plan. Actually, Ivan had similar suspicions about Albert but through recent events, he was confident that Albert was totally on his side.

When he got to Albert quarters, he entered quickly and simply told Albert to meet him at the sea-side entrance at 2:00 a.m., no later. "Bring only what you have to and include a few tapes. Have the entrance security off at that time." With no more said, he went back to his quarters and dumped the critical information from his computer on to several discs. He would leave the secure computer open until he left the room for the final time in case there was any last-minute change in plans.

He sat and thought for a while, then decided that he would invite Anna to his room and perhaps he could invite her to stay the night. At least that way he would have her in his control when the time came to leave. That would assure her departure without permitting any time for her to warn others if that was her motive.

When Anna arrived as invited, she seemed a little confused by Ivan's behavior. He seemed nervous to her and they normally met at non-work times in her quarters.

"Is there something wrong, Ivan?" Anna asked.

"Nothing at all," Ivan responded. "I have a nearly full bottle of vodka here and I suddenly felt the urge to share it with you. We haven't had a personal moment in some time, and I felt that tonight might be a good time for that." "You know I'm always ready for that, Ivan, but I have been in the laboratory all day and I need to clean up a little. Is it okay if I use your bath facilities?"

"Certainly, Anna. As a matter of fact, I am in the same condition. Perhaps we could shower together."

"Wow, Ivan," she giggled, "you certainly are in a different mood today. Showering together sounds like a great idea."

"Let's have a drink first," Ivan responded. He wasn't sure of what he had requested. He had in all his years never showered with a woman. How would that work, he wondered, but knowing Anna, he believed that she would lead the way on all of this.

They drank vodka slowly and perhaps because of Ivan's excited state of mind, it had a rapid effect on him.

"To hell with the vodka," Ivan said, "let's hit the shower."

"Again, wow," Anna replied, "you are in a rare mood today."

The shower experience was an event in itself for Ivan. Anna was completely aware of Ivan's lack of sexual history and her shower performance actually sent Ivan into a state that he had never before witnessed. He was spent, exhausted and weak and as they exited the showed into the bedroom, Ivan needed to sit at the edge of the bed for a while to get his head back together. This wasn't the first time Ivan was affected by tension and excitement mixed with alcohol. His head was pounding and the last thing he wanted on this night was to get sick.

They eventually fell back into the bed together with Anna making all of the lead moves. But Ivan simply could not perform. All of the emotions of the day and the knowledge of what tonight would bring along with the unbelievable treatment he received in the shower had taken its toll.

Ivan felt weak and spent but he still had his senses and knew that he couldn't let this situation get out of control. He suggested that they move to the living area to talk for a while until his brain recovered to its normal state.

Within minutes, they began to talk.

Ivan turned to Anna and asked, "What are your intentions when this assignment is completed, Anna?"

She replied, "You made me a proposition a few days ago about going to your hideaway in Vermont with you. Were you serious, Ivan?"

"Of course, I was serious, Anna," Ivan responded, "but you never really responded to my question about that."

"The time was never quite right for a response," Anna said. "I have grown very fond of you Ivan. We have never uttered the word, but I think I am in love with you. I have struggled with that feeling because the two of us have been cooped up in this facility, working very closely together and we have had emotional moments, but I was not sure if my feelings were simply a result of the situation or you really meant something special to me. I have concluded that I really have fallen in love with you. Out in the real world, people might not understand our relationship. You are much older than I, but as time has passed, that age difference has seemed to make little difference, at least to me." Ivan held both of Anna's hands and looked into her eyes. "I have never really known what love felt like. As far back as I can remember, I have been totally dedicated to my job. None of my early experiences in Germany and my early years being raised by my aunt and uncle never exposed me to real love being demonstrated. Also, with the suspicious tendencies that my father left me with, I never allowed myself to get close to anyone, feeling that a closeness would eventually come back to bite me.

"But, when you and I are in one of our emotional moments, I get a different feeling. None of that other stuff seems to matter to me. Is that love, Anna?

"I don't really know Ivan, but I'm willing to take a chance with you that it is."

They embraced and sat there quietly for a few minutes, sipping their drinks.

The mood suddenly changed when Anna asked, "I remember in our recent discussion about the work that the other two scientists were doing, you mentioned to me that you had indeed developed the antidote to the drug we have been developing. Is the true, Ivan?" Ivan was suddenly taken out of his emotional trance with that question. All of his doubts about Anna had suddenly returned. Why the hell is she asking me that question at this time? But he decided to answer it truthfully. "Yes indeed, I have developed a solution to the problem of recovering from the drug. It isn't exactly an antidote, like something that you will inject into a person, it is a process of sort of shocking the brain emotionally, telling the brain to reject the effect of the signals that it is being sent by the nerve where the drug was applied. I have written a complete record of my research on that subject. That is why I got into the subject of human trials with Topolski and Bechert. I know all about the brain and the nervous system from my years of research on neural networks, but to prove my theories in this case I believe that some simple test on human is needed. For some reason the other two scientists object to that type of testing.

"The drug that we have developed here is a relatively simply chemical compound. Its value and danger is in the method of application. If too much of the drug is administered, it could be possible for the individual receiving it to die or at least to never regain memory or even body function. Also, the same effect could be realized if the drug is applied to the wrong area of the body.

"My solution to these possibilities is to pre-condition the brain through simple mental exercises to reject the more dangerous elements of this drug. It's kind of like getting a vaccination against a disease. I believe we can also obtain the same effect on the brain by some fairly simple stimulations of specific nerve endings that can be accomplished in a non-intrusive manner." "That sounds almost revolutionary, Ivan. Do you intend to share that work with the others?"

"I don't think so, Anna," Ivan whispered, they have different motives than I do here."

"Where do you have all of this documented, Ivan?" Anna asked.

Ivan hesitated. That was the question that just changed his mind about Anna's loyalty. After the conversations that we have just had about love and the future, to ask a question like that showed her real intent, to get access to the material that I had been holding back.

"I had the complete file on this sent to my new facility in Vermont. I have managed to get a message to my son Michael, telling him how to get access to it if anything were to happen to me."

That last part wasn't exactly true. That is the reason Ivan wanted to get in contact with his son, so get that message to him, but that has not happened yet. No need to let her in on that Ivan thought.

Anna's mood now went back to her normal seductive style. She turned on the charm and before long they were back in the bedroom. By this time Ivan had recovered all of his senses so they could enjoy the next hours together.

But there would be no sleep for Ivan. He saw that Anna had fallen off to sleep but he got up, dressed and gathered a few things that were close to him. He planned to wake Anna about 1:30 and convince her to dress and accompany him to the sea-level floor. He wasn't sure how he would do that, but he had time left to think about it. Anna slept while Ivan sat by to make sure she never left his sight.

The hours and minutes seemed to drag by for Ivan as he waited for the hands on his watch to so slowly move toward the 2:00 a.m. zero hour. At about 1:15 he heard Anna rustling around in the bedroom, possibly looking for him. When he appeared at the bedroom door fully clothed, Anna was surprised.

"Ivan, you are awake and fully clothed. What's going on?"

Without thinking of a better answer he replied, "I am so excited about your willingness to someday go with me to my hideaway in Vermont, that I was overcome with this sudden feeling of romance and thought it would be wonderful if you and I could go down to the lower level where we could sit and overlook the ocean. We have never once put ourselves in a romantic setting like that in all the time we have been here. I know is nearly 2:00 a.m. but I couldn't sleep, and no one will be awake to see us there. What do you think?" "Now that I'm awake it's fine with me but we will have to first stop at my quarters so I can put on a jacket or a sweater. It's normally a lot colder on the lower level and having the chills would spoil the setting."

"Okay," Ivan replied, 'but let's get moving before we lose this middle of the night environment."

Ivan didn't want to seem too hurried, but he didn't want Anna to delay anything.

"Let's stop by your quarters and quickly get a covering for you and then go on down there"

He felt that he needed to be at her side at every point here just in case she suspected something and decided to alert the others.

They entered her quarters and she grabbed a jacket, put on some makeup, took her purse, and took Ivan's hand, ready to go below.

They entered the bottom floor area at about 1:45 and stood for a moment at the glass door that overlook the beach and ocean. The skies were overcast so there was no moon. The ocean appeared like a dark carpet and the heavy doors prevented any sound of small waves hitting the beach. Even with no moon and near silence, there was an atmosphere of romance between the two of them, and they held hands and stood very close together.

The door at the rear of the lower area slowly opened and Albert was about to enter, and he caught a glimpse of Ivan and Anna standing at the door. He immediately knew that this was part of Ivan's plan to take Anna out with him, so Albert just waited behind a partially open door until the time came for action.

At 2:00 am Ivan put his arm around Anna and led her to a sofa. "This is a beautiful setting, Anna," Ivan whispered. "Let's sit and relax and enjoy it." Anna complied without hesitation, leaning her head on Ivan's shoulder. The glass door suddenly open revealing five men dressed in dark clothing wearing black hoods. Colonel Overton went directly to Ivan, grabbing his hand to help him rise from the sofa. Without a word, Overton led Ivan out the door and out of sight. Mike Atwater and Chris Jenkins grabbed Anna who seemed to be in a trance not knowing exactly what was taking place since everything was happening so fast. At the same time Albert Brokow told Mike who he was and asked if they needed any assistance finding the two other scientists. Mike shook his head no as Albert handed him two key cards, one for each of the scientist's room. Without speaking a word, Hank Farber grabbed the two cards and Mike and Jenkins led Brokow and Anna out of the building. So far so good, there was hardly a sound made by anyone and except for a few words by Albert, no words were spoken.

Hank Farber and Ashiem went immediately to the elevator moving it up to the 4th floor. With silent precision they each entered the room of one scientist, moving directly to the bedroom. When they arrived at the bedside, they immediately placed tape of the scientist's mouth and bound their hands almost simultaneously pulling them up out of bed before they were entirely awake. Before leaving the room, each scientist had his head covered with a hood and they proceeded down to the lower level and out the door. Both scientists were in such a state of shock that they offered little resistance. Searching the two was simple because Topolski slept in pajamas and Bechert was naked. Unfortunately, since the men didn't anticipate that, the scientists would have to make the remainder of the trip as they were until it was possible to get them some covering.

Overton was long gone with Ivan and the other two boats left in different directions as ordered to meet their pickup vehicles.

The extraction had gone off without a hitch.

Unknown to the team, a plan was in place for a Navy SEAL team to arrive at the facility within minutes after the extraction and before the rest of the residents awoke. Their purpose was to get the computers of the two scientists from both their quarters and of possibly their laboratories. That mission was also a success.

CHAPTER 38

EIGHT DAYS AFTER the extraction, Colonel Overton walked into a room in Langley Virginia at a CIA facility. In the room were all four members of the extraction team plus Anna. There was some light chatter among the team as Colonel Overton entered the room.

"Gentlemen, and Lady in this case, you did a magnificent job with the extraction operation. Almost everything went off exactly as planned. Anna, I must apologize to you for keeping you in the dark on these plans, but we felt it was better that way. The two scientists have been taken to a friendly nation where they will be interrogated and treated appropriately. Albert Brokow is being processed in order for our government to honor its commitment to him. It will be a few days before he can join you. Unfortunately, there was one glitch in the operation." Colonel Overton walked over to Mike Atwater, leaned over the table and said softly, "Mike, I'm sorry to have to tell you that your father did not survive the extraction. The excitement was too much for him, and he had a heart attack and died on the recovery ship." Colonel Overton's words were broken as he gave Mike the terrible news.

Mike didn't react immediately, but Anna shouted, "Oh, no, he can't be dead."

"Unfortunately, he is," Overton muttered as he continued to stand facing Mike Atwater. Anna appeared to be having a breakdown, pounding on the table. Hank Farber tried to comfort her, not understanding exactly why she was reacting as she was.

Mike Atwater suddenly jumped up from his chair, he threw his briefing book across the room and shouted, "Son of a bitch! That was not supposed to happen. How the hell did you let that happen, Colonel Overton? He took this very dangerous assignment and apparently performed it way beyond expectations, even putting himself in a position of serious danger to get the information that the CIA wanted. You mean to tell me that after going through all of the stress of this assignment, he died when it was finally over?" Colonel Overton responded, "Unfortunately, Mike, we don't always have control of what happens to our bodies. Your father died a hero, providing his country with information that will have a profound effect on the future of world peace. You may not know the extent of the importance of his work right now, but in time you will see it all play out. We understand that he had been previously warned about high stress situations, and he had previously witnessed mild reactions to that type of stress. He never told anyone about those reactions." "I don't give a shit about the future playout, Colonel. My father is dead now, today, as we sit here gloating over our successes. What success does he ever get to gloat over?"

Mike slammed himself back into his chair and sunk his head into his arm on the table. The rest of the room remained quiet until, one by one, each of his team members quietly rose, approached Mike, and gave him their condolences and left the room.

Anna was the last to rise. She came and sat next to Mike, putting her arm around him as though to sooth him. "Mike, I understand your grief. I also grieve for Ivan's loss. He and I became very close during our time working together. Our relationship became a loving one. He spoke often of you and how proud he was that you were succeeding in your chosen field as he did in his. We should think about his successes, not the grief of his death. That might help us get through this trying time." Mike remained quiet and still until he rose and left the room without uttering another word to Anna.

Admiral Farber spoke to each of the team members by phone. He informed them that the recent work that they had done had and would continue to have a very significant effect on American foreign policy in future months. He told the team to take some serious leave as a reward for their work and to rest and enjoy some time off.

He told Mike Atwater that his father had previously requested a very quiet funeral and that would be accommodated at Washington National Cemetery within days.

The funeral was held with Mike and Anna attending along with two government representatives.

Mike, Hank, and Anna hung out together for a few days while on leave, periodically discussing some of their work. Anna indicated that she had been recruited by the CIA specifically for this assignment and she would probably not continue working for that organization. Her future was in question, but she would continue to miss Ivan and the work that they had done together.

She had mentioned on several occasions that Ivan had told her of his plans to live out his life in the solitude of the facility that he had constructed somewhere in the Northern United States. On one occasion while the three of them were in a pub having a beer together, she asked Mike if he had ever seen that facility or knew anything about it.

"Yes, I have seen it," Mike replied. "It's quite a place. If you ever wanted to get away from the world, he picked the right spot. He isn't even sure what country it is in, either Canada or the US."

"Did he ever talk to you about his work?" Anna asked.

"I wouldn't understand it if he did," Mike responded. "At times he left me files that he thought I might want to study someday, but that's about it. There is some material at his new facility that I want to go over but that can wait for the right occasion. I'm not exactly sure what the hell I'm going to do with that facility. It's so special a facility that the government might even have an interest in it. I'm just going to let it sit for now and see what turns up. There is some unfinished business that I have to attend to up in that area related to my cousins who managed the construction of the facility. I might consider attending to that soon." "Mike, if you do go up there, would it be possible for me to tag along?" Anna asked. "Ivan mentioned it so many times that I have a fairly good idea what it is like but seeing it might be a nice memory to carry of your father."

Hank piped in. "Why don't I rent a plane and fly up there and we can all take a look?"

Mike replied, "Well a plane can get you to St. Albans, but you need a helicopter to get you close to the facility. I remember that there is a helicopter landing pad about half a mile from the facility, and I believe we would have to walk the rest of the way, but it is an easy walk. If you guys want to do that, I'm game for it while we have some time off. It might be a fun couple of days." Anna excitedly said, "Let's do it, then."

Hank said, "I'll check out the rental situation for a plane and helicopter and let you know what I find out.

A day later, Hank indicated that he had made arrangements for a plane to St. Albans and a helicopter at that facility. The only complication is that he would have to be checked out in the helicopter by the rental agency which was certainly not a problem. They set a plan in effect to leave for Vermont in two days.

CHAPTER 39

THE TRIP FROM Washington National Airport to St. Albans, Vermont, took about 4 hours in the Cessna 310 that Hank Farber had rented. They had planned to leave early in the morning to ensure that they had plenty of daylight to make the trip to Vermont and still have enough time to check out in the helicopter and get to the mountaintop sight.

Hank Farber had purchased local sectional charts of the St. Albans area and marked the general location of the site as best he could with the information that Mike had provided him. From Mike's previous trip to the site with the Goldblatt brothers, he believed that the helicopter pad was on the US side of the mountain with the site located several hundred yards from there on the other side of the Canadian border.

They boarded the helicopter about 1 pm so they would have plenty of daylight to make a two-way trip. The trip was mostly Mike and Hank conferring about the charts, to locate the landing site. Anna sat in the rear seat and said nothing during the short trip.

"That looks like the landing site, Hank," Mike shouted, pointing to a flat clearing near the top of the mountain. "I remember that there was a big run of white birch trees adjacent to the clearing, and that was a very outstanding marker that stood out from the green pines behind the birches."

Hank mad a quick circle of the area and proceeded to make a very slow descent.

The helicopter touched down without as much as a bump and Hank quickly turned off the rotor switch.

No sooner than he'd hit the switch, Anna reached forward and slapped a patch on Farber's neck. Hank almost immediately passed out. Mike was sort of stunned by the happenings. He had not seen Anna attach the patch and he motioned to Hank as though to try to help him.

As he did this Anna slapped a patch on Mike's neck, and just as Hank had done, Mike immediately passed out.

Anna quickly sprang into action. She felt for a pulse on Hank Farber's neck, but she detected none, so she assumed that he was dead. She could only hope that Mike would not suffer the same fate. She needed Mike alive so he could guide her to the material that Ivan had sent which contained the analysis and results of Ivan's work on the antidote to the drug.

For months, Anna had been carefully reading all of Ivan's work about the drug that they had developed. She had little technical background, but she understood from her discussions with Ivan, that if this new drug was not properly applied, it could have devastating effects on its victims. She knew that the drug would seriously affect the victim's memory and Ivan also had told her that too much applied improperly could result in the death of the victim. That was apparently the case with Hank Farber, and she hoped that it would not be the case with Mike.

Anna exited the helicopter when the blades had completely stopped. She realized that Mike was still alive since he would occasionally move some part of his body. For what seemed like hours, Anna tried to revive Mike and eventually he opened his eyes but only to show a blank stare. He couldn't speak and he seemed to have no control of his body parts. As Anna tried to unbuckle him from his seat and let him get out of the helicopter, his legs simply folded, and he fell to the ground.

Anna managed to drag him up against a tree and she left him there in order to look for some pathway to the hidden facility. Eventually she did find a well-used path and she followed it for quite a while before she saw an old cabin, at the edge of a clearing. The cabin was small but well-built and in fairly good repair. This cannot be the hidden facility she thought, it looks like an old hunting camp or a miner's shack, but it was in good condition. She entered the unlocked front door and much to her surprise the cabin was nearly fully furnished and stocked with supplies. She had heard stories about mountain people who had hunting camps that they always kept open and stocked as a safety measure for other hunters who might be lost and need shelter. She assumed that this was such a cabin. She could use this cabin for shelter as she waited for Mike to recover some of his faculties and help her find Ivan's hidden facility. She had no idea how long it would take Mike to recover, if she could even get him up here to the cabin and then what his reaction would be to the situation. She knew the drug could have an effect on his memory, but she had no idea of how long that would take. Had she applied too much of the drug she thought? She just didn't know but she had several alternative plans made that took into account many of the possibilities. The most important thing that drove her was her assignment to get that information about the drug antidote and all of the remainder of Ivan's filed information.

All of this was Anna's alternative plan. She never expected that Ivan would not survive the rescue. She had agreed to live here with him and in that case, she would have fairly complete access to the facility and the information that Ivan had sent there and all that he still had in his head. She knew that this was going to be a long-term process getting everything from Ivan, but her assignment as a Russian agent was considered a long term one. Once she managed to get everything she wanted from Ivan, her direction was to kill him. His unexpected death required that she quickly make alternate plans as she was doing at this time.

Anna walked back to the helicopter. Mike was conscious but he didn't recognize her at all. He had no recollection of any of the recent events, he didn't know his name. He could speak but even his words sounded unsure. Anna managed to get him to stand and she helped him slowly walk with her back to the cabin.

She now had to develop a plan to get Mike to a point where he could lead her to the hidden facility without remembering everything that had transpired. She had no knowledge if that would even be possible so she would have to play it by ear at each step of the way. She didn't know if this would take hours days or weeks, but here she was, and her assignment was clear. Just let Mike rest and try to nurse him back so he could be useful to her.

She told Mike that his name was Mitch Waters and her name was Jessica. She simply pulled these names out of nowhere. She developed the story that they had been on this mountain for a long time, living together and loving together. Each day, she would walk him down a short trail to the edge of a clearing overlooking a beautiful small lake. She would talk to him, but he wouldn't remember any of their discussions from one moment to another or even remember that he had known her from the previous day. How long old this process take? Anna had no idea, but she knew that she had to make it work so he could find the secret facility and also the critical files that Ivan had reportedly sent there. She needed these files to effectively complete her assignment with the Russian government.

CHAPTER 40

A T THE CIA headquarters in Langley Virginia, Admiral Farber had just been briefed by his counter terrorism unit, informing him that Anastasia Meinkoff (Anna) had indeed been performing as a double agent for the Russians in order to ensure that her father remained in good standing with the Russian hierarchy. Throughout her assignment in Iran as Ivan's assistant she had made regular contact through her Russian handler back to the Russian KGB through her father. Admiral Farber knew that Anna had been debriefed upon her return but was released as the other members of the rescue team had been to take some significant leave.

At nearly the same time as Admiral Farber had completed that briefing, he received a message from his staff that his son Hank Farber had rented an airplane at Washington National Airport and flown with two companions to St. Albans, Vermont. At that airport he rented a small helicopter for a pleasure trip around the area. Both aircraft were overdue for return. Vermont FAA officials had received no reports of an ELT signal from the helicopter indicating that it had trouble or had crashed. The Cessna that Hank had rented was located at the St. Albans Airport. Since the weather was clear, Hank had not filed any flight plan, so officials had no knowledge of the where the helicopter had flown.

Admiral Farber immediately contacted Colonel Overton to see if he had any indication of the plans of the two team members. Overton indicated that he had overheard Hank and Mike discussing a fun trip to Vermont and that Anna was tagging along.

Farber immediately realized what was happening. Ivan must have given Anna the impression that his new facility in Vermont contained some important information about the work that they had been doing and she was attempting to find the facility and collect that information. That would certainly place both Hank and Mike in serious danger if they discovered her plot.

Admiral Farber's office made immediate contact with the Surface Intelligence Division to get satellite images of that area in order to locate the helicopter. Within minutes, he was told that the helicopter had been located and appeared to be intact showing no indication of damage.

That news was somewhat of a relief to him, but the circumstances of the whole situation were strange. Knowing the history of the two men involved who had become very close friends in recent months, he believed that there was a plan of some sort being hatched between the two men. Whatever that plan, they were not aware of Anna's status and that placed them in danger.

Admiral Farber contacted the resident FBI agent in the St. Albans area and briefed him of the situation, providing him with the coordinates of the helicopter's location. The FBI agent was briefed as thoroughly as possible in the time permitted. Farber asked that a ground party go to the site, locate the two men, and arrest Anna. He felt that any airborne approach might set off an alarm with Anna, causing her to react unpredictably.

When the FBI rescue party reached the helicopter, they found Hank Farber inside in an incoherent state, but he was alive. The team's medics took Hank back down the mountain for medical help.

The five remaining agents spotted the well traveled trail and followed it to the cabin. There was smoke coming from the chimney and with only one entrance apparent they broke into the cabin as Anna and Mike Atwater were sitting at the table eating. Anna made a rapid move toward the cabinet as though going for a weapon. Mike seemed unaware that a trauma was taking place. Anna was placed in handcuffs as the remaining agents attended to Mike.

The lead FBI agent grabbed his radio and called his headquarters to inform them that the men had been found alive and Anna was in custody. For a moment the agent was silent, listening to the directions that he was being given. "Roger, sir," the agent responded as he walked over to the rear window. "I do see the lever," he responded while pulling down on a red lever that stuck out from the wall. There was an immediate sound of a motor and the rear cabin floor opened up to reveal a stairway. The lead FBI agent signaled everyone to follow him. When they reached the bottom of the stairs, they entered a pleasant looking living area. Seated on two chairs facing in an opposite direction were two men who immediately rose and walked toward the group. Anna screamed "Ivan! Ivan! You are alive! You deceived me, you bastard!" Ivan immediately went to his son Mike, hugging him tightly. Mike immediately recognized his father and they went into an embrace. The shock of seeing his father immediately snapped Mike out of his state of trance.

"How did you do that, Ivan?" Anna asked.

"I told you recently that there were several ways to achieve an antidote to the drug. One of those ways was to shock the brain into its normal behavior. That must be what happened here. I finally got my human test of my work."

Ivan continued, "Mike, I want you to meet my new friend Albert Brokow or as he is now known, Andrew Brody. He served me well in Iran and he will help me in my work in retirement here on the mountain."

Ivan walked over to Anna. He kissed her lightly on the cheek whispering in her ear. "You served me well Anna, but you were the one who was the deceiver. Now you must pay the price for your deception."

EPILOGUE

THE SIGNIFICANCE OF Ivan's work and the efforts of the special CIA team were never made public as fact but they had epic importance to world events. Ivan was recognized by the President with the presidential medal of Honor, the highest award that a civilian can receive in the United States. The award was given posthumously because to the world, Ivan was dead. That was part of his original agreement with the Government.

The efforts of the civilian soldier team had far reaching results. The South African government announced shortly after the Angolan rebel attack on their facilities, that they were abandoning all research on the production of Nuclear materials. They never re-started that effort

Due to the teams continuing work after Ivan rescue, the team produced all of the evidence needed to uncover the arrangements that led to the prosecution in the Iran Contra scandal. The team discovered the initial evidence that the US was selling arms to Israel who was then selling them to Iran at a significant profit. That profit was passed along to the US where it was sent to Nicaragua to support the Contra rebels.

With all of it activities in the Middle East the team uncovered many illegal activities associated with the Oil cartel which was controlled by Saudi Arabia, the largest oil producing nation at that time. Several US Congressmen were censured and two were forced to resign from office for assisting in price fixing activities.

As part of the CIA's extraction plan, a team of Navy seals entered the building where Ivan had worked, the next day after the extraction. Most of the innocent residents of the building had no knowledge of what had taken place the previous night. All of Topolski's and Bechert's files and computers were taken and later revealed the Middle Eastern countries that had been recipients of the lethal gas. The CIA believed that all of the gas had been destroyed but history later proved that not to be true.

Ivan's direct activities and his discovery of the Russian-German scheme to produce and sell lethal gas to Middle Eastern dictators was used by President Reagan as a bargaining chip with the leaders of both countries. He promised to keep the evidence hidden in return for an agreement from the Germans and Russians to tear down the Berlin wall. As a direct result of that threat, the wall was opened in 1989 and began to come down beginning in 1990. This was one of President Reagan's most significant actions of his entire two term presidency.

Shortly after Ivan's extraction from Iran, he was told of crimes against him committed by his cousins Johathan and Samual Goldbladt. They had embezzled more than thirty million dollars of Ivan' funds, by manipulating the books as the price of gold escalated more than three hundred percent. Ivan was never able to face his cousins because of his original agreement to disappear. All of the legal activities against his cousins were carried out by his son Michael. As a result of family plea bargaining, Ivan received a settlement of ten Million dollars cash paid over a 5 year period and half ownership in their paper company placed in the name of his son Micheal. The government insisted that the Goldbladt brothers serve at least five years in a federal prison for their crimes.

Largely due to the efforts of Admiral Farber much of the corruption within the CIA was uncovered and those effected were removed and several served prison terms for their acts. Also Admiral Farber was successful in establishing more stringent oversight of CIA activities, especially with programs that were given "super secret" status.

Before President Reagan served out his second term, Admiral Farber was made Chairman of the Joint Chiefs of Staff and served in that capacity until his retirement.

Both Mike Atwater and Hank Farber remained in the services of Grey Skies, eventually becoming executives of that organization. Michael retired from Grey Skies five years later to spend full time in Vermont near his father where he took over as CEO of Mountain State Paper Company.

Anastasia Meincoff was convicted of crimes against the United States and through diplomatic arrangements, was sent back to Russia. She mysteriously died less than a year after her return.

As part of President Reagans negotiations with the Russians and Germans. Dr. Elias Bechert and Dr. Alyusha Topolski were held in captivity by the United States for two years and then returned to their respective countries where they have not been seen or heard from since.

Most recently, a man named Andrew Brody published a book titled "Be Suspicious of Everything That Seems Too Good to be True." One might question who actually wrote that book.

ABOUT THE AUTHOR

JAKE BUSSOLINI HOLDS a bachelor's degree in electrical engineering and received executive education at Harvard. He has previously published eight books, two of which were awarded silver medals by the Nonfiction Authors Association. He is a retired senior executive of a Fortune 100 aerospace company.